WHISTLING JACK

by Josephine Gardiner

First published in 2022 by Hypatia Publications, The Hypatia Trust, Lower Ground Floor, The Regent, 54 Chapel Street, Penzance, Cornwall TR18 4AE

This edition published 2025

Josephine Gardiner has asserted her right to be identified as the author of this work © Josephine Gardiner, 2022

Quote from the story 'The Lighthouse Keeper' in *Tales of the Seal People: Scottish Folk Tales* by Duncan Williamson (Canongate, 1992), reproduced courtesy of Linda Williamson, copyright holder

Verse from the poem 'Precursors' by Louis MacNeice (Faber and Faber) reproduced with permission from David Higham Associates

Cover design by Miki Ashton. Nautilus image on front cover © Chris 73, Wikimedia. This Wikipedia and Wikimedia Commons image is from the user Chris 73 and is freely available at: https://commons.wikimedia.org/wiki/File:NautilusCutaway LogarithmicSpiral.jpg under the creative commons cc-by-sa 3.0 license

ISBN (paperback): 978-1-872229-80-5

Typeset in Garamond by Ben Corrigan

Notes on the Author

Josephine Gardiner was born in Oxford and has lived in London, Barcelona, Brighton and now Penzance, Cornwall. She was educated at London University, the Open University and Durham University and holds degrees in Modern History (BA) and Psychology (BSc, MA). Most of her working life has been spent as a newspaper journalist: she was on the staff of *The Times Educational Supplement* for thirteen years as a news reporter, sub-editor and feature-writer, and has worked freelance as a writer, editor, and translator. She enjoys long-distance train travel and wild places. Josephine is married to the sports writer David Ross and they live with two cats. This is her first novel.

For David

Contents

Precursors	1
Part 1: The Art of Trespassing	**13**
1	15
2	36
3	53
Part 2: The Queen of Pearl	**83**
4	85
5	103
6	113
Part 3: The Fall	**147**
7	149
8	168
9	183
10	206
11	235
12	247
13	267
Part 4: Whistling Jack	**293**
14	295
15	312
16	323

You know, it's very hard when you live in a lighthouse on your own out in the sea and there's not a soul to be seen or not a voice or anybody to speak to or anything, and you're on your own. Even a mouse would cheer you up! When somebody comes flip-flapping around the floor, especially a seal that you have just taken from the sea, it means so much to you – it means the world to you.
Duncan Williamson, The Lighthouse Keeper

In an age of extinctions, the jellyfish is blooming. One species, *Turritopsis Dohrnii*, has spread across the world almost unnoticed. Turritopsis is also notable for the ability, when threatened or damaged, to revert to a sexually immature stage – to childhood, if you like. It can do this indefinitely, making it biologically immortal.
Nankervis, K. and Garcia Delgado, M. (2012). The role of jellyfish in anthropogenic ecosystem collapse in the north Atlantic, a review. International Journal of Marine Ecology, 22.

Precursors

There is something I haven't told you about St Anthony. It isn't a secret, but most people come and go without ever knowing it exists, just as passengers on a night train are obliged to stare at their own bleached faces beyond the glass, trundling across the black universe in plastic seats. Until the power fails. Then, with the lights off, you look out with sudden interest at the hawthorn, the cow parsley, the solitary deer riding down a river on an ice floe, surprised to realise they had been there all along.

In the early evening of Saturday, May 5, 1821, Napoleon Bonaparte, exiled Emperor of the French, died on a remote volcanic island in the South Atlantic named St Helena. On the same date, and at almost the same time, a four-mile section of Cornish coast split off and subsided in one of the most significant landslips ever seen in Britain. The earth's crust twitched, and within a few minutes some five thousand years of modest, hard-won cultivation was torn up and thrown backwards into the fertile chaos of prehistory. The journalist reporting for the *Cornwall Chronicle* on the 'Trebeere Landslide' (which actually occurred several miles to the west of Trebeere, beyond St Anthony) was unable to indulge in any fanciful linking of the two events, because the news of Napoleon's death did not reach the British newspapers until two months later.

'On the evening of Saturday last,' begins the report on May 9, 1821, 'a catastrophic subsidence occurred in the cliffs near Trebeere, Cornwall, of such magnitude that some four miles of wood and pasture have broken from the main coast and are now separated from it by a dreadful chasm. While it is providential that no persons are understood to have perished in the disaster, a number of farm dwellings west of the village of St Antony [sic] have either collapsed or suffered such damage that they are no longer fit for human occupation. One person is reported to be missing since the time of the landslip, a dairymaid of seventeen years by name of Eliza Tabb. Her mother, Mary Ann Tabb, a widow of good character and well respected in the vicinity, is one of the unfortunate residents whose cottage walls have been cracked open by the force of the fissuring. According to Mr Silas Rowe, proprietor of the Bonaparte Inn, multitudes of visitors from outside the locality have started arriving in the parish to view the extraordinary spectacle, which he declares to be "a wondrous convulsion of Nature", and he wishes it known that he has prepared additional lodgings to accommodate this invasion of curious sightseers.'

Personally I prefer the eyewitness account of the day of the landslip given by the local curate, James Prideaux of St Anthony, which appears in his memoir, *Reflections of a Cornish Clergyman*. This memoir, or journal, was not published until 1914, eighty-six years after the author's death (the family probably had misgivings about scandalous aspects of the content), and any interest it might have attracted was drowned by the Great War. The book is entirely forgotten today, but there used to be a copy in the old Branwell Library in Trebeere, shelved in a back room where a gold clock ticks and eucalyptus leaves whisper at the windows. Prideaux writes as though he is reporting a recent event, but this may not have been the case, and he might well have embellished or added to his memories in the retelling:

The morning of May 5, 1821, a Saturday, was not marked by any unusual occurrence, it being fair and mild, the sea ruffled only by a soft air from the south. I took my habitual walk with Voltaire after a midday meal of cold bacon and cheese, choosing the lower path along the stream and through the spinney, where bluebells were still abundant in the shade. My grey summer coat, which I put on for the first time this spring, is tight under the arms, though it is not yet two years old. I had intended to continue up Torbett's Hill, but stopped to talk to Samuel Trembath, who was attempting to shepherd his hens back through the gate into the orchard.

Samuel, as I have noted in earlier pages of this journal, is the long-standing tenant of the glebe cottage, a man excessively troubled by his health. He obtains some relief by describing his many afflictions to those of us who are prepared to lend him the time, but I am always left with the impression that he expects more of me personally, as representative of the curative powers of the Church. Samuel's father used to be the Sexton here long ago and I suppose Samuel feels he has inherited an affinity for my more melancholy duties (our current gravedigger, by contrast, is a cheery fellow who comes over from St Dominic and talks only of his many children and their noble achievements).

On this occasion Samuel was complaining of a nightmare that he likened to the Day of Judgement, which had frightened him out of his bed at three o'clock in the morning. He dreamed he heard a fearsome commotion from the henhouse, and, suspecting a fox had gained entry, went outside to investigate. When he opened the henhouse door (in the dream), he found a wolf in there, a terrible creature as big as a carthorse, which then trapped him in a corner, preventing any escape. Just as the wolf bared its teeth and lunged for Samuel's throat, the henhouse began to creak and tilt, the orchard outside to crack and subside, whereupon a great hole opened in the grass, and everything began to slide down into it: hens, henhouse, wolf, apple trees, and Samuel himself.

Shortly after the nightmare woke him, Samuel continued, he got out of bed for a drink of water and felt a genuine vibration in the floor of his chamber; a grumbling sound, or, rather, sensation, that appeared to originate from deep within the earth under the house. 'I swear to God I was awake,' he insisted, 'when I felt the vibration.'

While Samuel spoke I looked across at his handsome russet hens, dipping in and out of the meadow flowers in the spring sunlight, and suppressed an impulse to laugh at his catastrophic dream, which struck me as singularly fitting to the dour character of the dreamer. However, in view of what was to follow that day, I am tempted to credit Samuel Trembath with uncanny prescience.

Prideaux goes on to describe a number of incidental meetings that afternoon, and some thoughts about his sermon for the following day (on the various reappearances of Christ after Easter), before reporting on the landslip itself:

Around six o'clock a strong wind came up from the southwest and I asked Dinah to bring tea to the study where a fire was lit. I was immediately disturbed by Voltaire, whining and scratching at the door, so I let him in and he came straight across to lie under my desk. I had scarcely sat down again when I heard a truly fearful noise, like the loudest thunder except that it continued for longer, and rather than coming from the skies it seemed to be resonating along the ground. A heavy shudder came from somewhere deep below my boots, travelling up my legs and spine and into my stomach. Our china (depicting Faith, Hope and Charity in rose and silver lustre) rattled and jumped in the dresser, the key swung wildly in the door. I hastened outside, the dog creeping behind me with his body low to the ground, but noticed nothing unusual apart from a clamour from the birds, which were surging out of the trees in black flocks like unfurling sheets.

The rumbling sounds and vibrations grew slowly fainter and then ceased, so I left by the garden gate and walked down into St Anthony. Women were standing about in the roadway outside their doors, looking to the west; none of them seemed able to explain the source of the peculiar sound, but were eagerly exchanging accounts of the trivial duties they had been performing at the moment when they heard it. At the Bonaparte Inn a small crowd of men had assembled by the porch. The noise, they said, was assuredly the first warning of an enemy invasion. I was about to join this discussion when a young fellow came running up the street from the direction of Torbett's Hill. It was Will Trevithick's boy, Adam. He was sweating, barely coherent.

'It's all gone,' he shouted, 'the cliffs, the woods, the sheep, gone into the sea, Hocking's fields have sunk, there are *mountains* in the sea, it's terrible up there.'

We marched in a body up Torbett's Hill and the first thing we noticed was a quantity of greyish dust hanging over the pasture and cliffs like a sea fog. At Hocking's farm the house and dairy doors stood wide open, cattle penned in the yard, dogs barking, but no man to be seen. The land beyond Churchtown Farm is a high grassy common which extends for some quarter of a mile before folding into hills and thick woodland, and it was here that we had the first intimation of the horror to come. Great cracks appeared in the ground, cutting across the footpath, some as deep as a man is tall, exposing the raw earth, as if the land had been attacked by a giant with a cleaver. Towards the cliff-edge on my left the pasture had folded and crumpled downwards to form a series of terracings in the manner of an Italian olive grove.

Nothing however could have prepared me for the spectacle that rose before us when we reached the top of the bluff to look across the miles of coastal fields, coverts, woods and small bays formerly known as Torbett's Green. It was unrecognisable, an insane landscape, a scene from Macbeth's nightmares, or from Hell itself. Slabs of cliff, hundreds of feet high, had split away and slipped downwards in massive sections like cuts of hard cheese, so that the old slope from meadow to cliff-edge was reconstituted to form a series of titanic steps, separated by chasms of exposed rock. I saw an entire wood uprooted: a broad river of black mud inching downhill, prickly with the branches of drowning trees. Streams, evicted from their stony beds, poured into empty space. This jagged prospect reached into the distance as far as the western headland and perhaps beyond, while just offshore, towers of rock stood in the incoming tide, like the Alps in the time of Noah. Orchards were marooned on the summits of these towers: apple trees growing stoically on, pink and white petals drifting over beehives and down to the turbid waters. Other men, bolder than I, were standing right by the nearest cliff-edge; I advanced behind them and peered over. Some fifty feet below us was a small house, half of it placid in its vegetable garden, the other half projecting over another precipice.

We doubled back to check the two cottages belonging to Hocking on the westward edge of his lands, and found them mercifully empty, though they were cracked quite out of shape, granite walls buckled and bulging. In the smaller of the two dwellings a fissure in the upper wall had opened wide enough to expose the bedchamber within: linen was strewn about, a washstand and pitcher lay across the floor, smashed in pieces. Matthew Hocking was already there, outside; red in the face, uncharacteristically silent, prowling round his wrecked domain.

The more I reflected on this cataclysm over the days and weeks that followed, the more astonishing it seemed that no deaths were reported. It was a true miracle, and I thank God for it today. We were left with a mystery, however. One of the now-ruined cottages on Hocking's land was the home of a widow with whom I was once acquainted, a Mrs Tabb. Her daughter Eliza, a dairymaid of seventeen years, went out that afternoon and never returned. She still has not been found, though there is no reason to suppose that she was on Torbett's Green at the time of the landslip. The mother, Maryann Tabb, is a comely woman of excellent temper with whom I have had several pleasant dealings, and unhappily she cannot return to her cottage or work any more for Hocking, and I am told she has been obliged to seek shelter with a relative in Trebeere.

I confess it interests me that our disaster should have occurred, as I discovered some nine weeks later, on the very day that Napoleon Bonaparte died in exile on an island four and a half thousand miles due south of St Anthony. I attribute this curiosity of mine in part to the strange Providence of our shared birth date: August 15, 1769. At the age of thirty-five, when I was a penurious curate at Crackington Haven, bent under the constant gales that bleak parish delights in, my Corsican twin had crowned himself Emperor; commander of a continent, he rode the tidal wave of revolution like a dolphin in a storm. I have found it wise to keep this grudging admiration for the Enemy to myself, but at night, when the candle burns low, I look into the shadows of the room around my desk and fancy that the death of such an extraordinary man might reverberate across the ocean floor in a last assault on Fate, a final message to the nation he could not conquer.

Unsurprisingly, Prideaux's whimsical theory was not included in any of the geologists' explanations for the landslip that emerged over the next century or so. It is curious, though, that he hears and feels the thunder of the falling cliffs just after six o'clock. Napoleon's death was recorded by doctors on St Helena as 5.49 pm; in 1821 St Helena's clocks were set to solar time, some 23 minutes behind the British clocks. It is also an odd coincidence that Napoleon's burial place on St Helena was a wooded valley owned by a family named Torbett. And now, down here in the Anthropocene, it's not so ridiculous to imagine a human author of a natural catastrophe; we are Nature, putting out the rubbish, running back indoors, blinds shut against the flickering trees, the ardent moths outside.

I've read most of the scientific accounts, and the best summary I can offer is that Cornwall, despite its granite ribs and spine, has faults and flaws – pockets of weakness in which layers of sandstone, limestone and shale interleave the tougher rocks, and the weakest of these vulnerable sections lies just west of St Anthony. The decade preceding the landslip was notable for severe winters, punctuated by a series of exceptionally wet, and then uncommonly dry, springs and summers. This repetitive freezing and drying and soaking would have created perfect conditions for catastrophic shear and subsidence, and then there is the question of old mines – redundant mineshafts were backfilled and forgotten, while others may be so old that no records survive of their existence, leaving a desiccated anthill under the elastic young turf.

Since Prideaux's time the miles of fallen cliffs, terracings, upheavings and crackings have grown green and luxuriant, sheltering exiled colonies of insecure and half-forgotten species in a temperate rainforest. Only the tallest of the granite spires rise above the sea of treetops and creeping vines, and on the forest floor a thick ferny undergrowth conceals the fissures and chasms, creating perfect natural traps for the unwary. All that remains of Mrs Tabb's cottage are three walls, four feet high, while the fallen house Prideaux describes has vanished without trace.

Too dangerous for councils or conservationists to manage, the landslip is one of the few entirely wild places left in southern Britain, certainly of such a size: walkers are warned not to stray from the single narrow footpath, there are no visitor centres, no cafés, no camping areas, no forest trails, no phone signal, not even a birdwatching hide. Minor rockfalls and slippages occur every spring, sometimes meriting a paragraph in the local paper, while significant landslides, though none as cataclysmic as the first, occurred in 1856 and 1901, pulling peripheral villas and cottages into the danger zone. These buildings have mostly cracked and fallen, though the plants from their gardens – monkey puzzles, palms, Jurassic tree ferns, a solitary blue jacaranda – escaped and prospered in the wood, surprising visiting botanists with sudden flourishes of Victorian horticultural taste.

Under the mattress of fern and moss, geological time ticks on, irregularly, until one day, with a faint sifting, a whirring like a cricket in the bracken, the hour is struck, the earth splits and the world is another place. The important thing about the landslip, despite its aspect of green and ancient peace, is that it has not stopped moving.

In the 1820s people started to refer to the landslip as the Great Fall. Today it is known locally as St Anthony's Fall, or more simply, the Fall. Eliza Tabb was never found, and a predictable thicket of myths grew up around her disappearance: she was waiting for a lover on Torbett's Green when the ground swallowed her up; she was murdered at a manor house by a local aristocrat who carried her corpse to the landslip by moonlight; she was pregnant and killed herself by throwing herself into a chasm – and so on. Her phantom is, naturally, supposed to prowl the green shadow in the deepest part of the woods. The thought of Eliza Tabb's ghost didn't worry me as a child, until Tracy told me that Eliza was looking for someone – anyone – in the trees, because she wanted to tell her story. If Eliza is still there, she has company.

Part 1: The Art of Trespassing

'Loyal and Unshakeable'
Motto of St Helena

1

I was eleven when I moved from London to St Anthony, and eighteen when I moved away. We arrived in the spring of 1976, the beginning of the longest, hottest British summer since 1727. That record is unbroken as I write, despite planetary heating, and the summer of '76 is still smugly invoked by older people as a gold standard to which no younger summer can ever hope to aspire, let alone surpass. Before you know it someone will try to tell you, with astonishing open-faced sincerity, that children were less 'disrespectful' in those days, or that front doors really were left unlocked and the false cream in dry pink cakes was delicious. Don't look back, Kerenza once said, unless you are prepared to keep your eyes open. She and Victor and Tracy, in their very different ways, were always bracingly disrespectful. The persistent sun that summer held none of the climatic dread that hot weather brings today, nor was there a premonitory sense of anything coming to an end in those last years of the 1970s; we were just walking into the fog, skirting the precipice, like everyone else in history has always done.

nts were Walter and Maria-Nuria Martins (she was 1, always known as Nuria). They named me Sally, a ward name for a sensible child, though it was falling out of fashion by the time I got it. I've had two surnames since then, but for the purposes of this story I will remain Sally Martins. They had no particular plan; the move to St Anthony was inspired simply by a desire for change, and in 1976 it was still possible for a teacher to support himself, an artist wife, a child, a car and a modest London flat, while still feeling able to take risks. We had originally been going to move to Wales, to a commune my mother knew of, but then my father chanced upon a job teaching 'humanities' at the further education college in Trebeere and the choice was made. I sensed something unusual was imminent because they both started acting out of character. My father, enemy of received wisdom, began to throw homilies and aphorisms into the conversation like holy water. I would lie in bed in the dark watching car headlights slide across the ceiling like giant yellow bats, listening to him on the phone in the corridor: 'Fortune favours the brave, time and tide wait for no man, we're all whistling in the dark.' When I asked if I could go swimming after school he barked, incomprehensibly, 'Carpe diem, Sally, carpe diem.' My mother, who was shy about using her Spanish in public, quoted Antonio Machado at the Edgware Road bus stop, where anyone might have overheard her:

Caminante, son tus huellas
el camino, y nada más;
caminante, no hay camino,
se hace camino al andar.

('Wanderer, your footprints are the path, and nothing more; wanderer, there is no path, the path is made by walking.') The poem loses its poetry in English, so it was lucky nobody asked her to translate

They would have hated the word 'parenting'. My upbringing was scrupulously non-prescriptive: I was advised to avoid aggressive dogs, fast cars, sweets and sweet-talking men, told not to lie or cause distress to others, but unless I gave them stark evidence that this guidance had been ignored, they avoided checking on me. I was a late child, an afterthought, or more likely an accident; cautious, timid even, with an appetite for order, a sensuous delight in neatness, a nose for clean scents. I was a reader, but without the reserve or independence of mind that is supposed to go with it; if anything, teachers thought me 'too easily influenced', and I was frightened of rats, precipices, the three minatory railway bridges at the top end of the Kilburn High Road, scorpions, mould, the Lenahan brothers in the next street, cows, ghosts, pylons, and the decaying mansions in St Stephen's Gardens in Paddington. Of these, I was most afraid of ghosts, though now of course I long to see them. I had limitless uncensored access to books and films, and a weak sense of my own relevance.

But none of that really mattered. I never needed my parents less than I did when I was eleven.

I should mention one peculiarity which, in retrospect, marked me out from millions of similar children, and had consequences in the years under discussion. Nobody talked about synaesthesia in the 1970s. Until my twenties, when I read about the condition in a newspaper, I assumed that everybody saw each number in a particular colour, that every letter of the alphabet and day of the week possessed an inherent colour of its own. It wasn't something you would think to mention. My version of synaesthesia is the commonest kind (some synaesthetes hear colours and taste sounds), but it gave me an unfair advantage at school, leading teachers to overestimate my intelligence. I was able to remember, accurately and with little effort, historical names and dates, poems, geological formations, quotations, biological terms, geometric angles and foreign verb tenses by summoning their unique shade or particular chromatic blendings. I scorned mnemonics, laughed at repetition. By eight or so, I had learned to keep my hand down in class, to pretend to forget – a child who recalls exactly what a teacher said months ago does not endear herself to the others (shameless hand-raisers were known as Hitlers). Occasionally though, this neuronal crosstalk misfired. There was a day when the teacher asked me to subtract three from nine. Silence and humiliation (I was around eight, not five), I couldn't do it. The 3 glowed with green light while the 9, ashen, withered before its radiance. That sum, three from nine, still provokes an amnesic stutter, a squeak of static, and I have to picture a row of three emerald 3s and remove one of them to create the blue 6. Nine itself is thin as a cobweb, incapable of containing vivid numbers.

And now I'm talking about distinctive traits, there's one more odd thing. Before I moved to St Anthony, long before the murder of Clara Selman, I used to dream, repeatedly, that I had killed somebody. I never knew who – the victim was faceless and nameless – and had no idea why or how I had killed them, there was no recall of the deed. The only knowledge was the irreversible fact of having done it, that I was on the run, losing myself in crowds of bystanders (coldly superior in their inviolate innocence) because I was condemned to death. But the dream lacked the stark primeval taint of nightmare; the texture was more of resignation, fate. Besides, it made waking up delightful.

The walk to nursery school took my mother and me along a terrace of tall, ramshackle, once-white houses. Each one had its own pillared porch like a private temple, its own flight of steps down to a basement crypt, and blue mornings blazed from the upper windows. A squalid street full of the mysterious and frightening beauty the world holds for a five-year-old. One day we turned the corner and saw that every house had been armoured in corrugated iron, black crosses painted on the pillars.

'They are condemned,' my mother said, fusing the image of that road with the end of hope, and, quite possibly, sowing the seed for my dream of the death sentence. The street remained like that for ages – under-olished, quarantined in purgatory. Deletions and eruptions in the London landscape occurred often, nobody ever told you why and you never asked. The city seemed to be engaged in a campaign of self-destruction, obeying commands from some distant war. Or perhaps the grown-ups were unsure if the last war was completely over. Towers of glassy flats burst forth, changing the perspective, confusing the eye, and these too had a punitive air – as if caravans were stacked in concrete to immobilise vagrant tenants. The blocks acquired a temporary look almost as soon as they were born; they knew theirs was an ersatz, emergency architecture with no long-term ambition. There were resurrections, too. The council would board up a haggard Victorian mansion, but the next time you passed by there were people in there, playing house – flickering shapes in candlelight, music, bedspreads across the windows. When the power cuts started we all had to use candles anyway, so these illicit houses blended right in. London in the 1970s was moth-eaten and provisional, sometimes malevolent, unselfconscious as a frontier town or a huge railway station, in a way that is impossible to imagine now. Everywhere it said *nothing lasts*, so I should have been immune to impermanence. These days I am less in awe of death. I remember what Tracy's grandmother used to say, her homily for introverts: 'Nothing is ever quite as bad as you think it's going to be before you get there.' Tracy herself wasn't entirely convinced of the truth of this, however.

Our London flat was in West Kilburn, then a treeless, rackety district, and it sold for less than my parents had hoped for. When we moved to St Anthony they were obliged to settle for a tiny house in Pellow Street, one of a network of granite terraces built for the Victorian working classes, hidden behind the more photogenic harbour. Shortly before we left the city forever I was taken out of school and we stayed in Trebeere while the bureaucracy of buying the new house went through; I would not join my Cornish secondary school until the following autumn. My parents rented a chilly holiday flat out on the road to St Dominic, full of exploding electrical appliances, and for the first week I was almost entirely alone in the daytime. I lost days on the shore, crept into woods that glowed with lichen and rang with birdsong; I read for hours, or lay staring at the sky through a lace of ash trees, hypnotised by woodpigeons. All the same, there was a whisper of restlessness, a question I could not formulate, an impression that I was missing something important: if I could only open my eyes wider, make some original leap of attention, I would see the underlying theme, something that would let me step inside what I was looking at.

If I saw an adult I hid. This is how I met Kerenza. On the path beside the railway line a man was approaching in the distance, so I slid down the embankment and behind a decaying shed to wait until he had gone by.

'What are you doing here?' A tanned muscular girl of about my own age crouched with her back against the shed holding a bottle of something pink. She was frowning.

'Hiding from a man. But I'm going home in a minute, when he's gone past.' Kerenza always compelled me to tell the truth.

'Where are you from?' she asked, alerted by my accent.

'London. But we're coming to live here soon.'

'London? Really? Why?' She looked at me with frank interest, pushing herself up against the wall of the shed as if she were growing out of the earth. Her narrow hazel eyes were set at an angle, tilted sharply upwards at the edge of her face, giving her a speculative look.

'We have to move house because our cat Ivan died,' I said.

'Why?'

'He was too old.'

'Do you go to school in a tube? Have you seen the zoo? Do you live in a tower?'

She bombarded me with questions and I was flattered. I realised this girl had never been to London; the idea amazed me.

She looked hostile again, raking brown curls off her forehead with long, elegant, dusty fingers. 'We don't go to London, we go to Bristol. It's almost as big as London, but much cleaner. And Plymouth. My mother goes shopping in Plymouth all the time.'

I asked her about these other cities, unknown to me, and she spoke for a while about their virtues: their glittering fairgrounds, their cakes with silver icing. Then I asked her name, and everything changed.

'Kerenza Nankervis.'

'Kerenza' was not merely a new name with a poetic sound. The two crimson Es lit up the hard blue K, changing the hue to violet, while the copper Z and assertive scarlet A completed the stained-glass-window effect. 'Nankervis', if anything, impressed me more. I knew it must be Cornish. It was mysterious as the wooded swamp I had been exploring, the R deep green as ivy, the vowels flowering scarlet, crimson and white around its central curve. Names, though, more than ordinary words, change their colour according to associations with their owners, while some, like Tracy (navy and gold), don't conform to their synaesthetic structure at all. But despite what happened later, the colours never drained out of 'Kerenza Nankervis'; it remained the most beautiful name I could imagine.

'Is that Cornish for Catherine?'

'No, it's Cornish for "love".'

While Kerenza was enchanted by my outlandish origins in Kilburn, London, I was bewitched by her name. Such are the odd catalysts for human relationships.

'Do you want some cherry juice? It tastes of soap.'

She told me about her home as we walked the straight path back towards Trebeere, between the railway and the sea.

'My father owns the Bonaparte. It's the biggest hotel in St Anthony, probably the biggest in Trebeere as well. We've got seventeen bedrooms. There's an assembly room, it's eighteenth century. Dad's going to open the restaurant again, to non-residents, it'll be miles better than the Crabber or Betty's stupid tea garden.'

I had no idea what an assembly room was, or the Crabber, but I'd seen Betty's Tea Garden, a caravan on a field that ran right up to the shore, tables scattered haphazardly over it.

'Are you Cornish then?' I asked, guessing the answer.

'Cornish! Of course. We go back to the Celts and William the Conqueror. Probably even King Arthur and Camelot. My parents got married by Dozmary Pool. I am pure Cornish. You're an Anglo-Saxon invader.'

A big church on a hill dominated the roofs of Trebeere ahead of us: straight-backed, long-necked, with turrets like ears – I told Kerenza it looked just like a llama and she agreed, laughing, while a train slid weightily past on our right, starting its long journey upcountry. Strange to see a train and not wish to be on it.

Few people can have been less suited to reviving a failing hotel than Raymond Nankervis. The Bonaparte, he told me later, was immensely old, and had originally been named, unimaginatively, the Old Ship. When Napoleon was defeated in 1815 the owner of the time had changed this to the Waterloo, a name that had failed to catch on. People started calling it Boney's End, then Boney's Bottom, and worse, so the landlord, for the sake of compromise and public decency, rechristened it the Bonaparte. After that, Napoleon's shade moved in as a permanent guest, his heroic features lingering in corridors and surprising you on landings: lithographs of Austerlitz or Borodino, reproductions of portraits by Ingres, Prud'hon and David, busts, bicorne hats and death masks.

Kerenza offered to show me around. I was thrilled – my parents had always preferred camping, hotels were a foreign country. I walked over to St Anthony the next morning and found the Bonaparte easily: a tall, pale building with four flattened Ionic columns on the facade, it took up a lot of space on steep John Wesley Street. She was waiting for me in the porch, reading a book about ants. In Reception a life-sized wooden statue of the Emperor directed guests up a wide spiralling staircase, lit by thin daylight from a glass cupola somewhere up in the roof. Everywhere smelled of cigars, brandy, woodsmoke, antique damp. Mr Nankervis sat behind the bar reading the *Daily Telegraph*; a big clock ticked, there was nobody else about. He looked up, smiling vaguely, as if he had woken from a long sleep.

'Hello there my lovely, back already? And who's this?' He was thin, with darkish, longish, undecided hair like Charles the First.

Kerenza did not smile. 'It's Sally Martins. She lives in London. She's eleven already. I'm going to show her the hotel. Is Mum back yet?'

'Splendid. London? Well. Always a compliment to have visitors from our distant capital. Make sure you take her into the Assembly Room; one of the finest examples of late-eighteenth-century panelling in the south west. And watch out for the ghost in the cellar, ha ha. Your mother is out visiting the good burghers of the town.'

'Dad. We want pineapple juice. For when we come back downstairs.'

To my surprise, Mr Nankervis put his paper down at once and stood up obediently, his long back bending slowly to reach under the bar. He put glasses, two small bottles of juice and a bottle opener in front of us. Kerenza's brusque manner with her father sat oddly with the enthusiastic account of his plans she had given me earlier.

Her bedroom, on the first floor, had two immensely tall windows overlooking John Wesley Street, each with its own cushioned seat; 'I can watch everyone from here.' I noted the absence of dolls with approval, though there were no toy animals either. Like me, she had a lot of books; I saw fewer stories and a lot of natural history. In the Neptune Room next door a big woman loomed out of the wall over the double bed, her bosom thrust forward, plump arms clasped in front, purple skirt carved in a wave behind her. 'It's a ship's figurehead.' There was a wooden sphinx guarding the foot of the bed in the Egyptian Room. 'That's a sphinx,' explained Kerenza patiently. I was more impressed by the precisely folded towels, the miniature soaps, the smoothness of the bedspreads. The rooms were all unoccupied. On the second floor the corridor curved and doubled back on itself, carpet became lino, doors opened on iron bedsteads and bare mattresses. The top floor was worse. We were right up under the beautiful domed skylight, dusty and cobwebbed close up. It threw its watery light on drifts of fallen plaster at our feet, while inside the rooms, curtain rails had broken from their moorings, the fabric lying in defeated coils.

'All this is going to be renovated,' Kerenza said grandly, 'Dad's having it done over the summer.'

She opened a final door at the end of the landing: a gloomy greenish bathroom, a plastic shower curtain with gold stars on it, streaked with black mould.

'Pull the curtain,' said Kerenza.

Crouching in the bath was a huge brown radio, two round dials on its face like an owl.

'Dad says they used that radio to announce Hitler. To declare the Second World War open.'

'Who did?'

'The Government. It was the only radio they could find, but it was called a wireless then. Don't touch! It's dangerous.' She hustled me back downstairs into her mother's bedroom (no hint of Raymond's brown-wool presence in here), sat me at a mirrored altar, baptising us both with pale creams and sharp scent while she explained why nobody was allowed to touch the wireless upstairs in case dead voices came back out of the past.

'It intercepts radio waves and stores them. But if you move it, they all come howling out.'

I knew it was Kerenza's mother as soon as she came clicking through the door, they were very alike, physically – the same triangular face and wide, precise mouth – but while Kerenza fixed you with a restless curiosity, her mother's attention skated crisply around anything in her path. Kerenza went on painting her face, I jumped up off the seat, but Mrs Nankervis hardly glanced at either of us, or at what we were doing.

'A truly terrible morning. A disaster. Unbelievable.'

She snapped her bag shut and placed it on the perfumed wreck of the dressing table. I looked forward to a story of a sunken ship or fallen tower. She addressed Kerenza. 'The council have got the planning form. Now they want to look at the whole hotel building, again, so that means more people trailing in here like last time, jumping up and down on the floors and lecturing me on stability of supporting structures and architecture, as if anyone thinks about architecture in the toilet! And after I'd wasted my entire morning up at St Luke's Hall, the man who finally saw me insisted I was Chinese. "Nankervis," he says, "I've got you down as a foreigner." He seemed to think it was funny. He was a Londoner of course. Where *do* they get them from, and why do they always pick on me?'

'Perhaps the council men will fall through the attic floorboards, all the way down to the bar,' Kerenza suggested.

Over the time that I knew Penelope (always Penny) Nankervis, she seemed to grow younger as the years passed, so at this point she was at her oldest. She had the careful patina, the declarative busyness, of a self-consciously adult woman. A hairband pulled pale hair off a big bare forehead and the hair, stiff as candyfloss, belled out over a triangular silk scarf printed with horses' heads. Her speech always held the promise (never fulfilled) of imminent upheaval – a power cut or a thunderstorm, all the exciting disruptive things you had to pretend to find a nuisance. 'There's total chaos at the hotel,' she would say if I met her in the street, and I would picture troops of shouting men destroying the smoky quiet of the Bonaparte's bar, white waves at the windows, foghorns, distant gunfire. I paid no attention to the content of what she said.

'Who's your friend?' she asked Kerenza as we walked out of her room.

Kerenza is quite famous now in the world of marine biology. She's a jellyfish specialist. She has published a swarm of papers, and treks across the world, warning presidents and policymakers about threats to fish and sea mammals: the warming water, the spawning plastic, the holes in marine ecosystems that jellyfish are perfectly equipped to slide into, evicting other life forms, colonising the water. If you care about the future of the sea,

Kerenza is one of those doing most to save it; she's the only one of us who ended up doing something genuinely useful. My difficulty is that I always suspected that she *liked* the jellyfish too much. As a child she was obsessed with *Physalia Physalis*, the Portuguese Man o' War, and there was something unscientific in her frank passion for the things. We never saw any (they are much commoner now, the hurricanes blow them in as backwash, along with the plastic), but she enjoyed describing them to Victor, Tracy and me: the bluish peaked bladder with its bloated sail, frilled like a pasty, stretched like a condom; the long tentacles that may detach from the body of the creature and lurk, venom intact, in banks of seaweed.

'The Man o' War is not a proper jellyfish,' Kerenza would explain, 'not one creature but a *siphonophore*. A colony of organisms existing together.' The tentacles leave agonising red welts on human skin, like whip marks, and their touch can occasionally be fatal. But what most unnerved me as a child was the creature's lack of will. *Physalia* does not swim like a fish, or even pulsate like a true jellyfish. It simply drifts with the ocean tides, trailing clouds of poisonous ribbons.

* * *

It was clear something was wrong as soon as I arrived at the porch of the Bonaparte a couple of days later. The door was propped open; angry shouts came down the stairs from the first floor, banging and clattering from the bar. A delivery man came out with an empty crate.

'You don't want to go in there just now, my bird, there's a bit of a racket going on.'

I went in anyway. Penny Nankervis was coming down the stairs with clothes folded over one arm. There was no sign of

Kerenza, who had promised to show me a rockpool she knew, where we would see a giant squid.

'I've come to play with Kerenza.'

I don't think she recognised me.

'Kerenza is going up to Bristol with me today to visit her relatives. You'll have to come back another time.'

I went into the Co-op opposite the hotel, then realised I had no money for chocolate. I would not go back to the flat, though; I walked downhill, towards the harbour. At once passionately bored, I turned my back on the complacent shimmer of the bay and went right, into a walled churchyard. It was more of a wood than a burial ground, headstones anchored in a lake of cow parsley: 'Gone but Never Forgotten', they insisted, 'Beloved Wife and Mother, Always in our Thoughts'. The older graves were more modest in their claims, with long, elegant letters, the few words generously spaced. There was an Arthur Wigge, 1774–1848; no inscription, just a carved picture of a tree, its branches wide and spreading, all the roots showing. I was interested by the graves of children, of which there were several: Rebecca Jane Pengelly, departed this life aged twelve years, 1804; Samuel Thomas Rosewarne, nine years, and brother Adam, three, 1825. It was quiet, apart from a blackbird, and the tree branches made sharp woodcut shapes across the path. Then I heard a laugh. At the far end of the walk a girl and boy sat in ivy on a wall, facing away. The girl's yellow hair fell thick and straight across her shoulders, striped with tabby shadows; the boy looked darker and was pulling irritably at his t-shirt. They were about my age, and were sharing a bag of sweets. Perhaps if I could sneak up on their indifferent backs and shout or bark, they would drop the sweets and run in terror. At some point during this adventure I lost my footing on the ridge of a horizontal tomb, falling quite hard against it.

They were beside me in a moment, one on each side.

'Are you all right?' said the girl. 'Can you see me?'

There was a slight graze on my knee.

'Keep calm,' the boy said firmly. 'I have to inspect the wound. What's your name? You have to keep talking, if you go unconscious it's dangerous. Can you hear me? I'm called Victor, that's Tracy Pender, Tracy without an "e". Tell me your name and address.' His voice was loud and over-deliberate.

I told him. Like Kerenza, he was intrigued that I came from London.

He sat down on Samuel Rosewarne's grave. 'What's it like? I'm going to live in New York when I'm older.'

'Do you still feel dizzy?' Tracy asked. 'Have a banana split.'

I hadn't felt dizzy to begin with. The solicitude was soothing, but I felt rather a fraud; they were enacting a private game – hospitals, or treating the wounded on a battlefield.

'Sally,' Tracy said when I was judged fit, 'we have to go and bury a dolphin. Do you want to come?'

It's extraordinary how easy it was to make friends at that age. Turn right rather than left, and your life changes forever.

From a distance the creature looked like a smooth boulder on the prairie of wet sand. We took off our shoes. The only thing I knew about dolphins was that they were not fish; this one was small, a baby, the skin bluish-black on top, paler underneath. It sat solid and undamaged, the thick dorsal fin pointing up and back. I was surprised by its beak lined with teeth like a dinosaur.

'Are you sure it's dead?' I said.

'You have to look at the eyes,' said Tracy, 'if there's no expression in its eyes, it's gone away.'

Victor bent over and peered into one of the dolphin's eyes, which was small, pensive. 'I think I can still see a bit of an expression.'

'What happened to it?' I asked.

'It got lost,' said Victor. 'Sometimes they're curious, they come too far in and they can't get back.'

'Like the seals,' said Tracy, 'they come for a while, then they have to go, but sometimes one stays too long. You have to help them get back out.' She moved her hand slowly across the dolphin's side. She might have been a hostess talking about her guests.

When they talked about burying, I had imagined we would be digging a hole in the beach, but Victor picked the dolphin up and we walked a long way across the wide sands and into the pale sea with it. The water was cold. We went in waist deep, all of us still dressed, my skirt floating out in a bell, and we stood there, Tracy and Victor looking out to sea, me looking at them, the sensation of limitless space. Tracy had long, wide, solemn eyes, the moss-green iris circled in black, and when she wasn't speaking her face had the inevitable, perfect symmetry of a cat's. She looked somehow familiar, yet unlike anyone else. Victor I was unable to look at directly at all, because he was a boy. My primary school was girls only, you denied the existence of boys wherever possible, it was tactless to mention them. I stole glances at him, his unusual eyebrows – straight lines over black eyes. Otherwise Victor was unremarkable, flush-cheeked, brown-skinned, his hair lighter than you would expect, given his eyes.

'It's too heavy,' he said. He was leaning backward, holding the dolphin out of the water.

'Be quiet,' said Tracy, 'I have to think of the words.' She closed her eyes, stretched out her arms and placed her palms flat on the sea. 'I am the Resurrection and the Life, he who believeth in me,' she paused, frowning, 'will come back.' Then Victor relaxed his arms and the dolphin slid into the lines of little slapping waves.

The wooded cliff edging the dolphin's beach had a curious half-cultivated appearance; hedges high as houses enclosed what might once have been tiny fields or orchards, paths appeared in the meadow and then vanished back into low-growing oak thickets. We came to a wire fence, full of gaps, but a fence nevertheless, and a big printed notice: Private Land. Trespassers will be Prosecuted. Tracy and Victor flattened themselves to the ground and slid under. There was a moment's doubt, and then I followed and we threw ourselves down in high grass.

Victor was looking at me.

'What do you think? Do you like it on this side of the fence?'

I said I did.

'What do you notice about it? Is it different from the other side?'

'Well,' I looked around, 'not really.'

'It's better,' said Victor, 'because we're not supposed to be here. Can't you feel it?'

'Me and Victor go trespassing,' explained Tracy. 'It makes things more interesting.'

Victor lay flat and rolled himself down the slope. 'You can come sometimes if you want. It's safer with three, because someone can be the lookout. I always have to do a lot of planning beforehand.'

I remember our first formal trespassing expedition being directly after the dolphin's funeral, but I suspect we may have waited a day or two. It was May and, unknown to us, the great heatwave had begun to cast its long spell over the country. Victor called it a training exercise, but it was more ambitious than I had expected: a self-important Edwardian mansion in Trebeere, a muddle of steeply pitched roofs and bulbous bay windows, 'Danger, Keep Out' on the gate, a couple of skips screening the front door. A toilet, cut off at the neck, lay among formal islands of rhododendrons. Apart from a white cat watching us from the garden wall, the place was deserted. We got in through a side window and found ourselves in a cavernous hallway. The building had been stripped to the bone; even the wallpaper was gone, leaving bare plaster and a churchlike smell of stone dust. 'Hello?' Victor shouted, checking. The grandiose staircase had no banisters; we stepped delicately up, pausing on the third floor to peer into rooms without floorboards. Tracy and Victor danced along the joists in one of these rooms, pausing in the middle: 'Look, you can see all the way down to the ground.' The stairs to the fourth floor, the attic, were narrower and had whole steps missing; a wind came sighing and keening under the eaves and I thought of Kerenza Nankervis and how her hotel got sadder and gloomier as you went upwards. We sat in a row on the window ledge in one of the attic bedrooms, facing out, our legs hanging over empty space, trees under our feet.

I was full of terror and delight; I wanted to get out, and I wanted to stay forever. Again there was the unfamiliar sensation of space, of ownership, of time simultaneously paused and racing forward. Beyond the trees were rooftops, dark peaks against the pink evening sky (like the Andes, where I planned to live), and my future hovered just above them, waiting, intricate and boundless, already written but unread by me. How extraordinary that I was in the world at this precise moment, that I had managed to be born at the perfect time in history, out of all possible times it might have happened. I had missed the Tudors with their axes and burning stakes, I had avoided the Black Death, I would never have to do needlework or go to a school like Jane Eyre's, and because of penicillin, I would not die of diphtheria like my mother's Aunt Candela. I had even escaped the Nazis, who my parents remembered from their own childhoods. All I was required to do was to keep walking towards the mountains and the stories would spring up on either side of the road like a pop-up book, becoming more exciting with each page. These thoughts passed in seconds, as we sat balanced in bright air above shadowed lawns, aware also of the great husk of the house behind and beneath, its powdery stone breath at our shoulders.

'Whenever you see "keep out", or "private", or "no trespassing", you have to go in. It's your duty,' Victor said.

'It's like honour,' said Tracy, 'the point is to be where we aren't meant to be, and see things no one else sees. And when we leave, nobody knows we were ever there.'

Tracy spoke with a rhythmic seriousness; Victor by contrast was quick, uneven, apologetic.

'That's why they put "private",' he said, 'to stop you seeing the interesting stuff.'

'Like spying? Have you ever been caught?'

'No. It's easy if you're careful, if you plan it properly. But there was that woman once...'

They collapsed into laughter at the memory of some angry person who had come running out in her dressing gown at the last minute, and they swayed about on the sill, legs kicking out over the void.

'It's not just houses,' Victor said. 'There are loads of places — boats, the sheds on the railway line, dangerous parts of the woods.'

I thought of London and the condemned houses, the fathomless basements and gaunt back gardens. I had played around them, of course, with friends; we may even have gone inside a couple of times, but nobody had ever defined what we did with a word as sombre and grand as 'trespassing'.

A man was standing under the horse chestnut, far below, looking up at the house. He was in shadow, half hidden behind the trunk. Perhaps he sensed I'd seen him, because he abruptly straightened himself, stiffening his shoulders as if he were putting on a coat, and strode out into the light.

'Hey,' he shouted up, voice cracking, long face absurdly foreshortened, 'come down, get out of there! The whole building could collapse at any moment. Come down at once!'

We skittered down the stairs like tomcats, holding our breath as we ran – fast, tense, careful, intent on getting far enough away so we could start laughing in peace. I didn't tell them I had recognised the man. It was Raymond Nankervis, Kerenza's father.

When I returned to London with my parents to prepare for the final move I still hadn't seen the inside of our new house in St Anthony, or been consulted on its suitability, though I knew where it was. On the other hand I had been promised a proper compass in a silver case. The city was already unnaturally hot – aggressive orange tulips in the parks, petrol and lilac on the air, litter shifting and stirring across the wide windy space outside the pram shop on Kilburn High Road, the Lenahan boys standing against the billboard by the newsagent, flamboyantly bored – and I would never have noticed any of these things if I hadn't known I was leaving them behind. As our life disappeared into cardboard boxes, Ivan's hairy black ghost kept appearing around the edges of things, taking the shape of dark cardigans and old handbags; might he come back to life, like the dolphin, only to find us gone? My mother arranged for me to say goodbye to my friends at school and we went in together one lunchtime, when everyone was outside in the shade of the big sycamore. Several people asked me when I was coming back, and I had to explain that I wasn't. How casually I abandoned them, Miranda, June, Wendy, Marie; we promised to write once a fortnight, and I never saw or heard of any of them again. It was during this last period in London that I must have received the letter from Tracy.

I always expect to find that letter again somewhere, like a delayed message from a ship at sea, falling casually out of a book or an old wallet. When you move house every few years, things are repeatedly transferred and reshuffled in and out of cardboard boxes; papers are just 'paperwork' to the removers, who shove it all together – letters of love and condolence, bank statements from busted banks, cancelled passports, cheerful holiday postcards from your dead parents – though usually it is the most boring item that rises with bland impertinence to the surface (why has *this*, of all things, survived?). Perhaps the real letter would be disappointing, but I don't think my memory of it is romanticised; I can see the laboriously rounded script we were all taught to use back then, its sharp backhand slant, the lavishly capitalised nouns like an exercise in German, the many spelling mistakes. Tracy wrote that she and Victor had been trespassing again, and had found a white palace out on the Fall. It was dangerous, and she was only telling me because I was not a 'tell tail', and they would not be going back until I returned, because it was more exciting when I was there. The letter had a postscript, I think, a sentence about seeing hundreds of seals near the Fall, and green lights in the sea, but I may have imagined that. The suggestion that things were more interesting when I was around would have been gratifying, especially as Tracy told me this was confirmed by Victor, a boy of legendary disobedience. It would have given me the exotic idea that I might be important in other people's lives. I had known Kerenza, Victor and Tracy just under two weeks: three new friends, all good-looking, all of them willing to do things I would never dare to do alone.

2

People from St Anthony (originally 'Davas St Anthony' or St Anthony's Sheep) will tell you that the place isn't what it was, but they used to tell my parents the same thing, and I can't think of anywhere that has changed less in thirty-five years – at least to look at. It has two harbours: the old one – the one visitors come to see – is almost circular, its walls of massive rectangular stones set vertically in the manner of an Inca city built to withstand earthquakes. The 'new' harbour is a working fishing port. A third harbour, half a mile or so to the east, belongs to the market town of Trebeere, always a metropolis to us. These three havens form an enclave of perceived self-sufficiency, somewhat apart even from the general isolation of the far west, with a sense that the inhabitants watch the world as they watch the sea, with wary detachment, the hope of being forgotten by the tides of history. A tendency to hide its finer architecture behind warehouses, supermarkets and boat sheds has done much to save it from the artful self-consciousness that has stripped the spirit from similar places. My only fear, at eleven, was that I wouldn't be allowed to stay.

My father tore out the orange-brown carpeting at Pellow Street and dismantled the turquoise kitchen cupboards. My mother bought a new toaster and an Indian bedspread to cover the stains on our sofa. She planted herbs in pots for the tiny granite courtyard at the back. Then they seemed to lose momentum. Books on politics and social history (my father's) outgrew their shelves and fell about in shaky piles all over the kitchen and up the staircase, fighting for space with my mother's unnerving sculptures. A large goat, constructed of wire and cloth, occupied most of the front room. We were the only people in our street without curtains, so when passers-by looked in, the goat stared right back at them, its horizontal pupils defying evil eyes. My bedroom was the attic. I put a chair under the skylight and stood on it to look out over a descending cordillera of slate roofs. Beyond them, seeming to rise above them, was the sea: Lantern Bay opening itself to the Atlantic, the chimney of the house opposite just obscuring the triangle shape of St Materiana's Island. There were usually two or three cargo ships anchored out there in the bay – dim hulking presences in the daytime, but at night, when sea and sky become one dark void, they lit up yellow and pink like dance halls, floating over the houses. The ships would remain there for days or even weeks, a mile or so offshore, and I wondered if the sailors ever came into the harbour in little boats, or if they just stayed on board, dancing with each other on the decks at night while a band played 'Sailing By'. Later, it was Tracy's father I imagined out there, looking back at St Anthony through his telescope, trying to find the courage to visit his daughter. A morning always came when I stood at the skylight and the great ships had vanished, without warning, on their way to Rotterdam or Valparaiso.

The first person I saw after we moved in was Kerenza. I was halfway down John Wesley Street when she shouted down from her window at the Bonaparte.

'Sally, come up!'

I was nervous about seeing Mr Nankervis, in case he recognised me from the hollow house in Trebeere. Sure enough, as I crossed Reception he came loping out of the bar. He appeared, however, to be positively enchanted to see me.

'Sally, my dear, we're delighted you've returned to cast your lot among us here in Cornwall, the last refuge for the sane in the rising tide of concrete brutalism they call the modern world. Can I get you a cup of tea? Or some more youthful cocktail? Kerenza is upstairs in her room.'

She was sitting at a small table by the window, books open, looking more precise and definite than I remembered, her oak-brown curls penned severely in by slides. I suspected she hated those curls. She came straight to the point.

'Which do you like best, butterflies or moths?'

'Moths.'

'What's your favourite one?'

'The hummingbird hawk moth,' I answered firmly. 'I've seen them, in Spain. I heard them singing.'

The previous October, when General Franco was dying, my mother had taken us to Barcelona, perhaps as an anticipatory celebration. I had been puzzled by a thin piping music coming up from the street below our apartment in the mornings: five slow descending semitones in a high minor key, repeated. It was a painfully desolate sound, a primitive lament piercing the roar of scooters and buses on the Via Augusta round the corner. I kept leaning over the terrace rail to scan the street, but was never able to identify its source. On the last day I was on the terrace listening to this piping when a cloud of big, plump-bodied moths came out of nowhere to feed on a potted jasmine. More and more came down from the blue air, vibrating airborne mice, probing the white flowers, stirring the scent. I ran in to tell my parents.

'But the tune's nothing to do with moths,' they said. 'It's the Knife-Sharpening Man.'

My father took me down in the lift to the street where, by the kerb, a man sat on a moped, his back to the handlebars. I watched as he picked up a knife and held its blade against a thick spinning stone attached to the bike behind the seat.

'Look, Sally, his little pipes are there on the seat. He plays them so people in the flats know he's here.'

After that my parents talked often about the Knife-Sharpening Man, *El Afilador*, and his eerie tune, surprised that I was not more enchanted by the sinister fairy-tale echoes in his name and function, but I was unconvinced by this unmasking; the man was too sunburnt and ordinary in his sweaty t-shirt, the music must have come from the moths. I didn't tell Kerenza any of this, but she seemed satisfied with my answers and gave me a book, *The Moths of the British Isles*, by Richard South.

'Macroglossa stellatarum. It's on page 51. The book smells of mothballs, which is quite funny.'

I stuck my nose in the pages. 'It's OK, I like the smell.'

I still have that book, with 'M. L. Gladstone, August 1917' written inside the front cover in sepia ink.

Kerenza showed me her new camera.

'Uncle Maurice gave it to me. He's horrible, but he's quite rich. Aunt Pamela is worse, though, because she always asks what I'm *doing*, and what I'm going to *do* today. She comes into your room without knocking and stands there, blocking the door, sighing and hovering.'

Kerenza didn't ask me about London or our new house on Pellow Street, and volunteered nothing more about her stay in

Bristol. She disliked small talk, and somehow I suspect she still does.

'Sally, I've seen you with Tracy Pender and that Victor.'

'What? Do you know them?'

'I know everyone. Do you know what happened to Tracy's mother?'

I knew Tracy had no sisters or brothers, that she lived with her grandmother, but I had never given her parents a moment's thought.

'She went mad. They put her away. In the loony bin, but it didn't work. Then they let her out again and she committed suicide. She jumped off the harbour in the middle of the night, in a storm. Tracy was five.'

The loony bin. It would be out on the moors somewhere, a lonely brick prison amid heather and bog, with a great looming chimney like the derelict engine houses I had seen near Redruth.

'What about her father, was he there?'

'No, he went off with a woman from Falmouth. Maybe that's why her mum turned into a loony. Or maybe she was mad before, I can't remember. And Tracy's gran eats seaweed and talks to dead people.'

'How do you know all this?'

'Everyone knows. Mum knows. Also, Victor's father was in prison. He stole a car with some gangsters. Mum says they are rough. And why does Victor Jordan play with girls, anyway?'

I like to think I defended Victor and Tracy, but the memory isn't there. Kerenza asked me what I did with them, where we went, what we played. I found myself telling her about the trespassing. Why did I do that? Sometimes I think everything that followed hinged on that little betrayal. Kerenza had an ability to extract confidences; you felt she already knew what you were withholding, so that it felt deceitful, foolish, to keep quiet. But the real reason was pride. I was surprised and pleased to have climbed over walls and under fences, explored abandoned houses, entered forbidden places and ignored warnings. I saw myself as newly bold and athletic, and was ready to show off this heroic persona. Kerenza, unfortunately, was there, waiting. At first I wasn't unduly worried, because I knew Kerenza didn't go to the same school as Tracy and Victor, and assumed, in my city way, that people from different schools were unlikely to cross paths. I could keep my friendship with Kerenza separate.

I saw Tracy later that week when she invited me to tea. Number Five, Glebe Lane, was even smaller than our house, on the western edge of the village, built into the hillside. A flight of slate steps led up to a wooden porch; inside was a low-ceilinged room, rather dark, panelled in narrow strips, a staircase – more of a ladder – in the centre, a lean-to kitchen at the rear. Their furniture was odd, painted black or green, then painted again with insects, flowers and birds in white, red, violet. Tracy said her grandmother was out at work in Trebeere, which surprised me. Not having grandparents of my own, I imagined them to be immobile figures, permanently indoors, existing only in relation to their grandchildren. It was the first time I had been alone with Tracy, without Victor, and we found ourselves suddenly shy; already it was impossible to think of one without referencing the other. She made conscientious cups of tea and produced plates of saffron cake, but seemed more at ease in the sloping patch of ferny garden at the back. Snapdragon, their silver tabby cat, came padding briskly out of the bushes, then turned on his heels when he saw me, pretending he had forgotten something important under the lilac.

At my primary school in London we had divided ourselves into 'Sinners' (the majority) and 'Saints'. I was a Sinner, perhaps because my admiration for order did not translate into an ability to be tidy, and I could never refuse a dare. These labels settled on each child in organic fashion – it was difficult to be sure exactly why you were in one group rather than the other, and impossible to escape your category once it was assigned. The unhappy Saints would protest and strive to simulate naughtiness, but in vain – it was a life sentence. I was having trouble fitting Tracy Pender into this system. She seemed at the same time much younger and much older than me. Her gentleness was disconcerting, at odds with her trespassing – she was the first to enter forbidden territory, she ran faster than Victor and was much less anxious about being caught. Faced with authority she turned poker-faced and placid until the authority stopped talking, then she would ignore it, politely. I waited for the little flickers of malice, familiar from school – the barbed compliment, the comment that left a sting – but these never came, and gradually I came to feel a deep relaxation in her company, aware only of her voice, rain on the roof, the words like fingers, slowing the heart, stroking my hair.

That day she talked mainly about Victor, how they had known each other since they were six, how he was already an uncle at eleven, how he had walked across a concrete bridge on the wrong side of the railings, high above the A30, and how he couldn't decide whether to be a sailor, an explorer, or a film director when he grew up.

'His dad mends roofs. He can go miles high without being scared. Victor used to be terrified and his dad laughed at him, but now we go trespassing he's got better at it.'

Tracy's room, at the top of the ladder-staircase, was full of iridescent seashells. All sizes, hundreds of them, fixed to the walls, to picture frames, around the doorway. The skylight lit the shells from above, so the air danced with prismatic fires – silver, white, touched here and there with green or lilac – the colours eloping together to form new ones that have no name, no place in the rainbow. I had the impression of being inside a mirror.

'I collect them,' said Tracy, 'my nan and my mother did, too. I expect it's a family thing.'

It was crucial, she said, to check each shell to make sure there was no creature living in it. I had already been told this by my parents, as many children are, but Tracy sounded too emphatic to be repeating something. She raised her voice, scowling, 'You'd be stealing their house, and they'd die.' She picked up a big bowl-shaped shell, its violet-green hue deeper than the others, telling me her father had brought it back from abroad, 'So I don't know if he made sure it was empty or not.'

I looked down at the floor, noticing for the first time that Tracy's clothes and books were strewn over it like seaweed, flowing out from a big tartan suitcase in the corner. There was no other furniture, apart from the bed.

'Where is your father?'

I recalled what Kerenza had told me about Tracy perfectly well, but already I was good at pretending to know less than I did, in order to listen to a different version.

'I don't know. At sea. Not fishing boats, he works on the merchant ships, all over the world, as far as Plymouth and South America. But I haven't seen him since I was four.'

'Do you remember him?'

'No.'

'What about your mum?'

'She died. She was poorly and she died.'

'Do you remember her?'

'Yes.'

I still have the two shells Tracy gave me that day.

They are on the windowsill in front of my desk, flat like placemats, the former homes of some type of oyster. They surprise me every time: extreme beauty thrown into the world from the sea, uncelebrated by artists, dismissed by jewellers, worth less than five pounds, radiating light. Mother-of-pearl – nacreous aragonite – is one of the toughest materials in nature – it doesn't crack.

The inevitable meeting between Kerenza and my two newest friends, which took place in the botanical garden in Trebeere, was less awkward than I had feared.

Kerenza already knew them slightly and she chatted with confidence, asking questions, laughing, telling stories about people they all knew in St Anthony, so that Victor and Tracy were drawn out of their shyness and the association soon seemed quite natural. Kerenza was also tactful; we had been on our way to inspect an empty cottage, and she said casually that she had heard, from me, that Tracy and Victor were good at exploring. Not trespassing, exploring. So of course she was invited along. The cottage was the last in a row of five, with planks of wood nailed across the front door. There was no way in at the front unless we were prepared to break a window, so we climbed into the back courtyard. It was Kerenza, the new recruit, who pulled at the back door, forcing the rusted hinges to allow enough space for us to squeeze in. The place was smelly and dim; cobwebs hammocked the windows, the ceiling sagged, I thought of rats. We had to shove a wardrobe aside to get up the stairs and its doors flew open to reveal a shiny picture of a woman showing her bottom.

'Did you hear about the family in Trebeere who moved into a new house and kept hearing mewing noises, even though they didn't have a cat?' Kerenza began.

She had already told me this story, though I had been trying to forget it.

'They looked everywhere for the cat, all round the house, in the cellar, in the attic, but couldn't find anything. The mewing always came at night, in one particular bedroom, where their little boy slept. In the end they had to get builders in to see if it was trapped behind a wall. When the builders knocked a hole in the wall, they found a skeleton of a cat.'

Victor laughed, too loud like a bark, and asked her which house in Trebeere. Tracy said nothing, her face expressionless. I decided to tell Kerenza about the Knife-Sharpening Man, later, when we were alone.

Downstairs, Kerenza picked up a cup and threw it into the sink. 'Let's go.'

'Why don't we try a proper house?' she said when we were out amid dustbins and valerian flowers in the alley. 'One that's lived in. Then we could have a look at all their stuff. It would be more interesting. Like real spies.'

'Because there would be people in there, stupid.'

'Not if they're at work. They might forget to close their windows. If we got in here, we could do that too.'

Victor looked interested. 'It would take a lot of planning.'

'No it wouldn't. There's a house behind our hotel. It's a man and a woman who go out in the morning together, there's a way in down the side. Come on, I dare you.'

Kerenza, early the following Saturday, took us into a larder behind the back kitchen at the Bonaparte. From the window you could see into the narrow street that ran behind the hotel, and she told us to watch the door of a tall house opposite. It felt important, standing there in a row with the others, noting any movement or change; it felt like work. After about ten minutes a man and a woman came out, fiddling with bags and keys, and walked off up the street. Tracy watched the front while Kerenza led us to a back door, where she produced a key from under a flowerpot. She seemed to know her way about. When Tracy came back, Kerenza let us into the kitchen. It all smelled of fresh paint, clean sheets and new carpet; this house was sleeping, not abandoned, and this changed the flavour of the trespassing experience. The fear of being discovered was intensified, but the sense of taking possession was missing; here we were intruders, and with this came resentment, the need to shout, to disrupt these placid rooms. It would only have taken a little push, perhaps from an angrier child, to tip us across another threshold into destructiveness. As it was, Victor opened the fridge and took out a jar of peaches which turned out, revoltingly, to be pickled in brandy. He dropped the jar and it smashed on the tiles in a pool of volatile syrup, lending an undertone of hysteria to our explorations upstairs, where we opened cupboards in the bathroom, peering at shaving soap, a scent spray called Rive Gauche, anti-fungal cream, 'intimate deodorant' ('It's for their vaginas,' Kerenza said) – all the absurd and slightly disgusting appurtenances of adult culture. But it never occurred to me to be disappointed by what we found in these houses, because, as Victor and Tracy had promised, I was seeing things I was not supposed to see, and before long we were sure to uncover something magical and extraordinary. Kerenza challenged Victor to find the next trespass: 'You've got a week.'

* * *

While Kerenza spoke about her family with an unnerving lack of inhibition, and Tracy was mentioning her cat and her grandmother more often now that I had been to her house, Victor never talked about his home at all. He might as well have been an orphan, a glamorous solitary boy from a storybook. As it turned out I met the family by chance. Victor, Tracy and I were going up Carne Hill when we passed Denise, Victor's eldest sister, coming down on the same side with a crying child in a pushchair. Denise was dark, carelessly pretty, but her eyes were walls, blocking you out.

'Vic, you better get home. Mum needs you to go to the chemist.'

'Why can't Paul go?'

'Just get home, Vic.'

Victor's house was on the estate at the top of the hill. The front garden had a pram in it; I looked under the hood and saw an electric drill curled up there.

'Wait here, I'll only be a minute.' He disappeared inside, but then the door opened again and a big dark woman stuck her head out.

'Well don't just skirtle about out there. Come on in for your tea, now you're here.' The chemist seemed forgotten.

I was amazed at how crowded it was. Their living room was big, but with Victor's father, Keith Jordan, his mother Bridget, his older brother Paul, his sister Andrea, Andrea's boyfriend Matt, Andrea's baby, Denise's husband Mike and their little boy, two neighbour women who were just leaving with their children, it was more like entering a full classroom at school. A long table was spread with sandwiches, bowls of crisps, biscuits, and in the centre sat a big crystal dish of ham and lettuce with sliced beetroot bleeding purple all over it.

Years later, when I read Philip Larkin's poem 'Afternoons', I thought of Victor's sisters, Denise and Andrea. In 1976 they were nineteen and sixteen years old. Denise was already married with two small children, and Andrea, who was engaged, had a baby son. They seemed always to be anxious and distracted, speaking in short bursts, repeatedly interrupted by the needs of the children, and the talk was only of babies, food, shops. They stood on the sidelines, the next generation at their tired young feet, evicted from their own lives. For me and Kerenza, they came to represent everything we did not want to become, and for Victor, one of the many possible fates he feared for Tracy.

Chairs were pulled out and we all sat at the table, apart from Victor's mother who returned to her armchair by the fireplace, surrounded by piles of library books, facing us all. She was high and wide as a wardrobe, black-eyed, commanding the room.

'Good Lord, Tracy, look at the state of you! What on earth have you been up to? Look at your hair, like a bird's nest.'

Everyone turned to look at Tracy's hair, which was nothing like a bird's nest, but was tangled nevertheless with burrs and skeins of sticky goose grass from that day's trespassing.

Mrs Jordan then ignored Tracy for the rest of the meal and turned her attention on me. 'Who's your friend, Victor?'

'Sally,' I said, before he could answer. My accent betrayed me once more, and the questions about London followed. Victor's father, slimmer and seemingly younger than his wife, looked up from his paper. A high voice, birdlike.

'London! I know it. We did a bit of work up there a while back, '73 or '74. Demolitions. Massive she is. Very nice for a visit, I'm sure, but I wouldn't want to live there.'

'Last I heard, they hadn't asked you,' said his wife.

'More incomers, eh?' Mr Jordan was looking at me. 'Just what we don't need down here.' He had a way of saying everything as if it were a joke, so it took a while to wonder if maybe it wasn't.

'So, Sally,' Bridget continued, 'what do you like doing with your time?'

'Well, I like reading...'

'Ah! What are you reading now?'

'*The Lost World*, it's by Conan Doyle, there's a forest in the Amazon and some dinosaurs...'

'I don't know it. I like thrillers.'

Bridget Jordan asked questions and then cut you off and answered them herself, at length. This suited me well, excusing me from talking, allowing my attention to travel unsupervised. She outlined the plot of her current book, *Cover Her Face* by PD James ('the murder victim's called Sally'), before suggesting that if I liked reading, I should talk to Victor's older brother, Paul.

'Paul's the real reader in the family. He's sensitive. Ask him anything: history, geography, chemicals, figures, outer space. Up at the school they're saying he could be university material. That's what they said, word for word, university material. Think of that! I'm not sure where he gets it from.'

'Not from you, at any rate,' said Mr Jordan. 'Thrillers! Rubbish, you read. As if there wasn't enough to shock you in the real world.'

'At least I encouraged him to read, not like you with your nose in the paper, takes you all day to get through it.'

'He hasn't got into trouble yet, there's that to be thankful for.'

'No, and you'd know all about that.'

While the parents snapped reflexively at each other I looked over at Paul. He was a big, slow-moving boy in his mid-teens, with the dark eyes and high colour shared by the whole family. I was intrigued at how, with such similar features, he could look so unlike Victor. He was cutting up his ham and beetroot with care, and did not seem inclined to share any of his formidable knowledge. Denise's two-year-old son Jason, a startlingly beautiful child, wandered around the table, stopping at each person, holding up a red toy car. 'Look! Look! Look!' Nobody looked.

Just before we left, Mrs Jordan sent Tracy up to the bathroom to tidy herself. 'You don't want to frighten your grandmother, she's had quite enough of all that.' She turned to me again when

Tracy disappeared up the stairs, lowering her voice conspiratorially, as if I were a grown-up.

'It's not everyone would do what Hazel Tabb's done, you know, at her age. Bringing up a kid over again, and a teasy one at that, after what happened with Tom Pender and Irene. It's lucky Hocking let her stay on at Number Five after old Tabb died. Grace and favour, like, Hazel can't be paying much rent.'

Baffled, I nodded wisely, and when Tracy came back downstairs, gold hair brushed straight, Mrs Jordan opened the front door.

'Well Tracy, we haven't seen so much of you lately. Still away with the seals?'

Outside, hundreds of feet below us, a trawler was leaving the harbour – a distant inconsequential object like Jason's little car, its bobbing progress barely noticeable, but the slow rhythmical clack of the diesel engine was loud, throbbing in the evening air, disconnected from its source like a sound effect imposed clumsily on film.

'What's the lost world?' asked Victor.

I told him about the Amazon in Brazil, how a remote plateau had become separated from the rest of the tropical forest for millions of years, and how a brave group of explorers set out to prove that dinosaurs still lived there.

'Did they find them?'

'I'll lend you the book. I've already read it three times.'

It occurred to me that this was the first time Victor had said anything since we entered his house.

A week passed and Victor met Kerenza's trespassing deadline, but the house he had identified didn't look worth the trouble: a pebble-dashed semi-detached on one of the no-man's-land suburban avenues between Trebeere and St Anthony. He had been watching it – the people always used the car when they went out, he said, and mornings were best because the car was always gone. He had the times written down in an exercise book, and a toilet window at the back was loose, which would allow him to lean in and release the larger window. I was right, though; inside, the place was the least interesting we had seen: brown, bookless, fussy china crinoline ladies placed wide apart, all of it tidily becalmed as a waiting room. The only tempting thing was a zoo of tiny glass animals in a glass cabinet in the bedroom. It was there that we heard the door of the room close, the click-snap of a key.

We turned, appalled, staring at the door. Tracy crept up to it and gently took the handle, pulling it towards her, turning it both ways. We were shut in. I tried the door again, rattling and wrenching it. Someone on the other side cleared their throat, and I jumped back.

'It's locked, you can't get out. I've rung the police, so you'll stay in there.' A high, querulous voice, a woman's.

We sat on the bed in front of the glass animals in their glass prison until the police car crackled to a stop on the gravel outside, and when the two uniformed men came into the room we were still sitting there in a row. A grey woman was peering up through the banisters, clearing her throat repetitively, behind the police. In the police car, pressed up against a window, I watched the normal world flick by: a fat man outside the post office with a dog, a couple kissing outside the Ruby Tiger Inn. A child, grasping his mother's hand, smiled and waved at me when we paused at a zebra crossing.

They made us wait for ages at the police station, the air filled with typing and telephones and dry-paper seriousness. Policemen, and an occasional woman, would come past, cross to a bank of steel cabinets, open one, riffle about, slam it shut and walk out again. We were taken out one by one, and I was horrified to see both my parents there at a table in a windowless room, sharing the same baffled expression. A policewoman told me to take everything out of my cardigan pocket: moss, and 20p. She asked about the house. What had I been doing there? Nothing. My parents kept interrupting, what do you mean, Sally, you must know what you were doing. The policewoman ignored them and faced me – had I taken anything, how had we got in, surely I realised it was private. 'Whose idea was it to enter the house?' That last question was the most difficult. Whose idea was it? I had no idea.

We were only given a caution: we hadn't stolen or damaged anything, none of us had attracted the wrong sort of attention before. The woman who had locked us in the bedroom was a neighbour with a set of keys; she had spotted us from her garden. The worst part was the policewoman's lecture: did I realise an elderly couple lived in the house, could I imagine how frightened they would have been if they had surprised us in their bedroom? How I would feel if they were my own grandparents? I didn't tell her I didn't have any. I have no memory of any specific punishment afterwards, though I imagine my comings and goings were restricted for a while. What I do remember is my parents saying, over and over, 'But why were you all in someone else's house? What on earth were you doing in someone else's house?' Once Kerenza had overcome her anger at Victor for choosing an unsuitable trespass, she talked about her own parents' reaction quite often, describing, with a suggestion of awed relish, the fury on her mother's face, the shouting, her father forced away from writing his book on Cornish noblemen to take a phone call from the police, and how funny it would have been if the old couple had really found us in their bedroom. Tracy said she had been made to read the Bible. I don't know what happened to Victor, because he never spoke about it for six years, by which time the police had different, more frightening, questions for us.

3

1827 – A Resurrection

In December 1826, five years after the Great Fall, the parson James Prideaux ended his long bachelorhood and married, after a short engagement, a woman named Geneva Thomasin Florey, widow of a Trebeere brewery merchant and mother of a son, Henry, who was studying law in London. At fifty-one, Geneva was not much younger than her new husband, but he writes in his journal of her 'abundant chestnut hair' and 'pure green eyes reflecting the serenity of her disposition', so it seems to have been a love match. He is quite taken by the romance of her name, speculating on its possible derivation from Guinevere, or the birthplace of Jean-Jacques Rousseau, though he fails to note that the city of Geneva was also the home of Predestination. To her family and neighbours she was known more prosaically as Jenny.

Geneva, according to Prideaux, 'possessed a great aptitude for drawing, and an unusual desire for extreme solitude and tranquillity in which to practise this talent'. Only one example survives of her work, to my knowledge – a small ink and wash drawing of two seals, seen through a screen of leaves on a rocky shore; it is delicate but energetic in its precision, and now hangs in the Branwell Library at Trebeere. Not long after his marriage, Prideaux convinced himself that Geneva was in need of respite from the hectic life of a small rural parsonage and decided to buy a granite cottage in a remote spot on Torbett's Green, two miles beyond St Anthony, not far from the edge of the Great Fall. Here the couple could retreat at will, beyond the reach of social cares and duties. The place is very ancient, he writes, situated in a hollow or fold in the landscape, hidden by a thick growth of trees and brushwood:

> It lacks all amenities of civilised life apart from a spring, which supplies the water to the well, and a fire of the most antique type. The front of the house looks directly to the south west, to the bay and the open sea beyond, with the noble headland at St Anthony obscuring every sign of human influence in the wider aspect, just as the woods protect it from the curiosity of wandering strangers close by. I shall construct a veranda at the front, and cover it in glass, so that my dear Geneva may sit outside among vines and flowers even as the storms rush in from the Americas.

In March 1827 he visits the market town of Trebeere to conclude the business of buying the cottage, which had belonged to a reclusive widow. The sum paid was very little even by the standards of the time; presumably the extreme isolation of the tiny property, together with its nearness to the landslip area, made it an unattractive proposition to all but the most eccentric. Prideaux continues:

The land agent is a Richard Jenkin, a gentleman I have found to be agreeable and punctilious; he assured me again that the little house, though primitive in construction, is solid, and that its distance from the cracked and ruined landscape of the Great Fall is sufficient to obviate the danger of subsidence in the future. On my earlier visits I had walked all around the building and its environs, measuring the distance from the first crevasse, inspecting the ground, parting furze and bracken for signs of fissuring or instability, and found nothing to alarm me. With the business concluded to my great satisfaction, I walked out into the early spring sunshine, my imagination creating the moment when I would present Geneva with the keys to our charming haven, and I foresaw an evening there, the two of us sitting enclosed by my veranda, watching the sea turn silver beyond the apple trees. It was in this agreeable frame of mind that I entered the Bell and Candle to toast my success. The sullen fellow who served my ale had pouchy features like melting wax and, too late, I regretted my choice of tavern; I had forgotten that the Bell is a place where the fetid sawdust is sweeter than the malodorous customers, many of whom have business in the butcher's shambles to the rear. On my way to a table by the single window, I almost fell over a pail of slops. 'Bucket!' shrieked my host from his stool behind the taps.

I had not been seated more than a minute when I became aware of being observed from behind, an unmistakeable creeping sensation between the shoulder blades. A woman sat alone in the dim of the corner, and there was something familiar in her shape and aspect. She gave me a watery smile, raised herself up off the settle and came over.

'You don't want to mind Paulie, he can be quite obliging if you ask nicely.' She turned and bawled back across the room, 'Paulie! A jar of your best stout porter, Sir! The reverend gentleman is buying.'

With some dismay, I recognised my companion as Maryann Tabb, but Good Lord how changed she was! The handsome dairy-woman of my memory was woefully marked by Time, more than you might expect for the six years since I saw her last: the features coarsened, creamy complexion sallowed, grey eyes rimmed with red. She wore a dark gown, cut very low and shiny with wear, her bosom half-covered by a thin grey shawl or fichu, like a cobweb. I suspected she planned to ask me for more than a pot of ale, but she surprised me by asking after the health of my wife Geneva.

'What a blessing, I said, when they told me you had wed little Jenny! After so many years as a strict bachelor, and Jenny herself widowed just a year. They say the late weddings wear the best in the end, flowers and fripperies long forgotten, and yours is the tardiest I've ever heard of, but it did surprise me somewhat, you with your particular ways and tastes, choosing that quiet woman, little Jenny.' (Geneva, incidentally, is a moderately tall, well-built woman.)

'She did well to wed Ted Florey, I should think,' Maryann continued, 'but nobody supposed her likely to marry again, least of all her family.'

Paulie the candleface pushed past my shoulder and dumped a pot of ale on the table. Maryann interrupted herself to take a long draught.

'You will already know that Jenny is a cousin of mine.'

My face informed her this was not so, and her eyes turned shrewd.

'But of course. Her mother was Laura Pender, aunt to my mother, Jane Pender as she was, God rest her. Always looked out for my mother, Laura Pender did, dear of her, she was devoted.'

I had reason to doubt this, based on what Geneva had told me of her own mother's volatile character, and while Maryann spoke, I considered how strange it is that the loveliness of a woman's features can veil the hints of guile and rancour in the words she utters. I recalled my past association with her, when we used to meet in the copse by Hocking's farm, where Maryann, with the bloom of summer on her face and hair, her voice murmuring with the bees around us, would flatter me and spin diverting stories about our neighbours. I had taken this as evidence of the innocent amiability of her character, the brave cheerfulness of a woman prematurely widowed, and believed her to be as even-tempered as the dairy cows she milked (although, now I remember, Maryann herself insisted that cows were by nature 'quick-tempered and contrary').

She spoke to me now in the same manner, smiling all the while, but her words, without the softening influence of Beauty, were insinuating rather than soothing, and under the honeyed protestations of affection for mutual acquaintances hovered the faint odour of ill will, mingling with the less timid stink from Paulie's bucket. While I understood this as a consequence of her reduced circumstances and the influence of the wretched squalor in the air around us, I had the impression that there had always been a sour undertaste to Maryann's sweetness, and that it was I who had chosen not to pay heed to it.

In an effort to divert her attention from the subject of Geneva, I inquired as to her fortunes since the Great Fall, but I had no sooner asked when I remembered the loss of her daughter Eliza, who has never been found. This tragic circumstance had quite escaped my mind, and I regretted the uncharitable drift of my earlier thoughts.

'Hocking wanted no more of me and cast me off altogether,' she replied. 'The farm was half destroyed anyhow, he lost much of the pasture and half the beasts, so there was no work for me, and when there's no work there's no house, no home, though you wouldn't know about that, because I reckon your Good Lord is a better sort of landlord. Hocking wouldn't even let me go into the cottage to collect my pots and linens, he said it was too dangerous with the crackings, though when I looked past him into the passage I could see my jacket and Eliza's brown cloak hanging just so behind the kitchen door; it wouldn't have hurt him to let me go in for those.'

'What did you do then?'

'Went to Bessy in Trebeere, left word with Hocking to tell Eliza where I had gone, if she returned.'

Where, I asked, had she supposed Eliza was?

'Hocking said he saw her walking up Torbett's Green to where the woods get thick, around midday. He said he had often seen her with a young fellow there, a shipwright's 'prentice, but I'd never seen any such lad, nor heard of him. Myself, I think Eliza was over to Trebeere all along, and she left for work upcountry. We had not been seeing eye to eye, you see.'

'Why was that?'

She paused, and suggested I might like to refresh our ale, so I wasted some minutes trying to attract the notice of the dismal Paulie, who was enchanted by some new clients, a rabble of hawkers, butchers and traders shouting and jostling around the taps.

Maryann drank as if her second draught were the first in a fortnight. Her cheeks sucked inwards as she swallowed; she was thinner than I remembered.

'What you don't see, and never did, is how it is for us. Hocking was the same as most governors I've known. I expect he still is. Not the worst by a long mile, but he expected extra work, if you take my meaning.'

'As well as the dairy?'

'I mean evening work. Domestic duties. There are many ways, Jim, for a woman to pay the rent.'

As a younger man I would have reddened at this. I glanced about in fear that we had been overheard; her voice was growing in volume.

'Good Lord, Maryann. Matthew Hocking is a married man! Of course you refused.'

'Refuse? How long do you suppose I would have been top dairymaid and housekeeper after that? With a whole cottage, and just me and Eliza to live in it? We lived like gentry up there, compared to how I'm situated now.'

'I'm sorry. I wish you had confided in me.'

'If I had, then, would you have wanted me?'

I thought it best not to reply.

'His wife knew, Lowdie. But she knew better than to argue, the fussock. Talked sweet as violets but always made sure to send a rotten egg up to me and Eliza.'

She hesitated, looked aside, then faced me. 'That's not the whole of it, you see. Hocking had tired of me some months previous. He was set on Eliza. It was all right to begin with, he was courting her, coming back from Trebeere market with cologne and fancy handkerchiefs, raising his cap off his baldy head whenever she crossed the yard with the pails. But she wanted none of him, she was that proud. There was no talking to her.'

A distant but uneasy memory came to mind at this moment, and I took refuge in conventional reaction.

'No talking to her? You must have looked for ways to protect your daughter. Why didn't you seek me out? I would have helped you, as far as I was able. I could perhaps have spoken to Hocking.' As I said this, I was thankful that I had never been required to undergo the embarrassment of performing such a favour. Matthew Hocking I have long considered a graceless, ill-natured fellow, quite unprincipled. I avert my eyes when I see the heavy use he makes of sticks to drive his cows and pigs across what remains of Torbett's Green, though it cannot be denied he has made a success of Churchtown Farm since his father died. The older Hocking was a more companionable man, but he dragged the place almost to ruin with drink and cards. Maryann's face soured and she slammed her jar on the table.

'You don't listen, do you? Eliza was gone seventeen. Not a child. It was not hard work I was asking her to do, just to lie with him once or twice a week, and the man was quick with the business, too. Hocking didn't want me, and we still had our keep to find. Besides, what would you have done, Jim? Had me and Eliza in to stay at the parsonage?'

When I looked across at the coarse, pitted faces around me, the talk loud and brutal in drink, a piercing image came to mind of the perfect seclusion and wild beauty of the little house by the Fall, of Geneva's eyes that held all the green stillness of the forest in them, and I was reminded again that two kingdoms have always existed side by side, the natives of each strictly bound never to cross the frontier. Somehow, I had stepped over without being aware of my trespass. I wished only to escape, return to my wife, leave the Bell and Candle and its benighted patrons forever, but Maryann had summoned Paulie over (she seemed to have some sort of hold over him) and ordered more drink on my slate. From a distance, Paulie's melting lineaments collapsed and blurred in the poor light, giving the queasy impression that he had no face at all.

'Any rate I've had no sight nor word of Eliza since. She always had more time for horses than Christian people, but she was a sharp girl in many ways,' (I noticed how she spoke of Eliza in the past tense) 'and while not handsome exactly, she will have found herself a fellow, or work, one of the two or both, somewhere across the county.'

Maryann then abandoned the subject of Eliza and returned to her own situation. She was living, she said, in a rooming house close by the tannery, on the marshy land at the eastern end of town.

'It stinks mightily day and night, thanks to the muck and piddle they soak the skins in, but the room is dry. Bessy couldn't keep me for long, and I've spent a good while far away – Wadebridge, Camelford, all over. Paulie gives me a little work in here, and there's the fish as well, that's how my hands are as they are.' I looked – her hands were scored with pinkish cuts and little white scars. 'They make us work too fast. My fingers get cold, and the knife slips.'

I reached for my hat and prepared to leave; she took hold of my wrist.

'It's providential you came in here when you did, Jim; we should renew our relation. You're welcome to call for me of an evening, if your fancy takes you. We could light a kisky[1] fire between us, I'm sure.'

All the wheedling smiles were back, and I attempted to throw her off.

'But I owe, James. And you have a debt owing to me, for all those pretty summer evenings. We're almost family now, with you married to my cousin. Creeping Jenny, dressed in yellow. Does she know of our friendship?'

I handed Maryann the money I had, snatched up my hat and Jenkin's legal papers and scuttled to the tavern's back door. This time I kicked the bucket over entirely, sending a river of filth across the sawdust. I found myself in Pound Street, at the narrowest point of its long high-walled descent to the sea. The sun on the roof-slates was white, hard as iron, blinding, but it must have rained while I had been inside, for the setts were sticky underfoot: dried blood from the morning's slaughterings had liquefied once more, coating the roadway in a reddish dew. I took the shore lane back to St Anthony, and I was walking fast, trying to put the unfortunate meeting out of my mind, when a thought occurred to me, a memory of that day of the Great Fall, when I had looked through the cracked façade of Maryann's cottage into the bedchamber with its smashed pitcher and scattered linens. Maryann said that when Matthew Hocking had refused permission to gather her belongings from the ruined cottage, she had seen her coat and Eliza's cape hanging in the passage. I wondered why, if Eliza Tabb had left St Anthony for ever before the landslip occurred, she had not taken her cape with her.

---

[1] Kisky: dry, brittle stems of umbelliferous plants in autumn, such as cow parsley (S. Martins)

* * *

The more I read of James Prideaux's journal, the more I doubt whether he ever intended to publish it, at least not in the form it eventually took. The book is absurdly long, and perhaps I am the only reader to have persevered to the end. I was around sixteen when I opened it one day in the Branwell Library, and at that age I obeyed a self-imposed rule to finish any book I started. I would return to it intermittently, discovering a soothing pleasure in the placidity of Prideaux's early life. The extracts I include here probably give a misleading impression that he was wholly concerned with dramatic incidents or inner conflicts, but for much of the first two-thirds he is preoccupied by the minutiae of local affairs in his various curacies, travelogues (never very far), minor flirtations, observations of the natural world (these lack specificity and are somewhat sentimental), disquisitions on church architecture and long-winded accounts of perceived slights from local gentry and tight-pursed parishioners.

He presents an unfeasibly buoyant and positive picture of himself in these early sections – reading them today, you'd be reminded of social media posts – and there are unexplained gaps when he writes nothing for months (more than five years in one case). But he has an unusually sharp memory for conversations, transcribing all of them apparently verbatim, and tells us he has been doing this since boyhood. It was this that inspired a fellow feeling in me: I also have an over-efficient memory for conversations long past, though unlike Prideaux I never wrote them down; they simply exist, loitering in the mind like radio waves in space.

The sections that would have embarrassed his descendants, who proceeded mainly from a cousin's family, are slipped in without preamble, written when the strange pressures of his later years overcame him.

I like to think that a mischievous young descendant of Prideaux's read the manuscript and had it published surreptitiously in 1914 to embarrass a conservative parent, and this theory is bolstered by the poor quality of the printing: the typeface is off-puttingly tiny and tightly leaded, and the whole shows signs of haste and careless proofreading.

The five years between the landslip in 1821 and his marriage to Geneva in 1826 seem to have been the last in which Prideaux was modestly content. He was well settled into the curacy at St Anthony. His employer was the Rector of Boskerris, who bore the unfitting name of Laity (Prideaux never remarks on this; Laity is a common name in Cornwall). Silas Laity was elderly, rarely seen in the parish of St Anthony, the poorest under his supervision, so Prideaux, despite his meagre stipend, would have enjoyed a degree of independence as well as the use of the small parsonage house. But after the encounter with Maryann Tabb in the Bell and Candle in March 1827, the journal gives the impression of a man increasingly haunted by the consequences of a lifetime's inaction, his sins of omission. The entries grow more frequent, the style less stiff, and I am reminded of Goya's image of a man at a desk, writing abandoned, his head on his arms and his reason asleep, the room behind him filling with a swarm of bat-owl hybrids.

* * *

The Parsonage, St Anthony, April 23, 1827
The evening is advancing, it being well past seven o'clock, and the sun has retreated from this room, which faces east. I should not still be sitting here at my desk, I should be talking with Geneva in the bright parlour at the back of the house, sifting through the

commonplace occurrences of our respective days, my eyes resting on her strong features, drawing vigour from their imperturbable beauty. It was here, however, five hours since, that I saw the first harbinger of a visit, a visitor, a visitation, that has turned my day inside out and scattered my peace of mind, and now I find myself rooted to my chair in the dusk, afraid that the evening sun in Geneva's room would expose the turmoil behind my face.

I habitually work in this cramped room, preferring it to the slightly larger library next door, because the latter overlooks the churchyard and I would rather not have my faith constantly tested by the sight of those awaiting Resurrection. My desk is positioned directly in front of the window, beyond which is a short stretch of grass bordered by an old wall, much overgrown with fern, valerian and ransy[2]. This wall separates the parsonage garden from a footpath, set several feet lower than the lawn on our side. At around three o'clock I was seated here, as now, alone, reading the *Christian Observer*. Geneva had gone out to call on Amelia Cleer in town; my wife plans to revive the Sunday school in St Anthony, to have the children taught to write, as well as read; the idea has proved controversial, and she hopes to persuade Mrs Cleer to take her part, though I doubt if that lady will do so unless she is persuaded the venture will reflect well on herself. Something prompted me to glance up from my paper, and through the window I saw what appeared to be a coal-scuttle bobbing along the top of the garden wall.

It was not, of course, a coal-scuttle, but a lady's hat, in some drab material, of the ugly tunnelled shape that is unaccountably popular with women. I was surprised because the narrow footpath beyond the wall is frequented rarely, and then only by children. The coal-scuttle disappeared behind the holly bush to

---

[2] Wild garlic, also known as 'ramsons' (S. Martins)

the left of our lawn, but the sight, for a reason I could not identify, provoked a chill of unease. Moments later I heard the clicket on the garden gate, and Dinah knocked and announced that a parishioner, a Mrs Tabb, was here to see me. Maryann came into the study behind Dinah, in a blue cloak and the dark bonnet. I sent Dinah to bring us tea. Maryann was quite sober, her appearance somewhat improved since I saw her in the Bell and Candle. She removed the cloak and coal-scuttle, revealing tidy hair and a clean calico gown, and sat in my armchair. She began by excusing her conduct when we had last met, giving a convoluted account of some trouble with her landlord and her employer, before praising the comforts of my study and the elegance of the parsonage, when in truth it is plain to see this house is cramped and shabby, sorely in need of restoration. I could not avoid noticing how affected Maryann's gestures were, and how her big hands showed raw and red against the little blue flowers on her frock.

I let her chatter on until Dinah had returned with our tea, laid it out, and closed the door behind her. It is difficult to express adequately how dismayed I was by this sudden reappearance of Maryann in my house, my study. She had narrowly missed meeting Geneva, who only left for Trebeere at two o'clock. Dinah, who is an honest and unsuspicious woman, accustomed to visits from parishioners of all types, would not be inquisitive about Mrs Tabb, but she might mention the call to my wife.

'Where is little Jenny?' Maryann said. 'Over to Trebeere is she?'

I ignored this.

'Why are you here, Maryann?'

'Such a harsh question that one, I've been hearing it for years. I find myself in need of counsel.'

'Very well. What troubles you?'

'Strictly speaking, it's not a matter of me, but of what troubles a friend of mine, a young maid close to my heart.'

For a moment I thought she was going to talk about Eliza.

'I would be obliged to hear your opinion on her situation. Charity, for that is her name, is the daughter of a Christian family, a family living in a parish not far from this one for as long as anyone remembers. Her father was a cowman, a steady man known for his orderly work, and they had their own quillet[3], a sow, and hens, and grew almost everything they needed to feed themselves and trade a little extra besides. Charity had only one brother, her mother being delicate in the female way, dear of her, so Charity, not being required to care for a gaggle of little ones, had leisure to learn to read the Bible, *Pilgrim's Progress*, *The Faceless Huntsman*[4], and to write a little, and in time she grew into a fine-looking maid and followed her father into the dairy.'

I found my attention drifting from this tedious story, but at the same time Maryann's smooth voice (quite unlike Geneva's rapid, practical speech) was exerting some of the mesmeric power I recalled from our old association. I felt my shoulders dropping, the words sliding like silk across the skin of my back, my gaze resting on the top of her bent head – bronze lights in thick pale hair. I remembered that with Maryann I was never obliged to talk; she filled my silences.

'Some years ago they took her family's quillet away, I never did understand rightly why, but they said it was needed for the manor farm, together with the quillets of their neighbours. Charity's father tried to argue, but the Law found against him, and without the land his wages would not keep the family, so Charity

---

[3] Strip of land (S. Martins)
[4] Unknown (S. Martins)

was forced to leave her home and find a situation many miles distant. Charity worked hard and always sent her wages...'

I interrupted to remind her that I had claims on my time and would be obliged if she would address the matter of her friend's difficulty.

'Well, Jim, during the long years of the French War, she never ceased working in the dairies and in the big houses, putting money by in her teapot. Bread was mightily expensive, of course, but the parish was sometimes there when times were hard. Along came the Peace, which doubtless brought peace for some, but for Charity the battle began. Work became scarcer and scarcer, and wages smaller and smaller, and the governors harder, until she despaired of her life. But the Good Lord must have been watching over her still, for one day she met with a true gentleman, a man of learning, one who seemed to care for her, and she put her faith in him. She would bring him comfort, she told him, provided he never forgot her.'

Maryann replaced her cup with exaggerated care on its saucer, took up the pot and slowly refilled both cups, letting the placid reddish flow of the tea catch the light. The sound deepened the quiet in the room.

'Then came a great upheaving in the earth, a day when the wrath of God struck Cornwall like a... like a thunderous wrath. Perhaps He was angry about the War, or the Peace, anyway we had the Great Fall, which we all remember. Charity survived the wrath, in spite of being so near to it, and she waited by the willow copse for the gentleman to come. When he did not, she feared for his life, supposing he might have been walking on Torbett's Green when the hills fell towards the sea, and she went down to inquire after him in the town, but they swore he was in perfect health, and had gone away visiting. So she waited some more, and when he failed to ask for her, neglected even to send an inquiry, she fell into despair, for she had a secret she had been about to tell him.'

By this time of course I understood that Maryann had no such friend as Charity, and was talking about herself, despite the omission of Eliza, and of her own late husband, from the story. I held my tongue, however.

She looked at me, considering.

'Can you guess what that secret might have been?'

I said I could not, and I spoke the truth, however ingenuous that seems in retrospect.

'Charity knew she was carrying a child, and the child was the gentleman's child. When the days and weeks and months went by with no word from the gentleman, she sought refuge with a cousin, and was delivered of a boy at that lady's lodging.'

Maryann paused, smoothing the blue flowers over her knees.

'And she was delivered of the child, which came out lifeless, and it was put aside in despair, until a neighbour's girl took a notion to pick the infant up and shake it like a rug, whereupon the spirit jumped back in and the baby screamed. But with all of them in the little room, and the cousin most anxious about the landlord, Charity found herself cast out once more. You know of course that no landlord, no governor, would look at a woman burdened with an infant, so she took the road east, carrying the infant on her back, until after many hard miles she came to Redruth town. With the rain skeeting down on her head and her boots full of mud she climbed up to the Poorhouse and put the infant down, there on the step by the big door. She pulled on the bell and then went quick across the lane to hide behind a gate in a hedge. With one eye she peered around the gatepost and after long minutes the door of the Poorhouse opened and a tall man came out. He looked down at the infant on the step, stared around for a good while, and then looked again at the child, as you would look at a parcel of washing, and finally he turned around and shouted something back into the house, and a stout woman came and took the parcel in.'

We sat together in silence, the sun coming through the glass on the back of my head where the hair is thin, until presently I told her it was the sort of story that would need more consideration, or some such nonsense. Maryann departed directly, though not before I had passed her a little bag of coin from my desk, for that, I knew, was the true reason for this visit. Geneva tells me I am too susceptible to charm, to the outward appearances of things, too ready to believe the accounts people give of themselves, but I am not such a fool that I cannot see the lacunae in Maryann's tale of misfortune, the intent to influence my picture of the past. She is lying, of course. She tells me a history of her life that omits the most important events, namely her marriage, her widowhood, her absent daughter Eliza, her relations with Matthew Hocking, and greatly exaggerates an inconsequential association, one of countless such encounters in her life, in order to induce a perception of responsibility, of guilt, in me. I took care not to ask anything about the infant, which is no more than a phantom, a blackmail, a mockery.

Back at my desk I pulled this journal out (I keep it and all earlier volumes locked in a drawer), turning back six years until I came to my description of that terrible day in 1821. I saw that while I had written about the Great Fall, I had recorded nothing of its aftermath. The memory, though, is clear: as our party of menfolk walked home from Torbett's Green, we had found ourselves voiceless. No words existed to address the scale of the destruction we had seen. We came down at last into St Anthony, to the Bonaparte Inn, where people were still standing in groups in the roadway. They swarmed about us and pulled at our sleeves, demanding a report, but our replies were perfunctory, we were intent only on seeking the familiarity of our own homes. I remember there was a boy weeping, a big heavy lad, but nobody laughed at him. When I reached the parsonage gate I discovered that my coat had split open at the seams, under the arms, as if in sympathy with the cliffs. Dinah was standing on the path in the dusk outside the front door. She was drawn and anxious, her apron dirty.

'But where is Voltaire?' she said. 'Is he not with you?'

Over the next week of days and nights, we searched the village, Dinah and I, for the dog Voltaire. Back and forth through the spinney, all around the harbour, westward along the shore to Penglaze Point and then eastward to Trebeere. I often imagined I saw his big brown shape in the distance, his triangular ears like two pyramids on the top of his head, only to be disappointed. Once, and once only, I ventured up Torbett's Hill and a little way across the open green, calling for him in the wind, but I could not force myself to go any further, to look again over the broken cliffs and wrecked woods. Voltaire never returned. Dinah believes he had followed me up to the Fall that day, tracking our party of men, and had then become lost. Perhaps the revolution in the landscape upset some orienting mechanism in his anatomy – the scent of safety.

It was an obscure sense of shame about my excessive grief for the dog, as much as the shock of the Great Fall itself, that prompted my temporary flight from St Anthony. And Dinah would not let the subject alone. 'Did you not look behind you?' she kept asking. I hadn't, because I never do. Since youth I've had a horror of being followed, and a superstitious idea that if I do not look back, I will be safe. But that should never have applied to Voltaire. I went to stay with my good friend Daniel MacNamara at Fowey, and the short visit lengthened to a month during which I submitted to the healing effect of his kindness, and the tactful presence of his fine wolfhound. Daniel is the only man I know who fully understands the bond between Man and beast, without resorting to feminine sentimentality. He teases me about my faith, demanding to know the place of animal souls in Heaven:

'What use is a Paradise, a Heaven, without a dog at your feet? Will we have woods without fowl or deer? Meadows without bees? A sea without seals?'

Daniel used to hand me a whisky in the evenings while we watched the leavings and homecomings of ships past Polruan Castle, and he encouraged me to talk about the Great Fall, which I did, no doubt boring him to perdition. He told me that his parents also witnessed a frightening phenomenon afflicting Trebeere, back in 1755. Its distant cause was an earthquake a thousand miles away at Lisbon. Daniel's father remembered seeing the tide go out in Lantern Bay, much too far.

'Mother and Father were recently wed, living in that draughty house above St Dominic, overlooking the sea. Papa went outside to enjoy his pipe and was astonished to see the bay quite empty, sand and mud exposed far beyond St Materiana's Island. An acreage of brown stumps appeared: drowned trees from an ancient forest. Then, at intervals, long horizontal swells came back in, frightful waves not content to extinguish on the shore, but instead continuing, pushing forward into the low-lying parts of the village, across the pastures, flooding everything. Mother saw Papa in the garden, kneeling in the grass by the drying linen, praying. It must have seemed like the end of the world. Many people drowned, and the rotten smell of the water, the dead beasts, hung over the fields for months.'

I've heard mention of this incident before, but while Daniel was talking, a most unwelcome image came to mind of the marsh below my own childhood home at St Dominic. A swamp where stunted trees twist out of brackish pools. A place haunted by the thin bleak call of the moorhen, where a child once stumbled and drowned.

I should have been more assiduous in making enquiries of Maryann when I returned from Fowey that July and relieved Timothy Mason[5] of his extra duties, but I found myself immediately overwhelmed by the needs of my parishioners, needs which had multiplied and changed since the Great Fall. The people were coming to me with questions about the cracks in their walls, the mystery of God's will, the strange behaviour of their pigs, spectral visits from long-dead relatives, and, above all, their own bad dreams at night. It was as if Samuel Trembath's premonitory nightmare of the wolf and the falling henhouse had flown from his mind to take root and grow in the sleeping souls of his neighbours. My own nights, by contrast, were unusually peaceful at that time; the upheaval seemed, contrarily, to settle some disturbance in my spirit. Only recently has my insomnia returned.

Some weeks after my return to St Anthony we had to revise our happy conclusion that nobody had died in the Great Fall. There was, it transpired, an encampment of gypsies on the far side of the landslip area, four or five miles west of St Anthony, where the most severe collapses and fissures occurred. Nobody knew how many gypsies there were, guesses varied from a small family to a hundred people. It is impossible to establish the facts of the matter. They might have moved on; they may never have been there at all.

Geneva is rare among women in that she never questions a man's need for solitude, perhaps because she values it herself, but even she might wonder why I have been closeted here so long this

---

[5] Mr Mason was the curate from St Dominic parish, about six miles from St Anthony (S. Martins)

evening. It is almost dark, and I must stop writing and persuade myself that this visit will most likely not be repeated, and thank the Lord that I now have the means to dampen Maryann's wilder accusations with a little money. I cannot be the only man in my position who has been plagued by parishioners, or wandering vagrants, whose balance of mind is disturbed.

* * *

Tuesday May 1
This morning, as I drank my tea, I re-read what I wrote last week. I said that when I looked up to see Maryann's hat moving along the top of the wall, I had been reading the *Christian Observer*. I was not, in fact, reading the *Christian Observer*, although we do take that periodical at the parsonage; I was reading a novel, *Paul and Virginia*[6]. Why, in a private journal, should I have felt impelled to make such a trivial pretence? For whom was the deception intended? Not my readers, for there are none; not God, for He knows my literary weaknesses. It was an attempt, I concluded, to hoodwink myself, as if with ink and paper I could create, by changing details imperceptibly, a more conscientious version of my character, and that if I did this subtly, by degrees, the Universe and I would both come to believe it the real one. Today it was as if I awoke abruptly to a certainty that nobody was observing me, and nobody had ever been, and I realised that I have lived my whole life with the belief, so deeply buried that it cannot truly be called a belief, that my every thought is being recorded, collated for review at some later date. I wouldn't confuse this with my faith in God, for it was no Recording Angel I had in mind, but some

---

[6] *Paul et Virginie,* by Jacques-Henri Bernardin de Saint-Pierre, 1788 (S. Martins)

lesser being, a pallid functionary or scribe assigned to my case, existing merely to collect evidence and pass it on. I wondered then how many of my most secret thoughts I have cut, trimmed, or embroidered to suit this fancy of a recorder, like a seamstress working for a ghostly tailor. The idea passed in an instant, but within that moment I had the impression of looking down, with vertigo, on a primitive, incoherent landscape, much like the one I had seen on the day of the Great Fall.

Paul and Virginie was a favourite from my youth, and the subject of my first conversation with Geneva. I met her at a party given by the Trebeere Literature Society at the Bonaparte Inn last June. It had been years since I attended one of these events, which were less formal back in the 90s when I went regularly with Arthur Wigge and others (we wore our Radical dishevelment with pride in those times, shouting poetry and politics with our boots on the tables). My old evening coat was loose at the cuff, tight in the shoulder (Dinah is not a talented needlewoman) and I was in two minds about going at all. As it was I arrived late to find the rectangular Assembly Room grandly full, the mature generations disposed around the periphery under the brass sconces, the centre of the floor blooming with the young and the fresh, the maids' gowns luminous as sugared almonds.

I was irritated to find that Arthur, who had persuaded me to attend, was nowhere to be seen. The first person I recognised was Amelia Cleer: long thick neck like a white goose, small fair head with its prominent, vigilant eyes, the eyes of another bird entirely. In an attempt to avoid her, I made for a table at the far end of the room, laid out with cold mousse and miniature pies, where people were seated. I dislike engaging in social intercourse while standing. At that moment I was caught in a press of people with the same idea in mind, and I found myself penned between Edward Boase and, inevitably, Mrs Cleer. Old Boase, a prudent man, concentrated on serving himself a generous number of the tiny pies, while Amelia Cleer pronounced herself surprised to see me at a literary gathering.

'I had no idea you took an interest in the fine arts, James, I never saw you as a man of letters. Which of the nine Muses do you follow? Do tell me it is Terpsichore.'

Amelia smiles as she speaks, her teeth a yellow fence protecting her words from those who might seek to return their sharpness. I was unpleasantly aware of her bare upper arm pressed against my sleeve, the chill flesh specked with small raised pimples.

The arrival of Lord Sorleigh (the doorway is at the opposite end of the room) provoked an absurd scramble among my fellow diners to abandon the places so recently won, pushing chairs aside in a bid to position themselves on the aristocratic side of the chamber. Most tried to disguise this ploy with excuses, but not Amelia: her eyes cancelled my face, her attention flew across the room, landing on Sorleigh's noble blue overcoat, his distinguished jowls resting slack on the silk stock. Amelia Cleer is a wealthy woman; she has no need of crumbs from Sorleigh's table, so her eager reverence for 'the people who matter' never ceases to puzzle me, but I should be grateful, for it was Geneva Florey who took her empty place beside me. My new companion wore brown velvet, accentuating auburn hair, while her arms, unlike Mrs Cleer's, were covered, though her bosom was not. I caught drifts of Geneva's scent: almond with something resinous behind it (turpentine, I discovered later). Geneva was of the perverse opinion that a literary party is an opportunity to talk of books, and tried to interest old Boase, who had remained seated, in a new entertainment from America about Mohicans. When I volunteered a comment about virgin forests this led quite naturally to *Paul and Virginia*, which, to my delight, Geneva had also read. Since then the book has held a special place in our affections, and was the inspiration for our purchase of the sanctuary in the wild wood, which I have named Geneva House.

When Maryann's bonnet made its unwelcome appearance outside my window last week, I was, therefore, lost in the perfumed forest with the tragic young lovers, Paul and Virginia, dreaming of how I could recreate their Paradise around our own retreat, quite unable to collect my thoughts in time to challenge Maryann and dismiss her story for the concoction that it was and is. I determined to be more resolute if she made another appearance.

This she has done, this very morning. I was upstairs when I heard the clicket and saw, from the landing window, her hat coming to the porch. It was only a quarter of an hour since Geneva had left the house with Dinah to visit Arthur Wigge; Maryann must be watching the parsonage from some hiding place in the trees. I did not sit, when we entered the study, nor did I offer her a chair. She too was terse in her manner, making no mention of cruel misfortunes or lost infants. Instead she told of a debt she owed to Paulie, who had 'helped her in her time of sorest need', and she suggested I supply her with regular payments, rather than occasional gifts, implying that this would be a return for the debt I owed her. I ridiculed the notion of any such obligation, and conveyed my revulsion at the thought of filling the pockets of the loathsome Paulie, advising her to cut all ties with the man. Meanwhile I opened the study door and began to usher her away as swiftly as propriety allowed, for I knew that Geneva and Dinah would not be out long. We had reached the porch when she stopped and faced me. Geneva is not a short woman, but Maryann is much taller, her eyes level with my own. Unusual eyes – a very pale grey, with dark bands encircling the irises.

'You made a lucky marriage, James. I know how you were situated before, and I know old Teddy Florey's money is now yours. It's only fitting that you spare a little of it for me, who was your support in your loneliness.'

Like most women, particularly those of her station, Maryann's understanding of money is primitive. If I find myself more secure after my marriage, I also know that part of what we have has been committed to the purchase of Geneva House, and another part to the updating of the parsonage. Geneva meanwhile sends an allowance to young Henry, and her many plans and interests mean that she takes note of our outgoings. While she would never question occasional expenses (the repairs to Geneva House have given me a cover) I am certain she would not overlook regular extractions of large sums from our account. I suppose I should have tried to explain these realities, but it was hard to know where to begin. Instead, as I watched Maryann's retreating shape on the path, I was, unaccountably, shaken by an impulse to call her back inside. With her departure came a sudden thinning of the air, a depletion, the ghost of winter afternoons in childhood long ago when the last guest had gone and boredom rustled like fallen leaves along the corridors of my parents' house.

In the space of a few paragraphs, I see I have fallen into the same habit of evasion that I began by admitting. Two evasions. The first concerns Maryann's daughter Eliza. Eliza Tabb came to see me once, asking for help, shortly before she disappeared six years ago. I had not thought of this at all until I encountered her mother again in the Bell and Candle. It must have been around Easter 1821, a fortnight before the Great Fall. I was prowling the lanes, lost in thought; that year I had been more than usually preoccupied by the various accounts of the Resurrection, how the inconsistencies in the four Gospel versions make the whole – contrarily – more plausible, just as a group of sailors will give differing descriptions of a rough voyage, while preserving the central fact of the tempest.

A tall young woman, low-browed, dun-haired, heavy-footed, in a brown triangular cloak like the December Moth, Eliza Tabb came up the glebe lane and planted herself in my path. We had rarely exchanged more than a brusque greeting before, though I used to see her from a distance, stumping across Churchtown Farm with her pails. She was direct, her speech a mix of local dialect and some incongruous words she considered fitting for a clergyman. Matthew Hocking was 'pressing his liberties' on her, she announced, and she was weary of 'boosing up her virtue'.

'He calls us both Mary,' said Eliza, 'says he's no memory for names. I'm Brown Mary, and my mother is Yellow Mary. Only now she's Old Yellow Mary. As if we are cows.' She then embarked on a long digression about how she disliked working with cows, and had been promised a position with the horses, a strange ambition for a girl.

'But he wants to keep me near, where he can watch. Sends me alone to the shed at dusk, for any trifle, and then there's the big shadow of him blocking the door. He's setting a springle for me, Mr Prideaux.'

The springle is a cruel little wicker trap placed for small birds in the grass: the bird's neck is enticed into a noose, which then snaps tight. Eliza delivered her speech as you would hand over a package, in her bald flat voice, so unlike her mother's. In short, God help me, I did not like the girl; I was unclear what she expected me to do, and was distracted by her mention of the springle, a word I hadn't heard since boyhood. Perhaps she asked me to confront Hocking, or speak to her mother, but the words escape me now, it was six years ago after all. The meeting did not seem important at the time. And within two weeks the Fall had swept everyone's inconsequential daily concerns into the sea.

The other question relates to Maryann herself. I have been trying to understand the source of my strange terror at the sight of her. The shock when I encountered her again in the Bell and Candle was not occasioned simply by anxiety that Geneva might learn of my former lover's existence, or threaten my always-insecure position as curate. Nor is the foreboding that has followed it merely a revival of the oscillating repulsion and attraction Maryann has always provoked in me (which makes the attraction all the stronger when it happens). This dread is new. It comes in part from Maryann's apparent indifference to the fate of Eliza, and from the abruptness of her visits, but most of all it is because for a long time, years, I had convinced myself that Maryann was dead. After a few discreet enquiries when I returned from Fowey in 1821 revealed nothing, and after months and then years passed without word of her, I drew a conclusion. I have become *accustomed* to her being dead.

Part 2: The Queen of Pearl

O that the rain would come – the rain in big battalions –
Or thunder flush the hedge a more clairvoyant green
Or wind walk in and whip us and strip us or booming
Harvest moon transmute this muted scene.
From 'Precursors', by Louis MacNeice

4

We used to play, at my primary school in London, a game called 'levitation', more picturesquely known as 'Light as a Feather, Stiff as a Board' One child lay flat on the floor and the others knelt around her, placing two fingers just under the prone child's body. We then closed our eyes and chanted, 'She looks ill, she's ill; she looks worse, she's worse; she looks dead, she's dead'. The body, defying the gravity in our voices, lifted in the air quite easily, and the phenomenon is explicable scientifically as a form of distributed force. But my memory presents a clear picture of children remaining afloat, three or four feet above the ground, sometimes halfway to the ceiling, after our fingers were withdrawn I recall floating myself, the sensation of relaxing into a cushion of tensile air, like seawater, then turning my head to look down on the partings in my friends' heads below me, their hands passive on their laps.

The game was one of a number of occult activities we engaged in at that time. There were tarot readings, of course, but also prophetic dreams, visions, telepathic messages sent between bedrooms at night, upturned cups that spelled out useful advice from spirits. The ghost of a Victorian child spoke to us through a drainpipe in the school playground; a wolf leapt out of the lavatory when you pulled the chain, then chased you upstairs. One child, Marie, had lived in the previous century as a consumptive baker's boy in Blackburn (she was precise about the location): 'I'm standing in a wide street holding the horse's reins. There's a van behind the horse with trays of bread in it. It's a blue sunny day, but icy, people and carts moving about. I can hear church bells ringing and I've got a temperature, I know I'm not going to live very long.'

There was a curious absence of wonder in our response to these phenomena. We discussed them with the same offhand fatalism we would apply to the school timetable, or the sudden Godlike power cuts that had plunged our homes into thrilling dark a few years before ('Here comes a candle to light you to bed; And here is a chopper to chop off your head'). We were eleven, or nearly, a peculiar age. Paused before puberty, we had become expert at being children, and our minds, for the last time for many years to come, were turned outward to the light of the universe, rather than inward on the self. We shared a strange aloofness, a detachment: at eleven you don't need to suspend disbelief, for the presence of other worlds is axiomatic, immersion in them utterly serious, though by this time a fair amount of general knowledge has been caught up in the current. Those solid facts spin and jostle in the water, harmless, sometimes quite interesting, but no use in a storm. If any adult had asked us if we believed in ghosts, gods, demons, witches, cryptids, we would have answered no, of course not. We would not have believed that we believed in them, either. And there was nothing exceptional about the London school – my new friends in St Anthony displayed the same insouciant double consciousness, the same cool indifference to authority and family, a blithe unconcern for anyone who was not also eleven.

This is the source of my difficulty when I try to reconstruct our days on the Fall, to distinguish between what I remember now and what we saw or thought we saw then. The problem is not one of blackouts, repressions, or fugues – the facts of the past stand straight as a copse of larches, but other things have grown there in the green spaces, lit by shifting beams of light from another era, a more primitive state of mind.

Betty's Tea Garden was run by a woman named Maggie Hart (I'm not sure if Betty ever existed). Maggie had rusty hennaed hair and a weakness for hideous tie-dye t-shirts, but, most unusually for caterers in those days, she actually liked children and young people. She used to lean out of her caravan window with a broad smile on her long yellow face as she slipped an extra drink or a Penguin biscuit into your order. Her tea garden served as a meeting place for anyone in St Anthony too young to pass in pubs and too old to be held in the parental orbit. She must have done well that summer.

It was Tracy who suggested it was time for us to go to Geneva. We were at Betty's one afternoon, bored, sheltering by a hedge from the ferocious sun. The sea, just yards from our table, was surprisingly rough for such a fine hot day: blue and white, loud and restless under a steam of spray. Kerenza was trying to disconcert some of the other customers by creeping around and snapping their food with her Kodak. Term was nearly over and a respectable period had elapsed since our humiliating capture in the pebble-dash house.

'It's the most beautiful place in the world, but nobody ever goes there,' Tracy was saying, 'a hidden palace. I told you about it, Sally, when I sent you a letter. Victor and me found it after school one day.'

'You found it, really. You already knew it was there,' said Victor.

'Nan told me. She says there used to be people living there. She calls it "Geneva". But it was you who thought what we could do there.' She looked at Victor. 'You *reconnoitred* it.'

I liked the name Geneva: reddish brown, shiny as a fresh conker.

Kerenza knew about the Fall, but not the house. 'Geneva?' she said. 'Is there a lake?'

'There's a pond, I think,' said Victor. 'The point is, nobody goes there, nobody'll know we're there. But it's far, you have to go right up Torbett's Hill and a long way past the last house.'

'We don't care how far it is,' said Kerenza. 'Is it really a palace?'

It was, for us. The real forest, the Fall, introduced itself via a stretch of abandoned road – a straight narrow lane, telegraph poles running along on the right, their incongruity emphasising remoteness. Trees gathered and thickened on both sides, arching across to form a green tunnel, cool and quiet, discouraging talk. Those telegraph poles, with their looping, whistling wires, were outposts from the world we were leaving behind, the guides who lead you so far but no further before they stop, turn back, surrender you to the unknown.

We had crossed a plateau of uneven grassland to get here, and, before that, walked westward along the coast path beyond the last house, Churchtown Lodge, a former farm on the brow of Torbett's Hill. The silent road and the telegraph poles ended as suddenly as they had begun; now there was only a narrow path that descended sharply amid twisted oaks growing tight together, hairy with lichen, luminous in the dusk. Ferns covered the earth and the trees bent their mossy arms to let them climb onto the branches, where they grew in rows like green owlets, no space wasted in a display of extravagant fertility. As we went deeper the trees became taller, more confident, the species more various, soaring up the steep inclines so that they appeared many times their actual height. Creepers hung from their summits in great theatrical curtains. We had seen no one after passing a woman with a dog on the plateau. I was aware of the sea in glimpses to the left, through a net of ash leaves, and I could just distinguish its rhythmic sigh from the rush of the wood.

After walking for so long, Kerenza and I were beginning to doubt the existence of a palace. It was still invisible when Tracy and Victor turned left, off the path into dense undergrowth. We edged past brambles, climbed over fallen trunks and heaps of stone, slipped under what might once have been a fence, and pushed out into a clearing. I saw a small white house, low-built, protected on three sides by the woods. The fourth side faced the coast, the ground floor enclosed by a glass veranda held up by slender iron pillars like the front of a temple, a graceful effect countered somewhat by patches of rusty corrugated iron on the main roof. Between the veranda and the sea was a narrow meadow, full of foxgloves and another flower I didn't recognise: angular, ruby-red. And there were woodpigeons, so many of them; I was used to their dreamy call and response, an echo of an echo, but this was something more powerful and insistent, an orchestra: we have always been here, they sang, since the beginning of time, and we always will be here.

Something was odd about the meadow: rumpled as an unmade bed, it was split across in several places by gashes in the turf. One or two of these fissures looked quite recent – you could see the bare earth – and, further away, the ground had split into descending terraced sections. The glass veranda sloped to the right and was almost detached from the house at one corner. Its doors, and the door to the room beyond it, were open.

'Come in.' Victor and Tracy were already inside.

'Wait' – I was whispering – 'there's somebody living here.' It was clean, white, far more orderly than my own home: green wicker chairs arranged in a circle, a lamp with a glass shade on a table, a red rug on the floor, an ancient foggy mirror and a clock (stopped at twenty-two minutes past eleven) on opposite walls. The scent of trapped sunlight.

'There's no one,' said Victor, 'they've gone.' He pointed at a notice propped against the fireplace, black on yellow: Danger. Unsafe Structure. Keep Out. The people had walked casually away into the wood, abandoning everything, leaving it for us.

Kerenza tried the tap in the kitchen at the back, and water came out in jerks after a series of rattles and throbbings in the pipe. 'The toilet works too,' said Victor, 'but it takes ages to fill up again. And the bath's cracked.' Corners and angles in this house broke the rules of geometry and perspective, so when you thought you were walking flat you found you were going uphill or down. I was reminded of a ship: the rooms, the house, the garden and the forest seemed to be moving together like the sea, and, like the sea, nobody owned it. Upstairs were two rooms; one, overlooking the bay, had a bed in it and shells on the windowsill, the other, at the back, was darker, the wood growing close against the wall. Branches pressed on the windowpane; I looked straight out into an empty bird's nest.

The end of the garden had collapsed in a slope of rubble and gorse, so the shore was reachable only via a detour through an ilex copse. We passed a female statue made from opaque white marble, dense as solid sugar. The statue's feet had vanished in a crack between roots, so she grew straight out of the ground. She might have represented Persephone, Flora, the Virgin Mary, or Mnemosyne (which would have been apt), but I said the marble was like Kendal Mint Cake, and she was known as the Mint

Woman thereafter. Tracy wasn't sure whether the Mint Woman had cast a spell on the garden, or if she had witnessed the Great Fall and been turned to stone. A thin crescent of beach appeared below the statue, trees growing right up to the rocks and sand. 'I've seen seals here,' said Tracy. 'They like it because it's private.' Kerenza thought she saw a starfish, but the light was fading, and it was almost dark by the time we got back to St Anthony.

The discovery, the taking possession, of Geneva felt momentous even then; we knew it was a turning point, deserving of reverence. At the same time, more instinctively, we shut the door on the adult world and locked it behind us. We didn't go every day; we made sure we behaved normally to our families, paying our dues. I allowed Kerenza's mother to take me, with her daughter, on an expedition to St Ives (Penny Nankervis had entered one of her phases of random benevolence), Victor went diving off the harbour with boys from school, Tracy came to tea at my house, and I was polite to my parents' friends from London who came to stay at Pellow Street. This was a happy time for my parents: my father was free to read and write before the autumn term began, my mother had returned to her sculpture and was meeting local artists. She was fascinated by Picasso's *Two Women Running on the Beach*, exploring it in her own work as obsessively as Picasso dissected and recreated Velasquez' *Las Meninas*, her art being the only way she referred to the Spanish part of herself. Apart from the mystery of the trespassing incident, they were pleased I had found new friends so quickly, spending all my time outdoors. My father had met Kerenza's parents at the Bonaparte, and while I imagine they had little in common, there would have been a mutual sense of reassurance. The extreme heat induced a languor and a laxness in the adults that summer which was easy for children to exploit. Conversations in shops only had one theme: the uncanny persistence of the heat, the water shortages, the tropical nights. As children, we simply accepted it. It was hot, it would always be hot, and if it was too hot, you walked into the sea.

But our parents might have been amazed, perhaps mortified, to know how little we thought of them, or talked about them.

The four of us were workmanlike in the way we organised the days. We got up at dawn to evade the curiosity of other children or teenagers and their tell-tale threats ('Where are you going with all that stuff?'), meeting at the foot of Torbett's Hill where hawthorns stood up to their waists in mist. There we conducted an inventory of the supplies each had brought. Kerenza was particularly useful in this respect; if she said she was going to bring something, she did. She provided, at intervals, a camping stove run on methylated spirit, saucepans, cutlery, firelighters, charcoal, matches, soap, vegetable oil, toilet paper, eiderdowns, a tin opener, and a generous supply of tinned and packeted food, all of this presumably taken from the hotel stores, though we never enquired. Victor contributed a paraffin lamp, sheaves of comics, and occasional packets of Embassy cigarettes. I took my silver compass and *The Moths of the British Isles*. We saw almost no one. It was too hot for serious walkers, and the holidaymakers rarely strayed more than a few hundred yards from the beach and harbour, regardless of weather. Victor and I once surprised an old man in a copse of holly. He glared, holding a trowel up in front of his face, like a crucifix. We ran, then stopped to spy on him from behind a screen of leaves, throwing sticks at his back as he stamped off in the other direction. We treated any other rare visitors in the same fashion. The wood wanted us to be there, and we shared its authority over intruders. Another time, a large brown dog startled us when it burst out of the undergrowth onto the Silent Road. No owner appeared and it ran off, triangular ears erect, in the direction of St Anthony.

Victor had finished reading *The Lost World*. The jungle chasms and looming crags, the moths, the primitive tree ferns, the hosts of creatures and spirits inhabiting the Fall rose up around us, growing through the book's fertile pages and daring us to continue the story until we had summoned prehistoric monsters from the quiet mossy ground. Victor was Lord John Roxton, who walks across a tree trunk suspended over an abyss ('He must have had nerves of iron,' Victor quoted approvingly), while I was the journalist, the terrified narrator, Edward Malone. We re-enacted scenes from the book, scenes which were transformed by our explorations into new stories of our own. I grew close to Victor at this time. Under the shared canopy of Conan Doyle's novel he sensed the fear in me, extending a hand in benevolent encouragement. 'Well done,' he said as we inched along a precipitous path, 'you've outwitted the tyrannosaurus. Don't look down.'

There was a particular tree that had no convenient lower branches but was smothered from base to summit in a cloak of old man's beard. We climbed right up this creeper, using it like rigging on a mast; when the tangled mat began to creak and give way, we sidled across to a fresher section. The secret was a light touch, not to linger too long in one place. Victor showed me how to hang in this fragile hammock like Orion falling through the night sky, arms and legs outspread to distribute the weight. I saw the sea across the treetops, glimpsed the ground impossibly far below, and I found I was relaxed, not afraid. For years, the image of Victor in the wood, enlisting me as a partner in a battle with unseen enemies, was a sort of template of masculinity. I did not see at the time that fear recognises fear, and the fearful take comfort in helping the terrified. Don't look down.

To tease Kerenza, we cast her as Professor Summerlee, the dryly sceptical scientist in the book. She swore she hadn't read it, until her irritation with the Summerlee appellation betrayed her. Kerenza was already a scientist anyway: she kept a notebook stuffed in the pocket of her ragged jeans, her camera round her neck. She was the only one who would climb right down into the crevasses in the ground, inspecting root systems, and while I merely stared at unfurling ferns or creeping wrens with unfocused enchantment, she wanted to understand their behaviour, their place and purpose in the wood. Ants prospered in the dry heat; Kerenza sliced the top off one of the biggest anthills with her penknife and we watched as the intricate metropolis marshalled itself to repair the damage. A cataclysm whose author was inconceivable to the ants, and therefore irrelevant.

'Why did you do that?' I asked.

'I was just curious.'

'I wonder what they think has happened, who has done this.'

'They don't think like that,' said Kerenza. 'They just concentrate on putting it right.'

* * *

There was no question of refusing to spend the night on the Fall, and I can't remember whose suggestion it was. Once the idea had arisen, it solidified into a commitment, with a reality beyond the four of us as individuals. We dare you. It was easy to deceive the parents. We said we were staying at the Bonaparte Hotel with Kerenza, and Kerenza said she was staying with me. If by some ill luck Mr or Mrs Nankervis were to encounter my or Victor's parents, then we planned to say we had made a mistake and had been at Tracy's. Mrs Tabb, Tracy's grandmother, didn't have a telephone, and I had an odd feeling she would not betray us anyway.

Until then, the constant presence of the others had allowed me to hide unease; I had escaped from myself. When there are four of you, in daylight, nothing really bad can happen, but the idea of being out on the Fall at night, in the cracked house with its wild geometry, was different. Even for adults, it would have been different: we were two miles over steep uneven ground from any road or house. It would take a while to seek help if anything went wrong.

The Fall had already presented one disturbing face. Kerenza and I had been pursuing some project of hers concerning the insects known as pond skaters, which took us to the two pools in the subtropical ravine just beyond Geneva (we called them the Shadow Pools). It was quite late; the evening humid and steamy. As I sat waiting for Kerenza to finish, I looked down into the water just where a shaft of sunlight was hitting it and saw an animal's footprints moving, independent of any animal, along the sandy floor of the pool. The prints were perfectly clear, exactly like those of a small dog, and it was only the pulsing jerkiness of the gait which explained their source as shadows of the pond skaters on the surface. I was about to draw Kerenza's attention to this ghostly effect when I glanced across the pool. A blue light had appeared near some reeds on the other side, like a cold candle on the water, and even before I shouted to Kerenza, the light had grown bigger, writhing and sliding erratically towards me, its arms raised up. We dumped everything and ran. Just before we reached Geneva she stopped and pulled at my sleeve. 'It was only methane.'

'Who's Methane?'

'Marsh gas, nothing to worry about.'

I didn't, but only because by this time the Owlman had more power. It was my father who told me. He had picked up a leaflet on a recent visit to a country church at Mawnan, near Falmouth, and, knowing I enjoyed ghost stories, read it out at supper. Earlier in the spring, two sisters named June and Vicky, aged twelve and nine, had seen a birdlike shape as big as a man, hovering over the church tower. They were so alarmed by it that the family cut their holiday short. Not long afterwards, two different girls were camping in the woods near the same church. One of them, named *Sally*, my father emphasised, heard a hissing sound near their tent. She turned around and saw a long-eared owl as tall as a man, silvery grey, with glowing red eyes. The girls weren't frightened, assuming someone was playing a joke, and they laughed at the strange figure, whereupon it rose up in the air, black pincer claws hanging from its body.

'It's a complete load of nonsense, of course,' my father said, 'but what's interesting is how a story like this gets repeated and people add more detail all the time. Before you know it, you've started a nice rural myth, especially if you give the creature a spooky name like "the Owlman".'

'But what *is* he, really?', I insisted, unimpressed by scepticism.

'Oh, a ghost, for certain. Probably the ghost of a dinosaur.'

He would not have told me at all if he had had any idea I was spending time out on the Fall. It was unnerving that the creature was appearing to children and teenage girls, in daylight, and so recently. And Mawnan was only a few headlands away from St Anthony. I was fond of owls, but if an owl is blended with a man, and appears outside your tent, a shadow comes gliding across the mind, with a hissing sound. When I told the others about the Owlman I was surprised to find that both Kerenza and Tracy already knew about him (I had been looking forward to Kerenza's hoot of derision), though Victor didn't: 'Why does he only appear to girls?'

'Because he's a man,' we said. 'He's lonely.'

On the veranda step we sat watching light leak away from the world. The sky turned from rose to lilac, pale green to indigo; lost definition and the whole wood simplified itself into banks of shade. The sea had a pearl haze on it, and when this dimmed, lamps from a cargo ship blinked yellowish through the mist. Even at night it was exceptionally hot, but Victor had made a fire, a double layer of bricks with a drain cover suspended over it, on which we cooked soup and beans. We boiled water for tea on the meths stove and lit the paraffin lamp, mainly to see how they worked. The plan had been to sleep inside the veranda, or in the front room, but in the end we spread the Bonaparte's eiderdowns on the grass just outside the house. This, we told each other, was because of the heat, but the truth was that Geneva had changed with the dying of the daylight; when I went back into the kitchen to fill the saucepan the darkness had condensed in the eccentric angles and corners, the brambles outside the kitchen were now thorny fingers reaching through the window. It was not sinister exactly, because I knew the house so well, but the beauty of the place had retreated somewhere unreachable.

Nobody was tactless enough to draw attention to the owls calling from the trees behind the house. Instead Tracy started talking about seals. When the seals come, she said, they arrive at dusk, so no one notices. They could be down there already, on the shore.

'They were here a long time before the people. Grey seals usually, but sometimes rare seals visit from other seas and oceans. Those ones are called vagrants. If you live by the sea, you can change into a seal when you die, and sometimes people come back.'

'Come back how?'

They come ashore, she explained, and shrug off their seal coats like guests arriving at a party. 'They dance with you on the

'You can tell when they're coming because there   the sea. But they have to go back before   en want a seal to stay, so they hide its coat,   ed on land as a person for a while, but they   looking for their coat, and as soon as they find it they race back into the sea, without saying goodbye.'

'How do you know all this?' I said. She sounded certain as a teacher.

'I heard about it when I was small. My mother read it in a book. They're called selkies. And they know we're here.'

'Have you seen them?'

She had.

'Are they dangerous?'

'No. I don't think so. They help you if you're lost at sea. But you shouldn't stop them from going back. Then they might be dangerous.'

'Do all dead people change into seals?' Victor asked.

'Only the good ones.'

Kerenza was interested in the details of the transformation from person into seal. 'Does it happen as soon as you die, so you wake up and see your feet changing into flippers? Which parts of the body change first? Does it hurt? What if you die in Birmingham or London, miles from the sea?'

Tracy couldn't answer the question about distance, but she said that once you were in the water, 'the sea soaks into your skin and the human part soaks out. It's like dreaming.'

The thought of the seals and selkies out there, slippery spirits of long dead people arriving on our beach to dance, hand in cold wet hand, was only slightly less alarming than the Owlman, but at least it offered a choice: if something came out of the wood, I could get into the sea; Tracy would know what to do. We slept in a row under the eiderdowns, pressed close. That night I learned that there is no darkness, provided you stay outside. The dark was trapped indoors and stayed there: when we turned the wick down on the lamp the shapes of the plants crept back out, shyer versions of their daytime selves, while the palest flowers found courage in the night, glowing long after all colour was gone. I woke shortly before sunrise to see a great horned creature in the grass a few feet away. We regarded each other for seconds, minutes, hours – it was hard to tell. It was a stag, but until it had gone, I could not name it, nor even imagine that it could have a name, it defied categorisation.

The night on the Fall was judged a success, and was repeated. As July merged into August and the rainless heat intensified, we began to spend most of our time on the little beach below the edge of the meadow. From here Geneva was invisible, hidden behind upheavings of cliff and wood. I took my transistor radio with me if we were to stay overnight, a prophylactic against the Owlman, though the reception was intermittent. If 'Dancing Queen' came on we sprang up and joined the spinning bats in the dusk, turning cartwheels, bouncing on spongy turf over rifts and cracks. It was around this time that Tracy told us she had written a story. She climbed into an arthritic apple tree and read it to us, her congregation, sitting below. It was so still you couldn't hear the sea; the only sound apart from Tracy's voice was from the small stream in the woods behind Geneva. What appears below is as accurate a replication as I can manage; I should add that I read the story more than once, after Tracy had finished and left the paper lying on the grass.

Whistling Jack and the Queen of Pearl

Once there was a boy named Jack who lived in a village by the sea in Cornwall. When he was still small he walked into the woods on his own. In the deepest part he heard music coming out of the moss on the ground. On the way back he whistled the tune so he wouldn't forget it, but when he got home he found he couldn't speak, only whistle. His nan was cross. Jack grew up into a handsome man, but still he could only whistle. He learned to whistle so well that it was almost like a song, but not quite. He whistled at the women in the village, and soon they all wanted to marry him. But first Jack wanted to speak again.

Whistling Jack got a job on a boat and saw the world. If he had a break for tea or a cigarette, he leaned over the side of the trawler and whistled to the seals. In every harbour, there were women who wanted to marry him. One day the boat came to a remote island. The other men stayed on the boat, but Jack got off to explore. A beautiful woman was standing in the seaweed, singing. She had dark skin and black hair so long it reached her feet and flowed away into the water, and she wore a crown of bright green sea lettuce. She gave him a shell that shone with light, but no colour. 'When you get home, look into this shell, like a mirror, and you'll be able to talk.'

When Jack got ashore, he went home to his nan and stared at his reflection in the shell, and sure enough, he could speak, and he talked to his nan about pilchards. But Jack couldn't forget the strange woman, and when he had a day off he sailed to the island on his own. She gave him another shell, and this one had purple, red, blue and green, but no light. She said, 'Look at your face in this shell and you will be able to sing.' When he got home he went to the pub, looked at his reflection in the shell, and sang 'Don't Fence Me In' for everybody there.

The next time the men went out they were caught in a terrible storm. Blue fires burned on the masthead and

Whistling Jack was washed overboard. He thought he was dead, but three seals came up from the deep and carried him to the island, where hundreds more seals were gathered. When the woman appeared, Jack asked her to marry him. 'I am a seal,' she said, 'and if you want to marry me, you will have to die on land so we can both live in the sea.'

Whistling Jack said yes. At dusk the woman took out a sharp pearl knife and stabbed Jack in the heart. His blood flowed out onto the grass and tall violet-red flowers grew there. The woman took Jack by the hand and they walked into the sea. His blood flowed into the waves and through the seaweed, mixing with the light on the water. They both changed into seals. After they disappeared under the sea, the air turned ice cold and the water froze with Jack's blood in it. When the sun rose in the morning the sea melted again and the tide went out, but the white light and the colours had frozen together into the seashells like a rainbow, and now they're called mother-of-pearl.

The whistling jack (*gladiolus communis, subspecies byzantinus*) is a plant with magenta flowers and obscure origins that flowers in Cornish hedges and gardens in late spring and early summer. The name may derive from children using the stalks as whistles, though we never did. They grew all round Geneva, and there was something about the beauty of that particular shade of red (the colour combines the scarlet in A or 4 with the raspberry-crimson of E and 5), especially when seen against bright green, that set my nerves singing. The story still seems a strange one for an eleven-year-old to have written, a just-so story, *The Little Mermaid* inverted, the man sacrificing his life to join a phocine lover. It would be easier now, from the distance of decades, to interpret it; Tracy's lost parents are there, perhaps, under the sea, and echoes of her grandmother's Christianity, but at its centre is the boy without a voice, who must look at his reflection to find words.

After Tracy's story I stopped going to the shore by myself. There was always a wave in the distance that looked bigger than the others, pregnant, coming nearer, and perhaps when it reached the beach Whistling Jack would rise up out of the sea with a round empty hole where his heart should be, and then he might change again, like the Owlman, into something unspeakable.

With the others, though, I was not frightened. Over and over again we enacted the story on the shore, taking turns in the roles of Jack, the Queen of Pearl, the seals, the fishermen, Jack's nan, and the people in the pub. We swam out, once or twice even at night, to save sailors and entice villagers into the water, casting off our sealskin bathing costumes, draping broad ribbons of kelp across naked bodies. Characters were added, subtracted, altered; we stretched the story to accommodate books and films, television programmes and pop songs, but it always ended the same way, with the knife and the transfiguration. Tracy brought her seashells from the house down to the rocks and stored them there.

5

Sunday, August 22nd, 1976 was hot, of course it was hot, but the air felt stiller, thicker, than on any of the days before it. It might not have been stiller or thicker, it may have been no different from any other day that month; what I remember now is not what I would have remembered a week later, or at seventeen, when other people were compelling me to remember. It is not exactly what the others remembered. Out of all the afternoons of my life this is the one I have revisited most, which no doubt makes it the most vulnerable to distortion. Who is to say that each time you recall an event, an image that defines a life, you don't unconsciously add, decorate, or delete a tiny detail, a splash of light on a wall, a woodlouse on a pad of moss, so that as the years accumulate, the picture, the memorial ecosystem, becomes quite different. But this is all I have.

We started for the Fall much later than usual because Victor and I were told by our respective families to stay at home for lunch. My parents had friends from London visiting for a long weekend. We met up at Torbett's Hill after four, so we must have reached Geneva at around five o'clock. The intense quiet inside the house was soothing; Victor made tea on the meths stove, and we sat politely in our sitting room like grown-ups, talking about earwigs, and how odd it was that certain words, *earwig, trousers, skeleton, stoat*, are inherently funny. On the walls and windowsills the usual green lacewings had been joined by swarms of ladybirds – mats of scarlet and black the size of dinner plates. I had never seen so many in one place.

We almost didn't go down to the sea at all, but Kerenza said there was not much point walking all the way to Geneva unless we actually did something, so it was decided we would have one swim and then go home. As we passed the Mint Woman I saw the tide was a little way out, flat, opaque, pale as milk. A rounded bluish shape floated just beyond the waveline, in a nest of seaweed and rocks. My eyes couldn't make sense of it. Some kind of boat, or a lilo? A black head. A seal? We walked up to the water. It was a woman. She lay tilted slightly on her side, unmoving, her eyes open and looking straight at us, alert, intelligent. Her mouth was also open, as if forming a question, and her dark hair coiled out around her head and into the emerald gutweed draping the rocks. She had a dark blue dress on; I stared at this soaking dress as it moved in the pulses of the tide and wondered why she hadn't taken it off before she went swimming. We stood there in the shallows, watching, and because we were so still the little brown seashore birds came darting back across the seaweed, mouselike, and I saw one of them use the woman as a bridge across the pool. Victor bent over and pushed down gently at the woman's shoulder, so she moved on to her back. Her bare arm, which had been lying across her body, slid slowly back into the water, as if she had forgotten it belonged to her.

'Maybe we should do something,' Victor said.

Tracy looked at him, walked away, disappeared under a bush, and returned with her cupped hands full of iridescent shells. She began to place them, one by one, on the woman's chest and hips and forehead, anywhere that was not covered by water. 'We need some whistling jacks,' she said to me. I went up off the beach to pick some. Most of the flowers were dried up, but after what seemed a long search, I found two or three in the shade.

As I was coming back I steadied myself with one hand on the Mint Woman's head and looked down. Tracy and Victor were standing in the water facing each other, one on each side of the woman in the sea. Then, as if they were acting as one person, I saw them bend and crouch over her, their heads blocking my view. I couldn't see Kerenza. When I reached the beach, the two of them had moved back onto the sand, motionless, waiting for me. I paddled into the water and threw the crimson flower spikes across the woman's dress. Kerenza was somewhere behind us in the trees; she had said nothing at all.

As we walked up to Geneva I turned back once to look; the tide must have been coming in, because the whistling jacks had floated off the woman and were drifting on the surface of the rockpool. In the house, suddenly infected by a common idea, we began to hunt for moths. We lit the lamps to attract them – the thick trees always brought the dusk down early at Geneva. Victor gave a running commentary on every specimen he found, moth or otherwise, Tracy put her face close to each insect, as if she were trying to learn them by heart. Kerenza found a big Emperor moth on the veranda, a female, pale grey bordered with charcoal, white and rose. Four wide eyes looked back at us from its four wings, each one unblinking, impartial, the iris greenish and outlined in black. I opened *The Moths of the British Isles* by Richard South. The Emperor was there (*Saturnia Pavonia*), and I set out to find more living moths on the walls to match the watercolour pictures, but was spellbound instead by the colours of the moths' names on the pages, singing their own story: the Poplar Lutestring and the Brindled Green, the Satin Carpet, the Ruby Tiger and the Rosy Footman, the Vapourer, the Silvery Arches and the Pale-Shouldered Brocade, the Stranger, the Anomalous, the Confused, the Glaucous Shears and the Clouded Drab, the Suspected, the Dark Dagger and the Dusky Sallow, the Death's Head Hawk Moth, the Uncertain.

On the way home I lagged behind the others (talking was forbidden on the Silent Road, so I often lost myself there) and stopped to chase a green moth into a stand of holly. The holly opened on a small round clearing, where a man and a woman were lying on the grass, clasping and gripping at each other, sighing and breathing in a loud way. The woman had no clothes on except for her bra, and the man was naked. I didn't recognise him, but the woman was Penny Nankervis. Of course I knew what they were doing: trying to have a baby. I was astonished however that the lovers were lying down, having previously imagined that sex was done standing, face to face, arms by the sides, polite as strangers at a bus stop. For people, grown-ups, to perform this embarrassing act stretched out on the ground seemed shockingly self-indulgent to my puritanical mind; I pitied them. I wondered briefly why Kerenza's mother would want to get another baby, but that was nothing to do with me. Sex wasn't interesting, though I knew the world believed otherwise; adults would say I had undergone a *rite of passage*. Such things were momentous and strictly private, so I said nothing to anyone about the Rite of Passage, even the others.

Earlier that same Sunday, at around 1.30 in the afternoon, Clara Deborah Selman, aged seventeen, left her home in St Dominic, a village to the east of Trebeere. She was walking to meet her friend Sandra Jenkin, who lived close to Trebeere town centre. Clara was wearing a blue denim sleeveless dress with steel buttons on the front and she was carrying a fabric bag with an Indian embroidered pattern. It was a journey of just under a mile along quiet, but not deserted, roads; it should have taken her around half an hour. Clara never arrived at Sandra Jenkin's house. Sandra, who spent the afternoon sunbathing in her garden, assumed Clara had changed her mind, so the hot afternoon drifted amiably by until 7 pm that evening, when Clara's father rang Sandra's house to ask if his daughter had set off for home, because supper was almost ready. Just after midnight, Mr and Mrs Selman called the police.

The girls, Clara and Sandra, had been out in Trebeere the previous evening, Saturday night, together with Sandra's brother Michael. They had been in a pub called the Schooner, and then moved on to Cinnabar's, a club. At the club, according to Sandra, two boys, Dan and Sebastian, had joined them, and the latter had shown some interest in Clara. The girls left the club together at around eleven, without the boys ('we were getting bored'). Clara's father had picked her up by car, and Sandra walked home.

The first newspaper article, reporting Clara Selman missing and describing her clothing, appeared in the regional paper on August 24th. On Wednesday, August 25th, there was a second report:

> Cornwall Police confirmed today that a body, believed to be that of a young woman, has been recovered from rocks west of St Anthony, near Trebeere. The discovery was made on Tuesday afternoon by Albert Rundle, 69, a retired labourer from Trebeere, whose hobby is dowsing for treasure on the shore around Penglaze Point at St Anthony. The police spokesman was not able to comment on any connection between the discovery and missing St Dominic schoolgirl

Clara Selman, 17, who has not been seen since Sunday afternoon.

They confirmed it the next day, though, when it was clear that this would be a murder inquiry. That was when the regional TV stations picked up the story, and the national press followed close behind. The cause of death was not disclosed, though the post-mortem indicated that Clara Selman had died of 'asphyxiation' rather than drowning. There were 'some signs of struggle', and a knife wound to the abdomen, but this was not severe enough to have caused death. She had not been raped.

It's not difficult to unearth reports on the case in newspaper archives, while online there are dozens of True Crime sites where you can find sections devoted to Clara Selman and 'the Cornish Landslip Murder', usually with the addition of some pious moralising about parental supervision and arch references to her good looks and respectable background. I've read them all now, but I read nothing at the time, and I don't remember seeing any of the television reports. Perhaps my parents turned the news off as soon as this story came on, or never turned it on – during that blazing summer televisions were silent much of the time. It was six years later, in 1982, before I read a newspaper report about Clara Selman.

The day after we found the woman in the sea we went back up to the Fall. I had lost my compass and wanted the others to help me find it, though we never did. None of us said anything about what we had seen the day before. The Silent Road was silent, the trees still green and cool, though the meadow grass at Geneva was paper dry and patched with scorched flowers; it whistled with crickets and rasped against my bare legs. The Mint Woman had sunk a little further down between the roots of the ilex, the tide was high on the shore. There was nothing at all in the sea.

Kerenza rang me at home.

'I've been thinking,' she said, 'about the Emperor moth. The eyes on the wings. They're human eyes. There's a pupil, then an iris, with white around it in a long eye shape.'

I reminded her of what we both knew about moths, that the false eye patterns were mimicking a fierce animal, as a defence against predators.

Then she told me something I hadn't known: that among mammals, only humans have white permanently showing around the iris. 'So the Emperor moth is mimicking us. Not just any old animal, us.'

It was Friday or Saturday of that week before my parents, and the rest of the population of St Anthony and Trebeere, properly woke up to the drama in their midst. I was told at breakfast that I would not be going out to play with my friends, because we were going on a family drive to look at north Cornwall. Another day, a little later, I was sitting at the kitchen table, drawing cats. My mother said that if I was going out, I was not to go anywhere near Torbett's Green or the Fall, not even to go up Torbett's Hill.

'Maggie Hart's seen you with other children on Torbett's Hill several times. You're not to go near it.'

'Why?'

'Because something happened, someone was hurt. The police are busy up there, trying to find out what went on.'

'Who was hurt?' I thought of the Owlman, and the Rite of Passage.

Finally she told me.

'It was something horrible,' she said, 'they found a girl on the rocks out by the landslip, dead. She was only seventeen. It's dangerous on the Fall, the ground's unstable, there are derelict buildings out there, too.'

I knew what 'derelict' meant, but I never connected the word with Geneva, and 'seventeen' meant as little to me as twenty, or fifty, would have done.

'Sally,' my father reminded my mother, 'is an intelligent girl. She wouldn't do anything stupid, don't worry her unnecessarily.'

'Really? What about that house in Trebeere?'

'That's over, Nuria. She learned her lesson.'

'Do you think,' I said, 'that Ivan would mind if we got another cat?'

Over the following weeks, the police traced and interviewed Dan and Sebastian from the Cinnabar club, questioned the bar workers at Cinnabar's and the Schooner, talked to Sandra Jenkin and her brother Michael, Sandra's father Peter, Clara's ex-boyfriend Chris, Clara's father Colin Selman, Clara's mother Pauline, and Albert Rundle, who found Clara's body in the rocks off Penglaze Point. When these people turned out to have been elsewhere that Sunday afternoon, or in the company of one or several others, the police interviewed them all again: a web of connections with an invisible spider.

Frustrated, they began to go through the files on local offenders. The greatest mystery was how Clara, who lived in St Dominic, east of Trebeere, had ended up in the sea almost six miles to the west, beyond the village of St Anthony. There was no reason for her to have been on Torbett's Green or the Fall; nobody remembered her showing a particular interest in the area, and she had no friends or relatives in St Anthony itself. Penglaze Point, where her body was found, marks the start of the landslip section of the coastline; it's much closer than Geneva, but still remote: almost impossible to reach from the cliffs and woods above it, and cut off from St Anthony's westernmost beach by a hill of boulders. The police could not imagine how anyone could have led her, or dragged her, down through the steep thickets of stunted oak and bramble, across rifts and chasms to the jagged rocks below; perhaps, they wondered, her body had drifted in the currents from somewhere else, or maybe she had been taken there by sea. So they searched the harbour vessels, interviewed yachtsmen, harbourmen and trawlermen, the professional skippers who took teams of men far out into the Atlantic, the dinghy fishermen and tourist trippers who puttered around the local coves on a weekend, and hope flared for a week or two, a new man was taken in for questions, the papers reported a fresh line of enquiry, before everything went quiet again. As weeks became months, the newspaper articles got briefer and then ceased altogether. The people of St Anthony and Trebeere returned to their lives of complex obscurity, while Pauline and Colin Selman were left alone on the wicker sofa in their brand-new conservatory, without their only child. Nobody forgot, however.

The hot weather finally broke during the last week of August, the first week of the search for Clara Selman's abductor. I woke one morning and the square of sky above my bed was not blue, as usual, but grey as the slate roofs opposite. At breakfast the kitchen was dim as December; we had to turn the light on to see the numbers on the toaster, while outside in the courtyard a nervous gusty wind tipped at the sheets on the line so they lay like flatfish across the neighbour's wall. The first thunderstorm cracked into life later that morning. It was exciting at first, and a relief; the rain extravagant and tropical. Steep streets became torrents and a petrichoric steam rose from the scorched pavements and burned grasses. People opened their front doors and stood looking up, children ran out to dance in water racing down the gutters. Soon the sea joined in, slapping up around the harbour steps, breathing salt into wet air. Within a couple of days, however, all spells were broken: windows slammed shut, televisions came on, cats woke up frowning, lovers were left waiting alone in car parks, absences had to be explained.

As the wet Atlantic systems followed one another through September and October I discovered a more typical Cornwall of mists and gales and weeks of damp, of sudden rainbows and days that began blue and changed to rain and back again ten times before the evening. Dandelion, charlock and groundsel returned to our pavements to defy the tidy-minded council, while out on the Fall the water drenched the forest and seeped down through layers of earth and rock, reanimating streams and flooding cities of ants. Geneva creaked and shifted and sighed on its rheumatic foundations, and then, like a tough old woman, adjusted itself to the new shape of the world. By some unspoken agreement we avoided the Fall that autumn, but we started going back again in the winter to watch the storms from the veranda. And Geneva was always there, in the back of our minds, a promise of escape, should we need it.

6

1827: Blind Bocka

The Parsonage, St Anthony, Thursday May 10
Geneva House, our retreat in the woods, is everything we hoped it would be. The veranda is almost complete, thanks to the craftsmanship of Peter Trembath, grandson to the Samuel I have already spoken of. The work has proved more costly than anticipated, because of the time and labour involved in carrying the construction materials up the hill (by cart), across the cliffs and through the wood (donkey), but every time I visit I am surprised afresh by the picturesque location. The spirits of Paul and Virginia, were they searching for a sanctuary here in Cornwall, could not have wished for a more faithful echo of their tropical paradise. We have also acquired a young dog, a herding hound named Ossian. He is paler in colour than Voltaire was and lacks Voltaire's grave good sense, his ability to anticipate my intentions before I knew of them myself, but they share the same erect triangular ears.

Geneva spends whole days up there, as I thought she might, occasionally with Dinah, and once with her ghastly friend Amelia Cleer, who rode out there on her high horse, arrayed in a crimson habit, but usually she is alone with Ossian. She is working on a series of drawings. I had supposed these would be panoramas of Lantern Bay, but what she has produced are small, detailed studies of seaweed, and of the seals which she says visit the tiny cove below the house. Indeed Geneva has become somewhat obsessed with these clumsy sea creatures, speculating about their customs, attributing to them mysterious powers. I have yet to see a single one, however. Not even a dark head in the distance. It is as if the seals sense my arrival and make a hasty retreat into the deeps. Sometimes I think they are phantoms of her imagination.

Yesterday I arrived home after six o'clock from a fractious meeting with the parish concerning arrangements for poor relief. The talk had followed a pattern I have been noting lately, with men proposing that generosity in the rate merely encourages vagrancy and indolence.

'If the alternative were only the Poorhouse, then we would see a scurrying, a sudden access of miraculous ingenuity in finding work,' said Abel Copthorne, whom I had always supposed a more large-spirited man. We did however agree to provide boots for the widow Alice Tehidy, and I was able to secure help for John Menhennett to repair his roof, which is sagging like a netful of fish.

Geneva had been up in the woods all day, alone, and, having spent most of the glorious afternoon shuttered in a dim room, I was somewhat irritated not to find her back when I returned home. I was in the kitchen with Dinah when a hard rapping on the front door startled us. Dinah opened it, Ossian blundered in past her skirts, and I saw Geneva, her hair disordered, mouth set, in the company of young Peter Trembath, who was carrying the carpet bag Geneva uses for her drawing materials. Trembath told me that he had been leaving his grandfather's house when he was surprised to see a lady and a dog running down Torbett's Hill, and when the lady fell and dropped the bundle she was carrying, he went to her aid, and recognised Geneva.

She had told him little except that a strange man had disturbed her up on the cliff, and she had asked him, Trembath, to accompany her back to the parsonage. Geneva was silent throughout this explanation. I sat her down when Peter left, poured her a brandy, and sent Dinah out. Geneva is not a woman who is easily frightened, so I was anxious to know her account of what had happened. She recovered fast with the spirit, and spoke in her usual abrupt, practical manner.

'My afternoon was productive. I began a drawing of the big female seal. I sat behind the gorse where she could not see me, parting it to get a better view, and cutting my arms on the thorns in the process.'

Geneva's forearms were indeed scored with red marks above her gloves, and I was reminded of Maryann's coarse red hands with their pale scars.

'After an hour or so I climbed back up to the house to release Ossian, who was shut in the kitchen because his yelps disturb the seals. I saw one of those big moths with human eyes on their wings, the ones you call Emperors, inside the glass on the veranda. I made a quick study of it, but the sun was low over the trees, so I packed up and started for the village.

'As I walked with Ossian I was thinking only of my drawing of the moth. When we reached the place where the stream crosses the path I heard something, a crack and a rustle, and Ossian stopped short and growled. I expected to see a deer bounce out, but it was a man. He stepped through the elder bushes, right in front of us Taking him for a common pedlar, I wished him good evening and walked briskly on. Meanwhile Ossian was growling and barking, I could tell he was trying to decide whether this fellow was friend or foe, he's still such a young dog. But the man walked with me, crowding me on the narrow path. I made some trivial remark on the weather, and said that my husband (I did not name you) was coming to meet me, that you should be here at any moment.

"'I know him," the man said, "your husband, the honourable *Reverend* Prideaux. I see him all the time, doggetting along, out of the churchyard, into the alehouse, in and out the spinney, never looking further than his own nose."

'The fellow had a most disagreeable way of speaking, as if he already knew all about you. He walked the rest of the way with us in silence, through the woods and across the open green, matching his steps to mine, always jostling me and Ossian off the path. We came to the grove at the top of Torbett's Hill where he turned abruptly and seized me by the arm, his other hand grasping my hair at the back. He pushed his face into mine.

"'Tell your man Prideaux he needs to pay more attention to his debts. Tell him we have a big box of stories, and only have to open it to let them all out."

'By this time Ossian was wild with barking and the man turned to kick him. As I fought to free myself from his grip he tore my shawl off, scratching my chest, and I started running down the hill. I didn't stop until I slid in a cowpat and dropped my bag. All my sketchbooks and pencils spilled out and that's when Peter Trembath saw me. I looked back and the man had gone.'

I asked her to describe the man.

'Ugly. Remarkably so. About forty, short, thin, but the facial features were puffed and loose, bloated, as if the skin were falling from the skull. The forehead, though, was smooth as a child's.'

Paulie.

Geneva looked up at me. 'Who is he? How does he know you?'

I replied that from her description, I suspected that he was a labourer, a man enslaved by drink, who had done a little work coppicing on the glebe twelve months past. 'I should never have employed him,' I dissembled, 'because he would not accept the terms we had agreed, and for months afterwards he returned at intervals to ask for more money.'

'But you do not owe him money?'

'The debt is a chimera, the product of his addled mind.'

'What is his name?'

'It was something unmemorable. Brown, I think, John or Jack.'

'What did he mean by a box of stories?'

A box of stories. That was the phrase that disturbed me most in Geneva's account, apart from the encroachment of Paulie, who now provokes a revulsion in my imagination beyond anything he achieved in his flesh I said I had no idea. Reassuring her as best I could, I told her I would take every precaution to ensure the fellow never came near her again, but in the meantime she was not to go to Geneva House alone. At supper I was able to divert Geneva's questions from the phantom glebe-cutter into talk of cultivation of the glebe itself. Geneva wants to plant the small pasture, beyond Samuel Trembath's cottage, as an orchard, and is urging me to write to Boskerris for permission. I held the conversation on the theme of apples and damsons until she looked up and said, 'I trust there is no connection between what happened today and that strange woman, that parishioner, the one Dinah says is always calling?'

Early in our courtship, Geneva and I vowed that we would not press for details of our respective sentimental histories; we would each protect the privacy of the other, and create a modern npathetic minds. I was presented with the of her marriage to Florey, the history of the birth (arduous), and so forth, while she listened account of my antique friendships with Maria, Tabitha, rtain doctor's parlourmaid at Crackington Haven. I can't recall the exact reasoning behind this smooth elision of the past, and wonder if it was a mistake, because our conversation now feels tethered to the quotidian and practical, fenced by common sense to the point where any voiced doubt, regret or idle fancy, however tenuously connected with buried love, suggests a want of tact. And in the wake of this discretion a heavy silence has crept into the parsonage, settling in pools around the chairs and curtains. When I envisage introducing the subject of Maryann, her reappearance, the visits and payments, the absurd rewriting of history that it would involve, my courage shrivels, and the moment, if there was ever one, has gone.

Thursday May 17
A curate without connections is scarcely more fortunate than a travelling pedlar. We have no land, no permanent income or home. We can be evicted on a whim after forty years' staunch service or after mere months, and whether we are conscientious or lax, loved or loathed by the people, our destiny remains in the palms of patrons and employers. An itinerant and precarious life, then, and with time I grew to resent the unspoken but firm requirement, upon arriving in yet another new parish, to appear brimful of energy, surprise and gratitude. None of this ever emerged in my writings, and in early years of this journal I discover a man I do not recognise: glossy with virtue, jauntily sanguine – a fetch of myself. I envy him, this handsome wraith, while knowing I had always been lying; a curious sensation. For a long time I watched for any opening nearer Trebeere, and when

Silas Laity, a cousin of Lord Sorleigh's, became too rheumatic to make the journey to St Anthony from Boskerris, I was able to slip in here as curate. Amelia Cleer thinks Sorleigh and Laity assumed I was connected to the well-born Prideauxs of Padstow, a story which she delights in spreading far and wide, though I never made a secret of my pedestrian origins.

We never see old Laity now, and I try not to dwell on what may happen when he dies. I lost hope of being appointed Rector long ago, and the reason for this may not only be my lack of breeding. When I returned from Cambridge in 1791 I was twenty-two years old, pulled this way and that by a storm of dangerous ideas, haunting the reading room at the Bonaparte (then the Old Ship) as the news from France became astonishing.

Not one revolution but an avalanche of them: between one newsbill and the next they wiped the bloody stage in Paris clean, last month's actors recast or dead. I used to walk up on Torbett's Green and turn my face towards the French coast to catch some breath of Revolution in the wind, convinced that my individual existence was of great consequence to History, that a silver path would be shown to me when the moon rose. I also talked. Too freely, perhaps. Even Trebeere had its political societies, sometimes disguised as literary meetings. Being young, and often drunk, we never considered who might be listening.

Arthur Wigge was one of those I talked to, and he is the only friend I have left from those days. More like an owl than any man I have seen, Wigge is small and round in person, his face spherical also, the eyes large and slanted downwards at the outer corners, the nose long and slightly hooked. This resemblance creates the expectation of watchful wisdom, and in the months after my marriage I felt this to be fulfilled. He was legal adviser to Edward Florey, and a support to Geneva after Florey's death. With Geneva he is gently sardonic, affectionate, and he still finds me mildly diverting, I hope. But I have never been able to decide where Arthur's heart lies, or his opinion. He is deeply rational, yet at supper he always fills an extra glass with wine 'for passing spirits'; he lives alone apart from a manservant, never the same one for long, for they never appear much inclined to serve. In the past he wrote constantly, in a poetic, inflammatory style I would recognise in broadsheets and pamphlets, the articles getting fiercer as our early hopes dimmed and even meetings were forbidden. These days he tends to be judicious and guarded in his talk, but print is another matter: a few years ago some French duke was stabbed to death in Paris by a Bonapartist named Louvel, and our English journals were much occupied in condemning the murder. I was sure I recognised Arthur's accents in the *Royal Cornwall Gazette*, and I was so struck by the unsigned article I cut it out and kept it. The author tells us it is his 'painful duty' to report a crime more typical of revolutionary times.

'We live in times of extreme danger,' he warns officiously, requiring 'unwearied vigilance on the part of Princes.'

But the article concludes thus:

'The state of France is but an eruption in a remote extremity of that smothered fire which is gathering under the surface of the whole extent of the Continent. We are yet walking over the ashes of the Revolution, and too many of us do not seem aware that they are rekindling as embers beneath our feet.'

That paragraph sounds just like Arthur, and, as with Arthur himself, it is ambiguous. It might be no more than a conventional advisory to the guardians of Order, but the image he invokes creates the impression, surely most encouraging to a Radical reader, that the whole of Europe could be set afire quite easily: all you would need to do is light a candle and leave it burning in an empty room.

I am still unsure if Arthur Wigge reported my youthful views to anyone with the power to influence my career, or whether he pressed my case, seeing the advantage in having a reforming spirit, however ineffectual, at the parsonage in St Anthony. Our friendship is not of the sort where such frank questions can be asked (though it was, at one time). I suspect he was instrumental in arranging that first meeting with Geneva at the Bonaparte, and I know he encouraged our engagement against Amelia Cleer's advice, taking a mischievous pleasure in thwarting that lady. Now I am torn between the desire to tell my old friend (my only friend?) of my predicament with regard to Maryann, and the suspicion that somehow he might already know.

Tuesday May 22

I was correct in suspecting that Maryann might be watching the parsonage. She marks our comings and goings, notes when Geneva leaves me here alone. She must hide in the hawthorns at the edge of the spinney. Each time she appears, the interval between Geneva's departure and her own arrival is briefer than on the previous occasion; she is taunting me by shortening the odds of a meeting between them. The situation is bleaker than I had thought, for me and for Maryann, and the worse it is for her, the worse it becomes for me.

Geneva left for Mrs Cleer's house at five to ten this morning. At five past, I sat down at my desk in the study, glancing out at the chilly garden, which was being soaked monotonously with rain. Almost instantly, its shape distorted by the drops sliding down the glass, the black coal-scuttle came into view, moving across from right to left, creeping along the top of the wall.

'Mrs Tabb to see you.' Dinah's glance at me, as she turned to leave us in the study, was quizzical.

As Maryann placidly divested herself of the dripping cloak, revealing a gown of cheap red stuff, low cut, wholly unsuitable for the weather, I felt a mounting rage, more intense than any I can remember experiencing. I opened the door again, checking the passage to ensure that Dinah had retired to the kitchen, then I shut it, faced Maryann, and remonstrated with her in language I am ashamed to repeat, calling on her in the name of God to cease all these intrusions into my life, swearing that if she sent the craven Paulie to frighten my wife again, I would not be responsible for the consequences.

Sometimes I think Maryann is some sort of mimic or chameleon; she appears in as many varieties as Cleopatra. Today, in the face of my fury, she was soft, submissive, subtle. She stood quite still while I expressed myself, and made no attempt to argue. Her voice, when it came, was little more than a whisper, obliging me to bend forward to hear her, which of course forced me to modify the harshness of my words in reply. She professed ignorance of Paulie's wicked intimidation of Geneva, so I had to recount the whole story; she insisted it must have been a private initiative of Paulie's, because she lacked the power to direct or influence any of his actions. She put her hand to her neck and abruptly sat at my desk. To all my insults regarding Paulie, which continued to pour from me in a torrent, she agreed wholeheartedly, nodding her head up and down; he was ugly, stupid, sneaking, boorish, unscrupulous, verminous, violent, a rat-toothed hagfish... there was no epithet I could summon that she would not approve. When she finally spoke, she painted herself an innocent, in thrall to Paulie, as badgered and oppressed by him as I was by her.

'He holds my debt over my head like a sharp shovel, creeps into my bed quiet as a grammersow[7], there's no end to it, and if I do not find something for him, whenever he calls for it, which is every week or more, he makes me pay, one way or another. He is a cruel man, Godless, but I never saw it.'

I told her she should have heeded my advice and cut herself off from him. She ignored this, and then suggested something so unwholesome that I hardly know how to write it. Paulie, she said, is exploiting the hold he has over her to sell her, or persuade her to sell herself, to the journeymen, traders and seamen who pass through Trebeere. I stepped away from her and stood against the bookcase.

'Have you no family, Maryann? Didn't you tell me you had a brother?'

'Lost at thirteen. Brain fever.'

'What exactly happened to your husband? Did he leave you completely unprovided for?'

Something passed across her face, blurring the angles of it, but only for a moment.

'Dick Tabb was a good enough man, but raw, even younger than I was, and careless. They went out for mackerel off Penglaze Point, it was November. All men lost. But that was years ago. I don't think of him now.'

I was about to ask her again about Eliza. I had some idea that if she could find her daughter, or discover where she had gone, or even work on a plan to look for her, a little light might break into her life, and distract her from mine. I might have offered to help her search. But Maryann was looking at the rain, and she said, without turning round, 'I called him Jack, you know. Your boy.'

---

[7] Woodlouse (S. Martins)

Geneva House, Wednesday May 30
I have moved my chair and table outside into the shade of the ash tree, to escape the tropical heat under the veranda's glass and the hellish hornets that blunder in. Geneva is at the shore, and I have tied Ossian on a long rope to one of the orchard trees, so he cannot follow her. Like Ossian, I don't often accompany her down there, because I have no wish to repel any of the living subjects of her art. Geneva makes light of my idea that I have a discouraging effect on wild creatures, but in gloomier moods I think there is truth in it, that in Nature there is some primitive intelligence that recognises me as an intruder. This afternoon however I am surrounded by beauty: moon-daisies, foxgloves, the violet spikes Geneva calls whistling jacks; all these create a pleasing background for the jasmines and vines we have planted here together. A harmony of God's Creation and Man's design; only a lunatic could wish to be anywhere else.

A moment ago I was looking across the bay to the headlands down the coast, noting that they were almost lost in haze, and I was reassured by this vagueness, for when hills are outlined clearly, when distant churchtowers appear precise as an ink drawing, then it is certain that bad weather will follow soon, even if the sky is blue. Perhaps memory obeys a similar rule, for the closer I approach my death, the sharper the early pictures are.

At eleven I was unusually tall for my age: my wiry black hair sprang out of my head in all directions like a clump of rock-samphire, adding false height for good measure; my voice was deep, and I had a reckless physical courage. All this gave me a spurious eminence among the other children of St Dominic: my pronouncements, if not acted upon, were at least listened to with respect. At that time our games centred on a family of six boys and one girl, all very near in years, with the rest of us serving as their reserve troops. I shall refer to these children as the family

Smith, which was not their name, because they may yet be living. Mabbott was never a member of our little band; he had a reputation as a tattletale, a spoiler of mischief, unworthy even of a Christian name. Mabbott was also, God forgive me, a most unprepossessing child: his pallid face, with its full, downturned lips, had a fixed expression of complaint, together with a permanently swollen aspect, as one who has just left off weeping. A face, it seemed to me, that tempted cruelty. He was ten years old, not stupid, but he never accepted his exclusion, instead returning again and again to whichever copse or barnyard the boys had elected for sport that day. There he would hover, on the periphery, pleading for a role, a task, and sooner or later the Smith children would encircle him, chanting, taunting, serenely patient, until Mabbott lashed out at them. The sister, who was older, would then upbraid Mabbott, quite unjustly, for his snappish temper. The Smiths were not inclined to violence, they had no real need of it; all they had to do was slouch there and allow Mabbott to unravel.

And where was I at these moments? I was the watcher, standing just outside the circle on a little mound of raised ground. As I watched I was filled with a dangerous glee offered by the spectacle of humiliation, a sense that Mabbott's abject character excused me from any obligation to pity the prey. But I think I was watching, or listening, for something else, too: a sign, a voice, warning me that teasing had become torment or torture, exceeding its justifiable limits. How, though, would I recognise this signal that a border had been crossed? I never could decide, and I never once stepped over to help Mabbott.

The day it happened was a Saturday, it must have been late January 1780. It had been an odd sort of morning from the start. A cart drew up in the road outside while I was dressing, and I looked down to see three dark hats come up the path below my window. When I arrived downstairs the visitors had already disappeared into the dining room and the door was firmly shut, serious voices humming and murmuring beyond it – my father's among them. In the kitchen Lucy was setting out my breakfast. Two hens came in from the orchard, poking their way through the curtain that hung in the doorway. Lucy chased them out, flapping her apron, cursing them in a harsh manner uncharacteristic of her. Then she gave me two boiled eggs instead of one, which I took to be her revenge on the impertinent hens, and she put the honeypot, which was reserved strictly for Sundays, on the table in front of me.

I was about to complain about the eggs being underdone when the curtain parted a second time. A black horse entered the room; a horse somehow malformed and foreshortened about the head and snout, a monstrous, hulking spectre with amber eyes. From the pantry, Lucy heard the clatter of my spoon on the slate floor.

'It's your uncle Jacob's dog, he won't hurt you,' said Lucy, 'a German mastiff or Danish mastiff, I forget which. His name is Captain.'

I was to take Captain out, she said, occupy myself outside, because my father and uncle had matters to discuss, and I was not to disturb Mother, who was in bed. I gathered that this plan had been arranged betimes, for she handed me a satchel of bread and cheese 'for your dinner'. After a nervous half hour with Captain, I was enchanted to discover that Lucy was correct – this vast black dog with lion's paws was a gentle and courteous companion. I took him for miles around the copses, along the stream, and whenever our path narrowed, he would shift his towering flanks aside to let me pass in front. It was well after noon when it occurred to me what a splendid impression Captain would make on the Smith boys, and so we set off back to the village. By this time both the dog and I were covered in winter mud – it was smeared over our faces, crusted in our fur and hair. Captain, I would tell them, was a wild dog from the German forests; I was the only one capable of taming him. I found three boys behind the churchyard, and soon a small crowd had gathered in awe around my dog, just as I had imagined. Mabbott was not among them.

'We've sent Mabbott into Sorleigh's Wood. To find the silver muskets,' said the biggest Smith.

'What muskets?'

'And the silver cakes and the gold puddings,' added a smaller boy.

'He's been a while,' said the first, grinning. 'You should take Captain with you and flush him out.'

The further I went into the trees with Captain, the more noble my task appeared. The leafless wood was damp and hushed in the failing light, but it was not large (nothing like the forests around St Anthony); I would find Mabbott soon, and, like a benevolent huntsman, offer him a little bracing advice about his strategy with the Smith boys. Already I was feeling a surprising new warmth flowing from myself to Mabbott: he needed me, I would be his older brother, his saviour. But it was taking longer than I thought, and the dog seemed uneasy. I started calling Mabbott's name through the trees, and Captain echoed me with melancholy howls, each one becoming throaty and guttural as it died away. I suppose I should say that Mabbott found us: a stick snapped and the child lurched from behind a bush twenty yards ahead; he paused for a moment and I saw his bared teeth in a white face, and then abruptly he screamed – a high rabbit shriek – and ran downhill, away from us, away from the village, towards the marsh. I heard the sporadic crash of his footsteps grow fainter, and then there was nothing except the wintry cry of a moorhen from some distant reeds.

There is a peculiar terror in the realisation that you are the source of another's terror, as in those dreams in which you discover that you are already dead, inspiring horror in the living. I turned and ran with the dog back to St Dominic.

At home I was told to go straight to see my father in the dining room. Where had I been, they asked distractedly, your uncle Jacob thought you'd lost the dog. No one remarked on my wild and filthy appearance. The dining room was like an ice-house, the hearth stone cold; there was a bleak smell of soot around my father, who was standing against the chimneypiece, the table with its solitary candlestick between us. His voice was flat. My older brother Robert, he said, had died fighting the Spanish, somewhere off Portugal, at the battle of Cape St Vincent. It was a great victory, fought by moonlight, and Robert was a hero, and I was not to disturb Mother, who was still in bed.

I felt nothing. I had not seen Robert for over a year; my mind's eye settled, absurdly, on the cowlick that interrupted Robert's hairline, sending the hair up in a crest. I wondered if I would still be allowed to go to Trebeere market to see the accordionist with the dancing monkey Lucy had told me about. Robert had been dead two weeks when my family heard the news; all that time, while I had been playing, studying, sleeping in my box-bed by the window with its view of St Materiana's Isle, Robert, who was afraid of nothing, had been lying under the cold sea. How, I wondered later, had I failed to sense something amiss, some echo of this catastrophic change in the world? He was not even killed in battle, it transpired, but died the previous day of the smallpox, which had been infesting his ship, HMS Bienfaisant. I suppose they tipped his body into the waves with the others.

They found Mabbott's corpse early the next day, Sunday, in the flooded marshes between the village and the seashore. My family knew I had gone searching for him, but I hadn't told them I had seen him. Everybody was unusually gentle with me, as if I had suddenly become an invalid, or a much younger child: I was not to worry, they said; I had shown commendable courage, the only boy to go looking for Mabbott, and this bravery took on a retrospective glow in the village when news of my bereavement spread among the neighbours. Our kindly young curate, Mr Bugloss, started taking an interest in me, the brotherless boy Samaritan, from that date, paving my way to the future with lessons, books, letters of introduction, and soon it was easy to persuade myself that all this was my due.

The Smith children wasted no time in enlightening me as to the cause of Mabbott's panic – the reason why I, with my filthy face and monstrous dog, had been chosen to go searching. When they told Mabbott to look for the mythical silver muskets, they had also warned him not to stay after sundown, in case of Blind Bocka.

'Blind Bocka's a huntsman, a ghost with no face,' explained one boy, smiling at me cheerfully.

'No, it's more like a scarecrow,' said the other. 'And he has no eyes so he always walks beside his horse, a black horse with no head.'

It has been years since I thought about Mabbott. I was wondering why he should have come to mind just now when I tripped, mentally, and recalled Maryann last week, telling me how her own brother died young, and of her husband's death at sea, his fishing boat sunk off the very same headland I was looking at. Here was yet another circumstance linking me to her, but there was something else, something behind this thought. My gaze was pulled, as if by the same quiet force that warns the seals, to the purplish spikes in the long grass under the trees, the whistling jacks, and with this came the memory that Mabbott's unused Christian name had been Jack, and I thought of another Jack, a boy in Redruth Poorhouse.

The Parsonage, St Anthony, Thursday May 31
I sat immobile under the ash tree at Geneva House yesterday after writing the previous entry, reluctant to raise my eyes from the page, possessed by the notion that if I were to do so, if I were to turn my head and look across at the hedge, I would see a coal-scuttle shape moving through the leaves. There was nothing in the hedge, of course, but I can't escape the knowledge that Paulie has tracked us to Geneva House, and I fear the sense of retreat is permanently damaged. Each day I spend up there, each hour, each moment, will contain the possibility that Maryann, or Paulie, or both, might appear, like Blind Bocka, padding along the path over the cliffs, into the wood, pushing the trees aside, walking out of the shade onto the grassy slope by the veranda.

He would be around six years old, now, Jack, if he lives, if he exists or ever existed. I have no more evidence that the child is anything but a chimera than I did when Maryann first mentioned it. Even if he is real, or an infant existed once, there would be no means to prove it was or wasn't mine. Maryann never *explains* anything properly; press her and she lapses into silence. Besides, any search for answers would involve spending time with her, seeking her out, which would encourage her to mistake a request for information for an admission. But it is difficult to avoid wandering into speculation about the boy. Would he have my brown eyes or her grey ones, my dark wiry hair or Maryann's yellow silk? Might he have inherited my father's jutting chin, his interest in bees, or my mother's sharp memory, her broad forehead plagued by sudden violent headaches? All these conjectures, however, are only another form of self-deceit, for the truth is that an image has already taken root in my mind. I see a sturdy child with a square face, narrow grey eyes set rather wide apart, straight brows, coarse hair the colour of oatmeal. There is a suggestion of a cowlick around the hairline, but it is not my brother Robert I see, this child is quite particular, an individual, as if something beyond my understanding had painted him into being.

* * *

The Parsonage, St Anthony, Tuesday June 5
Arthur Wigge has started to come out to our church in St Anthony on Sundays, rather than his own parish church of St Luke's in Trebeere. He sits towards the back, on the pulpit side, half obscured by the pillar there. If I notice him at all, it is when his head bobs forward in a pecking motion to see his prayerbook: his eyesight does not match his owlish appearance. Last Sunday I was conscious of a change in the quality of his attention. My sermon was on Luke 16, and, still needled by the vestry meeting, I was talking about generosity, describing Dives the rich man and his brilliant purple cloak, Lazarus the beggar lying below the dining table, ignored, except by the dogs, who licked his sores (Luke leaves the dogs' motives unexplained; I like to think they demonstrated a fellow feeling the diners lacked). When the rich man awakes in Hell, he is told that a great gulf now separates him from all that is good, and nobody can pass to or from the place where he is. I encouraged my listeners to consider the gulfs most familiar to them, the chasms of the Great Fall, and how it would feel to be cast away out there, cut off from Christ forever. It was then that I noticed Arthur. He had moved right out from behind the pillar and was leaning back in the pew, his body at ease, short

wings folded on his stomach, but his face sharply alive, as if he had suddenly solved a riddle.

'A curious sermon, James,' he said, catching up with me on the lane, 'it made me quite nostalgic for my youth.'

I was unclear what he meant, unless it was a reference to the lax style of my preaching. I used to prepare my sermons with care, choosing texts according to the seasonal anniversaries in the life of our Lord, linking these to the commonplace travails of my parishioners, but recently I have found myself depending less on these plans and patterns, and instead I feel I am speaking from some other part of myself: verses from all books of the Bible surface without effort of memory; I combine them into new shapes, extemporise, add twists and flourishes, as if I were not in the pulpit but tramping the woods like some hedge preacher. Only the sight of a puzzled ruddy face or ugly hat recalls me to my reason and my duty, though I have been surprised to note that church attendance has improved and the rows of eyes below me stay open. Perhaps my old Cambridge tutor was correct: 'Do not explain it all too plainly, Prideaux; the rural parishioner expects some degree of mystification, a suggestion of the noumenal as well as the numinous, with a nice seasoning of Latin.'

Arthur invited himself to tea this afternoon, which we took in the front parlour with Geneva, and with Ossian, who worships Arthur immoderately, though Arthur's preference is for cats. The talk was chiefly of young Henry Florey, whose vague, fitful correspondence worries his mother, and of painting, which interests Arthur far more than the law. He was preparing to leave when he asked if he might speak with me in private, and I took him into the study. At once he pounced on the bookcases, opened the glass doors and bent double to peer at the titles.

'Ha! I guessed you would still have all this stuff.' He pulled a volume out. 'Ah yes – 1796, is it? No, 1799, *Biographical Anecdotes on the Founders of the French Republic*. I remember this, with the chapter on Bonaparte, quite a flattering portrait.' He ran his fingers along the shelf, his eyes an inch from the spines. 'And you have Paine here too, a bit dusty isn't he! And Rousseau, the old fraud. Puts all his children in the Paris orphanage to make room for little Emile, the paper child. But I expect you knew that.'

I did, and he knew I did. If Arthur had wished to discuss political philosophy, or ethics, he could have done so when we were sitting with Geneva. She is very well read for a woman.

'You know I read widely as a youth.'

'As did I, James, as you know. We lived through terrible years. For a brief time, ordinary souls were sailors on the tide of history. I don't suppose the world can ever be as interesting again. Perhaps I should write a memoir, I'll call it *The Sorrows of Young Wigge*. What do you think?'

I said nothing.

'Shall I tell you what I think? I think you are slipping back into those habits of thought. Perhaps you never abandoned them. Maybe you are at last emboldened, now the Bourbon king is back on his little square of the chessboard, and we no longer have to watch our words for sedition, or beware with whom we keep company.'

I had an awful suspicion that he had heard something about Maryann. Why, I said, was he asking me this, now?

He picked up his brandy and sat. 'Your sermons, for one thing. On Sunday we had Lazarus the Beggar, and last week the Rich Fool – most unnerving, that one, the idea of someone arriving in the middle of the night for your soul. But it's not just the subjects, James, it is a question of flavour. As I said, I was transported back twenty-five years. Are you troubled by your conscience? With respect to the poor and unfortunate?'

'No more than usual.'

He puffed himself out in the chair, his round face clouding, patting at the sides of his forehead as if adjusting a weighty headdress – a mitre perhaps, or a wig. He began by reminding me of his duty as informal trustee following the death of Edward Florey. He had been taken aback, he said, during his quarterly check on Geneva's accounts, now mine of course, to see the large sums which have been taken out at irregular intervals.

'If these big payments are all to young Trembath for works on that cabin of yours, then I think he is swindling you. The work should have cost half of that at most. But I don't believe Peter Trembath to be dishonest, and I have been puzzling and puzzling over who the recipients of this generosity could be, until Sunday, when I listened to you in church, and it came to me: you are distributing a private poor relief, from your own pocket! Which is admirable, but it is my duty to advise you that with all the expenses already incurred on the cottage, it cannot be sustained, not for another month, if that. When our dear Geneva was left widowed, I felt it my duty as a friend to protect her from the local vultures, and as a friend, too, I am urging you to caution now.'

Good Lord he can be pompous.

Wigge had only just departed when Dinah knocked. The butcher had called at the kitchen door while I was closeted with Arthur, and was 'most agitated' about his account.

Geneva House, Tuesday June 12
We spent the whole of last night out here at the house in the woods, only the second time we have done so, and the deep quiet has gone some way to soothe my spirit. I am mostly recovered from the embarrassment of Arthur's warning, and now consider it providential; the butcher is paid in full, Jordan the dairyman also, while the other tradesmen have accepted payment in part. I am resolved to pay closer attention to our household, and in time

our situation will improve. Far better that Arthur should think me an elderly Radical than guess the real reason for my profligacy. There have been no further visitations from Maryann, and there are moments when I dare to hope that she has gone from my life. Perhaps she has escaped from Paulie and left the district.

I lay awake for hours beside my sleeping wife, our window open, the warm air alive with rustles and squeaks, methodical siftings, sudden cracks. I felt the power of the forest, its indifference. It took no account of us in here; it was moving closer to the walls of the house, to the bed, ready to absorb us without a thought. These midsummer nights never become entirely dark: a diffuse twilight fell across the pillows, draining the red from Geneva's hair so that it looked quite grey, ageing her face. At around three o'clock I went down to the kitchen and walked outside with Ossian, who was delighted to have company so early. We sat together in the damp grass, looking south. The yellow moon, displeased by my intrusion, disappeared behind a cloud.

Just over a month ago we passed the sixth anniversary of the Great Fall, a day that must have been as unremarkable as any other, since I cannot remember it, but it means that Bonaparte has lain six years in his grave on St Helena. I have outlived him, my unknown twin. Last night however I sensed him still out there in the southern ocean, wide awake, staring north, his telescopic eyes disregarding me to focus on Europe, spread out behind my shoulders like a tablecloth all the way to Russia. I used to wonder how he reconciled himself to the contrast between what had been and what was, if he heard voices in the ceaseless churn of the waves, but of course he would not. Bonaparte would not waste energy on remorse, nor wonder if a lifetime might be warped by a trivial error made in boyhood. He was, is, my opposite, for the dead child Mabbott haunts me now, along with the living Maryann. When Geneva told me Paulie claimed to have 'a whole box of stories', my first thought was that Paulie somehow *knows* about Mabbott, an absurd fancy, but not a new one.

I failed, repeatedly, to defend Mabbott, choosing to preserve my standing with my peers; and when at last I strode into the trees to help him, I became Blind Bocka with his headless horse, the cause of his death. A death that coincided with my brother's (for years my imagination struggled to separate them) and brought me praise, sympathy, a mentor in the Church. Perhaps I have always been dimly aware that my curacy began with a misconception. As for courage, I have never trusted myself with it.

Dew had crept up the hem of my nightshirt. I raised myself slowly, an ungainly spectre with painful knees, and heard a subtle movement from the trees behind the house, a faint whistling breath, like the snort of a horse. Ossian remained placid, his nose pointing south to sniff the sea; he had heard nothing. I forced myself to cross the lawn, to part the thicket, inspect the dark path. The curious thing was my disappointment when I found no one there.

The Parsonage, St Anthony, Thursday June 14
In the afternoon I called on young Tom Menhennett. The poor lad does not have long. He coughs and laughs in the rank feverish dark with the hot day buzzing outside his shuttered window. Unaware of his condition, he tells me about his epic future on the sea, so it always seems tactless to pray with him. On arriving home I found Geneva and Dinah in the kitchen, where the air by contrast was warm and sweet, the talk animated. Dinah has been teaching Geneva the arts of baking. They stood together at the table, floury sisters in identical aprons. According to Dinah, who heard it at Jordan's dairy, a dreadful crime has been committed in Trebeere, a murder.

The victim is a cooper named Edwin Hookway, and it seems he has been slaughtered by his own wife. 'She murdered him in his sleep, plunged a knife into him over and over.' Geneva had the pastry dough in her hands, she was pushing its dimpled flesh into the ribbed china, pressing Dinah for detail. There is no doubt about the author of the crime. Dinah says the woman ran out into the street, covered in blood, where she gave herself up, shouting her deed to passers-by. I asked Dinah if she knew any more about the victim, or his family.

'Hookway's a Devon name. Most likely they're not from Trebeere. Hannah at the dairy is terrified, she lives close by Pound Street, where it happened.'

Dinah then made a long speech arriving at the somewhat obvious conclusion that she would never have expected such a crime to occur in a Christian neighbourhood like this one, and swore not to step outside the parsonage door until she knew the murderer was locked up. I asked if the woman had been arrested, where she had been taken, and Dinah, forgetting what she had just promised, said she would find out more at the Saturday market at Trebeere.

Tuesday June 19

Dinah did not go to market on Saturday, being plagued by a toothache, so we heard no more of the crime in Trebeere until yesterday, when Geneva returned from a visit to the draper. The supposed murderess, Janet Hookway, was arrested at the scene and has been taken to Bodmin. She is believed to have formally confessed the crime.

This evening Wigge called on us. He stayed only an hour, but it was a friendly visit, Arthur at his most owlish and witty, our earlier difficulty forgotten. He brought Dinah some rosemary cuttings from his garden, and a bottle of cognac for us all. He also left a copy of the *Gazette* in my study just before he departed, laying it down on the table with a little too much care, which usually means he has contributed to one of the political articles and wishes me to read it.

Wednesday June 20
I am still not absolutely sure, and of course I cannot ask. After breakfast I took my tea into the study, and picked up the newspaper Arthur left last night. My attention, straying over advertisements for coppice auctions, was trapped by this article. Even after I had read it halfway through, I was still planning to take the paper back out to Geneva to share with Dinah. I have now cut the whole page out and burned it, except for the report.

FEARFUL MURDER WITH FISH KNIFE
Trebeere, June 16

A most shocking crime has occurred in the parish of Trebeere on Wednesday 14th inst., in which Edwin Paul Hookway, potman, was viciously assaulted and murdered in his lodgings by a woman, believed to be his wife, Janet Hookway. There were several witnesses present immediately following the event, which happened at around four o'clock in the afternoon in a court to the rear of Pound Street. Mr John Capstone, aged 45 years, was attending to his business when he was surprised to see a woman run through the court, her apron copiously soaked with blood. The woman was observed to drop a knife onto the roadway, whereupon she sat by a wall in a crouching position with her knees to her chest. Nancy Hendra, aged 19 years, a hide-trimmer at Carr's tannery close by, was also proceeding along Pound Street at that time. Miss Hendra said that when she saw the blood, she had at first supposed the woman to be injured, and on going to her aid, the woman said to her, 'I have killed him, I have killed him, God have mercy.' Mr Capstone then secured the help of a Mr George Landry, and together they entered the court and the dwelling to find Mr Hookway lying on the floor with deep wounds to his throat and abdomen, such as might be produced by a sharp knife. He was dead. There was evidence of much drinking having taken place, according to Mr Landry, and the condition of the chamber was disordered and dirty as a pig-bed. The weapon, which proved to be a fish-gutting knife of the sort used by women on the quays, was retrieved by Mr Capstone.

Janet Mary Hookway, aged 45 years, also known as Mary Ann Hookway, was examined by the local magistrate, Philip Wickham esq., and has been indicted for trial at the next Bodmin Assizes. At an inquest held at the Cinnabar Inn before the Trebeere Coroner, Mr Laurence Starkie, on 15th inst., it was established that the victim expired through extreme loss of blood, and the accounts of all witnesses were heard and transcribed.

The past hours have been spent persuading myself that this is coincidence: the Pound Street area of Trebeere around Carr's tannery and the shambles is notorious for lawlessness and vice; a man named Edwin Paul Hookway is more likely to use his first Christian name than his second; there are hundreds of potmen employed in the inns around Trebeere and there was no mention of the Bell and Candle in the report. Furthermore, any local fishwife, in fact any local wife, would possess a fish-gutting knife; I only ever saw Maryann write her name twice, in short notes to me, and on neither occasion did she separate 'Mary' from 'Ann', and she never called herself Janet. Most importantly, she never mentioned any marriage, other than her original one to Dick Tabb. It seems incredible that she could have been married to Paulie, if indeed Edwin Paul Hookway was Paulie. I am praying that he was not.

Thursday June 21
Sometimes you only realise how little a person cares for you when you see them with someone else, someone new. Dinah came to work for me twelve years ago, soon after I took up the curacy at St Anthony. The parsonage, which must be the smallest and dampest in England, was in a parlous condition, and I sent word around the parish for someone to attend to domestic matters while repairs were completed. Dinah Pengelly was not too young, not too old. She had a grave oval face like a Mediaeval madonna, an admirable indifference to cobwebs and falling plaster, a firm manner with labourers. She did not pester me with questions, understood my need for quiet, and she was unusually fond of dogs. 'Well done, good and faithful servant; thou hast been faithful over a few things, I will make thee ruler over many things: enter thou the joy of thy Lord.' I entrusted her with many things, but there was no joy. After a year, I knew no more about her than when she arrived: that she had a married sister in Trebeere, she enjoyed baking but preferred to send the linen to the village, she disliked liver, even the smell of it, and she grew fragrant herbs outside the kitchen door. The more time passed, the more impossible it was to put our relations on a less distant footing. Our only warm conversations were about dogs in general and Voltaire in particular, and these ceased when Voltaire vanished in 1821.

I was resigned to this state of affairs until Geneva came to the parsonage. Within days my wife had discovered Dinah's interest in medicine and had given her a book on herbs, she had met the sister, and Geneva and Dinah went together to collect the new dog from a farm near St Just – I was simply informed of Ossian's imminent arrival. Recently Geneva engaged a young maid with the apt name of Martha to do the morning work, for Dinah has developed pain in her knees, which I knew nothing about. Most noticeable is the difference in Dinah's manner when she is with Geneva; she seems younger, light-hearted, volunteering an unsuspected variety of opinion and anecdote. I am often startled by the sound of her laugh, rattling along the corridor from the kitchen. I now understand why Arthur Wigge calls Geneva a natural democrat; she seems nearly oblivious to the distinctions that constrain the rest of us.

They are in there now, in the kitchen with Ossian, talking in hurried whispers. I have twice tiptoed out into the passage, as near to the door as I dare, but the door is oak and very thick, so it is difficult to make out the words, and I fear that Ossian will sniff me out and alert them. I have been trying to determine what Geneva knows or suspects, and I know this will depend on how much Dinah guessed about Maryann and her visits. Geneva has asked me no questions, and if she has been a little cool in her manner to me, preoccupied with her work, this is nothing unusual.

Yesterday Geneva went out just after breakfast. Before she leaves the house she always stops in the hallway to adjust her hat in the looking-glass, a very old glass which imparts an emerald hue to the reflection, like a pool in a wood. I was standing a little behind her, looking at my bush of hair (still hardly touched with grey) and her green face, when she spoke.

'You will be surprised what I have discovered from Dinah about our local murder. I am related to the murderess. Distantly. Through the Penders, my mother's family. She is a sort of cousin, Janet Hookway, though Dinah says she used to go by another name, Mary Ann. I do remember my mother talking about a little girl called Mary Ann.'

Tuesday June 26
I have received a letter from Bodmin. I have copied it here and destroyed the original, which is senseless because I would anyway have concealed it in this journal, where everything would be revealed were anyone to break into my desk; the existence of the original letter or the copy would make no difference. But I could not endure the thought of that rough yellow paper, the words in that uneducated hand, existing in physical form in my study.

> Good morning Jim
>
> You will have seen the newspaper. They told me my crime is written up in it for the world to read of, though I am not permitted to see it. Reverend Cauley who is the chaplain here tells me my case has stirred curiosity, and folk as far as Bude and Plymouth know my name and talk of me over their porter.
>
> You are surprised one such as I can write, but I told you I learned long ago at home. My mother taught me, and her Aunt Pender taught her. An art that never dies. You should have listened more. I draw my letters slow and the words creep like snails across the paper, but I have no other work so it is no matter. Here in this fine room I have my own time, hours and hours of it for the first time in years, until they stop the clock. A jest for you Jim.
>
> I am permitted to write to you because you are my parish parson. The chaplain will send you this letter. I have confessed all and expect nothing. I have a mouse with me in here, which is a comfort, otherwise I see only Liddicott the turnkey and Reverend Cauley, and Cauley not often. Cauley's work is to

bring forth remorse in me, and he is dutiful in the task, but dutiful in the way of a housekeeper, not a father. Likely he hopes you will win where he fails.

I have no remorse to deliver. I would gut Hookway again today and tomorrow and next week. Therefore Jim I have no prospects for the trial or hope of pardons. I cannot even plead my belly. The true purpose of this writing is to ask that you come to Bodmin on the last day. You will discover what day that is when the trial is done. The ceremony, for so I name it to myself, will be outside the gate of the gaol, where there is an open pasture. Liddicott says there is a hawthorn on a patch of rising ground to the left. Stand by it, quite still. I will see you Jim

I only fear those days beyond the trial, after the hour of my death is told to me. Old Cauley says all men walk in the shadow of death, but there is a hellish bitterness in having that hour made known. You can pray for me at that time. After it is done, well it is your choice Parson to pray or not. I will face a different Judge

They say it is fine weather out, but in here we are cold as a witch's tits. There is a fever in the gaol at present. Three men were taken out dead on Friday, so I half expect Providence to cheat the wigs of their prey.

I do not think of Eliza, who you were always so concerned about. I will confess another thing. I never wanted Eliza. I do not believe God intended me for a mother, but still He made me one, which is a puzzle to me. I wanted Dick Tabb for a while, and I wanted a house, a home, and books to learn, and work to better myself, but Eliza came too soon. In the end she never wanted me.

Two nights past I dreamed I was still a child, in my mother's old kitchen. Eliza was there, but we were the same age. We were chopping carrots. Waiting for Mother to come home. But then who comes skirtling in the door, not Mother but Lowdie, that fussock of Hocking's at Churchtown. Lowdie takes hold of the child Eliza, pulls her up and away over Torbett's Green and I shout after them, but the hill's too steep, I stumble and slide fast through the willows down to the sea.

My regards to little Jenny. How much does she know?

Maryann
Jim there was a name with the parcel, I put it under the wrappings.

It is true I never suspected Maryann could write anything more than a curt note. Nonetheless in copying the letter I was obliged to impose some literacy on the writing, which lacked all consistency and punctuation.

Part 3: The Fall

The Heart of the Wood

My hope and my love,
we will go for a while into the wood,
scattering the dew,
where we will see the trout,
we will see the blackbird on its nest;
the deer and the buck calling,
the little bird that is sweetest singing on the branches;
the cuckoo on the top of the fresh green;
and death will never come near us for ever in the sweet
wood.

Anon, Irish traditional, translated from Gaelic by Augusta Gregory, 1919

7

I was the least remarkable person in this story, and if I had never come to St Anthony the same things might well have happened, taking a slightly different shape. But stories are told by those who survive to tell them, people who keep a packed suitcase under the bed and hide in the hedge, listening.

At twelve I was evicted from the eerie self-sufficiency that we all had at eleven, becoming tearful and needful of my parents, just at the time when the world suggests briskly that you make bold steps towards independence, unfold yourself in the shared light of common sense, exams, clothes, periods, parties. From this time on I withdrew into books, preferring those from the previous century, so that the granite world around me often became as thin as paper. I'd be awake for hours at night under the skylight, keeping watch on the freighters out at sea. Their separateness felt like a promise.

At Joseph Carne Comprehensive, my new school in Trebeere, I found myself for the first time in a classroom with boys. They were shockingly different – unkempt and clumsy – but I liked their loud defiance, their frank irreverence for authority and reckless, polychromatic swearing: echoes of Victor's deliberate disobedience. Their contempt for neatness was also salutary; I learned to be less distracted by surfaces, wrappings and colours, to dive confidently into the heart of a question. You were supposed to ignore the boys in your own class, as if they were younger brothers; if you did risk expressing an interest in a male person, this had to be directed at the boys in the older groups. They in turn ignored us in favour of the sixth-form girls with their elaborate eye make-up and uncanny understanding of style. I saw much less of Kerenza, because she was sent to St Agnes, the private school, while Victor, because of his earlier birthday, was in the year above us. But Tracy was with me, sitting always at the back of the class, her presence like an underground river. Naturally I made other friends, as we all did – people who swam close for a while like coloured fish, before glancing off the glass wall and waving away.

We grew self-conscious. Victor and Tracy found each other so excruciatingly embarrassing at thirteen that they hardly spoke for a year. By fifteen they were a couple. Victor grew taller, broader and darker, but the red cheeks persisted, to his shame. If I passed him and his friends in the street, he would nod and say 'All right' like a statement. People seemed to like Victor, outside of his own house. Meeting him alone was easier; we chatted about books or films or music, the ennui of school, but nothing dangerous or personal. Whether I was with Tracy or Victor or Kerenza or all three, I never heard any of them mention the woman in the sea. It was not that we avoided the subject of Geneva and the Fall; we still went up there, and if we did not visit as often, that was only because there were more demands on our time and attention; there was no shadow over it.

In time I started to notice people, strangers, staring at Tracy, and I knew they were trying, as I did, to define exactly what it was about that particular arrangement of structure, features, colour and expression that made her face extraordinary. They would be experiencing the same sense of recognition: 'That's it, the theme, that's what all the other faces were trying to do.' She provoked surprisingly little envy in others, her looks being so far outside the normal range it would have been like resenting a lake because you only had a bath at home. Her effect on boys, apart from Victor, was also odd: the blonde hair, that trite bright signal, pulled them towards her like moths in dimmed pubs and dance halls, but when she turned to face them they would step back, unsure, unmanned, their ramshackle courage collapsing inward. Kerenza called it Tracy's Medusa Effect. Tracy also had no idea about clothes, which she viewed as camouflage, and no banter, tending to answer questions over-literally. Once I overheard a boy telling his friend that Tracy was pretty but half-witted. Kerenza by contrast was entirely witty: slim and elegant as a dragonfly, eyes sparking with sardonic deflection, she was studiedly flippant with the opposite sex, the transformation so disconcertingly rapid you would never guess this was the same Kerenza who still spent hours lost in the private lives of ants or jellyfish.

Halfway through my sixteenth year, my father was sent to Treliske hospital in Truro for a precautionary scan, after a winter cough refused to disappear with the coming of the daffodils. The diagnosis was lung cancer, and so began the journey down long corridors of shuffling walkers, through hanging strips of plastic, into the specialist wards, all different, all the same; the treatments and remissions, tubes in the flesh, flickering hope and clenched dread in the windowless canteen. After his death I was surprised to feel not sadness, but a scorching anxiety, mountainous and jagged, as if the worst was still about to happen at any moment.

Our house in Pellow Street seemed always to be full of people; they must have been relatives or friends, but I couldn't understand what they were all doing there.

Every death leaves a signature image behind it, distinguishing it from all other deaths you have known or will know, separate even from the person who died, although you don't find out what these pictures will be until later. In the case of my father there were two. One evening I visited him at the hospital on my own. He was in an old-fashioned ward with long lines of beds on either side. All the patients were gravely ill. My father pointed to an empty bed on the opposite side of the ward. The previous night, he said, at about eleven o'clock, the man in that bed had abruptly sat up and pulled his drip out. Then, swaying on his feet, he put on his trousers and jacket, swept his few possessions off the locker into a carrier bag, shouted 'Bollocks to this' and walked away. The dying patients in the lines of beds had shouted, or whispered, encouragement, and the man vanished, leaving a ripple of defiance behind him. The second image is of an afternoon in May when my father was out of hospital for a few brief days before he went back, probably for the last time. Somebody had organised a visit to a pub garden, full of flowers and people, bright as a fête. I went inside the pub to get a drink, and, coming back out, paused in the doorway, struck by something strange about the scene before me. My father was sitting in an upright chair in the centre of the lawn with a blanket over his knees. The people were still there, but they had dispersed themselves, by some unconscious process, into little groups on the periphery. There was a wide circle of empty space around my father, precise as a frontier, excluding everything but the hard spring sunlight on the grass.

I went with Tracy to the Fall, shortly after the funeral. It was months since I had seen Geneva. The woods pressed even closer to the walls of the house; a huge jasmine creeper had burst out of a pot by the veranda, rooted itself, and then crept back inside through broken glass, drenching the sitting room in its narcotic scent. It was clear that Tracy had been coming to Geneva on her own. A gleaming chambered spiral – a nautilus shell – sat on the table like a sea lamp, too beautiful for comment, while cairns of stones and frosted sea glass, emerald or sapphire, had appeared along the wainscots. But the centre of the floor was swept, the red rug lay flat, the green wicker chairs were still placed hospitably around the room in case a stranger should be passing by.

She told me that she had been there one day in winter and found some opened tins in the kitchen, a bed upstairs rumpled, the ashes of a fire in the grate.

'Like Goldilocks, except you're the bear,' I said, but I was uneasy. 'Isn't it a bit dangerous coming here on your own?'

'Everything is dangerous. If I saw anyone, I'd just go into the woods. They'd never find me. Come down to the sea. That's why we're here.'

The Mint Woman had gone. Tracy said she had just disappeared into a new crack in the ground, sometime in February.

'I was relieved in a way. I never told you, but I used to think the Mint Woman was a statue of Eliza Tabb.'

We stopped in the bracken above the shore. There were two seals down there, lying parallel on the seaweed, smooth, marbled grey. They lifted their heads up like babies on a rug, snuffing and shifting their improbable fatness, trying to get comfortable. They seemed not to see us. A few yards out in the sea, a third seal, dark Roman nose turned in profile, watched. Their whiskery faces had the fugitive familiarity of someone you used to know. Tracy whispered that the seal in the water had been coming for a while, but the other two were more recent visitors.

'I told them you were coming. They know who you are.'

Then she lost her footing, dislodging pebbles, setting off a tiny simultaneous vibration between the seals. The two on the shore undulated into the sea with surprising speed, and the three of them paused in the waves, regarding us. Their eyes looked melancholy, I thought, but having thought it, was irritated by my compulsion to impose human expressions on them. Perhaps the seals pitied us, the landlocked humans, jerky naked imitative apes, jacks of all trades, slow runners, amateur swimmers, mechanical flyers; a species without a niche, the measure and measurer of all things, homeless, destructive, full of dread and deeply angry.

Tracy saw me frowning. 'Maybe you should just try listening to them instead.'

I knew Tracy's intention had been to suggest the idea of return, that people, and animals, might come back, or move on to some different state, but it wasn't really necessary. It was years before I really understood that death might be permanent. Tracy, who had no concept of permanence of any kind, was never in any doubt about the presence of other worlds. With both parents gone, this was not surprising. Or perhaps she knew something I didn't.

* * *

'I'm on the bus and I see you with Tracy out on the sand, out beyond the harbour, and I think to myself that will be Sally, and I'm telling Rita, she's on the number 16 as well, how you came here all the way from London and Tracy is talking about you all the time.'

Tracy's grandmother, Hazel Tabb, spoke entirely in the present tense, and since her talk was thickly populated with people, and like Victor's mother she assumed that you knew the people she was talking about, I often lost my way in the jungle of her conversation. As a child I was more interested in her descriptions of Carmelow's bakery (the name a local corruption of Carne & Lowe's) where she worked, the saffron buns and heavy cakes, doughnuts and éclairs (my parents were strict about sweet things). I must have mentioned the curiosity of the present tense to Kerenza one day, because she said, 'Most of the people Mrs Tabb talks about are dead.' After that I listened a little more carefully, and when my father died, Mrs Tabb in turn became more expansive in my presence. With practice I identified snatches of memory from her youth: 'courting' on Torbett's Green, a boyfriend who was almost killed by a bull, a sister dying from a 'swollen throat' – she moved from the 1930s to the 1960s to this morning with no pauses, no time markers other than hours or days of the week, no borders between the living and the gone.

Once I caught her talking about Tracy's mother. Tracy and I were doing our homework together in her lean-to kitchen. It was getting dark, rain tapping on the tin roof. When Tracy went out to the Spar for milk and cigarettes before the weather worsened, Mrs Tabb came through and started chopping sea spinach and potatoes by the stove, her back to me. At first I thought she was talking to herself.

'Irene comes up the steps on Saturday with Tracy,' she began, 'the rain's running off the hill and down the steps like a river, so Tracy keeps slipping on the moss, hanging off Irene's arm, and Irene has that blue tartan suitcase, too heavy, I'm going out to help them in. Irene is talking too fast like she does, she can't sit still while I make the tea, dancing round the room, lighting cigarettes, touching everything, and Tracy keeps jumping up and down on the sofa, singing, shouting, and Irene says can I watch Tracy this evening because Tom's coming back. It's been such a long time, he's been over to Venezuela, but Irene's had a letter, and the ship's in the bay at five, and he's coming ashore at Trebeere in the launch. Irene has the case open on the floor and she puts on this short skirt and long boots, doesn't bother about stockings even though it's bitter and skeeting out, and then she sits at the table and draws black lines round her eyes and rushes into the rain for the bus. Tracy's restless after she goes, I'm up with her half the night telling fairy tales. Edie Cooper is on the steps in the morning, no rain now, bright and clear, the steps are dry, so Edie comes up quite fast but she won't come in. There's been an accident on the harbour at Trebeere. She always likes to pass the news first so I'm not really worried, but I'm thinking of Tom's ship. No, Edie says, not a boat, it's a young woman that's gone in the sea, and I'm not to worry, but Dan Ferris at the Schooner says the lads see Irene on the harbour wall after closing time. And Edie says her boy Martin will drive me over to Trebeere, just in case.'

The rain was loud on the roof. She was facing the room now, drying her hands. In the dusky light there was an echo – a trace – of Tracy in her face with its high rounded cheekbones and strong chin, green eyes staring unblinking at the door.

'Where is Tom?' I asked, unconsciously using the present tense.

'The ship isn't in at Trebeere, or in the bay at all. It's over to Plymouth, someone says, but I don't know if that's right either. I think he's staying in Venezuela.'

I looked over at the sofa. I had a powerful impression that I had actually just seen Tracy, aged five, wearing a red shift dress and purple woolly tights, jumping up and down on it.

My mother's financial circumstances, and mine, deteriorated sharply after my father's death. There were no savings; nobody expects to die at fifty-four. We were lucky to have the little house in Pellow Street, as my mother kept reminding me, but that was all we had, and there was still a mortgage on it. We learned the secret terror, shared by unmoneyed people everywhere, of the postman; the relief when he walks on by, his bag of bills and evictions going somewhere else, for today. My mother spent several weeks entirely indoors, numbing herself with vodka and Valium, talking on the telephone, and then reversed all that by going out early in the morning and walking for hours. I've no idea where. We said very little to each other, but slowly wove a net of tacit routines, like very old people, with times for going to the shop, cups of tea, or radio programmes. The radio was less dangerous than television, because if anything about cancer or hospitals came on, no images assaulted our eyes before we could jump up to turn it off.

After three months, she went to the jobcentre and accepted the first job she was offered, in a private old people's home called Willow Court on the Trebeere seafront. She came home drained and silent after her shifts, but after a glass of wine she told stories about the residents, and about her colleagues, some of whom could barely read.

'The senior care manager thinks "respite care" is spelled "rest bite". Rest bite! And she's my boss. And there's no union, what would your father have said to that?'

Sometimes I went to meet her at Willow Court. There were no willows of course, just some sad agaves in the front garden, their rubbery leaves shredded by salt winds. I noticed only what every young person notices if they enter an old people's home: television on in the daytime, upright armchairs in a circle, deflated people with the air of shoppers sheltering under an awning during a cloudburst – the same rueful patience: wait it out, it will soon pass. Willow Court's windows offered fine sea views, but the offer was declined; everybody sat with their back to the waves. Did they ever try to escape, I asked, thinking of my father's rebel comrade in the terminal ward. 'Only the ones who've lost their memories. They know something's not right, but not what. They're always looking for something or someone, so they walk away.'

Visits from my parents' friends grew less frequent and then ceased altogether. They were replaced at first by telephone calls and, finally, postcards, as the gap between our standard of living and theirs became wider, until we were cut adrift, watching the old world receding like cliffs behind a ferry. 'It's as if I'm a ghost in my own life,' my mother said. After school I would walk into the house to find her fighting with the Hoover or kicking at piles of clothes. The house itself developed malicious little tics, host to a more than usually dull-witted poltergeist: a door wrenched itself free of its hinges, light bulbs exploded in threes, pictures pulled their nails out of the wall and slid down with a crash, vinyl tiles recoiled from the kitchen floor. 'Pay no attention,' she said, 'don't give it the satisfaction.'

One evening she told me to help load her sculptures into the car. They were light, but awkward, and would only fit on the back seat when we bent the wires out of shape, tearing the cloth flesh; we had to tie an angel and a bull on the roof rack. She said we were going to the rubbish dump, but after driving about for a while she realised she didn't know where the dump was. Instead she pulled up on a lonely stretch of shore beyond the railway tracks. The tide was out and we carried the sculptures across the flat wet sand until we met sheets of water sliding in, and we arranged them there in a rough circle: the goat, the angel, the running women, the bull, the seal, and a giant wren. A few days later, she sold the car.

It was after my father died that the dreams came, though I only had one about the Fall, in which blue methane was seeping out from the hole left by the Mint Woman, assuming her shape. The other dreams were all of London. I was with Tracy, looking for seals in the decomposing streets around the Harrow Road and Portobello; she kept urging me on, down basement steps, along windy avenues, until we came to a dark square, and we looked up and saw Victor in one of the peeling sooty mansions, leaning out of a high window.

Like my mother, I started going for long walks, alone. It's surprising we never met each other. One cold still day in October I went a long way out on the Fall, past Geneva, beyond the Shadow Pools. I was some four miles from the nearest house at this point, and was about to turn for home. On the path about fifty yards ahead was a woman, taller than me, but young. She paused there for a few moments, brown hair tied loosely on her head, facing to the right, into a copse of larches. Then she walked into the trees. I assumed she was following her boyfriend who was already hidden in there – very occasionally, we would come across couples out on the Fall, usually tourists; local people avoided the place. What struck me as odd was the way she was dressed on such a raw day: a thin longish dress in dull red, her calves and lower arms bare. I had a coat and scarf over jeans and jumper, trainers on my feet. When I reached the place where she had been, I looked into the larch copse expecting to see her and a man. There was nothing, just the empty grassy rides between the trees. I noted the incident as unusual and continued with other thoughts, passing no one on the long way back. It was not until I reached Torbett's Hill that I felt a rush of unease and began to run. That was the only time I have ever encountered anything that could conceivably have been a ghost. Since then I have never stopped looking.

While my mother's life, and mine, had become sadder and narrower, the reverse was the case for Penny Nankervis. Her appearance changed: the big bare forehead, the hairbands and sleeveless polo necks were gone. She now wore her fair hair longer, with a soft fringe, and her formerly wide trousers had been fashionably drainpiped. From a few yards' distance she looked more like a member of the upper sixth at school than Kerenza's mother. She also had a job; this was at Hocking, Simpson and Boase, an estate agent in Trebeere. One morning, in the post office, Penny invited me to dinner at the Bonaparte, acting as if she had just that moment been struck by a wonderful, spontaneous idea. It was for a Tuesday evening, the quietest night of the week, and Victor and Tracy would also be there, 'so you won't feel out of your depth'. Mr and Mrs Nankervis must still feel sorry for me because of my father, I thought, but Tracy and Victor's invitation was unexpected. Kerenza suggested that her mother had only just realised that they were acquainted with her daughter, and had felt obliged to offer some sort of formal acknowledgement.

'She notices things about a century after they happen, and then she keeps reminding you about it. Uncle Maurice and Aunt Pamela are coming down from Bristol, so it'll be really boring.'

Penny certainly had an impressive ability to exclude the irrelevant; she walked with me some way along the street when we left the post office, talking all the while, quite undistracted by the seagulls fighting over chips in the gutter, the smell of soap from the launderette, a racing ambulance, 'You Drive Me Crazy' blasting out from a workman's radio.

'Just be yourself,' my mother said as I left the house in high shiny shoes, and I clacked downhill towards the Bonaparte, my new tights already slipping down to form a web between my thighs, with this advice bumping stupidly about my mind like a bluebottle.

Victor and Tracy, just arrived, were standing nervously beside Napoleon in Reception, laughing and picking at each other's clothing. Tracy was in a curious dress: green velvet, sleeveless, waistless, with a ragged fringe around the hem; I think it must have been her nan's. The dress matched her eyes, but not her feet, which were in brown desert boots; she never wore heels ('What if you suddenly have to run?'). Victor's shirt was ironed, but tight, its ice blue inflaming the russet in his cheeks, while Kerenza, who danced out of the bar to hurry us in, wore her old black jeans with a scarred leather jacket. Kerenza's clothes would never dare to argue with her physical person, they obeyed the shape and tone of her, and when I looked at her I always thought of a phrase encountered only in books: 'self-possessed'. To possess yourself, to be certain of this ownership, familiar with the sharp outline and solid form of what you had, confident that your property would not dissolve or subside in any weather – that seemed to me a worthy ambition, and without elusive and unlikely goals I was never happy.

Raymond Nankervis had made only modest headway with the renovation of the hotel. The air of offhand, mismatched grandeur (velvet curtains, gold Regency mirrors, Formica tables), which I found so relaxing, had not changed since I was eleven. A few rooms on the second floor were now prepared for guests, but the third floor was untouched: the 1930s radio still sat in the bath broadcasting historic silence, bedrooms were disturbed only by the salt wind rattling eighteenth-century window frames. Nor was there any sign of the formal restaurant Kerenza used to enthuse about. Only the large bar with its aromatic wood fire was attracting customers with any frequency, and most of these regulars were elderly couples who spoke to Kerenza's father with the fluttery deference typically reserved for aristocrats or royalty.

We were to sit at a table opposite the fireplace, properly laid with daunting cutlery. Among the many prints of shipwrecks around the room were two portraits of Napoleon, facing each other on opposite walls. One was a reproduction of the painting by Antoine-Jean Gros of young General Bonaparte charging across the bridge at Arcola: dauntless, thin-faced and stormy-eyed. The other, by an artist I don't remember, was a charcoal drawing of the defeated emperor, cheeks full and sagging, his furious gaze turned inward.

Despite the lack of commercial progress, Mr Nankervis was in a sanguine mood that night, his attenuated face, with its drooping lines, almost animated. He spoke to Victor, Tracy and me as adults, filling our glasses with wine as he topped up his own, discreetly avoiding irksome queries about school. He told us he was still working on his history of the county's Great Families (the capital letters were implied by his emphasis) and the manor houses they lived in. Outlandish names floated around the table over the onion soup like tropical butterflies: Carlyon, Vyvyan, St Aubyn, Trerice, Lanhydrock, Restormel, Cotehele – and, less poetically, Sorleigh; the Sorleighs who had owned large chunks of St Anthony and Trebeere for the past three hundred years or so.

We even had waiters, a boy and girl, who were to attend to us and, if any drinkers called in, to the bar. Only Penny could have hired a sixth-former and a former sixth-former to wait on a table that included pupils from the same school, without seeing any potential for embarrassment. She may have wanted to impress her relatives, but more probably she was simply practising, and our dinner was a trial run for a future restaurant. One of these casual staff was Carole Carr, who had left school a few summers ago. Carole always addressed you as if you were nine, and slow for your age. The other was a boy named Thomas who was still at school; I had admired him for at least half a term. Thomas brought chicken in a basket to our table, his dark-lashed gaze pausing on Tracy, and then briefly on Kerenza, sliding fast over my head. Carole came round with a plate of garlic bread. When she reached me, she withdrew the plate just before my fingers closed on a crust.

Kerenza's uncle Maurice was her mother's brother. He sat through Raymond's Great Families with fulsome patience, fingering his tie and napkin with small white hands. When Raymond finished, Maurice gave the tie a stern flip and embarked on a series of enthusiastic descriptions of Cornish beaches, monuments, scenery, attractions and excursions, as if we were the newcomers, in need of holiday advice. The Cornish accent was not what he had expected, he said; it was weaker than those of Devon and Somerset. Raymond agreed: 'It is watery, yes, diluted, as if it had been left to soak too long in the sea.'

'Of course, none of us are Cornish at all, are we,' Pamela broke in. 'Maurice and I are from Stroud, originally, and Penny too, and even you, Raymond, you only moved here after Kerenza was born, if I remember. Although you've got that wonderful Cornish name, of course.'

'Nankervis: valley of the deer, or stag. I'm a returned exile, Pamela, that's the truth of it. My branch of the Nankervis clan migrated to Bristol and Birmingham in the mid-nineteenth century, part of the Cornish diaspora. A most industrious lot, my ancestors, Methodist and methodical. I'm just reversing the process, as it were, in retreat from the relentless ugliness and suburban blight of the twentieth century.'

I glanced at Kerenza behind her fall of hair, bent over her plate. She was, it seemed, an 'incomer'; almost as much of an outsider as I was.

'Tracy here,' Raymond continued, 'also has an interesting surname, don't you? Pender, if I remember rightly, is from the Cornish *pen dyr*, and means "end of the land", or is it "head of the land"? Very apt, anyway, considering where we are.'

Tracy started. She had been silent until then, absent as a stone saint in her green dress.

'Pender was my father's name,' she said, speaking like an interviewee. 'My mother's name was Tabb, and it's my nan's, too.'

It was unfortunate she said that, just then, because it brought Maurice back into the conversation.

'Tabb? That rings a bell. Yes, I've got it, it's what I was reading on the way down. Eliza Tabb, the ghost who haunts that landslip near here. Maybe she's a relation of yours, Tracy, ha ha, you never know. You really should take a look at the book, all of you, it tells you about the landslip, St Anthony's Fall they call it, and all the myths and folklore and so forth.'

He poured himself another wine and launched into an exposition of the geological underpinnings of the Fall, getting himself somewhat lost along the way. I was aware of feeling uncomfortable while he was talking, a steady hardening of the heartbeat. Carole and Thomas had put dishes of baked Alaska in front of us; it was delicious, but the meringue was getting prickly, hard to swallow. I felt, at first, a simple irritation with this uncle who was blundering around our secret territory, exposing it to prosaic daylight – the invaded sensation I experienced when someone talked casually or critically, or even too perceptively, about one of my favourite books. But it was not only that. Nobody else was talking, and everyone except Maurice and Pamela was concentrating on the food with unnatural earnestness. The impression that I was not the only person who was tense amplified my own anxiety, as if a thread of disquiet linked everyone at the table except Maurice and Pamela, and Maurice, the more he talked, was pulling it tighter.

I made myself interrupt with a rather flat version of the Owlman story, in the hope of diverting the conversation to the Falmouth area where the Owlman had appeared. The Owlman had lost his power to frighten me. Not because I was older (which is no guarantee), but because I associated it with my father; it was his story, I just passed it along. 'Nobody is more intriguing,' he used to say 'than the atheist who has seen a ghost.' Victor, Kerenza and Tracy piled in with hectic enthusiasm, adding absurd embellishments to the Owlman's appearance, and Penny, who always appreciated a change of subject, suggested that the Owlman could be a woman, 'a jilted bride, come back to haunt the church tower'.

Raymond lit a cigar; manly common sense drifted across the table in its bookish cedar perfume. Perhaps I had imagined the tension. He turned to Maurice.

'It's because the landslip has been inaccessible for so long, Maurice. The Fall has become a kind of repository for local myths and legend, a hinterland of half-remembered history. In the 1920s, for instance, there was a rumour that a couple of panthers had escaped from a travelling circus and bred out there. And there's a Wandering Boy, too, an older story about a lost child who roams through the trees with a lamp, singing, like a will-o'-the-wisp, or jack-o'-lantern.'

'Or Jack the Ripper,' Kerenza shouted rudely. She had been immersed in blowing crumbs of meringue across the tablecloth.

'People want myths and riddles,' Raymond continued, paying no attention, 'it's an instinct, they go rooting after them like truffling pigs. And all these stories are similar.'

He said the Owlman reminded him of Goethe's poem about the Erlking, in which a man rides through a darkening forest holding his small son on the saddle in front of him. The child sees the Erlking and his ghostly daughters come out of the trees, hears them promising dances and colourful flowers beside the sea, but the father says it is only the wind in the leaves.

'It's just the primitive fear of the woods,' Raymond concluded abruptly, having noticed Penny tapping her fingernails on her glass.

'Why would anyone be afraid of the woods?' said Tracy.

'What happened next?' I asked.

'The boy died. Dead on arrival. He was right, the father was wrong.'

'But what about Eliza Tabb?' said Pamela. 'She was real, wasn't she? What happened to her?'

'Probably nothing very dramatic,' Raymond said, 'it was just after the landslip happened in 1821. Eliza was most likely somewhere else altogether, or maybe she fell into a crack in the earth, who knows. The surprising thing is that there were not more deaths. There's a theory that some gypsies were camped on the edge of the Fall on the far side, out to the west, but no record of whether any of them were killed or not, or how many were there, because, well, they were itinerants.'

'Gypsies!' said Maurice. 'That's it. I'll bet Eliza was kidnapped by gypsies, or ran away with them. There you go, I've solved your local mystery.'

'Well you haven't really, no,' Kerenza replied, 'that's just another stupid myth, since we're all talking about myths. Easy to blame people who travel around, after they've moved on.' She turned from Maurice and looked straight at her father. 'Especially easy when nobody was bothered if they were crushed by the Fall or not.'

'So the Fall is still too dangerous, inaccessible,' Pamela went on, 'none of you have ever gone there? It seems a bit of a shame. I wouldn't mind having a look, at least.' Her blouse had a big bow at the neck, like Mrs Thatcher's, which kept flopping off her bosom and towards her plate when she leaned forward to speak.

Penny straightened up, placed her shapely hands flat on the table, and seemed to make a decision.

'Pamela. The thing is, there was a tragedy out there more recently, just a few years ago. A girl was found dead, murdered. They never found out who did it. You may have heard about it on the news. So I think people around here tend to avoid the place, avoid the entire topic.'

'Oh heavens,' said Pamela, and I thought she and Maurice would both take the hint and shut up. Not Maurice; he spooned more baked Alaska onto his plate, stared unseeing at the defeated Napoleon, and began again.

'Yes, that's right, what was the name? Caroline something? I forget. And they never caught the killer? Pretty slack of the police, as usual. The girl was found on some beach out there if I remember. How on earth did she get there? I mean, think about it, how did the murderer physically get the dead body onto the landslip, drag it through all that wasteland, onto the beach, if the whole area is a dangerous minefield? Or maybe the bloke strangled her in the wood, perhaps he was someone she knew, took her out for a picnic lunch. Funny place for a picnic, though, from what you say.'

Pamela dabbed at her blouse with her napkin, then turned to Mr Nankervis. 'Well, Ray, I must say I admire the way you find the time to study the local history as well as running this place. I don't know how you do it.'

8

Our English teacher was Miss Rescorla. Her first name might have been Nancy, but the idea of her even having a first name felt indecent. She was tall, old in an ageless way, armoured in the stiff suits of the early 1960s. On winter afternoons the setting sun slanted through the classroom window and lit the chalk escarpments of her face with a rosy flush, like a mountain above the treeline. Nobody liked her exactly, a fact of which she appeared unaware, and to which she would in any case have been utterly indifferent: she was incorruptible, treating every pupil with a cool, unswerving fairness. If this was a conscious strategy it was a clever one, because it meant her students competed to stand out from the others, always in vain. On a simpler level I suppose the absence of favouritism made us feel safe.

Miss Rescorla had two passions, two topics guaranteed to ruffle her equilibrium: irony and hens. She spent much class time wrestling with the various forms of irony, her fear that we would misunderstand, and now that we were starting the lower sixth and studying Thomas Hardy, the explosions were frequent. Someone only had to pretend to confuse irony with sarcasm, or coincidence, to ensure that fifteen minutes of the lesson disappeared. Conversely, if you wanted to lift her mood, you asked after her hens. She kept a flock of them at her home in the glebe cottage at the bottom of Torbett's Hill. The hens were free to wander over her orchard and out into the lane and we often waded through them on our way up to the Fall. But even this topic had pitfalls. It was from Miss Rescorla that we learned about the industrialisation of animal farming that had been creeping across the country throughout the 1970s, Miss Rescorla who opened our eyes to the way hens and pigs were vanishing from the lanes and fields into flesh factories. She became enraged if anyone referred to hens as 'chickens'. 'Chicken is the meat. The living birds are hens, the males are cocks, and the young birds are chicks, or, sometimes, chickens You wouldn't call cows beefs, would you, or pigs, porks?'

She was right, in retrospect: the substitution of the word 'chicken' for 'hen' in the English language roughly parallels the removal of hens from the open countryside.

One day these two themes collided for Miss Rescorla when she went to Thomas Hardy's birthplace at Higher Bockhampton, in Dorset, to inspect it for a possible class visit. There she found a concrete embodiment of irony 'as if in mockery of the promise and fitness of things': an agricultural horror in the birthplace of a poet with an eye both for irony and the hopeless fate of living creatures in the face of money and machines.

'I walked away from Hardy's cottage to explore the woods,' she told us, 'which were beautiful, but I was suddenly aware of a ferocious stench. I tried to escape the trees, looking for the lane, and there, right in front of me, were rows and rows of sheds without windows, behind a high wire fence. I'm surprised there weren't watchtowers. A battery-hen farm. It's only a short walk from Hardy's cottage. They've hidden it, but they can't hide the smell. Hens never smell bad – if they do, there's something wrong.'

We should ignore Bockhampton, Miss Rescorla suggested, and look instead at Boscastle, in our own county, the village where Hardy had met his first wife: 'I'm rather surprised none of you have bothered to go before now.' The opportunity to do this arose sooner than I could have foreseen. Not long after the dinner at the Bonaparte, Penny Nankervis, our existence still fresh in her mind, offered to take us on what she called a business trip up the north coast. She was to inspect and value some houses (Penny called houses 'properties' – she must have been one of the first people to do this) for Hocking, Simpson and Boase, assessing them as suitable candidates for conversion to holiday lets. Perhaps she asked us, rather than Kerenza's friends from her own school, because she barely knew our families, so there was less chance of anything being reported back. Or it might simply have been another sudden flash of goodwill.

Penny had also rung my mother and offered me a 'little job' as a chambermaid at the Bonaparte, which I accepted, telling people it was for clothes money rather than admit the cash was needed at home. Every Saturday I hauled baskets of linen around the corridors of the hotel, stripping and making beds with a woman called Mavis, about whom I remember little except that she told me one day that she had not been to Truro for thirty-five years. 'It was Christmas, just after the war; I bought a red dress and matching shoes.' Truro is just over half an hour on the train from Trebeere. I never saw Kerenza when I was working. She had a good deal of natural tact, and I imagine she made sure she was out on Saturday mornings. I hoped the job would be a chance to indulge my curiosity about the lives of strangers, to uncover evidence of unnatural habits, but the guests were mostly disappointing, leaving only dirty plates, wet heaps of towels. I would sometimes find a little pile of change on the dresser, but no note addressed to me, no hidden map of adulthood.

The trip to Boscastle had been planned for early December, but for various reasons of Penny's we didn't set off until the morning of December 31st, New Year's Eve. Two whole nights away from St Anthony, in the middle of winter: we were excited after all the delay, and the evening before the journey I went with Tracy to Victor's house, where we would wait for Kerenza, then go out. Kerenza was late. Bridget Jordan was in her customary position by the gas fire. Her black hair now had a white badger stripe on one side, but otherwise she had changed little, her big russet face a waspish apple. The Jordans were watching a programme called *Angels*, about nurses. Bridget turned to me.

'Do you fancy nursing, Sally?'

'No.'

'So what are your plans then? After school?'

I mentioned university. She approved; she could certainly see me as a career girl, she said, glancing slyly at her husband, who frowned, leaned forward and launched dutifully into the attack, looking at his wife, not me.

'University's pointless for her,' said Keith Jordan, 'because, like all women, she'll just drop everything when she starts a family.'

I wasn't offended; it was interesting to hear myself described as a woman, not a girl; to experience the dissociated sensation of seeing myself through the eyes of others, like watching a hairdresser's face in the mirror while you tell lies about your social life. Or the time someone described my dead father as 'jovial' – not that he was gloomy, but the bland inaptness of the adjective revealed how casually people miscast the minor characters in their lives.

Victor however lost his temper. Sally is not just any old woman, he said, you can't predict what she will do.

'By the law of averages,' said his father, who was fond of citing that particular law, 'she will get pregnant, she will want to, and all that university will be wasted. It's her destiny. Look at Andrea, always about to nip up to London to be an actress. Didn't get very far, did she. It's the same for us men in the end, you can't fight nature, that's what we're all here for.' (Andrea at that moment was in the kitchen, I hoped she hadn't overheard.)

'You won't find out what real love is until you're a parent, Sally, that's true,' Bridget agreed. 'Wait till you have a baby, there's nothing like it. I used to spend hours sniffing Paul's head like it was a fancy perfume.'

'What's the point of being born,' Victor shouted, 'if the only reason you're born is to get pregnant, and the only point of them being born is to have children and die and so on forever?' Victor ran out of breath. His ability to reason aloud never survived long under the onslaught of his emotions.

'Men don't get pregnant at all, Victor, in case you hadn't noticed,' said his mother, 'and maybe there isn't a point, who says there has to be one?'

'Yes there is,' her husband insisted. 'The point of life is to continue the line, the point of life is life.'

'So there's no difference between us and insects.' Victor stood up and hurled his empty can across the room, where it bounced off the top of the television, just missing the faces of the Angels. Bridget threw up her hands in mock despair.

'Nothing wrong with insects,' Mr Jordan said placidly, and repeated his aphorism with evident satisfaction: The Point of Life is Life.

The doorbell rang; relieved, I jumped up to let Kerenza in. In the hallway I noticed some big studio photographs had appeared on the wall: Denise and her entire family, Andrea with her son as a baby, Paul with his certificate. Victor was not featured. The sitting room was unnaturally quiet; Kerenza knew she had missed something. On the way down Carne Hill, Tracy turned to Victor.

'When Snapdragon was run over, everybody was very nice to me and Nan. They said he was a lovely cat, and it would take us a while to get over him. But that wasn't enough. They felt sorry for us, not him. I wanted Snapdragon to matter, his character. I thought he should matter *in himself.*'

December 31st was gloomy and raw from the beginning, the road darkening under a charcoal and yellow sky as we drove north, but Penny was in an airy mood. She was a better driver than either of my parents had been: fast and efficient, her shiny nails clicking lightly over the controls. The car was soft, quiet, scented with new plastic. I had the passenger seat in front so it was me she chatted to about Boscastle, and because, unlike Victor's mother, she expected attentive responses, I was unable to lapse into the comfortable absence I normally enjoyed on journeys.

'You'll love it, Sally, it's a bit remote of course, but picturesque. Plenty of scenery, if you're into that. I think it's got a lot of potential. The cottage is very quaint, and I'll be looking over a couple more properties tomorrow. Mark thinks it's a fantastic opportunity, so I won't be around much, you'll have to entertain yourselves. Kerenza's been before, so she'll show you around.'

'Potential' was a teacher's word that peppered my school reports; I wondered how it would apply to places.

'Mark?' Kerenza leaned over the seat from the back of the car.

'Mark Hocking, of course.'

'You seem to know a lot of Marks.'

'Well I wouldn't be talking about Mark Boase, would I? I don't suppose he's spotted an opportunity since the last war.'

Old Mark Boase was the senior partner at Hocking, Simpson and Boase. He was sometimes in the Bonaparte's bar, round and courtly, holding the door open for you.

'Is he going to be there,' Kerenza asked, 'Mark Hocking?'

'Yes, briefly, tomorrow. To check one of the properties over.'

'Oh. I hope everyone likes big rocks and steep hills, then,' said Kerenza.

We stopped once, at Port Isaac, where Penny left us in the car while she called on another estate agent, and bought us tea in plastic cups. 'Not on the floor!' she said to me when I'd finished. 'This is a new car! Just throw it out of the window.' Then we were speeding along a straight road over high, empty country. Huddles of short, stoic trees appeared now and then, black branches stretched horizontal to the earth. There was no traffic, the rest of the world having sensibly shut its doors on the dim day, the death of the year, and this heightened the mood in the car; we were a ship of reckless sailors heading straight into a gale. Tracy and Victor were talking about a book of ghost stories by EF Benson, and whenever we passed a particularly bleak farmhouse they described the spectral characters who certainly lived there. The coast reappeared abruptly, a long way below us, and the road fell over the brow of the plateau into a tunnel of oaks. It was dusk and had started to snow – always a major event in temperate Cornwall – by the time we stopped in the village. Penny unlocked the cottage and told us, as if she had just remembered, that she would be staying at the Valency Hotel down on the harbour. We had it to ourselves.

I opened my bedroom window and the rush of an unseen river came in from somewhere down in the valley. Boscastle rang with the sound of moving water. It hurried off the hills (higher, grander and steeper than those at St Anthony), cut through woods, threw itself off cliffs and slid in sheets over slate rock in a race for the sea, which received it in a narrow, fjordlike harbour. The house itself was cool, white, sparsely furnished; its similarity to Geneva was noticeable, though nobody mentioned it.

That evening was the last the four of us spent together entirely happy. Snowflakes hung in the dark air as we walked down to the harbour, swarming round the streetlamps like white bees. The Silver Seal Inn was almost full and we got the last table. I had never seen Victor so talkative, lit up by something I did not recognise, and this was before he finished his first drink. He was, half seriously, complaining about films we had seen at Trebeere's film club, the only cinema showing what they called 'art films', although they reached us long after the rest of the country had seen them.

'Why are there so many films about young people in the past, even if they're new films? As if they're trying to make you nostalgic, and you do feel nostalgic, but about a time when you weren't even born. What's wrong with the present? When are they going to make films about us, now? And why always America, not Poland or Wales or Ecuador?'

'Or Trebeere. It's because in America people our age are important,' said Kerenza. 'At the centre of things. They have special dances, and they all have cars, even when they're still at school, can you imagine? If they made films about us, they'd have to do it at bus stops. I don't feel important, do you?'

No, we all said.

Going to the cinema with Victor was always a tense experience. He came out in a terrible mood – silent, furious. Later though, he might refer to the film in glowing terms. I didn't understand it until Tracy explained that he couldn't bear the perfunctory return to the street, its insolent sameness: 'He says it's like playing a single at 33.' It was formlessness that upset Victor, he always wanted a plan, a pattern, a story. As an only child without cousins, I was fascinated by the shifting alliances in Victor's family, the parties of neighbours processing like a carnival through their front room, the resentments and affections that glowed like magma under the chat, Mrs Jordan's ability to cast her children in the wrong roles in the wrong play – Andrea, restless and confused, was 'a homebody', according to Bridget, while Andrea's sharp-tempered sister Denise, who lost interest in her handsome children as soon as babyhood had past, was 'a born mother'. Victor's father made a point of being kind to me (apart from the occasional jibes about incomers), making positive comments on my appearance, but I understood that he was trying to press my case to Victor, in preference to Tracy. Meanwhile Victor's brother Paul had left home and was training to be a dentist in Truro, and while this was evidently satisfactory, it was not enough to compensate for Andrea's failure to marry her boyfriend, and Paul's absence drew attention to Victor's indecision about his own future. Victor had a propensity to attract the ire of both parents, and both of them disapproved of Tracy Pender, for reasons I did not fully understand. Paul himself had tired of the role of perfect son and was collecting a series of the most unsuitable girlfriends he could find in Truro; this in turn had improved his relationship with Victor, who sometimes went to visit him there.

'Maybe Victor will make films about us,' said Tracy, 'and people in the future will complain about having to watch people from now, and being forced to feel nostalgic about them.'

Kerenza widened her eyes theatrically. 'None of that matters, because at midnight, three hours from now, everything will suddenly change.'

A barmaid in a dress made of green leaves put a plate of free sandwiches on our table, 'Video Killed the Radio Star' came on the jukebox, a complete stranger bought us brandies; it was as if we were being welcomed into a benevolent club.

Penny joined us once, briefly, with Mark Hocking. Mark had a rolling walk, as if the bulk of his shoulders troubled him, though when he removed his jacket the shoulders were quite narrow in their striped shirt. I had watched him crossing the room behind Penny, arranging his capable features into something appropriate for teenagers. A handsome face, tanned and wide-mouthed like a man in an advert, but the eyes were so small I wondered how he could see out of them. He asked us loud questions about school, until Penny reminded him we were underage and could he for God's sake keep his voice down.

'Roger. Say no more. Your secrets are safe with me. We've all done it. I remember the Wimpy, Coke and ice cream in the same glass and a crafty dash of something else, puff of pot round the back. I could tell you a few tales about nights out in Trebeere that would literally make your hair stand on end, though the town isn't what it used to be, of course. You should have seen it a few years ago, it was hilarious, much more going on. We're only here for Trebeere! Happy days. Loved my schooldays. Joking aside, make the most of it, you'll never have so much fun again.'

Mark put a £20 note for us on the table when he left with Penny, so it was less easy to laugh at him.

Outside the Silver Seal the new year was spread out before us under the night sky like an empty page. With all detail blurred in whiteness, the street, woods and looming hills had expanded to fill the world, so that where we were was the only possible place to be, impossible to imagine anything existing beyond it. The last few revellers were up to their knees in snow: a man in a rabbit costume, a witch in red satin, the barmaid wearing antlers, two figures in long black cloaks and beaked masks like Egyptian birds of prey. A boy spun in circles with a plastic blow-up sex doll, swinging it by its pink handless arms. Their voices followed us all the way up the steep lane out of the valley, as they danced and laughed and fell down.

During the night the temperature plunged. I woke late into padded silence and thought myself alone in the house until I found Kerenza in bed, reading. She said Victor and Tracy had gone up on the cliffs – surprising, they were normally the last up. We made tea and then walked down the lane together, the only sound the tight creak of snow around our shoes. Kerenza was indifferent to weather of any kind and conversation about it bored her, so I made no comment on the crystal trees under a fairy-tale blue sky, or the hundreds of streams and waterfalls turned to glass, moss and creeping jenny petrified inside them.

She peered up at the rockface beside us, which was draped in icicles, some six feet long.

'Slate and granite. Did you know Cornwall is the most radioactive place in Britain? Radon gas everywhere. Decaying uranium. You can't see it or smell it, but it seeps up out of the ground and hangs about in people's basements.'

'Is it dangerous?'

'Yes.'

It would only have taken a second for both of us to slide unnoticed off the shiny sloping quay into the sea, so we kept close to the cliffside, weaving our way through the giant icicles as Kerenza tried to get me to understand the concept of radioactive half-life. I kept thinking of Mark Hocking's too-white, radioactive teeth.

They were a long way up on the headland. I wouldn't have recognised Victor from such a distance, but Tracy's hair caught the sun. Bent forward, using my hands like an animal, I crawled up the narrow path cut into the side of the hill, rock cliff to the left, smooth precipice straight down to white-capped waves on the right. Meanwhile Kerenza walked steady and upright in front of me, far more like Lord John Roxton than Victor ever was. Tracy and Victor watched us approach but made no effort to come and meet us. They looked solemn; I wondered if anything was the matter.

'We've got something to tell you,' Victor began.

'A decision,' said Tracy.

'We're getting married.'

A black monklike bird fell headfirst off a crag on the other side of the harbour. I thought: I'll always remember this. 'Very funny. Have you both gone mad?'

'No. It's sensible. We can't imagine marrying anyone else, so what's the point waiting? Why wait until something goes wrong?' Tracy's voice was flat in the still air, snow blotting the echo.

'Why wait? You're sixteen, that's why,' said Kerenza.

'I'm seventeen,' said Victor. 'Tracy will be seventeen in May. And people can get married at sixteen. Anyway,' he added vaguely, 'this is just a declaration, like reading the banns, or something.'

'You still have to get parents' permission,' I said.

'And your parents won't give it,' said Kerenza.

'So we'll go to Scotland to do it. We'll get the night train to Glasgow. You can come, of course.'

The night train, the dining car, sleeping compartments, wolves, insomniac lamplit stations at three am, *The Lady Vanishes*.

'Yes,' I said.

Kerenza was sculpting a ball of snow in her gloves. She threw it out over the precipice. 'You need money for all that. But congratulations, anyway.' She examined the huge horizon for a while, then turned and walked away down the path, adroit as a goat, her shape dipping neatly around slabs of slate.

'I don't see why you have to get married,' I said. 'Nobody gets married anymore. It sounds frightening, final.'

The three of us were lying on our backs in the snow, facing the blue, smoking.

'Yes, that's the point. It would be like jumping off a cliff,' Victor said.

'That's the part he likes,' said Tracy.

'Also,' Victor went on, 'if you're married, people take you seriously. We wouldn't just be Tracy and Victor, we'd be Mr and Mrs Jordan. They would have to listen.'

I laughed. 'You won't start talking about freezers and furniture?'

'We won't need furniture,' Tracy declared. 'Chairs turn up, sometimes you use them, sometimes you don't. But you need to get a passport, Victor. I've got one.'

'For Scotland?'

'Venezuela,' said Tracy, 'in case we need to go further.'

'Usually there's too much furniture. Think of the front room at my house,' said Victor.

I felt they were being rather literal. I told them I was going back down to look for Kerenza, but I wasn't, I wanted to walk and think.

'Do you think Kerenza seemed annoyed?' I said.

'About what?'

'You getting married.'

'She shouldn't be,' said Victor. 'It was her idea.'

People had come out into the snow – mostly couples, young, old, middle-aged. With their bulky clothes, their faltering movements in the simplified landscape, they were like children outside a nursery school. They slid hand in hand down the paths, embracing under the icicles by the river, a conference, or confluence, of lovers. Few people smile at teenagers usually, but they smiled at me that day, and not just for the new year; no traffic was getting in or out, we were cut off by drifts, temporarily dependent on each other. I thought I heard or felt a low whispering, a reverberation from the massed hills, the earth emboldened by human silence. Tracy and Victor's announcement broke a spell, time would no longer be tabled, wrapped in segments; a story was going to unfold, my friends were going first, we would become important. I would just stand to the side and watch until I saw my part, and then step forward at exactly the right time.

I went back up to the house to see if Kerenza was all right, but there was nobody there. I forced myself to go out again, despite the cold ('Never waste a blue day,' my father would say), but by afternoon both sky and snow turned ashy grey, and when I checked again she was in her room, on the bed, cheerful, a glass in her hand, reading a biology reference book.

'Hi. Do you want some of this whisky? Plankton prefer the sea to be cold, you know. It's to do with currents and nutrients.'

'They'll love it here, then,' I said.

The next morning Penny had to get help from men with ropes to haul the car up the 1:4 hill through weeping ice. It was all melting. Down in the harbour the icicles slid off the black rocks, a shower of glass knives menacing any lovers still lingering beneath. This time I sat in the back with Victor and Tracy, Kerenza in the front with her mother. The warmth of the car and Penny's voice, the words barely audible in the back, induced an irresistible drowsiness. Tracy and Victor fell asleep quickly, leaning against each other, and I fell into a doze, waking for a moment to see the auburn streak of a fox along a white fence. The fox made me think of hens, and when I thought of hens I thought of Miss Rescorla and the connections with Thomas Hardy we had ignored during our time in Boscastle. It occurred to me then that Miss Rescorla might not consider it an auspicious place to announce a wedding. When I woke again we were already passing the railway sidings at Trebeere; it was raining, time had quickened, and Penny was still talking.

9

I'm one of those people who smell books as soon as they open them. Cedar, moss, damp plaster, camphor, hay, plastic, tobacco, mildew, the chemical gloss of fresh ink on shiny paper – all are welcome. A book's unique smell persists in memory long after the pages are read, flavouring the content forever, defying subsequent editions. But James Prideaux's journal is the only book I've encountered whose scent changes as you read it. The carnation and clove perfume may have been what encouraged me to start reading it at sixteen; this is joined, around the time of Prideaux's marriage, by a damp salty note. It took me a while to identify it as seaweed, and in the later chapters this begins to dominate, finally becoming unpleasant, a whiff of rotting kelp.

I read the book slowly, as I've already mentioned, its effect soothing at first, then intriguing when I realised that our Geneva was named after his wife, and Miss Rescorla's cottage had once been the home of Samuel Trembath. Even when Prideaux starts to describe Maryann's intrusions into his life I felt only a mild amusement. It was heartening to have this evidence that nonfictional adults – even old ones from the past like James Prideaux – were pursued by embarrassing misadventures, and were so anxious about imagined consequences that they would go to ridiculous lengths to conceal them from other old people. It was an echo of the glee I had experienced when we trespassed as children, the way the cracked houses with their decapitated toilets and abandoned furniture undermined the serene edifice of adult authority, collaborating with us in irreverent laughter at the chaos that waits underneath.

This detachment crumbled when I came to the entry where Prideaux recounts the episode with the child Jack Mabbott. The fact that he was eleven when it happened, his status with the other boys, his failure to act in Mabbott's defence, the faceless huntsman Blind Bocka in the wood, the way the adults in his life misinterpreted everything – all made me uneasy, though I couldn't have said why at the time. And there are other things in the journal, uncanny details that I cannot explain even now.

It must have been shortly before the dinner at the Bonaparte when I read the section about Mabbott, and I would have been reading the parts that follow below when we returned from Boscastle – during those weeks in 1982 when the road ahead darkened for us.

* * *

1827: *'She could have been anyone'*

Bodmin, July 26
I thought I had arrived at the place in good time, but already there was a great multitude assembled under the racing clouds, trampling the meadow to filth. I identified the hawthorn tree on its small hill easily, but was obliged to push and shove past people

to reach it. When I found a space under the branches, I was informed by the man beside me that I had just missed the first execution of the morning.

'A cracksmith from Mawnan. Nineteen. They had to drag him up the steps' I followed his gaze and saw the gallows some hundred yards away, a raised platform with a single beam above, surprisingly makeshift and brittle. It reminded me of something: the wicker bird trap, the springle, hidden in high grass. There was no sign of the cracksmith, they must have taken him down.

I had lodged at an inn, the Indian Queen, after reaching the outskirts of Bodmin late the previous evening. I did not sleep, of course I did not; it would have been a kind of blasphemy, with Maryann living the thin agony of her last hours in a cell half a mile from my room. The vigil was not easy. I sat at the table on the hardest chair, I read parts of Job, and Corinthians; I prayed, paced the room, turned my chair around to avoid looking at the bed, pinched the flesh of my arms and dipped my finger in the candle flame whenever waves of sleep threatened to swamp me, which they did at ever shorter intervals as the minutes crept towards the dawn. I was disgusted by the power of this bodily need, my inability to share the suffering of another human soul, even through the paltry offering of my wakefulness; wakefulness endured in a comfortable room which I was at liberty to walk out from at any time. The inn was quiet except for a longcase clock in the hall downstairs. Its slow hollow tick penetrated the walls of my chamber, eating the night away in rhythmical measured bites. Time itself became a physical substance, as if the clock were contriving to stretch it, but each time the hour struck I jumped, for it seemed but a few minutes since the last time, and the deep musical chimes set my heart racing in my chest. The dawn came in cool and grey, but presently a wind got up and the sky broke apart in patches of blue and white: a bright breezy morning, the sort of day when men feel hopeful.

A stout woman was moving around the field handing out sheets of printed paper, one of which she thrust at me, then demanded money. It was a broadside: 'Execution by Public Hanging, on 21 July, 1827, of Alfred Warren, thief, 19 years, at Bodmin gaol'. The paper included an absurd woodcut of a figure hanging on a rope, and a souvenir verse, which purported to be a transcript of Warren's last words from the gallows:

As I bow my head in shame,
I beg you don't forget my name,
But look into my empty cell,
And shun the path that leads to Hell.
The hour draws near and 'tis too late,
I must accept my dreadful Fate,
But as I look Death in the eye,
I lift my face to God on high,
Forgive me Lord the wealth I stole,
Wash clean again my blackened soul,
May Jesus my last words receive,
And grant me yet the last reprieve.

My companion under the tree, the man who had spoken before, watched me reading.

'Lovely bit of poetry, isn't it? The printer makes all they up in advance. Looks foolish if there's a pardon, though, or the rope breaks, or the hanging gets put forward. The lad never said a word, died quick. Now we wait for the coxy backjowster[8].'

---

[8] Saucy fishwife (S. Martins)

I tried to fasten my thoughts to Maryann, to advance my spirit from my body to her side, but was constantly distracted by the horror of the crowd, which was thickening by the minute. I have always disliked multitudes, and this was the largest I have ever had the misfortune to find myself in. The noise was ceaseless, a deafening babble, punctuated by yelps and whoops, barks, shrieks of laughter, snatches of song; the sounds rising and falling across the wide space, stirring up the grey mass of close-packed people which swayed below me in the breeze like a field of mildewed barley. Just in front of us was a large party of young men and girls. They were acting as children will when they band together to defy their elders: arms linked, they bawled and roared and jigged about, the maids as loud as the men, and then one of their number would admonish the rest in a falsetto voice, 'This is a solemn occasion! Hush, you Godless smellymidges!', whereupon they all affected to compose themselves: stiffening their shoulders into a rigid posture, clamping their lips, blowing out their cheeks, eyes bulging, until one of them burst forth in raucous laughter, followed directly by the rest in a chain of hysterical bellowing. This mummery I saw repeated over and over.

Other spectators were more respectable: men in good summer coats, women in tidy sunbonnets and clean gloves, a farmer with a broad merry face who was the spit of Abel Copthorne. Why were they here? Dogs ran in little packs among the people, and there was a surprising number of children. A meagre boy of eight or nine years, his complexion the same putty colour as his hair, was peddling refreshments. He ducked around the legs of the crowd, pulling a small wooden cart, or hurdle, on which were displayed a number of dough cakes. This cart was decorated with coloured ribbons in homage to the carnival occasion; they were tied to the shafts and the base, and to the spokes of the wheels. Also attached to the cart was a tiny child, a girl of around three, presumably the boy's sister: she sat beside the cakes, secured to the frame by a string, and the same bright ragged ribbons and bows were fixed in her hair, to her dress, along the string, and around her ankles. The boy had something wrong with his speech, a lisp, he was calling out 'hevva cake' or perhaps 'have a cake'. He made his way towards our group under the tree, dragging his grotesque carriage, and pulled at my sleeve, 'Mister, Mister.' His face, puffy and disconsolate, reminded me of Jack Mabbott's.

The tone of the noise changed. All the heads before us were facing one way, towards the gaol. There were jeers, shouts of 'Hats off!' then a frantic hushing among the watchers. A looped rope had appeared on the beam while I had been distracted by the boy and cart, and a short procession of dark-clad figures began to pass across from some hidden door in the gaol's facade, bobbing along towards the wooden platform. The wall of people in front and below me restricted the view, creating the curious impression that the little figures were cut off at the waist, like puppets, Punch and Judy. I made out two men in front of this cortège, perhaps the Sheriff and an assistant. Then came Maryann in a charcoal dress, between two guards. She was taller than either of them. The chaplain, Reverend Cauley, grey hair flapping, walked to the side of her with his Prayer Book. Cauley would have been reading the burial service, but it was not audible. Maryann moved stiffly, her arms pinned in front, the two guards close beside her, protective, as if helping a frail lady across a busy thoroughfare. They disappeared from view when they reached the foot of the platform, but after a few moments reappeared mounting the steps, and then all stood in a row behind the rope, joined by a short stout man, who stood off to the side. The chaplain was still reading, verses blowing away in the wind, but a few words reached us, trespasses... the power and the glory. There was a moment when Maryann might have been facing me, looking over. I couldn't make out her features, she could have been anyone. I stood as tall as I could, and for an absurd instant wondered if I should raise my hand, but, thank heaven, thought better of it.

Then the short man walked forward; I had the impression he had no face, until I realised he was masked, and then they put a white hood like a nightcap over Maryann's head, so there were now two faceless figures on the stage. There was something odd about the shape of her dress, and I saw they had tied it close to her legs, to preserve her modesty in the windy morning. The stocky gentleman, the hangman, placed the rope over Maryann's head. He stepped back to the left and bent over, as if he were pulling something up off the floor. After that it happened very fast: a thud like a closing door, not particularly loud; she dropped downwards to the level of her knees, the rope jerked and tautened, she spun once, twice, I shut my eyes. I opened them to see the hangman run neatly down the steps and disappear underneath. Presently he reappeared on the platform, pulled his leather waistcoat straight, then followed the others down the steps again and away.

For a while I remained motionless under the tree, my back to the gallows, eyes on the grass at my feet. I could only think about the grey dress Maryann was wearing, that it would still be perfectly serviceable, and that someone somewhere must have made that garment, sewing it cheerfully with good strong stitches to withstand years of wear.

A kind of elation had taken hold of the crowd. Ale was drunk, pies consumed, there was an eruption of singing and shouting and running about. It was as if the people realised, with a most unfamiliar clarity, that they were still in possession of their lives. But within half an hour the mood soured and a peevish discontent made itself felt, a mutter of drunken insults and petty argument.

The spectacle was done, and perhaps the watchers had an intimation that what they owned had lost its lustre. I was now alone on the little hill. In the distance a knot of big lads descended on the boy and his cart. They snatched the cakes and kicked the wheels until the whole contraption fell over, with the infant girl, screaming, still tethered to it.

As I joined the hordes walking away from the pasture, someone handed me another broadside. This one had 'Janet Mary Ann Hookway' printed blackly across the top, with her age, a short history of her crime, the date and place of her death, but the rest of it was the same as Alfred Warren's. The same commonplace 'last words' were there too, and when I saw the word 'path' in the fourth line, Maryann's image sprang up before me: Maryann on the sunken wooded path behind the parsonage, her ugly hat moving along the ferny wall. They had forgotten to replace 'wealth' with 'life' in the ninth line.

* * *

Geneva House, September 22
The autumn equinox, the first day of Vendémiaire, when history began afresh. On mornings such as this, when grass and ferns glitter with dew and the blue air is scented with coconut from the gorse, I feel I may survive my exile. I try not to dwell upon the coming winter. My joints are stiff, muscles sapped by fever. Salty mists make the linen damp, silverfish come wagging out of my books at night like misspelled words, and I do not know how long I will be able to pull the water from the well. Some mornings it seems simpler to walk to the little brook to fill a kettle, and I wash my pots and my person there at the same time; I am becoming less susceptible to the cold.

My nearest neighbour is Matthew Hocking, whose farm lies to the east, in the direction of St Anthony. His wife Loveday (the one Maryann used to call Lowdie) died not long ago, but in every other respect he has recovered remarkably from the effects of the Great Fall, when half his pasture slipped towards the sea. His fields have extended themselves inland, he has sucked the damp from meadows and commons, spread them with night soil, bordered them with ditchings and wire. You would not notice this incursion unless you had the leisure to look, which I do. Arthur always said Hocking was close to the Sorleighs, though I can't imagine why Hocking shoots from time to time in the woods around Churchtown Farm, sending black flags of birds over the trees and out to sea, and I see him occasionally on Torbett's Green, scowling along the frontiers of his land like an angry bullock, sometimes with his scrawny son. They both ignore me completely.

I have been living alone out here seven weeks and today is the first time I have touched my pen since the horror at Bodmin. I have discovered that it is quite impossible to write, to reflect, while life is hunting you, harrying you, forcing you to do battle with each passing minute, to live in a perpetual present, like an animal. My fellowship with Ossian, who shares this mode of existence with me, has deepened. Geneva has allowed me to keep him. He is a very ordinary dog, much less intelligent than Voltaire was, but his constant padding presence and relentless optimism tether me to my better self.

I spent a second night at the Indian Queen, after Maryann's death. While I had been tormented by unseemly drowsiness the night before the hanging, I was now unable to sleep. At around two o'clock a gale blew up: the vast mad emptiness of Bodmin Moor came banging at the shutters, kicking along the black road into town. I used up some hours writing an account of the morning, but I have no memory of how I passed the rest of the night, or of the journey home in the mail coach the following day, except that it rained, heavily and constantly. Arriving back at St Anthony in the evening at about seven, my legs were so feeble that I was barely able to tramp the muddy hill to the parsonage. I went straight to my study and sat for a long while staring out at the wet lawn, the empty sunken path beyond it, before I became aware of the clock striking into a profound silence, and I knew there was no one else in the house. I had a headache, which worsened if I moved. I was waiting, listening for the clicket on the gate, in dread of the moment when Geneva, or Dinah, or both, would arrive home, ask how was my trip to Fowey (I had lied about Bodmin of course), how is Daniel MacNamara keeping. Daniel moved to Dorset two years ago.

Eventually, driven by thirst, I stole out along the passage, a thief in my own house. The kitchen was in perfect order, unusually so: stove warm and ticking, coppers hanging in polished rows, floor brushed clean of crumbs and dog hairs. No cup or book sat on table or dresser, no apron hung in the dying sunlight on the wall. I found a similar state of affairs in the pantry: tidy rows of bottled peas and beans, pickles, fruit preserves, salted fish, spices; but no pie, no bread, no eggs, no cheese. There was a strong smell of cloves, which reminded me of Lucy's pantry long ago when I was a boy. I used to linger there in the buttery cool, listening to the hens in the orchard outside, their constant purring questions. And her pantry had a small hidden window, an open grating just below the spice shelf, where I sat and watched a universe of gold gnats stirring the evening air above the hens' backs, and if I waited long enough, I thought, God would appear in the gap between the apple trees, wearing a black broad-brimmed hat.

I was contemplating opening one of the jars when I heard a noise: the clack of pattens in the porch, then softer footfalls. Someone was moving about in the hallway. I stepped out of the pantry and the air split with a cry. It was young Martha Tippett. She froze for a moment in the half-light, one hand at her mouth, but collected herself admirably when she saw it was me. In her other hand was a basket, from which she took a package. She thrust this at me and spoke in a rush.

'I was told to bring this up to you, Mr Prideaux. There's four eggs, and steamed pork belly, it's still warm, a wheat loaf, butter, currant pudding, a big twist of tea, and I went for the hevva cakes but May Trevithick said they'd all gone by four.'

'Who? Who sent it up?'

'What? Oh. It was Jenny, Geneva, I mean Mrs Prideaux, Mr Prideaux.'

'Where is she?'

'Over to Trebeere. She made up the meat and bread and tea herself, and then she says I should get the cakes at Trevithick's on my way, and take the parcel up to the parsonage before I go to my mother's.'

Martha spoke as if I should already have known about all this. It was awkward to have to question her, and she seemed nervous of me. I asked her where in Trebeere Geneva was, and why.

'She's over to Mr Wigge's house, with Dinah Pengelly. She said if you want a fire in the study, even though it's quite warm out, I am to make it up for you.'

I declined the fire, and when Martha had gone I sat and opened the parcel, spreading the contents on the kitchen table. I could not summon the strength to light the lamp. I looked at the two hardboiled eggs, the pork belly in its greasy paper. The smell from the meat was sickening. I managed to boil a kettle, took a cup of tea into the study, and was abruptly stricken by a headache more severe than I could ever remember, a cracking, hammering pain. I lay on the couch with the cup beside me on the table, but when I attempted to reach for the tea I felt my skull would split apart. There is a looking-glass opposite the couch; it was too high to see my reflection, but I would not have been surprised to see jagged fissures opening across my forehead. I remained there all night. Once, just after the clock struck three, I got up and went to the wash-house, where I found a counterpane, and a bucket for my nausea. The night was warm, as Martha had noted, but I had started to shiver and jerk about, as if my bones were fighting to break through the skin.

It was Arthur Wigge who found me the next morning and sent for the doctor, though I remember only a confusion of shadows, voices, ague, and slow, painful creepings to and from the privy. During the first week I was frequently unconscious, consumed by nightmares, and I was ill for quite a long time; there was apparently some concern for my life. When the fever broke it was Martha I saw first, coming in and out with cups and pots and poultices. Absorbed in her nursing function she had lost her timidness, and I found her presence soothing. Thick chestnut curls, rosy cheeks and black lashes; it still amuses me how often these humble Marthas and Marys from the village outshine the young ladies of the county with their centuries of gentle breeding. Doctor Barton-Taylor was too abrupt with her I thought, so I took pleasure in correcting him, praising her skill and efficiency. Nobody can argue with the opinions of a sick man. Some time later I woke to see Arthur in the chair by my bed, actually the couch, which had been made up in the study where I first fell ill. He began, oblique as always, talking about a history he was reading on Charles I, comparing him with Louis XVI, 'that strange ability of kings to close their eyes when their kingdoms pull apart, and then to believe sincerely that the pretty pictures behind their eyelids represent the truth'. He settled a tray on my bedclothes, a cup of broth, spiced with spirit, balanced on it.

'I count myself among these blind men,' he went on, 'because almost everyone had a sharper view of the nature of your troubles than I did: Dinah Pengelly, young Martha Tippett out there in your kitchen, the landlord at the Bonaparte, good farmer Copthorne, bad farmer Hocking, the foggy Mrs Cleer, and, above all, your wife Geneva. As for me, as I told you once before, I was convinced, for a long time, that you were merely overtaken by some spiritual crisis.'

'Where is Geneva?'

'She's staying in the annexe. Dinah is looking after her, as I have no manservant at present.' Arthur lives in a solid granite house in Trebeere opposite St Luke's Church, and it has a sort of summerhouse or cottage behind it that he calls his annexe, in the walled garden.

'What precisely does she know?'

'You'll have to ask her yourself, but I think she suspected something amiss a while ago, and Dinah will have filled the gaps in the hedge. I think Dinah is very fond of her. I cannot be sure how Dinah knew, but I'm often taken aback by the mystery of how things become known in our part of the world; it seems unnecessary to say anything outright, the facts seep out and the *Gazette* is usually redundant. Before the first report on Hookway's murder was published, Dinah and Geneva had both confided in me, about you. I could not believe that, having seen the paper, you would still imagine that you could keep us in the dark, telling Geneva that you were going to Fowey that day. To Fowey, by the Bodmin coach! And you forgot you had already told Geneva that your Fowey friend had moved to Dorset. So there came a point when Dinah's loyalty to you was overcome by her loyalty to your wife. They have been living in the annexe since the day you left for Bodmin.'

I wondered if Dinah had always known that Maryann was not merely a visiting parishioner. 'Does Geneva refuse even to see me?'

'Why no, of course not. I will arrange it whenever you wish. She came here, twice, while you were ill, but on both occasions you were asleep.'

'Could you tell her to bring Ossian?'

Geneva came, and brought Ossian, who greeted me warmly. What she could not endure, Geneva said, without preamble, was the knowledge that I had poured so much vigour into the concealment, and that I had presumed she would set more store by a past impropriety than the plight of an unfortunate woman in moral and physical danger.

'Dinah told me the woman had been coming here, always when I had gone out, and that she had a desperate air, like a hunted creature. Dinah heard shouts, whispering, hours of it. She understood from the first visit that this was no ordinary parish call. Did you really think she would have sat dumbly in the kitchen, that she wouldn't have wondered?' Geneva pushed her curls off her forehead, which was slightly damp. She always had trouble restraining her red hair.

'When did you know?'

'When Hookway attacked me out on Torbett's Green. Dinah had told me your visitor was a Maryann Tabb, and I wondered if the woman could be the same cousin Mary Ann my mother had spoken of. I drew a conclusion. I asked you if there was a link with the man in the wood, I gave you the opportunity to tell me, then. After that I watched you lie. Then Arthur told me about the money.'

'The money. Yes, I tried to help her.'

'You tried to pay her off.'

'You would rather it had been public knowledge?'

'We could have helped her. Arthur could have had something done about Hookway. And it soon became public, in any case. Perhaps it always was.'

'Arthur could have *had something done*,' I raised my voice, which, being sore, came out harsh as a rook's, 'of course he could, he always can. And now you are living in his garden house. Is he in love with you?'

'Don't be ridiculous. Arthur loves only his cat, and perhaps his paintings. But he's kind; you seem to have forgotten how he laboured to bring us together, those supposedly chance meetings, the little suppers at his house, how tactful he was.'

I thought of Maryann, or rather, I saw myself thinking of her, as if I were looking down on myself in the bed from the ceiling, and I heard myself speak: 'Maryann was not an innocent young girl, Geneva. She was only a few years younger than you, and, incidentally, she had no regard for you. She had lovers, after she was widowed. I was far from her first. She was blackmailing me. You forget, we are talking of a woman who murdered.'

'You never met Hookway, as I did. The only person I've ever encountered who filled me with true dread, an apprehension of ill-wishing. Not just because he followed me in a lonely place – there was something stony, pitiless, about the man. And so ugly. Perhaps I would have done the same in her place.'

I thought it better not to mention that I had in fact met Paulie, that time in the Bell and Candle.

'Maryann had a daughter named Eliza,' I continued. 'She disappeared at the time of the Great Fall and was never found. Maryann never appeared even slightly concerned to find out what happened to her.'

'Really? Dinah heard that the daughter went upcountry. Married a shopkeeper from Taunton.'

'Dinah, of course, being infallible in these matters.'

Geneva said nothing for a minute. I sensed she was rehearsing a prepared speech, and indeed that was what I received.

'What I also cannot bear,' she said, 'is the knowledge of what happened at Bodmin gaol. The image in my mind. The picture of you, there, at a public execution. I have the idea that something grotesque and hateful has entered this house, my life, something that I would never have expected to be forced to confront, and it is you, James, who brought it in, you who opened the door to this shadow, and I think you did this, contrarily, by closing the door to me.'

After Geneva left, I recalled, with a sudden grief, those evenings on the terrace at Arthur's house last year: Geneva and I talking of Wordsworth and Coleridge while we ate Arthur's chicken pie and drank Arthur's wine, admiring each other's chiaroscuro faces through the cloud of moths spinning around the lantern, congratulating ourselves on the benign Providence that had brought two kindred souls together so late in life, and all the while Arthur had floated in and out of the velvety dark, absenting and presenting himself, supplying wit, encouragement and coffee with the delicacy of a jeweller adjusting a watch.

I suspected it would now be impossible to continue in my position in the parish, an impertinence to imagine I should presume to cure the souls of St Anthony when my own blew about like a dirty paper in the back lane. Arthur confirmed it: a letter from Lord Sorleigh had arrived.

'Of course I argued for you, praised your long service here, the affection the parish holds for you, but unfortunately your mistakes have proved quite convenient; Silas Laity has finally died.

And Sorleigh has someone in mind, a rector for both livings, here and Boskerris.'

He, Arthur, had talked to Geneva, and it seemed that I had a choice. Geneva House could be sold and I would move away from St Anthony, or alternatively I could live there, out on the edge of the Great Fall. I would be utterly dependent on my own resourcefulness, for no servant, no maid, would consent to stay alone with a disgraced curate, even in the unlikely event that they were prepared to reside miles from the nearest neighbour on the borders of a wild chaotic landscape viewed by most of the village with a sort of horror.

Geneva House, September 28

'Geneva House', I write at the top of the page each time I make an entry in this journal, as if I were seated in a graceful drawing room, something in the style of the Assembly Room at the Bonaparte Inn. This is not, and never was, a house, but a peasant's cottage of the humblest sort, built for a smaller race, and my vanity is mocked every time I knock my head on the lintel in the dark passage, or struggle to light the rudimentary stove. To think that I used to find the parsonage cramped, and resented the proximity of the study, with its big window and generous bookshelves, to the back parlour and kitchen where Geneva spent most of her time. Time with Dinah.

I wonder sometimes about the woman who lived out here before me, a Mrs Barrett, who always appears to my imagination as a youngish woman in a green gown and a flat straw hat. The land agent told me she was ninety-two when she died. Mrs Barrett would have seen the tidal waves coming in from Portugal in 1755 as well as the Great Fall sixty-six years later. How near the historical past seems when you consider it like this; you could stretch a hand behind you and touch the people there. Samuel

Trembath told me he remembered her a little, but nobody else has ever mentioned her existence. Did she have visitors prepared to make the arduous walk from St Anthony, or did she accustom herself to a life of profound isolation, becoming indistinguishable from the forest around her? Geneva once dreamed Mrs Barrett was still here, perched on a high branch of the ash tree like a woodpigeon. We used to search the place for evidence of her long tenancy, but there is nothing. No book slipped behind a cupboard, no loose floorboard hiding a cache of letters. The orchard, whose fruit startles me at night when it thuds on the grass, must be hers, and perhaps she planted one solitary whistling jack and watched over the years as the ruby spikes colonised the garden all the way to the shore. But I must cut these speculations off: they lead only to melancholy thoughts of the numberless souls like Mrs Barrett, or the still more obscure Mr Barrett, who have passed through this wood since the beginning of time, leaving no trace.

Whether or not Mrs Barrett had visitors, I do, and this is a surprise, especially as most of them are not the people I might have expected. Arthur Wigge is the least surprising, and has been twice. Given his intense dislike of walking I am flattered. It was Arthur who arranged the transport of my books, furniture (there wasn't room for much) and deliveries of provisions: a crate of bottled vegetables (perhaps he emptied the parsonage pantry), a couple of cured hams, salt pilchard, flour, oats, yeast, tea, fat, dried fruits. I have had to teach myself to light the stove with furze, to make a coarse bread, and cook simple meals. For now, I stew everything, but I plan to learn pastry-making in the winter. Arthur brought brandy on the first occasion, a copy of *Blackwood's* on the second. Our talk was carefully neutral. He told me the new incumbent is a Geoffrey Pardoe, 'a great man for the chase, hunts with Sorleigh at St Dominic'. This Pardoe will not be living in my old parsonage, but will remain at the superior rectory at Boskerris, and he has no plans to employ a curate, so the services here will be infrequent. There is somebody in residence at the parsonage though, a maiden aunt of Pardoe's who was, aptly enough, involved in some minor scandal upcountry. Perhaps Pardoe has a sense of humour.

'The Methodists are delighted, of course,' Arthur said. 'All those churchless sinners turning to the chapel, trooping in, conscripts to the great army of penitents prostrating themselves in luxurious self-excoration, each outbidding his neighbour in swooning declarations of sin, bowing low before the gentlefolk who hold all of them, especially Methodists, in contempt.' Arthur detests Methodism, though I am never sure if his objection is doctrinal, political or aesthetic.

We do not speak much of Geneva, who has understandably not made the long walk to this isolated place which bears her name. Arthur tries to interest me in the affairs of the world beyond Cornwall, in states and kingdoms and great men: a new Prime Minister has succeeded Canning, he told me last time, and a treaty has been signed with Russia and France, against the Ottomans and in support of the Greeks. All of this, once, we would have been able to discuss, but I feel myself too separate, too conscious that my grasp of the active, industrious world is gone. Arthur seemed to sense this detachment, and looked to the sea, flat and silver that day, framed by my thickets of dwarfish oaks.

'We have watched the tide go out, you and I, almost since this century began, certainly since the Wars, a long ebbing away, a disenchantment, and I know you felt it. But tides come in.' He began to talk, somewhat darkly, about discontents upcountry, rumours of assemblies in cities and gatherings in barns, new societies and old ideas, things, he assured me, that I would never read of in *The Times*, or the *Gazette*. I'm afraid I hardly listened; I wanted to tell him about something else, something with which, once, he might have helped me, but now I would have to do for myself.

But I mentioned other visitors. The first of these was a woman I barely knew, Ruth Rosewarne (I had to scour my memory for her name), who arrived with a cheese. I received her with some anxiety, anticipating that she would probe the reason for my exile, sniffing out information she might use later, for village gossip about Maryann or Geneva. Instead she told me about the new Rector. She called him 'Prudoe', and asked if he was a relative of mine. Pardoe, Prideaux, Prudoe, the spoken names sound alike.

'We seen him just the once. He's the face of a hare, and he's tall as a bocka, and we don't expect him again before St Martin's Day. We see his aunty, though, in the parsonage garden, scrantling about in the lettuces with her petticoat up her fundaments.'

Starting back along the path, she turned to me. 'Don't let them push you into the sea, Mr Prideaux.' I was bemused, but touched. Since then, the pattern has been repeated, a visit, usually from a person I had scarcely been aware of, every couple of weeks. It was not until the most recent of these, John Menhennett, father of poor Thomas who has now died, that I understood the source of the difference in manner that I had noticed in the first. Menhennett brought me an old shotgun wrapped in cloth, 'you'll need it for the rabbits', and told me, apropos of nothing, of how his family were forced off their land, obliging them to move around, each time to a smaller dwelling, and I was reminded of Maryann's story of Charity, which I had dismissed at the time.

'It was the wife said to come up,' said Menhennett. 'Take him something, John, she says, because I never thought we'd see a parson put out of his house and left out there by the Great Fall.'

They consider me to have been evicted; it is this which has induced the relaxation in manner, the levelling. I am seen, finally, to be a person who shares their condition, and the reason for my fall from grace seems less important than the simple fact that I am living out here. Perhaps I might acquire a reputation as a hermit, an anchorite with occult powers. Already I fulfil the conditions: set apart from the world, alone in the wilderness, and I have not shaved in weeks.

I must not pretend Menhennett's attitude is shared by the whole parish. To the majority, and certainly those whom Amelia Cleer describes as 'the people who matter', I am invisible. Amelia has returned my subscription to the Literature Society. She sent a curt note via Samuel Trembath, telling me I could call at the Bonaparte to collect the money still owing to me, which she knows very well I will not do. I imagine her at some bookish evening there, laughing at the nice coincidence that my fall should have landed me so near to the Great Fall. The only fall Mrs Cleer recognises is the social one; the Fall in Genesis, to her, is just a nursery fable for Sunday school. Samuel's manner to me is no different from usual, but since I pay him to bring my post, eggs from his hens, butter from Jordan's dairy, this is unremarkable. Samuel's grandson Peter, however, has twice walked straight past me without a glance, our days constructing the veranda forgotten, while the fellow Arthur hired to bring my provisions dumped all the boxes wordlessly in the bracken, declining even to answer my good morning. A bottle of brandied plums broke open. I have also received an unsigned letter, the contents of which were so violently rancorous that I felt ill all day.

September 30

Jack Tabb, Jack Pender, Jack Prideaux, Jack Hocking: this is the problem I have, attempting to guess which name Maryann would have chosen to write, on whatever she wrote it on, when she left the baby at Redruth Poorhouse. Pender was her mother's unmarried name, but I have no idea of her father's, the one Maryann bore before she married Tabb. Geneva would know, the one person I can never ask. As far as I am aware Maryann had not met Hookway back in 1821, and in any case it is most unlikely she would have given the baby his surname, but I cannot afford to discount any possibility in my search. I have considered that Jack may not have been my child: the most probable alternative of course being Matthew Hocking; Maryann had every reason to convince me of my paternity, rather than Hocking, both for her own sake and the child's. It also occurred to me that Maryann may never have given birth at all, given her advanced years, and that the child was Eliza's, from Hocking. This might explain Eliza's sudden disappearance, but I am not inclined to credit the theory: Eliza was stubborn in her resistance. I believe Jack is Maryann's, and while I cannot be sure the child is not from Hocking, she told me her relations with the fellow had ceased when he tired of her, long before I lost trace of her. I run through these speculations in order to placate my reason, but it is a somewhat mechanical exercise, for I know, in the warp and weft of my body and soul, that Jack is mine.

It is a great relief to have written that paragraph, to have been able to do it in so matter of fact a style. Odd though that this rational attitude was made possible by a night phantom, a dream. I had expected, in the long weeks alone up here, to dream of Maryann: Maryann in the willow copse on Torbett's Green, in my study at the parsonage. Or some gaudy horror from the day at Bodmin. Instead my rest has been disturbed only by dreams of parcels, bedclothes, wrappings. Two days past I dreamed that Samuel Trembath came banging on my door in the middle of the night. He had a package from the village. I jumped out of bed, in the dream, but could not find a candle and became confused in a labyrinth of dark passages, overgrown with creeping plants (the house seemed to have become much bigger). When finally I was outside, I shouted in vain at Samuel's retreating figure on the path, and woke. It was on the day following this dream that the flesh and blood Menhennett came to my door with the shotgun, and there was something about the careful way he unwrapped it, folding back the chequered cloth with his broad red hands, that unlocked my mind. I turned back the pages of my journal and found my transcription of Maryann's letter from Bodmin gaol, with its cryptic postscript, the sentence that has been hammering, *rapping*, on my door: 'Jim there was a name with the parcel, I put it under the wrappings.'

Strange are the barriers the sleeping soul erects to obscure the truth from itself, the way that revelation arrives wearing a mask, and while I of all men should not be surprised by this phenomenon, I cannot understand what purpose the camouflage might serve. With the mind cleared of quotidian chatter, when reason itself is asleep, why wouldn't the spirit seize the chance to speak plainly?

I intend to start, naturally, with a visit to Redruth Poorhouse. I am under no illusion that I will find Jack still there after six years, but it is my hope that there will be some functionary, or inmate, who can tell me where he is now. I have resigned myself to making a number of expeditions, and after examining my finances, I consider that I can afford to make one journey, including two nights at an inn, every two months. I will shave tomorrow, using the greenish looking-glass I brought with me from the parsonage.

10

It was about a fortnight after we returned from Boscastle when Kerenza rang me and asked me to come to the Bonaparte after school. I imagined she would want to discuss Victor and Tracy's engagement. Had it really been her suggestion, and why was she now, as I suspected, less enthusiastic? I had armed myself with an array of arguments in their defence, with literary and historical precedents as ammunition.

What Kerenza wanted to talk about was something quite different. She fetched coffee from the kitchen and sat me at a table in the empty bar, the reproach of a Hoover moaning somewhere upstairs. I noticed a notebook on the table. As always, she launched straight in.

'What exactly do you remember about that day on the Fall, when we were eleven?'

'What day?' But I knew.

'The day we found the body in the sea.'

I glanced around as if to check that the bar was empty, aware even before I did it that it was the trite reaction of a guilty person.

The first image that came to mind, if I thought about that day (which was almost never), was of the naked Penny Nankervis and her unknown lover, screened by curtains of ivy, the scene my eleven-year-old self had termed the Rite of Passage. The second was of seals, the third, moths. Those things, at the time, had been important.

'Not much. We found something on the beach, in the seaweed. It was hot. There were flowers, tall red flowers, we put them on the water, and we saw moths, hundreds, an Emperor. It's a bit vague.' I was throwing colour into the gaps, to cover the grey centre of the memory.

'I don't believe you,' Kerenza said. 'What do you remember about the body?'

'There was someone floating. Maybe. Why? What do you remember?'

'I remember a woman in the shallow water on the little beach. A blue dress. She was dead — at least I think she must have been dead. It's perfectly clear. I'm fed up with pretending nothing happened, all of us just wandering along for years and years like we never saw anything, never talking about it. We were eleven, not five.'

I didn't think I had been pretending. Nor had I forgotten. What I had not done was separate the image of the woman in the sea from the mosaic of pictures from that summer. It was not even close to being the sharpest of the memories: the Mint Woman was clearer, her blind white face in the deep green shade of the ilex; Tracy was more vivid, reading her story, blowing out the candles to save the moths. I saw Victor in a tree, dangerously high, and heard his laugh when I shouted, 'Don't look down.' I told Kerenza this, and that I had never thought about it in a deliberate way, it was so long ago. And, I might have added, things that are not spoken about, even to yourself, become indistinct. They lose substance.

'I wasn't sure if it was real,' I said, 'or if it was just me. We saw so many things, we made them up. I remember hundreds of seals, but I don't know if we actually saw any.' I paused, looking up at a colour print of Napoleon at Eylau, stained snow on a battlefield, dead men and dying horses, random fires around a church. 'I remember going back to Geneva, the day after, and there was nothing there, the beach was empty.'

'There wasn't anything there,' she interrupted, 'because she'd been washed down the coast a bit towards St Anthony, to where they found her, at Penglaze Point. Clara Selman. It must have been her. You must know it was her. She wasn't really a woman, either, she was only seventeen, in the sixth form. Doing A-levels like us, but at William Noye in Trebeere. At least admit you know it was Clara Selman.'

Kerenza offered me a Camel, I lit one, she didn't. I asked her how she was so certain, and she told me she had looked it up in the library – the history of the case, the investigation, the suspects, the failure to find out who killed Clara Selman.

'That's the point, Sally. They interviewed a load of people, they even arrested someone, a bloke called Michael Jenkin, but he didn't do it, they never found out who murdered her. There are no newspaper reports after 1977, except a very short one in 1978 basically saying nothing. I've got copies of the articles upstairs. Look at this.'

She opened her notebook and took out a folded sheet of paper. It was a photocopy of a newspaper photograph. The caption underneath read, 'Clara Selman: teenager's death unexplained', and the girl in the photo was looking at something away from the camera, her mouth open, as if she was about to argue. There was too much light on her face, but there was something familiar about the way her hair curved away from a point in the centre of her forehead, like Snow White. The hair was paler than the hair of the woman in the sea. But then I had only seen it wet.

'I don't know,' I said. 'I can't remember.'

She folded the paper up again. 'Who was the Mint Woman, anyway?'

'The white statue. She was sinking into a crack in the earth.'

'I don't remember that at all. You remember a statue, but not the woman in the sea?'

While we had been talking, while I was emphasising just how little I remembered, images came in behind my eyes, one or two at first, then a swarm: white rooms rippling with light, the steamy green quiet in the woods, the smell of methylated spirit, the Owlman, three seals looking back at me from the waves, a rounded arm sliding into a pool, Tracy and Victor on the shore, dressed in seaweed, enacting the story of Whistling Jack.

'I'm not sure what happened when. It's all mixed up.'

Kerenza sat back and looked straight at me for the first time, her tilted eyes friendly. 'Well, don't worry about it too much. I just want you to think about it. I don't want to be the only one thinking about it. Then tell me what you remember. And why we didn't report it.'

'I thought you'd asked me over to talk about Victor and Tracy getting married.'

'There's not much to say. They won't do it, it's a daydream. They're sixteen, seventeen. We're young. Why can't they just go out with each other for a while like everyone else? She's not pregnant is she?'

Kerenza was the only young person I remember who was fully aware of being young, at the time, while she was young. She would say 'only seventeen' where I would think 'already seventeen'.

I said I didn't think Tracy was pregnant, though, naively, the thought had never occurred to me.

'Victor told me it was your idea,' I said.

'I wasn't serious. You were up at the bar that night in Boscastle and we were talking about Victor's parents, how they think Tracy has bad blood, how he has to pretend he isn't going out with her. So I said, why don't you just get married?'

I dare you.

'Perhaps they want to be independent.'

'How? What would they do? Where would they go? There's three million unemployed. Victor doesn't know what he wants to do, and Tracy, well, she's good at art and craft, but that's it.'

'My mother's an artist,' I said.

'Perhaps Tracy could be a muse, with her looks. An artist's muse, or a writer's. Muse, inspire, breathe in, in a musical museum. There were nine of them, daughters of Zeus and Mnemosyne, that's Memory to you. What does a muse actually do, though? I'm never sure.'

'Amuse?'

'No. The words *amuse* and *muse* have different roots.'

Kerenza did this often — took hold of words and shook them until all the little etymologies and masked meanings came scuttling into the light. A muse, to me, was just a blue word, a lilac statue.

'Neither of their families have any money,' she went on, 'and Tracy's family is weird. Her grandmother spends her time talking to ghosts at the Spiritualist church, her mother took an overdose, her father vanished. I don't think Tracy or Victor will ever leave St Anthony.'

'I thought her mother jumped off the harbour in a storm?'

'Nothing so dramatic. She went off to Falmouth and took some pills in a bed and breakfast. That's what Mum said, anyway.

There's a secretary in Mum's office who was at school with Irene Pender.'

'But it was you who told me she jumped off the harbour.'

'Then I must have made it up. Or perhaps Tracy made it up, or someone else.'

To ask Kerenza if I could borrow her photocopied cuttings would have been out of the question, an acknowledgement that I was interested, worried, that I was prepared to think about that day on the Fall, that I remembered. Instead I wanted to have read everything she had read, to know what she knew. So I went to the main library in Trebeere and asked where the copies of old newspapers were, for 1976. I told the librarian I was doing a project about heatwaves for geography at school, though she had not asked and made no comment. She told me to wait.

It was unusual to be in Trebeere Library for a conventional purpose. I preferred to buy paperbacks if I could, because I resented having to give books back. If I did have to borrow, I used the old Branwell Library in the botanical garden. Trebeere Library was for truanting; Victor said I was the only person he knew who minched off school in a library. On these occasions I would hide at the back in the unfrequented Poetry and Literary Criticism section, writing up overdue homework or reading novels beside the ticking radiators, while the massed ranks of books in their rigid bindings, stuffed with centuries of polished thoughts, looked down on me with sad puzzlement.

I feigned interest in the leaflets by the desk (local history, domestic violence, pottery classes) while the librarian fussed around retrieving my newspapers. Finally she thumped some heavy red folders down on the table with a warning about not eating and drinking while I used the archive. I had asked for the local paper, the *Cornish Times*, the regional *Wessex Press*, and one national, which turned out to be the *Guardian*, for the second half of 1976. I carried them to a secluded corner of Poetry, and spread some collected works of Tennyson around the table to give the impression, if anyone should pass by, that the newspapers were not particularly important to me.

The *Cornish Times* had the most articles, although they were mainly short: two blocks of text comprising one fact and a couple of denials. I found four reports in the *Guardian*, each one with new information in the first few lines, then a recap of earlier ones in the subsequent paragraphs. But the *Wessex Press* included interviews and features as well as news. First I studied the pictures. Most of them used the one Kerenza had shown me, but there were two others. One showed Clara looking very young, in a halter-neck dress; she stood between her parents at some sort of outdoor party. In the second photo she was around my own age. She was sitting in a greenhouse, smiling up at the camera, with *The Age of Reason* on the table beside her. I recognised it from the cover design, Picasso's *Guernica*, the same edition as mine.

The newspapers seemed anxious to emphasise Clara's respectable background. She was an 'attractive and sensible teenager', a 'promising pupil', taking A-levels in French, English and German, hoping for a place at Exeter University. One report included a photograph of her parents' house taken across the garden hedge, another of the harbour at Trebeere, which was described as a 'tranquil seaside town'. Her father Colin Selman was a 'prominent' local solicitor. Perhaps it was the blend of attractiveness and respectability that ensured that there was more detail about Clara Selman than was usual with murder victims at that time. Her 'hobby' (a word I loathed), according to the *Wessex Press*, was German cinema, and she hoped one day to become a film director. Like Victor.

I read all this with detached interest, as if Clara Selman were a person in history or a character in a novel, until I found some quotations from a 'close friend'. This friend was not named; it may or may not have been Sandra Jenkin, the girl Clara was out with in Trebeere the night before she disappeared, in the same clubs and pubs I now went to, the friend she was walking to see on the last afternoon of her life.

'Her name was really Clare, but she thought Clara sounded more foreign. She was kind, quite serious, always reading, but she liked dancing and going out too. She had terrible taste in music, Tammy Wynette and that sort of thing.' And then this odd detail: 'Clara was never careless like me, all her work had to be perfect, in order. She stuck flowery plastic covers on her school books to protect them.' I looked at the photo again, and Clara had moved nearer, closer to her name. There were hints of a contradictory personality: German films and country music, Sartre and obsessive neatness; a faint signal from the person she might have been, someone I might have liked.

I took the bound volumes back to the main desk without making any photocopies, and then replaced the Tennyson books, but I had already flicked through one of them, pausing, by one of those chances that are not really chances at all, on another dead girl, Claribel.

Where Claribel low-lieth
The breezes pause and die,
Letting the rose-leaves fall:
But the solemn oak-tree sigheth,
Thick-leaved, ambrosial,
With an ancient melody
Of an inward agony,
Where Claribel low-lieth...

I liked the surprise: the dour black cover, the sheet of tracing paper veiling the poet's serious, bearded face ('frontispiece') with its downcast hair (he looked rather like Raymond Nankervis), and then suddenly, inside, there was Claribel: the living words, hypnotic, intoxicating, faintly ridiculous – a mourning oak, lisping lines and booming beetles.

* * *

Victor was on the phone, from a callbox. 'Sally? Can you come and meet us at Betty's?'

The afternoon was gloomy and raw, I didn't feel like leaving the house, and said so.

'Come on. I'm dying of boredom. Denise is at home with the kids and keeps going on about what they did at Christmas. Christmas! It's almost February, for Christ's sake. And we've got some news, me and Tracy.'

My mood, not high to begin with, sank. Kerenza must have talked to Victor or Tracy or both, asking about Geneva and Clara Selman. I was still thinking about what I had read at the library, and I didn't want to imagine how Kerenza's probing questions would affect Victor and Tracy. Particularly Tracy. It was even nastier outside than I thought and I had forgotten to change my shoes – high heels with pink fish embedded in the plastic uppers. My feet were wet and icy by the time I reached the quayside.

In winter, Betty's Tea Garden, still run by Maggie, moved indoors, sharing space with a clothes shop on the harbour. To get to the café section you had to walk through rails of anoraks in elderly shades of grey, mushroom and powder blue; the tables were arranged under a big window at the back with the sea directly below. In rough weather, when the tide was in, you could drink your tea amid the rubbery chemical scent from the anoraks while waves smashed against the glass. I blundered past a display of rainhats and found the two of them sitting at the window table, talking to Maggie, who was standing with her back to the sea, mug in hand. Maggie Hart was one of those who inform any passing stranger, with portentous gravity, that the place you are in is situated on an important ley line. On this occasion she was explaining how her sister's labour had started when the sister's husband's car broke down on Torbett's Hill.

'The Mini couldn't cope with the steepness and started sliding backwards. They rolled down and crashed into Miss Rescorla's gate, and then Karen's waters broke, right there in the front seat.' She paused, rolling a cigarette, her many bangles chinking and clacking on her arm. 'I always say everything happens for a reason. It turns out there are two ley lines going through St Anthony, and one of them runs right up Torbett's Hill, through the Fall, and connects up with the Foolish Virgins on the other side. So if Tony hadn't turned up Torbett's Hill by mistake, Karen could have popped it out on the A30, and God knows what would have happened.'

I was willing Maggie to shut up and go back behind the counter, scanning Victor and Tracy's faces for hints of anxiety, but they attended politely to Maggie's story with no sign of impatience.

'Was your sister OK?' Tracy asked.

'Yes she's doing great, and the baby too. Miss Rescorla came out and drove them to the cottage hospital in her Morris Traveller. She's good like that, Miss Rescorla, quite sensible for a teacher, dear of her.'

The Foolish Virgins are a small circle of ancient standing stones out on the moor. I was unsure how they, or the ley lines, were supposed to have influenced the birth, unless one of them had sucked the car up the hill before expelling it into Miss

Rescorla's gate. Just before she went back to serve a customer, Maggie offered Tracy a Saturday job in the café, once the spring visitors started arriving. To my surprise, Tracy accepted.

'Well?' I said when we were alone.

'It's about Kerenza,' said Victor. 'I've heard something.'

'Not Kerenza exactly. Her parents,' said Tracy.

'They're splitting up, separating, divorcing, calling it a day,' Victor said, throwing synonyms around as usual in case people failed to understand him. 'Penny's moved out of the Bonaparte. She's living with another man.'

I tried not to look relieved. 'Is it that Mark we met in Boscastle?'

'I think so. Mark Hocking from the estate agents. He lives in the tall house behind the hotel, so she hasn't gone far. I think it might be the one we trespassed in once.'

'But that's not everything,' said Tracy. 'Her father's going out with someone from school.'

'What?'

'Carole Carr. In the upper sixth a few years ago.'

Carole Carr, who had waitressed at Penny's dinner party. I could not connect her with Raymond Nankervis, whom I regarded as old, older than the fathers of my other friends, older than my own father, who was dead.

'My mother heard it in the Nelson,' Victor continued. 'She was telling Denise, I was listening on the stairs. She says it's because Raymond never put enough effort into the Bonaparte. She thinks Penny has been having an affair with Mark for ages, but she only just heard about Carole. Raymond Nankervis is a disgrace, she says, and she won't be giving the Bonaparte her custom ever again, although she never went in there anyway.'

'No wonder Kerenza was strange in Boscastle,' said Tracy.

Kerenza must have known all this when we met at the hotel, while she was unearthing the question of Clara Selman, but she had said nothing. How long had she known? I remembered how she seemed to know her way around the house behind the Bonaparte when we trespassed in it long ago, and I thought of the time I saw Penny having sex on the Fall, on the day of the woman in the sea. I had never told anyone about that.

'So where's Kerenza going to live, with her mother and Mark Hocking, or at the hotel?'

'We should ask her,' said Victor, 'find out if she needs any help.'

'Don't just come out with it, though,' Tracy said. 'She hates pity. That'll be why she hasn't mentioned it.'

I was to meet Carole Carr again when I worked my next shift at the hotel. Mavis and I sometimes took our tea break in a secret place whose existence I had only discovered when I became a chambermaid. It was a tiny isolated room up in the roof, reached by a back staircase off the second floor. It was, naturally, undecorated, shabby and damp, but there were two comfortable armchairs. It was also a place of astonishing beauty: an octagonal cupola drenched in light. Mavis and I didn't talk much when we drank our tea up there, it was a moment out of time. That morning, however, Mavis was telling me about the glory days of the Bonaparte in the 1950s, when she had been a waitress in the restaurant. She broke off abruptly at the sound of quick footsteps on the stairs. Carole opened the door.

'What are you two doing in here? This room's closed for refurbishment. It's not safe.'

Mavis replied to the effect that if it wasn't safe, it had been unsafe for a long time.

'It's filthy, man,' Carole said, 'you'll bring dust and muck down on your clothes, and then you're going to be going in the guest rooms. You can have your breaks in the laundry, that's for staff.'

We followed Carole's narrow shoulders down the narrow staircase, Mavis clumping hard on each step. Carole was five years older than Kerenza or Tracy, but looked younger, with long hair of the pale dusty beige that is known as mouse, centre-parted and falling in tent flaps around a face bare of make-up, but her status as Raymond's girlfriend conferred authority. With Raymond himself, I noticed later, she smiled constantly, following him around the bar, into the cellar, up the stairs, complimenting him on his plans for the hotel, plans that sounded most unlike him, such as converting the Assembly Room into a dance bar. And she called Kerenza 'Kerry', which no one ever did.

At the end of my shift she put her head out of the dining room and beckoned me in, leaving Mavis to depart alone.

'Before you split, come in here a sec.'

She talked like an old hippie, as well as looking like one, peppering her talk with Americanisms. She produced two glasses of white wine, and as she leaned over I caught her scent – sweetish, meaty, slightly metallic: patchouli. I supposed that Raymond or Penny had mentioned something of my connection with Kerenza, that I was more than a mere employee, but she gave no hint that she recognised me either from school or Penny's supper. That happened quite often, though; I had a forgettable face. She was frank, almost intimate, about the weighty responsibility of running a hotel so soon after leaving school, and how a publisher was showing some interest in Ray's book (she called him Ray).

'We're getting the Masons in for dinners, and last week we had the St Dominic hunt. People who matter. Lord Sorleigh came into the bar after, with his wife, she's a model. He was amazed Ray knows so much about the history of Cornwall.'

As I was leaving she thanked me for my hard work, and then touched my arm, so of course I was touched; how annoying not to be free to dislike someone without reservation. I realised she hadn't asked me a single question, but I never minded that.

Kerenza came to see me at Pellow Street, unannounced, which was unusual. My mother was at her new job at the Trebeere Museum café and I was in the kitchen reading Prideaux's diary, which I had now removed without permission from the Branwell reference section, along with a book on the French Revolution, for a history project. I had a headache, the impression that my thoughts were taking place at some distance from my body, which itself seemed pinned too tightly to its spine. The revolutionaries were only a bit older than me; one named Saint-Just caught my eye because there is a town in Cornwall of the same name; he was twenty-two in 1789, Napoleon barely twenty. Perhaps I didn't have as much time as I thought, to decide what I thought. As Kerenza took off her jacket I resolved to be decisive, unlike James Prideaux. I cleared my books off the table and set about making efficient coffee in a pot.

'I'm sorry to hear about your parents,' I began, 'we were a bit worried about you. We don't have to talk about it now, though. Or at all. It's none of my business. But if you want to...'

She looked at me for a moment and then burst out laughing.

'Are you trying to be tactful? No need, I've known for ages. Not about Mark, particularly, or the dreary Carole, but my parents' affairs. My parents are hopeless. Or rather one is hopeless, the other is restless.'

'Really? How long?'

'Sometime after we moved here when I was a child. They're so different, I can't think why they ever got married.'

'What about Mark Hocking, do you like him?'

'He's all right. Boring of course, just talks about his office. But he never says things like "all in good time" or "hold your horses", he just does it. He's *dynamic*; that's Mum's favourite word at the moment, dynamic.' She paused, laughed. 'Coke and ice cream at the Wimpy! Do you remember Mark saying that in Boscastle? How embarrassing.'

Her father was more embarrassing, though.

'The hotel is a wasteland. Rooms rotting away. He only does enough to break even, keeping it open for withered regulars and a few summer tourists. Everyone else in St Anthony goes to the Nelson or the Crabber – they have live music, cocaine, red-herring pie, all the trawlermen blowing their wages. Mum could have made the Bonaparte work, but he wouldn't even let her put bathrooms in, in case it spoiled the proportions, then he wrote to the council to get the building listed. He's still grinding on with his history book, which nobody will ever read.'

'Have you?'

'What?'

'Read any of it.'

'Some. But the style annoys me. He says the grand houses "attest to a bygone age", and church towers "stand sentinel", and everything is always *bearing witness* to something else in the past. It's like being in court. He doesn't write like he talks.'

She wasn't particularly surprised, she said, about Carole Carr. 'Maybe he just prefers a young woman who doesn't argue. Carole won't stay, once she realises what he's like.' Kerenza pronounced the name Ca-*role*; 'If she wants to call herself Carol, she should knock off the "e".' Kerenza would be keeping her room at the Bonaparte and would also have a home with her mother and Mark Hocking in the house behind the hotel. Victor had been correct, it was the same paint-scented house we had trespassed in, the one

Kerenza had seemed to know her way around. 'I've got two rooms right at the top, almost a flat. They both feel guilty about me of course, Mum and Dad.'

It occurred to me that Kerenza seemed older than her parents, and I wondered what it would be like to have so much space, to have both your father and mother alive, plus a stepfather, and a stepmother just a few years older than you were; to be able to sit on a green island in the stream and watch the foolishness of your older relatives sweeping around you on both sides. Kerenza, as much as Tracy and Victor, opened windows on the future, and I looked out obediently at the view, following the direction of her pointing finger, but I never looked back at her properly, never questioned where her premature cynicism came from, or what might have compelled her to adopt it. It seemed authentic, different from the studied world-weary posing I heard at school. I read Kerenza like a book, that is, uncritically, with involuntary suspension of disbelief. If she said she was unconcerned about her parents, if she appeared always to be competent, uncompromising, without fear, then that must be how she was.

She put her cigarette out, gathered herself, and sat up straight; at that moment she looked just like Penny, closing a subject down, except that Kerenza always opened subjects up.

'I've been thinking again. I expect you have. Why didn't we tell anyone?'

Why didn't we tell anyone. Such an ordinary question, but I couldn't make sense of it. We had been children, probably nothing serious would have happened to us. We had never decided not to. We had never addressed the question – not because we didn't know what the question was, but because we had not realised there was a question. That is what I had been thinking, but as I talked to Kerenza I realised that I had been using the first-person plural in my thoughts, never doubting that we all remembered the same things.

It was the trespassing, I said. We had already been caught, we couldn't be caught again. 'And we didn't know who it was. We didn't connect it.'

'With Clara Selman's body,' said Kerenza helpfully, 'no. But even at the time, on the beach, you must have realised something was peculiar. What I've been thinking is, how did we know she was dead?'

The dolphin's skin gleamed, blue-grey, taut. How do you know it's dead, I had asked Tracy. *Look at the eyes*, she said. *If there's no expression in its eyes, it's gone.*

'What if she actually wasn't dead?' Kerenza continued. 'Did you check? Did Tracy or Victor check?'

I saw a rounded arm sliding across dark blue fabric into a green pool of seaweed; a gentle splash. It was as clear as a short piece of film. *She looks ill, she's ill; she looks dead, she's dead.*

'I know you were only eleven, Sally, but you must have seen dead animals. There were dead things all over the Fall, that dead fox in the shed at the back of Geneva with all the sexton beetles coming in and out of the fur...'

She was sitting there, meditative, staring out of the kitchen window at our tiny courtyard, telegraph wires and washing lines crossing the white sky above the alley. I dumped the coffee pot on the table and forced the plunger down, where it stuck halfway.

'What about you?' I shouted. 'Did you check? What do you remember?' I was suddenly furious with her.

She touched the top of the coffee pot to steady it. 'You have to wait till the grounds settle, otherwise the whole thing explodes. Look at all those jackdaws out there, on the roof. They don't walk, they bounce.'

I kept glaring at her until she resumed, evenly: 'I remember watching, sitting under the trees. I had a blister, one of my shoes was hurting and I was trying to pull it off. I'm not trying to catch you out, or accuse you of anything. I just need your brilliant memory. I want to know the facts, that nothing really bad happened.'

The primary school I went to in London had been a Church of England school. My parents, who were atheist, were under the impression this was just an antique label, a picturesque relic from the past. But the school took religion seriously. Every fortnight a different class performed a parable at assembly, rehearsed beforehand. We wore cotton tunics and tea towels on our heads, secured with canvas bands. When not in use these Biblical clothes were stored in a big black trunk, and because they were never washed, a musty odour hung around the Good Samaritan and the Prodigal Son, officious Martha and smug Mary, the Wise and Foolish Virgins. We were not offered much in the way of interpretation, so the moral message was often confusing (don't share your lamp oil with feckless people; leave the boring housework to your sister; behave as badly as you like and provided you eventually come back, you will be better loved than conscientious stay-at-homes). Sometimes, after these playlets, the headteacher would announce that money had been stolen from the cloakroom. We sat in tiers around her, rows above rows as in a theatre, so you were uncomfortably aware of your face being on view. I had never taken money, yet my face burned each time these crimes were announced, as if I had stolen from every pupil in the school. Perhaps this was the point, to instil a permanent sense of transgression, because whether you had done anything or not on this particular occasion, you had surely thought about it, and at some deep level you were stained.

When Kerenza said she was not accusing me of anything, what took shape was the idea that there might be something to be accused of, that something bad, in a formal sense, might have happened because of something we did or failed to do, and that a memory fluttered just outside the range of vision, as it does when you fall asleep in the early evening and wake in dark silence, experiencing for a few seconds a total amnesia, an absolute ignorance of who or what or where you are, knowing only that knowledge exists and that in less than a second it will slide back, mothlike, into the light. Whatever it was, this doubt, it was not past, not locked in a story or hidden in old newspapers in red binders; it was here in this room.

I returned to the French Revolution when Kerenza left. Paris under the Terror swarmed behind the historian's cool prose: the tocsin ringing in the narrow streets, the poisonous suspicions, betrayals and beheadings, young Saint-Just with his implacable dedication to the purity of truth, and I thought of Maryann Tabb in her cell at Bodmin, and the time I'd watched men and women filleting fish on the quay at St Anthony, how the knives flickered over the flesh, parting it so the spines sprang out, pearly and flexible, with pockets of blood between the vertebrae. Then I realised I was going to throw up. The flu came down in the sudden, violent way flu does, in a paroxysm of shivering and clattering teeth. It closed down our house for two weeks. When I had been in bed three days, my mother fell ill. The Rayburn went out and our rooms grew dank and cold; fever – an acrid feral reek – hovered on the landing. We took it in turns to creep down to the kitchen, pausing on each stair, to heat cans of chicken soup or fetch milkless tea and aspirin for each other. The telephone rang out into the silence; once or twice I heard somebody banging on the front door. Visions came: trees made of twisting flesh, wide flat fields where grey fungus grew in neat ploughed furrows. Two voices were in my head speaking over each other, one jabbering maddeningly fast, the other drawling so slowly it seemed that time itself would stretch and die – an aural hallucination I recognised from a description of fever in a children's book, Laura Ingalls Wilder's *Little House on the Prairie*, though I've never come across another account of this phenomenon.

But the fever had passed by the time I was visited again by the execution dream. This time, for the first time, the person I had murdered had a face and a name.

I was out of bed before my mother. Hollow, unsteady, I went to the Co-op to replenish our empty cupboard. The common day beat in, white sun of late winter flashing off tarmac and slate, traffic bullying along into John Wesley Street. It was after four and the pavements were thronged with people returning from school – loud, red-kneed, healthily cold. I was distanced by my absence, which seemed far longer than a fortnight, and obscurely ashamed of it. In London I could have walked out of the front door and lost myself at once amid strangers and complexity; here I had to pull a scarf across my face and slip down one of the cobbled alleys that connect the high street with the harbour.

Victor was there, hunched in a doorway with three other boys, smoking. He saw me and broke away, flipping his cigarette end across the stones.

'At last, Sally. Where have you been? Your mum told us you were ill, then nothing. I rang up several times, and me and Tracy came round to your house once as well.'

The other boys were making hooting jackal noises at Victor and me, so we were walking fast back up the alley.

'Yes, thanks for asking, I'm nearly better. But Mum's still ill. Can you slow down?'

He apologised, took my carrier bag, and I gave him as lurid an account of the flu as I could. He smiled but without looking at me, his black eyes distracted by some shadow beyond my shoulder.

'Have you heard from Kerenza since you got ill? She said she talked to you about something. Could we meet up later? If you feel well enough, of course?'

I said no, but he could come round the next day. I had a good idea what he wanted to talk about.

My mother was able to sit up in bed. She was in that cleaned-out, mildly euphoric mood which sometimes follows an illness, and I was afraid she would try to come downstairs when Victor arrived. When I told her he needed to talk to me about something private, she gave me a long look.

'Mum, Victor's with Tracy. He always will be. This is just something to do with his history project.'

'Don't let him tire you out then, you're still not well. And don't go out.'

When Victor arrived around six I closed the living-room door behind us, pushed him through to the kitchen, then closed the kitchen door. I had made a large quantity of toast, for which Victor always had a prodigious appetite. As usual he threw his jacket down and wrenched off his jersey, but without the normal exasperated energy. He asked for a beer and we didn't have any, but my mother kept a bottle of Cinzano Bianco in the cupboard so I poured us some of that. I had guessed correctly about the topic.

'I can't understand why Kerenza has suddenly started asking about it now. We were kids. Even if it was that girl in the paper we saw, or thought we saw, we didn't know anything, we didn't do anything.'

'She thinks that's the point, we didn't do anything. She wants facts, she hates anything to be hazy.' As I said 'hazy', I remembered a day on the Fall when a sea mist had come in, enveloping Geneva. I had thought it mysterious and rather beautiful, but Kerenza, uncharacteristically, had insisted we set off back to St Anthony immediately.

'But why now, after all this time?'

It might have something to do with her parents' separation, I suggested, or even his engagement to Tracy. 'And,' I added casually, 'because they never found out what happened. To Clara Selman. They never caught anyone.'

'I don't remember that much,' he said. 'It was always hot.' He paused. 'We were acting those weird plays that summer, in the woods, in the sea. That's what I remember – Tracy; Tracy with seaweed all over her, sleeping in the orchard. She made me put the lantern out, and the candles, because the moths kept flying into them. We saw glow-worms in the grass, or were they fireflies? And you dropped your radio into one of those cracks in the earth. It was still on, loud, and the music kept coming up out of the ground for days, "Dancing Queen", the shipping forecast, until it changed to static and the battery ran out. It was quite surreal.'

I didn't remember any glow-worms, or the incident with the falling radio, but let him continue.

'The story Tracy wrote, "Whistling Jack" – was the woman in the sea before or after that?'

'After.'

'Kerenza remembers that story, she mentioned it when I saw her.'

'So do I. It was a beautiful story.'

'Quite strange though. There was a knife in it. Blood. Kerenza mentioned that as well. A stabbing.'

'It was just a story, Victor.'

'Didn't we have a knife? Tracy had her shells everywhere, mother-of-pearl. But I think I also remember a pearl knife.'

Victor glanced at the door, and lowered his voice.

'What I'm really nervous about is if Kerenza tells the police.'

This was a new idea. 'Did she mention the police?'

'No. But the thing about the police is they never believe you. There's something I haven't told you about my father. He was in prison. Not for long, just three weeks, years ago. It wasn't his fault. His mate was having it off with the landlady at the pub. This woman, the landlady, lent her husband's car to the mate, and he went off on some trip in it with Dad and two others, but the husband came back early and reported the car stolen, and the police caught my dad and the other blokes in the car. The landlady didn't back them up, she didn't want her old man to know about her being unfaithful, and they were all found guilty of car theft and sent to prison in Bristol. Dad only got three weeks because he was eighteen. He didn't even know it was the husband's car, it was nothing to do with him really, but the police didn't believe him.'

Since then, said Victor, his father had a mortal dread of the police and warned his sons about the consequences of getting into trouble. 'Paul of course avoids trouble, or maybe trouble avoids him like Mum says, but Dad suspects me all the time. After we got that police caution with the trespassing, well, it was bad at home.'

Suspicion, verging on paranoia, was something of a theme in Victor's family. Bridget Jordan's concerns tended to the medical: chemicals in hair dye and make-up, poison in children's vaccinations, chlorine in the water ('How do we know what else they put in?'), and fluoride, which she believed was radioactive. She had fallen out with her son Paul, the dental student, over fluoride. On a recent visit to Victor's house, Keith Jordan had explained to me, in his even-tempered tenor, how the police force was run by Freemasons for the benefit of Freemasons, and how the Communists had recruited and trained a secret army, infecting every British institution. 'The damage is already done,' he said, 'schools, Parliament, the unions, the Church, even the railways. Scratch a do-gooder and you'll find a Communist underneath, it's been going on since the end of the war. You should know, Sally, you're learning history. You must have debates in class? Victor never has an opinion, most likely he never listens, or he doesn't have the sense to think about it.'

But I didn't have an opinion either. I never knew how to begin to answer when people asked me these sort of questions. A boy I knew was in the Young Socialists, but he never suggested I join; he told me I was a 'petty bourgeois individualist', which sounded bad. How did people create these opinions for themselves? Victor was good at history, but he used to say he disliked it. I dismissed this as affectation, though now I'm not so sure: 'It's stopped,' he said once, 'all the interesting things have already happened, and all the worst things have already happened. Nothing will change, nobody will dare to do anything, in case it starts a nuclear war, and if that happens, nobody will be here to read history.'

'Isn't that the point?'

'Nuclear war?'

'No, stupid, that it's stopped. It's history, past.' At that time I conceived of history as a sealed region, the Second World War serving as a grey no man's land separating it from the recognisable present.

'People in history looked forward,' said Victor, 'they thought there was something interesting round the corner. I can't imagine anything.'

I had meant to ask Victor some more about his specific memories of the day we saw the woman in the sea, but was distracted by his talk of the police. Instead I asked what Tracy thought about Kerenza's questions, what she remembered about Clara Selman.

'She hasn't seen Kerenza. She doesn't know, and I can't seem to ask her. She thinks Kerenza is upset about her parents splitting up.'

I thought she definitely should know, I replied, in case Kerenza surprised her by bringing the subject up without warning, as she had with me.

'It's difficult. She loves the Fall. I think she'd like to live out there, all the time. We still go up to Geneva. We don't do much, just the usual, drink, read, listen to music, other stuff, you know. Sometimes we lie in the bracken and watch for the seals; even if we hardly ever see any, we imagine what sort of person they would have been when they were people, and we talk about people in the village, from school, Maggie or Kerenza's dad or Miss Rescorla, and what sort of seal they will become when they die. It's just a game, but sometimes I wonder what she really believes. I know she goes up there on her own, at night even. We've had rows about that. Mrs Tabb never tells her she can't go anywhere, so she doesn't have to lie, like you and me. I've no idea what she remembers about the woman in the sea.'

'Clara Selman.'

'Maybe. We don't know. I can't think what would happen if someone started asking Tracy those factual sort of questions, about something horrible.' Victor was speaking haltingly, with long sighing pauses, pulling at his t-shirt. 'I think she would feel protective, about Geneva I mean, and, well, she might say something confusing. If people asked. I'm sure it's illegal not to report a body. Maybe we could go to prison.'

'When was the first time you met Tracy?' I said, to change the subject. I would go back to the library, later, and look up the law about reporting dead bodies.

'At school. I was six, we'd just moved back here from Falmouth. I started term late, I was the new boy. The teacher was called Mrs Gryce and she took a dislike to me straight away. One morning she told us to write a story about a holiday, or some stupid thing, and when we finished she collected the stories and read them out, one by one. When she got to mine, she said it was terrible, not what she asked for at all, and she picked up my exercise book and threw it at my head. She had those angry glasses that go up at the corners. She asked the whole class to think up a punishment for me. I remember the smell from the oil heater, and a different, sick smell from the crate of milk bottles next to it. There must have been twenty children in the room, but only one put her hand up, Marjorie, who thought I should miss playtime, which wasn't a problem to me because it was freezing out. Anyway, when Marjorie sat down, Tracy suddenly stood up and said she liked my story, and she didn't think I should get any punishments. Of course I never forgot her. It's one of my earliest memories. Think about what it must have been like to get up like that in front of everyone, to defend the new boy, with Mrs Gryce so terrifying.'

'One of your earliest memories? You were six not three,' I said unsympathetically. I was startled when Victor confirmed that he remembered almost nothing from before the age of six.

'I didn't even learn to talk until I was five,' he said. 'They thought I was backward.'

I told him I clearly remembered being two, maybe less.

'Mrs Tabo would say you're a reincarnation, you moved straight from another life to this one. Can I have some more of that horrible drink? It tastes of tin.' He swung his legs onto the table, his face somewhat brighter; talk of the past seemed to cheer him.

I poured the rest of the Cinzano and told him about my own first memory, aged two, under the same kitchen table we were sitting at, a stockade of legs all around, voices like gulls above my roof. I had been given a glass box (probably just hard plastic) with sugared almonds inside: iced pebbles in emerald, lilac, rose, snow white, morning blue. The box wouldn't open, and I didn't have words, so I pushed it upward at people's knees. A preoccupied stranger took it but handed it back unopened; the almonds trapped, enchanted in their glass casket, infinitely desirable in proportion to their inaccessibility. Later, when the words came, they arrived in colour.

We heard footsteps on the landing overhead and Victor stood up, retrieved his outer garments from the floor, then hesitated at the door.

'There's a couple of other things I never told you. Tracy's mother was in trouble, when she was a child. She was about nine and she ran away with another kid, a boy. He was younger. You can guess where they went. They were missing overnight, police searching everywhere. Nothing happened, they just strolled out of the Fall on the Silent Road in the morning and a woman walking her dog found them. Mum remembers it, because the little boy lived next door but one. A week later the little boy was killed by a car; nothing to do with Tracy's mother, but people seemed to connect the two things, and nobody was allowed to play with Irene Tabb after that.' The other thing, he said, was that Tracy was put into care when she was five, after her mother died. 'Only a few weeks, until Mrs Tabb could cope, but Tracy remembers it. A place in Redruth, and she went back again a couple more times, a few years later.'

After that I began to wonder if Victor was wrong in his protective attitude to Tracy, whether she was actually more robust than any of us. In Mrs Gryce's classroom, I would have been among the children sitting silent, neither complicit like Marjorie, nor courageous. And I thought of Tracy alone on the Fall. If I went up there by myself it was always in daylight, and I kept to the path, avoiding Geneva. Except once. The previous September I had decided to spend an afternoon alone there; I would work at the table, I thought, read, or do all my homework in advance and have an easy week. Perhaps I would pick apples, or blackberries, for my mother. I took a thermos of coffee. When I arrived though I found myself becalmed under the glass of the veranda, sweating in the greenhouse air, suddenly reluctant to step into the bright empty quiet of the sitting room. I looked at the green cane chairs, the mossy mirror, the clock that said 11.22, and I understood why nobody had ever disturbed us here. The veranda itself was now almost detached from the house. Beyond it, the slope of the sitting room floor, always noticeable, was sharper, rising up towards the main interior wall at an angle of ten degrees. To get into the corridor leading to the kitchen, you had to step over a hole two feet wide in which an elder bush had sprouted. Wainscots gaped, cracks crept like roots up white walls. The front section of Geneva, obeying the shifts in the earth beneath, was slowly splitting from the back, moving in the direction of the shore. Outside, recent fissures cut across older slippages, and a huge ash tree had joined the slide to the sea, its roots pulled up like a skirt behind it.

I saw it all with the eyes of a stranger, and no sensible stranger would step into this house, even if they ignored the isolation, the fence, the brambles, the council's warning notice. I did step in, however, and I made myself sit for a while at the table and watch a sapphire dragonfly flicker over the grass, the sea holding its breath beyond. How strong would you have to be to stay here for days and nights, quite alone, seeing only the beauty, not the danger?

On the way back, as the telegraph wires whistled along the Silent Road, I remembered Raymond's story of the Erlking and the dead child, and how Tracy said she sometimes saw the bushes stirring and rippling as she walked by, even on still days, as if something were echoing her progress. 'It's only the wind in the trees.' Like Tracy, I often felt safer in the woods than anywhere else, but there were times when I avoided looking behind me.

11

The police came a couple of days after my talk with Victor. I never had time to go back to the library and consult law books about dead bodies. Two police officers, a man and a woman, three firm knocks at the door. It was Saturday, early; my mother had just gone to work and I was expecting to see the postman. They asked me my name, my date of birth, and said they wanted to talk to me about some 'new information' relating to a death in 1976.

The police station hadn't changed since the time we were arrested for trespassing all those years ago. I thought I would see Kerenza, Victor and Tracy there, but there was nobody, and I was left alone in a room with a table and four chairs, wondering what they would think at the Bonaparte when I didn't turn up for my shift. A window of frosted glass, contorted in bloated swirls and crude blisters, projected a swarm of semicircular shadows on the opposite wall like the bacteria in my biology textbook.

The woman was Detective Sergeant Sharon Pengelly, and the man was Detective Inspector Iain Greaves, though I only discovered their names later. DS Pengelly asked most of the questions, sitting directly opposite, while DI Greaves, dark and neat, sat alongside her, writing notes on his knee, occasionally asking me to clarify something. They did not shout or fire off questions, but spoke neutrally, as if they were merely interested in my experiences and would like my opinion on their research. DS Pengelly was always very still; even her hands were motionless on the tabletop and when she blinked it was an event. She had a face that should have been allocated to someone less intelligent: snub-featured, broad, with eyes so wide apart it was impossible to look into them both at the same time. She poured me a glass of water, and after asking me again to confirm my age, date of birth and address, said that they had received new information relating to the death of Clara Deborah Selman in August 1976, which led them to believe that I had seen the body of the young girl on August 22nd, 1976, and could I tell them, from the beginning, what I remembered about that day. They called it a 'witness statement'.

My memory of the story I told has blurred with what I had said in the conversations with Victor and Kerenza, but it must have been something similar. When I had finished, they asked me, repeatedly, to repeat everything, including the full names of my friends. I guessed it was Kerenza who had come to the station with her 'new information', and though I had no idea how she would have presented it, she must have given our names, so I didn't hesitate. What time had we left St Anthony, what time did I think we had arrived at Geneva (they called it the 'derelict cottage'), did I see anyone else there, how long had we spent there before going down to the sea, and, over and over, what had I seen in the sea. The pressure of the questions brought some details into focus (the blue dress with the silver buttons, the long hair), but when they asked me what the others were doing, I was for a while unable to answer, the pictures would not come forward, and underneath was a tangle of unknowns – had the others already been questioned? What would they have said? At the same time I was trying to recall what I had already said to them. Why hadn't I taken Victor seriously when he told me he was afraid Kerenza would contact the police, and why hadn't we all talked about this openly, agreeing what we would say, when we had the chance?

Then came the question I had been expecting: 'Why didn't you tell anyone? Why didn't you report it?' I told them what I had told Kerenza, but in doing so I had to cut out all the parts that sounded stupid – the stories, the games, the fears, the imaginary inhabitants of the woods and sea. And with those gone, the reasoning behind our failure to say anything felt thin. I found myself repeating that we were eleven, we weren't sure what we had seen, we were scared that our parents would find out we had been on the Fall.

'How did you know she was dead?'

'We weren't sure, but she wasn't moving.'

'Did you touch her?'

'No.'

'Did anyone touch her?'

'I don't think so.'

'Did you know Clara Selman?'

'No.'

'Did Tracy Pender know Clara Selman? Did you ever hear her mention her before?'

'No, no.'

'Who said that you should not report what you found?'

'Nobody, or nobody in particular, it was all of us, we never talked about it.'

I kept checking the two of them for a reaction to my answers, the little changes of expression (encouraging, doubtful, interested, irritated) you would see on a teacher's or a parent's face, but there was nothing, it was like talking on the telephone. Nor did the questions follow from what I had just said; instead they doubled back on themselves, or ran off at tangents, nipping my attention at the heels, fencing it in.

'Did you see Victor Jordan touch the body?'

'He might have, once, just lightly.'

'He might have. Did Victor Jordan know Clara Selman?'

'No.'

'When did you all decide not to report it?'

'We didn't. It wasn't really a decision.'

'Did you see Tracy Pender touch Clara?'

'I can't remember.'

'Did you see Tracy Pender near the body?'

'Not really. We were just standing on the beach. I think we put some flowers on her, and Tracy put some shells on her.'

'On Clara Selman's body?'

'Yes.'

DI Greaves put his pad down and leaned forward, clicking his biro on the table.

'Who was Whistling Jack?'

'What? Nobody. That was just a story.'

'Whose story?'

'Tracy's. She wrote it.'

'Isn't it true that the story involved a knife, somebody stabbing somebody else?'

'No, well.' I gave them a rough outline of 'Whistling Jack and the Queen of Pearl', the words toneless under the striplight, dropping like coins before their eyes.

'The story was about selkies,' I added. 'We used to pretend to be selkies, people who change into seals.'

'Did you play with a knife?'

'No. There wasn't a real knife. It was just a game.'

He sat back, glanced at DS Pengelly, and she opened a folder and took out a plastic envelope. She slipped something from it, and placed it carefully on the table in front of me. It was a photograph.

'Can you look at this photograph, please, Sally, and tell us if you recognise anyone in it?'

I saw the shape of a young girl lying in a pool of shallow water, a rockpool. Clara Selman was slightly tilted towards the camera, her face half-covered in dark bands of hair. Bent over her was a small figure, a child with thick straight hair, hair so bright the photograph reproduced it as an undifferentiated blaze of light. The child was clearly Tracy, and from the way her arms were extended, it appeared as if her hands were hovering around the throat of the figure in the sea. There was nobody else in the photograph.

I found out later that I had been the last to be interviewed by the police. After Kerenza's initial approach to them, she had given her own witness statement. Her parents had been present throughout, because she, like Tracy, had not yet passed her seventeenth birthday, and she was considered a juvenile under the law. It was Kerenza who had provided the photograph. I suppose this should not have been such a shock, that a photograph existed. When she was eleven she used to carry that camera everywhere, the little Kodak her uncle Maurice had given her, taking pictures of ants' nests, jellyfish, moths – whatever struck her as worthy of record. I don't recall her taking pictures of any people, not even us, and she never showed us any photos from film that had been developed, but just because we didn't see her take any did not mean she hadn't done so when our attention was elsewhere. There would have been many opportunities.

After seeing that photo, the police had called Tracy in.

Tracy, who would have been taken entirely by surprise given that she had been excluded from our conversations with Kerenza and about Kerenza, denied that anyone was up at Geneva that day apart from herself. It was Victor who told me this, and Victor, interviewed later the same day, who put them right, confirming that all four of us had been there. He would have guessed Tracy would be wary of getting anyone else into trouble. Whenever I think of that interview, Tracy Pender and the broad-faced policewoman in that grey place, my imagination fails. I think of the questions about times and dates and decisions, joint agreements, knives and photographs, and then Tracy's answers – what would she have told them? What would they have made of Mrs Tabb, who sat in on the interview – Hazel Tabb with her infinitely slippery perspective on time and history? It was like trying to imagine a conversation between different species, and while Tracy herself believed such conversations to be perfectly possible, it is doubtful the police would have agreed. But I could be wrong, perhaps Tracy was able to make a clear distinction between her eleven-year-old self and the present one, perhaps she sensed that the police station was not the place to talk about the afterlife, selkies, or restless spirits, and confined herself to a simple account of what she remembered and what she did not. I reminded myself that Tracy's usual defence was silence.

My mother refused to accept that I had been on the Fall at all, particularly not on the day in question. She insisted that we – my parents and I – had gone to Falmouth, and then stopped at Mawnan Church.

'I remember it well because we had tea there, and Walter found that pamphlet about a giant owl. I told him off because I thought it was too frightening for you at that age. It wasn't until later that we heard about the missing girl.'

When I told her I had never gone with them to Mawnan, that the trip was earlier, and my father had told me the Owlman story in the kitchen at home, she wouldn't have it.

'You've got the times mixed up, Sally,' she said, reminding me of other times I had been convinced I remembered something – a fairground in Wales, for instance, which had in fact been in Sussex. 'The police must have just assumed you were there because you were friendly with Kerenza and the other two.'

That my mother could be so adamantly mistaken was unnerving, like the time Penny Nankervis, the prototypical grown-up, had insisted there was only one species of moth, the sort that ate her jumpers. It was tempting to give in, to agree with my mother's version, to say the others were lying or confused. It would have been easy. Perhaps she was right, perhaps I had not actually seen a woman, I was remembering a different day, or tales told by the others which I had confused with the Queen of Pearl in the story. My mother would go down to the police station and explain that I had been thirty miles away, and an alternative memory would form quite easily: a drowsy afternoon, a church in a wood, my father telling me about the Owlman over tea in Falmouth, the long drive back, arriving home to see the lights coming on around the harbour, far too late to see a corpse drifting ashore.

Once, early that summer when we were eleven, we had passed a police officer coming up Torbett's Hill as we were on our way back from Geneva. We had all frozen, the police station experience still fresh in our minds, but this was a different, elderly policeman, for whom we were unknown innocents. He warned us, indulgently stern, about the dangers of the Fall. When he turned to resume his breathy progress uphill, we had behaved strangely: Victor did a cartwheel and shouted rude words, Kerenza and I jigged about, making faces at each other, Tracy twirled and sang like a drunken ballerina. We withdrew into an adult's version of childish behaviour, meeting the policeman's expectations – children pretending to be children.

These strategic retreats were no longer possible now, and when I told my mother there had been visitors staying that weekend, Juliet and Richard from London, she was thrown off balance. Richard and Juliet had never been back to St Anthony since, and the fact I remembered them at all surprised her. Whatever I said, though, was received with incredulity. Why would I have been out on the Fall when I knew it was dangerous? Why was Kerenza Nankervis telling such strange stories to the police? What were her parents thinking of, and why hadn't they been in touch? Why were the police taking any notice of what we said – nobody in their right mind would pay attention to the memories of children, especially when those children were now teenagers trying to recall one lost afternoon six years earlier, a third of our lifetime ago.

Around lunchtime the next day, the police called me back in. This time my mother came with me to the station and sat in the waiting area. Most of the questions were about Tracy. They put the photograph in front of me again.

'Please look carefully again at the photograph. What was Tracy Pender doing with her hands?'

'She was putting shells on, mother-of-pearl shells, like the story.'

'What story?'

'Whistling Jack.'

'We've now read Whistling Jack.'

This threw me. Had Tracy kept the story? Or perhaps Kerenza or Victor picked it up off the grass that day, after Tracy read it to us. The idea of the police having it, handling the old lined paper, was somehow appalling.

'There is nothing in the story about putting shells on a body,' said DS Pengelly.

Tracy's story flickered and spat like a damp candle. I could not have retold it, then.

'Where were you when this photograph was taken?'

'I think I was collecting flowers.'

'Why were you doing that?'

'To put on her. Tracy said we should put flowers on the woman, whistling jacks.'

'In the story, Whistling Jack is a man. Was there a man with you?'

'No, it was just a story. Whistling Jack was the man in the story.'

'But you just told us the whistling jacks were flowers.'

'It's both.'

She asked me again about the flowers. They had looked up whistling jacks, she said, in a botanical book, which said that they flowered only in May and June. 'We are talking about August 22nd. An exceptionally hot dry summer. Those flowers would have been long over.'

I was silent, twisting at my hair, DS Pengelly still looking straight at my face.

'Sally. I want you to think very carefully, and remember that if you don't tell us the whole truth now, you could be in more serious trouble later on.'

DI Greaves, who had been leaning back as usual, sat forward and give her a sharp look which I could not interpret. She paused, then asked me to describe, again, what I had seen when I first came down to the beach. Had I seen her, Clara, move at all?

'When Victor touched her, I think I saw her arm move.'

'You saw her arm move. Did you see her move again?'

'No.' What if she had still been alive?

'So you assumed she was dead?'

'Yes, I suppose so. I didn't think about it.'

'Did any of the others tell you she was dead?'

'No.'

'So none of you checked to see if she was still alive? And you all left her there, and went back to the derelict house? You never said anything to anyone?'

She insisted I confirm all this, and then I had a moment of clarity, or rather an awareness of making a strenuous effort to translate my eleven-year-old mind by applying the wisdom of seventeen.

'I think we thought it was none of our business. We thought she was a grown-up, and someone, another grown-up, would already know about it, know what to do, and we should just leave it. We didn't realise it was important. We were not supposed to be there at all, on the Fall, like I said, and we were afraid of being found out, that seemed the most important thing.'

I sat back, dropped my shoulders, quite pleased with the maturity of my analysis, my ability to distance myself from the past. DI Greaves unfurled himself and bent his thin dark face towards me.

'Were you afraid of Tracy Pender?'

'What?'

'Did she ever threaten you?'

'No, of course not.' I almost laughed.

'You have told us it was her idea to spend time on the Fall. Her idea to go trespassing that time when you were all caught and cautioned, then her idea to break in to the abandoned house on the Fall...'

'We didn't break in...'

'...Her idea that dead people change into seals, and it was her story you all listened to, about Whistling Jack, the knife, the stabbing, and you all made a play, a drama, out of this story, you said, acting it out over and over again on that beach.'

'No, it was all of us, the story was just part of it, we all had stories, books, games – we shared them.'

'But Tracy started the games, didn't she? It was always her idea.'

'No.'

'Tracy Pender is very pretty, isn't she? You all admired her, followed her?'

'It wasn't like that.'

'So it was Victor Jordan's idea?'

And so it went on, in circles; every question I answered, every attempt to shut down one line of questioning, opened a door to another. They seemed determined to lead me to isolate one person from the others, and obsessed by the idea that one of us must have been 'the leader'. Once, though, DS Pengelly made a mistake. She suggested that Tracy, in her interview, had told a different version, she had told them it was I who had written 'Whistling Jack and the Queen of Pearl', that it was my idea to 'cover up' the body of Clara. This was such an obvious fiction that I relaxed and was able to say with confidence, 'I don't believe you.'

'Why not?'

'Because she would never do that. Betray anyone.'

'How can you be sure?'

'Because she's a good person.'

'Good people do strange things,' said DI Greaves.

They had asked me almost nothing about Kerenza, and it was this, the sense that she alone was somehow evading scrutiny, together with my own treacherous desire to please – to give these police, these adults, something – that led me to say what I said next. I told them how, on the day we saw Clara Selman's body, I had seen Penny Nankervis with a man in the woods on the Fall, and I told them that the man was Mark Hocking.

12

There is a widespread idea that people in small places all know each other, that we form a protective network, an extended family or tribe, each member taking a keen interest in the affairs of the others. In my experience this is not the case. Lives in small towns and large villages run along the same closed mappings of family, work, corner shop, pub, bus, supermarket, school and friends as they do in cities, just as foxes prefer to take the same narrow paths through the undergrowth, until their tracks look crisply demarcated, planned, like the efficient infrastructure of some hidden race of children. You could be a hermit as easily in a village as a city, though in the village it is perhaps more likely that at least one person would suspect you were there, the dog fox by the railway, the vixen raising cubs in the thicket behind the bowling green. It is only when something goes wrong that this changes and the community knitting gets tight.

The police had not called me back since the second interview. It was half-term, a week off, a relief not to have to face the possibility that people knew I had been questioned. On the other hand there was nothing to do at home, I was nervous about going out, and I had heard nothing from the others, no phone calls, no visits. It was as if they had been reclaimed and reabsorbed by their families, independence shrivelling in the first spell of rough weather. I called once at Tracy's house, but there was no answer. I got up late and paced around, making toast, interrogating and answering myself, prosecuting and defending, speculating on what the police thought, what might my friends have said, what they thought I had said, what were they thinking right now, where were they. From my attic I watched the street below for anyone coming around the corner, and by afternoon I was usually back in bed with the cat, clouds racing across the skylight, re-reading books I'd read many times; I had always preferred knowing what was going to happen. A brownish adolescent herring gull paced the roof opposite; it made a constant plaintive keening and whistling for its parents. There were no cargo ships in Lantern Bay.

The next Saturday however I had to go to the Bonaparte to make beds. Mavis and I were on the first-floor landing when we heard a police radio downstairs. I leaned over the banister. I couldn't see Raymond, but heard his slow, hospitable voice talking to the officers, his polite surprise. They would have found him in his usual foxhole behind the old bar, reading, making reverent notes on Grand Houses, though he was allowed this indulgence less often now that Carole was in charge. Mavis joined me at the banister and three heads emerged suddenly into Reception, two policemen with Raymond Nankervis between them, the hair combed thin on top of his head. Mavis knew, by some instinct shared by many in St Anthony, that it was about Clara Selman. They don't believe us, I thought, they must want to hear what our parents say. But Mavis said, 'I'm not that surprised.

All these young ones about the place all the time. The way he looks at Tracy Pender. People talk.'

Kerenza rang me. They had interviewed her mother, she said, and Mark Hocking. 'Mark's fuming. Someone said something, some busybody who thought they'd seen them both on the Fall on the day of Clara Seaman. As if anyone would remember that from years ago.'

Mark had been on the telephone to his solicitor, and had barked at his clients and lost a sale. Her mother on the other hand was calm. 'She's good in a crisis. But nobody's been into the bar all week. Not a single customer. There's a couple from Manchester staying upstairs, they must think the Bonaparte is the most depressing hotel in Cornwall. It probably is. And Carole has gone. Packed all her horrible reeking clothes and left, the day the police came.'

'But what were they talking to your father about?' Perhaps I ought to go back to the police, explain that they had misunderstood, that it was only Penny and Mark I had seen on the Fall that day, not Raymond.

'What do you think? They still have no idea who did it. So they're just looking at people to do with us, because we found Clara first. Dad's gone very quiet. He's started drinking Calvados in his office. He never does that. And he's had an anonymous letter, I found it on his desk. It's quite good, with words cut out of a newspaper like a punk record cover.'

Kerenza's dispassionate, pragmatic view of the world had, as always, a stabilising effect, dialling down the chatter of anxiety. I allowed myself to imagine a day in the future, all of us sitting in a row at the end of the harbour with our legs in the sun, laughing at the police, wondering how we ever thought any of it was our fault. I had planned to ask Kerenza a great many questions, about the photograph and Tracy's story and what had happened in her interview, but I was so tired.

When I returned to school Tracy and Victor were both absent. Everything else was ordinary, at least at first; everybody wrapped in reassuring self-absorption. Once, towards the end of the week, I walked by a huddle of fourth-years; one of them glanced over, a ripple of whispers passed through the group and they turned and stared. After that I started to wonder if the teachers seemed too carefully neutral; only Miss Rescorla, the still eye of every hurricane, was her pedantic, scrupulously impartial self. On the Friday afternoon I was cornered in the cloakrooms by a group of pupils in my year. They wanted to know about Tracy, was she coming back, had the police arrested her, what had she done, did she make me do anything, was Victor in trouble too? They seemed not to know the police had interviewed me as well, so I was able to plead ignorance. I was hurrying out, stuffing papers into my bag, when one of them called after me, 'What was Tracy doing in that photo?'

I soon discovered that everyone seemed to know about that photograph. I doubt whether anyone had actually seen it, but a description must have leaked out. The image of Tracy, her gold hair falling forward as she bent over Clara Selman in the water, had been discussed, reimagined, dissected, retouched – fingered by the minds of strangers just as thoroughly, if not quite as fast, as a photo would be shared between phones today. After that, the trickle of glances, whispers, rumours and evasions gathered force and became a cascade.

Miss Rescorla sent me out of class one morning to deliver a bundle of reports to the headteacher's office. She had been telling us about the hanging of Martha Brown, how the young Thomas Hardy ('he was exactly your age') had witnessed Martha's execution outside Dorchester prison in 1856, recalling later 'what a fine figure she showed as she hung in the misty rain, and how the tight black silk gown set off her shape as she wheeled half round and back'.

The headteacher's door was shut and I could hear her on the phone, so I sat on the chair outside to wait. This chair was set against a wall, near the reception desk but screened from it. The school secretary was talking to a woman, a parent or perhaps one of the dinner staff. It was the fervent hush in their voices that attracted my attention.

'There must be something to it, though, mustn't there,' the woman was saying. I could hear Mrs Marsh, the secretary, creaking her huge bottom around on her swivel chair.

'Well, Tracy Pender was always a teasy one, not quite with it, broken home, but I never picked up on anything really wrong. But the photo, yes, I heard she was doing something... it doesn't bear thinking about, does it? That poor young girl, Clara.'

I pictured Mrs Marsh's prominent eyes as she talked, eyes that were sorrowful and deeply sympathetic even when she was reminding you to fill in some form or other.

'Tracy Pender's mother was unbalanced, wasn't she?' the other voice said. 'I heard she jumped off the harbour wall. It was in the paper. And the grandmother, I don't think she's quite compos mentis. I expect Tracy told the police a lot of nonsense. Do you know anything about the others involved?'

'Victor Jordan's a bit of a tearaway, but nothing unusual. From a nice local family as well. And there's Sally Martins, quite a bright girl, but she's from upcountry. I don't know the other one. What on earth did they think they were doing?'

'They were old enough to tell right from wrong, that's for sure,' said the other woman. 'I know my two do, and they're younger than eleven. It must be tricky for the school, mustn't it? My husband says there's reporters around.'

A boy called Adam had asked me out. When he failed to turn up at our agreed meeting place on the harbour on Friday, I assumed he had gone on ahead to Betty's indoor teahouse. Adam wasn't in Betty's. I sat down anyway, inspecting the fretful sea, waiting for Maggie to come over. She didn't. I went up to the counter, where she was sitting on a stool, talking to another woman. She didn't smile, or say, 'All right, my bird?'

'A cup of tea, please, and an éclair.'

She got down heavily, moved over to the tea urn and clattered a saucer and plate on the counter. I still didn't understand. 'Maggie, is Tracy starting tomorrow or is it next week?'

'I've already told Mrs Tabb the Saturday hours are filled now. I'll bring your tea over.'

I drank the tea too fast, burning my throat, Maggie's hushed chatting inaudible through the screens of anoraks. But I knew exactly which clichés she would select: no smoke without fire, everything happens for a reason. I never ate the éclair, but I did ring Adam when I got home. He was polite, passive.

'I didn't think it was a definite arrangement. I ran into someone else after school.'

'Do you still want to see *The Day the Earth Caught Fire*? It's got tornadoes and forest fires, and the Arctic melts...'

He didn't really. It was an old film and sounded childish. And there was a lot going on at school – rugby practice, the play, essays. 'I don't think I'm going to have much time.'

On Saturday night I went out alone. I would go to the rocks by the harbour, smoke, watch the lighthouses flashing. Or perhaps for a drink at the Crabber, sit outside at the back, meet a trawlerman. It was barely ten o'clock, but the streets were deserted until Market Square, and the few people I saw there seemed to be already on their way home. The Crabber was also bleakly empty; I took my lager out into the courtyard, and, too late, spotted Geoff the Pylon there. Of unknown age, Geoff was a local authority on drugs; we had named him Geoff the Pylon in homage to his skeletal height and the airy vacancy of his face and conversation. He used to tantalise us, describing the manic delights of cocaine and speed, but all he ever supplied were dirty little nubs of cannabis. The conversation that followed consisted of me lying about foreign countries I would soon be travelling to, and Geoff explaining that he had been to every one, none of them were what they were cracked up to be, and that anyway they had sunk into fatal decline since his visit.

'You should definitely split, though. Lots of chins wagging about you right now. Just saying.'

I suddenly wanted to leave very much, just walk to Trebeere station and get on the first train out. Perhaps Kerenza was right and Tracy and Victor would never leave St Anthony. Maybe I should distance myself from them to avoid finding myself like Geoff the Pylon, years into the future, depressing young strangers in pubs with my reflex cynicism.

Crossing Market Square on my way back I heard the thump of a bin being overturned, a clatter of cans and bottles. A voice I knew shouted, 'Fuck off, fuck off, for fuck's sake,' and Victor emerged from behind the Ruby Tiger. He had a cut on his cheek and he could hardly move his right arm, but he threw the left one out and then tried to hug me.

'I terrified the bastards, Sally. They weren't expecting that at all, thought I'd just walk on by.'

He seemed elated, repeating himself, but not drunk. The streets were silent: I glanced down the alley – no sign of his assailants. I didn't need to be told that the fight was about Tracy. He had been on his way to see her, but Mrs Tabb told him she had gone up to the Fall. I discovered why he and Tracy had been so elusive – they had gone to Truro, Victor said, after the police interviews, staying in his brother Paul's student house near the hospital.

'It got a bit tense at home. Paul's been pretty good. We just turned up late one evening, but he opened the door without a word and made up a bed in the corner.' Tracy, he said, was in reasonable spirits. She has told the truth, he said, the way she sees it. 'This will blow over, Sally.' He was sure of this because he had worked out that all our stories for the police agreed with each other. 'That's what the police do, set people against each other, trap you, make you incriminate someone. But we didn't.'

The only worry was that a social worker had called at Tracy's house to talk to her nan, and he wasn't sure why.

'Would Tracy mind if I went round?' I said.

'Don't be stupid. She'd love it.'

Despite the low pay, my mother enjoyed her job in the café at Trebeere Museum, and she was making sculpture again – the same ecstatic running figures, but this time on a miniature scale, the animals larger than the people, a series she called *Añoranza y Saudade*. If it were not for my troubles, she would have been on her way back to a happier time, and she was more inclined to be sanguine about events than she would have been a few years earlier. But she warned me against going to see Tracy. She had absorbed the idea, probably from conversations overheard, that Tracy was, if not the cause of my difficulty, then somehow at the heart of it.

'Tracy has a troubled background. Perhaps you should let other people help her first, professional people who know what they're doing. She may be quite an unhappy girl, really. She's certainly difficult to get to know. And so unlike you. I never really saw what you had in common.'

'She doesn't seem unhappy to me,' I said.

She never seemed angry, either. It was the aspect of Tracy I found most puzzling. Where Victor was defiant, she was impervious; she did not react as young people are supposed to. Victor told me it had been no different when they were eight.

'The teacher sent us all outside to trap insects in glass jars. Tracy didn't like the idea, so she just lay flat on the floor. They shouted, argued, pulled her by the arms, the headteacher came, all the other children were standing round watching, but she just lay down again, eyes shut, her arms by her sides.'

Tracy was sitting like a gull on the top step outside Number Five, as if she knew I was coming, though Mrs Tabb still had no telephone. It was early March, bright but with a hardness in the air, a false spring. I climbed the steps and sat beside her. As usual, she started talking about me.

'Congratulations about the French Revolution. Vic told me. Why didn't you say anything?'

I had won a school prize for my history project. 'How are you? When are you coming back to school?'

'I'm all right. I told them the truth. But Victor was right, the police never believe you. They went to his house as well, asking his parents questions. You can imagine the row. That's why we had to go to Paul's in Truro, and then Paul told us they'd been to see him too, the police.'

I started telling her about what I thought had happened in 1976, before asking her what she remembered.

'I remember everything,' she said. 'We saw the woman in the rock pool. I thought she was the Queen of Pearl, she looked exactly the same. She was stranded by the tide. I put the shells on her, and you put the whistling jacks on her dress. Then we went back to Geneva and saw all the moths.'

I felt ridiculously grateful that she remembered the whistling jacks. After my last police interview I had looked up the whistling jack, *gladiolus communis, subspecies byzantinus*, in a botanical book, fully expecting to find the police had made a mistake about their flowering time. They had not. But if the whistling jacks had been finished long before August, what were we both remembering? Tracy was accurate about plants.

'Did you realise she was dead?' I asked. 'Because I'm not sure if I did.'

'I suppose so. She looked like someone who was changing into something else.'

I told her what I had discovered, in the library, about Clara Selman. Echoing my own thoughts, she said Clara sounded like someone she would like.

'Tracy, you do realise why the police wanted to talk to us?'

'She died, and they can't find out why.'

'Do you ever feel bad about it, not telling anyone?'

'No. We helped her to return to the sea.'

I had forgotten how confident, how unshakeably certain, Tracy was about ethical questions, her eyes with the same grave expression they had in childhood. Her account of what we saw was as uncompromising as Kerenza's; nevertheless I sensed a difference, though it was hard to define.

People, I said, were talking. 'At school, in the shops, about us. And they know about Kerenza's photo of you.'

'Don't worry, Sally, that always happens.'

* * *

Everyone said it was the worry over Tracy that led to Hazel Tabb's accident. She left work at Carmelow's bakery one afternoon and walked straight into the road. The driver slammed into her right side, and Mrs Tabb's colleagues saw everything from behind the cake display in the shop window: 'She was knocked flying, rolled over and over down the hill like a bolt of cloth,' one of them told the local paper. The lapse of attention seemed uncharacteristic of Hazel Tabb. I was never sure exactly how old she was: her face was ploughed with lines, but her body was supple and quick. She used to stride up the steep hills, laden with bags, like a woman of thirty, and Tracy told me her grandmother's hearing was so good she could still hear bats squeaking in the dusk. Nor did Mrs Tabb have any history of worrying unduly about her granddaughter. A month or so after the accident, Carmelow's was taken over by a larger bakery; I wondered if she had been told something that day, about her job. Perhaps the new owners required their shop assistants to use the full complement of English tenses.

She lived, but her hip was badly broken and she spent a while in the Truro hospital. During that time, many decisions were made by people in authority. It was decided, quite reasonably, that Mrs Tabb would no longer be able to manage the steep and often slippery steps up to Number Five. I suspect also that the unedited presence of the past in her conversation may have encouraged social workers and health professionals to make unsubtle judgements about her mental competence.

It is not difficult to imagine how it went:

'Mrs Tabb, Hazel, seems to experience difficulty in distinguishing clearly between her granddaughter, Tracy, and her daughter, Irene, who passed away twelve years ago, taking her own life. Several times during our interview, Hazel (they would certainly have referred to her familiarly as Hazel), in responding to a question about her granddaughter, talked instead about the daughter. On a prior occasion Hazel told an outreach worker that her daughter had disappeared into the woods with a four-year-old boy, which necessitated time-consuming checks with the police to confirm that the incident was in fact historic. Furthermore, she continually confuses past and present in conversation, even when talking about simple practical matters. This tendency was also noted by police officers during the interviews with her granddaughter Tracy, interviews which Hazel attended in compliance with the procedures for juveniles. Her grasp of the current situation is therefore fragile. She shows little understanding of the difficulties faced by her granddaughter and she appears to suffer from the delusion that Tracy, a vulnerable and unstable sixteen-year-old involved in a serious police inquiry, is in possession of some type of supernatural power. She permits Tracy to wander at will on the hazardous landslip area known as the Fall, even after dark, thus exposing her to serious physical risk. In view of this state of affairs we consider that Hazel Tabb is no longer in a position to take responsibility for Tracy, and recommend that she, Mrs Tabb, is found alternative sheltered accommodation with the local authority.'

This is pure conjecture of course – they may have said nothing of the sort. But the effect was the same, and when Mrs Tabb finally left hospital it was to a tiny bungalow, one of several supervised by a warden, at the top of the village on the same estate where Victor's family lived. She would no longer have to negotiate her mossy steps; she would however be faced with a journey of half a mile to the shops in St Anthony, via one of the steepest hills in Cornwall. I suppose Mrs Tabb imagined Tracy would stay on at Number Five on her own. It was Victor who told me about the accident and the bungalow, how he and Tracy had managed one visit to hospital, but after that I heard nothing for two or three weeks. If Tracy was perpetually absent, and Victor wouldn't keep me informed, I would just leave them to it.

A red armchair, a chest of drawers painted with bees and vines, a lampstand, a cupboard, and a matronly sofa stood about in the lane outside Tracy's house like cornered sheep – uneasy, but still vaguely hopeful. A man stood in the doorway holding a box of crockery; another man was jogging down the slate steps, big trainers pointing outwards, two of Mrs Tabb's high-backed kitchen chairs hanging off his arms. He swung the chairs onto the road and they skittered down the slope on their thin legs before falling against the sofa.

'Is there much upstairs?' he shouted to the man by the door.

'No, just a few knick-knacks.'

The bright furniture looked quite festive on the green lane. The men must be taking everything up to Mrs Tabb's new bungalow, I thought. Would it fit? Would they leave enough behind for Tracy? There was no sign of her. I stamped back down Glebe Lane lost in irritation; how dare that man use a repulsive term like 'knick-knacks' to describe Tracy's luminous shells. Near the bottom of the hill the pavement was blocked by the width of Victor's mother, Bridget Jordan, ploughing her way up. Victor's nephew Jason was with her. Now around eight, Jason was still remarkably good-looking, and I was encouraged to note hints of his uncle in his scowling, uncooperative demeanour.

'Aha Sally,' said Bridget, 'I thought it was you, doggetting down the hill. It's for the best, you know. Hazel hasn't been right for a while, gone a bit cakey. And as for *her,* well, she's never been a help to anyone. Best place for her, where she's to. But you with all your studying, life ahead of you, you could have your pick of friends. You need to learn to tell the pilchards from the pezzacks though, like I tell Victor. Some people are full of cobwebs and shadows.'

This speech of Mrs Jordan's being even less intelligible than usual, I thought little of it, but – again as usual – I was trailing in the wake of events.

A letter came for me at Pellow Street. This is the second of the two letters Tracy sent me, the one I still have. For the sake of clarity, I've adjusted her spelling and punctuation.

St Levan House,
Devonport Avenue,
Plymouth
March 21, 1982

Dear Sally,

I'm writing this at 2am. There's a dog somewhere outside. It's been barking for hours, the sirens excite it, it thinks they are wolves. It's too hot, radiators on even at night. Vic has been twice. I haven't told anyone here we're getting married. The first time, Paul drove him up, and then last Saturday he came by train. Everything here is new and everything is upstairs; downstairs it's just offices. It all smells of plastic, quite nice, like Play-Doh, or the groundsheet in Vic's old tent. The floors are thick blue plastic and instead of wainscots the walls curve into the floors like a boat, and some of the people here come from miles upcountry, as far as Liverpool and Brighton. Nan always says nothing is ever as bad as you think it's going to be before you get there.

We can smoke in the lounge and have baths whenever we want, although they won't let us stay in bed in the mornings. You'd like my room because it's so neat. The staff say we should feel free to make a mess, so everyone does the opposite. We have a competition for the tidiest room: we fold our towels into perfect squares and go round with a ruler to check our books are level with the edge of the desk. I nearly won the other day, but I had the window open and a bumblebee came in and scared the judge.

I'm older than most of the girls here. Mrs Barfield [I think this was her social worker] said it's because I'm a Transitional. Julie next door is only 13, looks about 10. She won't go anywhere without her duvet. She likes it here because at her last place, which was out in the country, they made them run round a field at night with just underwear on, as a punishment. We sit wrapped up like bears on her bed and do our nails. On the other side there's Maxine who's older but thinks there's a vampire living inside her alarm clock. If the vampire wakes up, it doesn't let Maxine go out of her room. Three of us went in there once when she was having a bath and took the alarm clock and hid it, we thought it might help, but then we found Maxine under the bed, curled up like a woodlouse. She said the vampire was angry with her for losing Time, so we had to put the clock back. The vampire is loud – I hear it at night ticking through the wall.

There's a man on the staff called Chris. He begins every sentence with 'if you just' – 'If you just go down to breakfast now Tracy because it's past eight,' or 'If you just clear your plates quietly after tea, girls, without smashing them.' It's catching, I've started doing it myself. When we knock on Maxine's door he says, 'If you just give Maxine some space, because she has severe mood swings.'

Mrs Barfield said to call her Amanda, they all say that, as if they are your friend. She came to the house after Nan had been a while in Treliske [hospital]. Victor had gone to see Steve [a friend] so I was alone. She kept fluffing her hair in Nan's silver mirror and told me I could pack clothes and photos and small personal things. We don't have any photos, but I took my make-up and a shell. I had to write Vic a note. Her car smelt of her dog, though there was no dog in it. She said I'd be shocked when I saw Plymouth as it is a proper city, so I told her I've been before, with my mother when I was four, but she said I couldn't possibly remember that. I didn't tell her I'd been once with Victor as well.

The worst thing is the road, right outside the front of the Home. Cars and lorries roar and grind along it all the time so we have to keep the lounge windows shut, but sooty stuff still comes in round the edges. There's a video shop on the corner outside, demons and blood and murderers, it smells of mushrooms. The man pushes up behind you when you're looking at the shelves, pretends to tidy the videos. We're not supposed to go in there at all. At night men come and hang about on the street below the lounge, and yesterday a lot of girls came in and pushed all the windows open. They leaned right out, shouting and screaming and swearing down at the men. 'Do you know those men?' I said, but nobody did, so I squeezed myself in with the others and started screaming too. The men shouted back up but we drowned them out, and then Chris came by and said, 'If you can all just calm down and close the window.'

I don't have school because I'm a Transitional, so mostly it feels like waiting for something to happen. Today I had to go to Mrs Carpenter's office, she's the Head of Home, to talk about my Framework. Call me Lorna, she says. Her office is nice – light, freesias in her vase, chairs like pillows – but I never understand what she's saying because she takes so long to say it. The separate words make sense, but once she stops talking I can't remember a single thing, so I just sit there, and at the end she is never as nice as she was at the start. I don't want her to think I'm rude, so this time I took an exercise book with me to make notes. This is what I wrote:

Transitional care

Care leaver issues
Develop a Framework to plan for the future
Evaluate emotional resources
Come to terms with the past
Appropriate attitude
Confront my sexuality
Develop an approach to managing reality
Denial

It didn't really help. I kept thinking about Victor, how he is everything I ever wanted. Ever since we knew we will always be together, it's like getting a huge present each morning that I never asked for or expected or deserved. Then I started thinking of being here and what Nan says about things never being as bad as you expect, and she's right, but only partly, although I've noticed something new: every time they talk about temporary arrangements, or call me a Transitional, I feel like dancing. The whole Home looks different, sparkling. When I know I'm going somewhere else, when something is ending, the place I'm in changes too and looks beautiful. This is a long letter Sally, all about me. When you come up with Victor there's so much I want to ask you.

Love from Tracy.

The visit to Plymouth was difficult. Victor and I went up by train. I paid for both of us, with my savings from the Bonaparte; his parents refused to fund any contact with Tracy, and the previous time he had avoided paying the fare by hiding in the toilet when the guard came round – you could still do that then. I had slammed out of the house after a furious row with my mother.

I had suggested that Tracy move in with us; she could sleep in the box room, or even with me in the attic. My mother had refused even to contemplate it. 'Tracy is in council care. It's not as simple as you think.' One part of me was relieved.

Victor's mood changed from station to station as we trundled up Cornwall's backbone. He was elated at Redruth, where he wrote 'Miss Froy Was Here' on the misty window, furious at Truro when we were told the buffet car was not going to open, depressed at Lostwithiel. By Bodmin Road he had decided to smuggle Tracy out of St Levan House, 'Or just walk out. Who do the bastards think they are?' But the Tamar Bridge subdued him – giant iron girders flashing past, the airy drop below us, tiered ranks of slaty streets. I saw grey warships out in Plymouth Sound and there were swans drowsing in the water a hundred feet below the train.

St Levan House was as Tracy had written, new and light, two glassy quadrangles one on top of the other, a small garden area in the middle, a big cheese plant in Reception, the Play-Doh smell. The first thing we heard was someone crying, far off. Mrs Carpenter came out of her office and ushered us in. All the residents were upset, she said, because two girls had absconded and had been returned by the police late last night. As Tracy had indicated, it took Mrs Carpenter about twenty minutes to convey this information. When we were seated opposite her she told us a bit about Tracy herself. 'Given that Tracy has no real family, I am trusting you both with this background.' We should be aware, she said, that our friend had experienced a lot of disruption in her life, was in denial about past events, and needed time to develop a mature outlook. She smiled as she spoke – not just between sentences, but continuously. Later, at home, I practised doing this in front of the bathroom mirror, but could never master it.

'Tracy has entered, or I should say re-entered, residential care within an unusual timeframe, that is, she is now approaching seventeen, and this of course is when our formal care role draws to a close. So with this milestone in mind we have focused chiefly on taking steps towards encouraging Tracy to develop relevant skills in order to facilitate her adjustment to the wider community and provide her with sufficient confidence to confront the challenges which lie ahead of her. Tracy has made good efforts to adapt to a residential setting in terms of integrating with the other girls, and has developed some positive relationships. Having said that, staff and backup team members have found her behaviours inappropriate at times and even challenging on occasion. She is often reluctant to engage with staff at all, and on a personal level I've felt she is not really happy participating in discussions regarding her future. You'll find Tracy in her room, she's expecting you.'

Blonde Mrs Carpenter, with her careful voice, her violet silk scarf and prolix gentleness – she was so far from my Victorian image of a children's home superintendent that I was inclined to like her, but Victor didn't: 'She's like Tippi Hedren in *Marnie*, or *The Birds*. I kept checking the wires outside her window.' After we left her office I realised we hadn't asked her where Tracy was supposed to go when she reached seventeen.

Tracy was dressed in a pink miniskirt and a black and white football shirt with two tiny seahorses on it. 'It's Newcastle United, someone gave it to me.' The shirt made her look like a novice nun. Victor made the atmosphere in Tracy's room impossible. He paced around the tiny space, lay on the bed, messed up her books and towels, was sullenly silent or constantly interrupting. If she turned her back on him, he leaned forward or angled his face in front of her. We had to talk over, across, and behind him. The bedroom itself was spartan, orderly as a soldier's tent. Tracy hadn't put a single picture or poster on the wall, there were no ornaments, no shells, no photos, no identifying marks. The place had no claim on her.

She saw me noticing *Macbeth* and *The Mayor of Casterbridge* on the desk, our A-level texts. 'Miss Rescorla sent them, dear of her. Fancy her knowing where I am.' None of the other teachers had been in touch. I left Victor and Tracy alone to allow their argument to take its course, and it started before I had closed the door, Victor roaring at her to walk out, Tracy protesting that there was nowhere to go, wait and see. Along the corridors I went, round and round the square, peering in through open doors that revealed bedrooms that were mostly as impersonal as Tracy's. A tall red-haired man was leaning with his head pressed against one of the doors that were closed, bending over awkwardly, pleading with its occupant, 'If you just calm down and act your age...'

Victor said little on the return train apart from mocking Mrs Carpenter's use of English ('*Inappropriate* behaviour. Inappropriate to what?'), but at Redruth he finally turned away from the window and told me that Tracy's house, Number Five, was for sale, and the estate agent was Hocking Simpson Nankervis, where Kerenza's mother and Mark Hocking worked (old Mr Boase had retired and Penny was now a partner. They had dropped the commas along with Mr Boase).

'Mum says it used to be a tied cottage. Tracy's granddad worked for Mark Hocking's father, and when her granddad died, he let Mrs Tabb stay on. Now Mark's running things, Tracy's gran is away up the hill, and Mark and Penny are going to do it up and sell it. Everybody wins.'

13

1827 – The springle in the grass

Geneva House, October 12

Alone in the forest, where the cry of an unfamiliar bird or a rustle in the trees is worthy of record in a journal, a man can develop an inflated sense of his own particularity. On arrival at Redruth I was rudely shaken by the press of humanity that assaulted me as soon as I left the safety of the carriage: a pulsing current of miners, engineers, masons, merchants, mountebanks and common labourers, my person imperilled by an army of overladen carts driven at speed along the narrow roadways. Every soul I saw was intent on urgent and serious business. It was alarming, but stimulating; a fierce unchecked energy runs through this town like a herd of bulls. The noise – the bartering, clattering, arguing and coquetting – continued all through the night, and I slept little in my hard bed at the Feathered Footman, humbled by the knowledge that the new century has advanced quite far without me. Like a vagabond child I slip through the curtain into a party for adults; I no longer signify among the industrious and powerful, but find a mouselike pleasure in scapegrace anonymity. I left Ossian in Wigge's care.

At breakfast I realised I had no idea where the Poorhouse was. A foolish shame prevented me from asking my landlord at the Footman, so I was reduced to accosting strangers on the street. The first three gave me a peculiar look, and denied all knowledge of the place; the fourth laughed and pointed me uphill: 'Down on your luck, Mister?' I followed his directions until the dwellings thinned out in rough, treeless moorland, misshapen rocks strewn around the heather like giant's teeth. I knew the Poorhouse before I came close, though there was nothing, theoretically, to mark it from its neighbours close by: it is a squat house of brick and granite, with a high wall extending from either side, enclosing some sort of yard with outhouses behind. Yet the scrubby grass shrinks from it, leaving a patch of bare earth in front.

I pulled the bell and waited on the windy step, keenly aware of the little parcel that once lay upon it, until a small door, concealed in the structure of the larger one, opened, revealing a bovine woman, very short and stout. Her unkempt appearance led me to assume I was dealing with a low servant, but this was Matilda Trefusis, the superintendent. I had a story prepared for this visit (I am always more confident in the guise of another): I introduced myself as a Mr Seal, inquiring on behalf of a gentleman friend who had lately discovered he might bear some relation to an infant boy left here in 1821. Her expression changed when she heard my accent, and I sensed that my imposture was unnecessary. I could have told her I was an agent of Satan and she would have tried to accommodate me with a suitable young boy, thus earning credit for lightening the burden on the parish. Matilda Trefusis ushered me along a passage into a high-ceilinged room which served as an office and smelt of mice.

'We don't have a lot of children here as a rule. The keener ones are 'prenticed out quick, or sent to service. This is Redruth, Mr Seal. Look around you at the workings. Engines! Mines! Copper! Plenty of employment for those that want it. What you see here is those that can't; the cripples, the halfwits, and the all-wore-out, which is natural. But we might have something: a woman came in last week that had a boy with her, nine years, brawny, but she can't keep him, state she's in. Very likely she'll listen to you.'

Mrs Trefusis spoke with huffings and sighings, as if language itself were an onerous modern habit, obliging her to make painful, costive quarryings in the pits of her mind.

I had to interrupt to explain, a second time, that I was looking for a specific child, an infant left at the door six and a half years ago; that while I did not expect to find him still here, I would like to see the admissions for that year, 1821, and any record of where he was subsequently sent.

'Oh, a particular child. Well, you should have said.' She opened a dresser, dragged out a set of ledgers and laid them on the table in a row. 'Name?'

I gave her my clutch of possible names.

She looked at me as if I had lost my senses. 'Jack Tabb, Jack Pender, Jack Hocking, Jack Seal, Jack in the Box, Jack o' Lantern, Will o' the Wisp, Wandering Jack! Have you a notion of how many Jacks pass through here? How do you figure to find a pauper child without a proper name?'

'Can you please look back to 1821?'

She returned to the ledgers, turning the pages with ponderous slowness, running her finger along the columns of names and dates. Minutes passed. Feet clattered along the corridor beyond the door, a man cried out in pain, somebody retched, a woman dropped something metallic and swore, water dripped. The finger of Mrs Trefusis came to an abrupt halt and its owner looked up.

'Wait! 1821? That's six years past!'

For a moment I hoped she had remembered something.

'Me and Trefusis never had the contract until 1823, springtime. We were still round the corner in Bride Lane. The parish was running the Poorhouse. They used to just pay us rent for the big house, this one. We have the three houses, see.'

I did not really see, but gathered the parish was no longer running the Poorhouse.

'Like I said, in the end they gave us the contract for housing the paupers, admissions, sustenance and clothing, doing all the real work. Saved them a heap of money. They pay us a trifle and we're just left to do the best we can. Trefusis says it's turned out more trouble than it's worth.'

I had heard of such arrangements. Wigge told me there had been a plan to offload Trebeere Poorhouse in this way, to farm the paupers out, but it had been voted down. I could not see why this should prevent a search of the records, however.

'Gone, Mr Seal! Gone! The churchwarden came for the old parish books. He's dead two years. We had to buy new books for the old paupers they left us with, write in all the names, then add the new ones that came after. Here,' she thrust one of the ledgers at me, opening it at the first page, 'nothing before April 1823.'

I asked her to check if there were any boys of around two years old still in the book in 1823. She was showing signs of irritation, flicking the pages, but her manner shifted when I hinted I would be making a donation for the inmates, and for her time. However, she found no two-year-olds at all for that year.

'Most likely, Mr Seal, if it was a mere infant that was left, then it would have been sent out, straight away.'

'Sent out?'

'Out to nurse. There's matrons that take them in, clean ladies as a rule, even if they expect rewards for what the Lord provides them free.'

I asked what happened to the infants, after they were weaned. She looked as if I had demanded the answer to some occult mystery.

'Well, that depends, Mr Seal, that depends on so many chances and fortunes and providential events. I'm not a prophet, Sir.'

Could she, I wondered, oblige me with the names of these nurses?

She demurred, but gave me one, a Mrs Edgcumbe. 'Selina, she calls herself, the fat fussock. She's over to Camborne now. Retired. Old man keeps pigs. Tell her I sent you.'

She was collecting up the ledgers, eager for my departure, but I remained sitting and asked if any current inmate had been living in the Poorhouse back in 1821. Again, the blink.

'As a rule, they come and they go, Mr Seal. Six years is six years. But there's Alice. She's in the back. Works with the linen.'

Mrs Trefusis led me out and waddled ahead down the passage, opening a door into a big rectangular chamber, coldly lit by windows set high in one wall. About thirty women sat close on wooden settles, bent over some sort of sewing task. They were mostly crooked and yellowed, one of them obviously some kind of idiot, but a few were younger, notably a girl so thin her skin appeared transparent. The expression on all these faces was the same, not unhappy so much as listless, and they hardly glanced up as we walked along the side of the room.

'This here's the women. Trefusis does the men.'

She bustled me out into a stone yard where a solitary woman, her back to us, was stirring something in a copper. There did not appear to be any fire beneath it, and the place smelt more like a midden than a laundry.

'Alice! This gentleman, Mr Seal, wants a word with you. Concerning when you were here six years back.'

Alice spun around, anxious as a rabbit.

I explained myself, and asked her if she remembered a baby named Jack arriving on the doorstep. 'It would have been late summer, or autumn of that year, 1821.'

'Yes, Sir, I remember. Was it a Sunday?'

'A Sunday? I don't know, perhaps. You remember a baby named Jack?' I was excited.

'Yes Sir, baby Jack.' Alice had black eyes, with heavy lids; it was impossible to read their expression. She was in mid-life, but seemed somehow younger.

'How long was he here? Do you remember any other name he had, a surname?'

'Macey, Jack Macey.'

'Macey? That's just your own surname, Alice!' Mrs Trefusis shouted, causing Alice to jump again.

'Please think, Alice,' I pleaded. 'Do you remember who took the infant in, who unwrapped him?'

'Yes Sir.'

'Who? Was there anything in the wrappings?'

'A seashell? Mother-of-pearl. It was Missis that unwrapped him.'

Mrs Trefusis interrupted. 'She means Mrs Ogilvie. Here before us.'

I turned to her, but she anticipated my question.

'Gone to the Canadas.'

I made a last attempt. 'Alice, where was Jack sent? When he left here, when he was put out to nurse?'

She looked at me. 'The Canadas?'

Mrs Trefusis threw her head back and laughed, her tiny eyes vanishing under the overhang of her brow. 'Alice will remember whatever you wish her to remember.'

As we re-entered the women's room, Alice called out at my back: 'Grey eyes. The baby had grey eyes.'

I handed Mrs Trefusis my donation in the porch. As I set off downhill, the Poorhouse door slammed behind me with a gunshot crack; she must have been expecting something more substantial.

The view to my left, over the hedge and across a broad valley, was shocking. I had not realised how extensive the mining is at Redruth, compared to the isolated workings on the moors at home. Field, stream and moorland have all been scoured away, leaving a brown desert on which a modern forest has grown: numerous engine houses like stretched chapels, each with its chimney spire, sprout randomly amid an undergrowth of sheds, iron gantries, giant wheels, chains, ladders. The dead ground is scored by rough roadways, pitted with stagnant pools; great pyramids of blackish rubble erupt everywhere – the wasted earth. By this time it was quite late in the morning, but silence hung over the scene. Where were the men? I looked for signs of life, of industry, but spied only a pair of horses, tied up by a shed, and a goat on the one remaining patch of grass. The people were underground, or indoors. The unnatural quiet, my elevated viewpoint, the radical transformation of the landscape – all brought to mind the scene from Torbett's Green on the first day of the Great Fall. While resting at a stile for some minutes I noted that there was, in fact, a sound: a distant machine, not visible, was making a slow, rhythmical clacking, like a muffled clock.

Wednesday October 17
By far the greater part of my day is consumed by domestic tasks. I am amassing a good stock of wood and kindling, learning to be

more accurate with the axe. The small outbuilding at the back of the house would be most suitable for storing it, but the roof leaks and since I do not have the strength to mend it, I am using the pantry. Woodlice and earwigs trickle out from this woodpile in the evenings, joining me at dinner; my dominion over the creeping things of the earth is failing, and they know it. In the early mornings, just as darkness pales and the wood begins to redescribe itself, I tramp into the trees with my sack, collecting dry furze and sticks, noting the location of larger fallen branches, for which I will return later. There should be a word for the colourless, timeless hour before sunrise, the hour of the Resurrection, when all men sleep apart from He who walks alone in the dew, and the wild creatures inherit the forest.

I have been experimenting with Menhennett's shotgun. Robert taught me to shoot, after a fashion, when I was a child, and I was surprised to find the skill returned quite naturally, though I had not held a gun in forty years. After a little practice, having fired on a good many innocent trees, I finally killed a rabbit. Ossian was less than useful: in the first place, it was difficult to persuade him to be quiet, and then he was excessively frightened by the noise of the shots. We reached the rabbit together, and I had to pull him off it. I am embarrassed to recall my delight, the inspiriting sense of competence, that I experienced with that first small rabbit, and was rather sorry that Arthur had not been there to witness it; I cannot imagine Arthur hunting in the wilderness. Skinning the creature proved more awkward: I made the mistake of trying to peel it with a knife, rather than easing the skin gently away like a coat; my hands were scored with cuts. It made a decent stew, however, and Ossian enjoyed the entrails. I might see if Samuel Trembath would sell me some hens, though I would need a henhouse, and now of course I cannot ask the younger Trembath to build one for me.

Since the day of the rabbit I have been taking the gun out once or twice a week, leaving Ossian in the house when hunger is stronger than my desire to teach him stealth. The results are almost sufficient for my needs, which continue to shrink in any case. Recently I wandered further than usual towards the north east and was stopped in my tracks by a deep fissure in the ground. Living here on the edge of the Fall I have developed an instinct for the presence of these earthy traps under the ferns, and have never had an accident. Supposing myself to be in deep forest, I was surprised when the trees thinned out beyond the crevasse. I heard footfalls, and the heavy frame of Matthew Hocking came stamping into view, hatless, on a lower path. I was looking down on his reddish scalp from a distance of around six feet. He was quite unaware of my presence, and the thought came to me that I could lift the gun, fire it into him and disappear into the wood, all in a matter of seconds.

October 19

I have been so tired since the expedition to Redruth that I have not found energy enough to write of a strange experience before I left, in September. After my success with the gun, I resolved to test my skill at fishing. Usually I avoid the little stony seashore because I associate it with Geneva, but the day in question was warm and brilliant, the sea blue-green as a peacock's throat, striped here and there with indigo. I sat on a tussock and, losing interest in the fish, returned to my book. When I next looked up, most of Lantern Bay had vanished behind a white screen of fog, the perspective radically foreshortened.

As I watched, the rocks and trees enclosing my tiny harbour turned vague and ghostlike, then they too disappeared, until finally even the waves on the strand, sucking and sighing just a few paces from my feet, seemed as insubstantial as the Classical sea in one of Arthur's paintings. Suddenly shaken by a notion that I too might disappear, I picked up my book, stumbled a little way up the path, then tripped and landed on my behind in the bracken. I was facing the shore. There were four seals down there, a few feet from me. One was heaving itself out on the pebbles, the others still in the sea, dark heads moving in and out between the curtains of mist.

The book was Rousseau's *Emile*. My idea is that I should use it to design Jack's education, so that when he arrives here everything will be in place. On reacquainting myself with the contents I have had to modify this somewhat; I do not find myself in agreement with Rousseau on all matters. I see no reason, for instance, to delay Jack's reading until he is twelve. He will learn to hunt and fish, to chop wood, to grow food and cook it, but he will also read the Scriptures, poetry, political and natural philosophy, *Paul and Virginia*; anything, everything, except for newspapers. I will ask Arthur to have the rest of my books brought up here. There is another question I am faced with, one which Rousseau failed to address. Jack will have been corrupted by his first six years, in ways I struggle to imagine. I will have to rinse away the taint of Mrs Trefusis and her ilk, start afresh with his instruction, as if he were a babe again. I'm not sure if this is even possible, so Jack will be something of a natural experiment. Nevertheless I will strive to shield him from the poisonous influences of the world, from the crowd at Maryann's execution, from Hocking, from the condescension of great families and the callousness of rich men, until he is wise enough to resist them. He shall live with me here out by the Great Fall, remote from Society, but close to the dangerous wisdom of Nature, from which he will learn God's purpose for all living things. He will learn to walk freely in the dark, which is never truly black when the other senses are sharp, and I will show him how next year's ferns coil tight and green even before this year's leaves are dead. We will find the Emperor moth with the human eyes.

I saw Hocking yesterday, on the path with his ugly son. I think they were flushing pheasants, beating at the bracken. The more I think about Matthew Hocking, the more I am convinced that he is the original source of Maryann's troubles, and, in consequence, of mine. His behaviour on the day of the Great Fall was odd. All of us who were on the cliff that evening stood together, quite still, speechless, frozen by the spectacle before us. The immensity and suddenness of the change washed all individual concerns from the mind, or at least from the mind of any man of normal sensibility. Yet Hocking never joined us. We saw him, and he must have seen us, but he stayed there by Maryann's cottage, blocking the door, walking around the back and then standing in front of the door again. It was Hocking's fields that were the most affected, his sheep and cattle lying dead below us, but he showed no interest in them. What was it that was more important? I am coming to suspect that Eliza Tabb never left St Anthony, never left that cottage, that something happened to her in there, shortly before the land split apart and began its slide towards the sea. The wreck of the bedchamber has also puzzled me; the landslip might have cracked the wall and smashed the pitcher, but why was linen strewn around? Hocking was guarding the place, so that none of us should come in.

There was a time, after Maryann's reappearance in my life, when I wondered if she was complicit in the disappearance of Eliza; now I doubt it, though I still wonder at her easy acceptance of the idea that her daughter had abruptly left the district, leaving her cloak hanging in the passage. Whatever the truth of the matter, I cannot ask her. Over the past six years the woods have closed in on that cottage; slates are missing; saplings and briars crowd close to the broken window, though the door is solid. In a few years, only the granite walls will remain and people will ask themselves whether it was a house for people or for pigs. I could try to search the place, but I would have to ensure that Hocking was not likely to be there, nor any of his family or field hands. At night, perhaps. I would need a lamp inside, which could attract notice. Besides, the walk from Geneva House is taxing, I would then have to walk back again, and Hocking was always cunning: there is no certainty that I would be able to determine where he hid Eliza's body.

Wednesday October 24

Arthur Wigge has been. I have told him everything, almost. It was late; the day, though warm, had been darkening since noon, clouds banking to great heights to the south, the bay an ill-tempered pewter. Fat drops of rain had begun to thud on the veranda's glass roof, something I always rather enjoy. I was drowsing over the Book of Job, that passionate dialogue between man and God. I am preoccupied by the verses after 9:11; He passes by, says the voice, but I do not see him; he snatches away, but who can stop him, and who will say to him, 'What are you doing?' It is Job speaking, yet I fancy it could as easily be God talking about us all, down here. His voice is too quiet for us, and is silent at the truly dangerous moments, those seconds when we should be most awake, because the ground is cracking at our feet.

Arthur came stumbling crossly through the undergrowth, his short arms beating at leaves and creepers. He had a large satchel on his back from which he extracted a bottle of wine, brandy, a roast chicken, bread, a blackberry pie. He is stronger than he pretends to be. Once he had recovered from the walk (he described it as 'loathsome'), his mood became expansive. I lit a lamp and we sat under the glass, the meadow an unnatural emerald green, lightning flashing at sea. I was enormously pleased to see him.

'Geneva has left us, for a while,' he said. 'She departed two days ago for London, with Dinah Pengelly. She is to stay with a cousin of mine in Clerkenwell, so she can be close to Henry, who is engaged to be married. I think there will be difficulties, however, as the girl's family are set against the match. Geneva is furious of course.'

'With Henry?'

'No, you fool. With the young lady's family. Geneva feels slighted on Henry's behalf. They are Crabbes. Their money is in sugar. She is worried Francis Crabbe will spirit Henry away to Jamaica, soak him in rum and slavery.'

Arthur, I know, thinks Henry spineless, or superficial, or both. I have not met my stepson: he never made the long journey down to St Anthony during the brief time his mother and I lived under the same roof. Arthur's mention of the tropics threw my mind back to *Paul and Virginia*, the novel that once seemed to connect me and Geneva. There is a curious incident in the story in which the children return a runaway slave to her owner. Virginia pleads with this owner to treat the woman kindly, and, moved by Virginia's beauty, he agrees. Later, though, we learn that the slave woman has been seen chained to a block of wood. The author intends this as an illustration of Virginia's purity of heart, but I always wondered why the children took the poor woman back at all.

Arthur was becoming melancholy over the end of my marriage. I have not seen Geneva since she came to the parsonage during my sickness, and my image of her is hardening, becoming polished like Arthur's rosewood chairs, glossy with beeswax.

'None of this was necessary. These sickening events, you living out here in this hovel. If you had only trusted her. I don't understand why you didn't. Geneva, Jenny, is the most tolerant, least conventional woman I know, and, besides, you were not married to her at the time of your relation with the other lady. I always thought you had so much in common, that Geneva would complement you, bring a melodic influence to your house, and I was so pleased to bring you together, to observe a meeting of sympathetic spirits. It wasn't only for your sake, either. Ted Florey was an honest fellow, the marriage a fine one, but he never understood his wife's unusual artistic talent. And yes of course Geneva would have told me of your difficulties, if you had confided in her. Did you think I would judge you? That you are the first in your profession to commit an indiscretion, to make an error of judgement about a woman? As for the unfortunate lady herself, we could have settled the matter privately, and you would never have needed to be troubled by her again.'

'Maryann was more than an error of judgement,' I said. 'She was a woman of some courage, some intelligence, too much perhaps, until she met Hookway, and he took the last of her strength. I had feelings for her.'

He looked up but said nothing.

'It is Maryann I think about now, not Geneva. In truth I hardly knew Geneva. That was my fault; I had been alone so long, and once we were married I never knew how to progress, as it were, beyond my basic duties to her. It was as if I had a pleasant guest in the parsonage, and my bed. I liked and admired Geneva, but that isn't enough. My guilt is for Maryann.'

'You feel no guilt about your marriage?'

'Geneva is protected, has always been protected. She walked from her father's house to Florey's, from Florey's to the parsonage, and now she has strolled through your garden house and thence to London. She has travelled past me. Maryann's life was something so different. She was like a woman fighting a war. You cannot imagine the contrast.'

I was aware that I had drunk a good deal of Arthur's wine. He poured me another glass. His eyes, with their hooded lids, had the familiar veiled look.

'Here, have some more chicken, and give some to Ossian. What would you have in common, James, with a woman who was fighting a war?'

'Nothing. That's the strangeness of it. Maryann was sly, evasive, harsh, even brutal. She was not particularly handsome. She was without culture or education and had no knowledge of the world outside Cornwall. But there was something else, something beyond sympathy or liking or physical admiration. An undercurrent. The air felt different when she was in the room, like a change in the weather. Why are some human beings impelled towards each other? One person rather than a thousand others, others with whom they have far more in common? The process does not seem to obey any reasonable law.'

Arthur smiled. 'You could say the same about friendship. True friendship is always inexplicable.'

That was when I told him about Jack. The storm beyond the glass was exerting its usual elevating effect on my spirits, and, with the wine, I felt reckless. He listened while I told him of my earlier wilful disbelief about Jack's existence, Maryann's letter with its cryptic postscript, my interview with Mrs Trefusis. I had begun an exposition of Rousseau's educational principles and how I planned to adapt them for Jack, when he interrupted.

'Stop. It seems to me that you have built a ship of paper here. Where is the evidence that the child was yours? That he is alive or ever was? Maryann had reason to create a mythical infant, to pin down your interest in her. Why did she go to Redruth Poorhouse, rather than our own in Trebeere? Why didn't she tell you the full name of the child? There are holes in this fabric, if I may adjust the metaphor.'

I was in no mood to be irritated with Arthur – after all, the story was new to him. I told him I had considered these questions, and how I had answered them. As for her choice to go to Redruth, Maryann was proud as well as practical. If she had left the baby at Trebeere, her act of abandonment would have become known, and before long she would have seen Jack in the street, or in the bleakly buxom care of some local Mrs Trefusis, or working in the tannery, or on the quays. Working for Hocking. I was speaking very fast, something about my conviction must have been infectious, for Arthur stopped questioning me and his expression became gentler. He promised to make inquiries, to travel, if necessary.

'We will proceed by elimination. I will start in Trebeere, and move outwards.' He was too tactful to add that this would involve money. 'What a pity that you could not have found this concentration, this energy, a long time ago. It might have been useful. Every man is guilty of all the good he did not do, as your old dog Voltaire once said. Why did you never go, James?'

'Go where?'

'To France. While you had the chance, before everything froze over.'

'We were at war for a good while, if you remember.'

'Not until '93. And you could have gone again in 1803, and even after that, it was not impossible to slip across unnoticed, and you knew French, at least on paper. Not such a terrible journey; the Channel is a mere canal in the oceans of the world, though I'll admit it can test the stomach.'

'It was still dangerous.'

'Everything is dangerous.'

I saw the consequences, though, I said. The tin-legged eyeless men, the mad men who swore they knew Wellington like a brother and saw the Enemy lurking behind every sheep. Widows making stew from seaweed and hairy nettles.

'And what of you? Why did you never step over the English canal?'

'I did. Three times. In 1790, as a boy, again in '95, and once much later.'

He had the grace to look away. He knew I was astounded.

'I can tell you the story if you wish to hear it, but not today. I must tramp back through your savage wood; I have a trap waiting at the Nelson.'

'In this storm? You are welcome to stay tonight.'

'No thank you. Too many rustling leaves. I would never sleep. And I travel upcountry tomorrow. In any case, the weather is passing. Look.'

A hole had opened in the cloud to the south, casting a circle of yellow light on the black sea. I accompanied him some of the way back to St Anthony. Pooled rain drowned much of the path and our progress was slow; Arthur told me there had been a landslip a few weeks ago, nothing serious, but enough to open some new cracks to the east. He stopped once, turning to me:

'Is there anyone else living out here at all? It's just I thought I heard voices this afternoon, when I was on my way to see you, just before I reached your house. Children's voices, coming from the shore. Laughter.'

'Not to my knowledge. It might have been seals. I hear them at night. They do sound quite human sometimes.'

I started telling him of my hunting adventures, the sighting of Hocking and my sudden desire to shoot him. I felt Arthur's interest quicken, but he said nothing more until the woods gave way to the open pasture, where we had agreed to part, and he stopped, breathless, glancing across in the direction of Churchtown Farm.

'Your splenetic neighbour may have cause to be afraid. There's a fever in the air, James, not new, but revived; something is stirring. Under the surface, so to speak. Gatherings. Fires. A sort of sabotage. Two barns near St Dominic, an empty house in Trebeere, a rick at Helston, and more out towards Falmouth. The trouble seems to be spreading east, but it started here.'

'Arsonists? What is it about?'

'Wages, or the lack of them. Evictions. You should know; it's about Maryann, if you like. What is singular is the matter of the letters. People are receiving rather frightening letters, all signed the same way: "Captain Jack". Your boy's name seems popular. We don't know about Sorleigh, but that old weathervane Copthorne has had one, and Hocking certainly has. So if you had obeyed your momentary impulse, it's unlikely that you would even have been a suspect, and there are a good many who would have applauded the deed. Captain Jack, James, Captain Jack.' He smiled, and made his ungainly way across the meadow.

Dark has fallen since I got back, but I am too cheerful to sleep.

October 25

The first thing I saw this morning was the full glass of brandy Arthur had left out for 'the spirits who might be passing by'. I poured it back in the bottle. I have a bilious headache, and am struggling to rid my mind of an unpleasant idea. I had been dreaming – at last! – of Maryann, and woke thinking of her, how tall she was, her sweet voice and rough words, and whether I will ever be able to separate my memories of our friendship from her terrible death. And whenever I recall the day of her execution at Bodmin, that pallid boy with the ribboned hurdle comes following close behind. My impression was of a sickly child of around eight years. Jack is six, but has two tall parents. Fate could surely not be so cruel as to allow a boy to witness, unknowingly, the execution of his mother, and to permit his father to walk by him in ignorance, with distaste in his heart.

October 31
I have been back to Redruth. Or Camborne, to be exact.

When Matilda Trefusis told me Mrs Edgcumbe was retired, she meant it literally. I found the latter lady disposed upon a couch. The light was low in this frowzy room, closed curtains drawing a veil over the pigs in the rough pasture outside. Buttressed by an opulence of stained cushions, embraced by garish shawls, she was nursed attentively by a slabfaced, hulking lad. Despite this, Mrs Edgcumbe did not appear unwell; she was generously built and her face was round, bearing traces of former comeliness.

'Draw your chair closer, Mr Seal, and call me Selina. Our names make us almost family, don't you think? Charlie, that's my precious boy over there, will bring us tea, unless you prefer gin or porter?'

When I told her my business, and that Mrs Trefusis had sent me, her mouth pinched up, but only for a moment; she heaved herself forward on the couch so that her bosom overhung it, and became coquettish, as far as indolence allowed.

'I am sorry you have wasted hours in such low company. Matilda is famous for sharp dealings; she lacks all daintiness and finer feeling.'

My efforts to direct her attention back to Jack, and the infants she had cared for, were not a success. Her reaction when I gave her my list of likely surnames was similar to that of Mrs Trefusis, and she took pains to emphasise the time that had passed since she had been a wet nurse.

'It was before my husband died. Since then, myself and my lovely Charlie have done well with our little farm; better, truth be told, than when William was alive, dear of him. As I always say, everything happens for a reason. And there were so many precious infants, and they were not here for long enough to recall any particular one. William used to say I was too soft-natured for my own good, but you can't become too fond, can you? My business was only with Good Families. They sought me out, I never had to advertise. I don't know why Matilda told you I would be taking in pauper infants from the Poorhouse, I expect it was just to vex me.'

'But where did the babies go, Mrs Edgcumbe, when you had finished nursing them, when they were weaned?'

'Go? They went back to their precious mothers, or to kind strangers, to fine families. They went all over the county.'

Did she keep a book, recording where they had gone?

'A book? I'm not a clerk, Mr Seal.'

'What about Jacky?' said a voice from the corner. Charlie, the precious boy, had not uttered a word until now. 'He was here a while, that Jacky.'

'Jacky?' said Mrs Edgcumbe. 'Jacky what?'

'We used to call him Jacky Piddle.'

Charlie and his mother both shook with laughter at this witticism.

'I'm sorry, Mr Seal. Yes, we did have a Jacky. Muddy-looking lad. But he left us two years back.'

'Where to?'

'Up Bodmin. To Annie Trelowarren. She took him along with Dorcas, Dorcas was only tiny. Annie wouldn't have kept him long though. She never keeps them.'

Bodmin. I could feel the onset of another sick headache; they strike me frequently since my illness. What was his second name, I asked.

'Well it wasn't really Piddle, Mr Seal.' (More laughter.) 'What was it, Charlie? Piddow? Priddow. Yes, Priddow.'

Prideaux.

November 1

Today I found something in the kitchen, behind the cupboard. A compass. The only trace of Mrs Barrett, perhaps. Tarnished, of cheap construction, the needle swings drunkenly; it has lost its bearings. Perhaps the Fall is full of lodestone. I chose to consider the compass a sign, however, for there is something else I must do. If I can find the courage, it will count in my favour. I should do it soon, before the storms strip the woods I need the cover of leaves.

November 4

What decided me last night? I have no real idea, I had been procrastinating. The moon was huge, the night clear. I had lit no lamps and a greyish light drenched the cold orchard like whey. Ossian was playing with the fox who has started visiting (I am careless with our scraps). They, the dog and the fox, were crouching flat to the ground opposite each other, silent, bushy tails outstretched, then both pounced out simultaneously between the apple trees, meeting briefly in the centre of the orchard with soft yips and snaps, the fox making little feints and bouncings over the dog's back, before they separated again, whereupon the dance began afresh. Excluded, I grew envious of their tireless absorption in each other, called Ossian and shut him in the kitchen.

I put on my oldest soft-soled boots, took up the gun for the reassurance of it, and padded eastward along the path. My eyes are now so attuned to darkness that I wished the moonlight were less bright; every few yards I was darting into shadows, freezing like a deer, listening. When I came to the limit of the wood I stood for some minutes looking at the ruined cottage; I had forgotten about the exposed stretch of meadow between it and my sheltering trees. I bent over like a beast and loped across. The door was nailed shut, so I pushed through a mess of briars to the side window, squeezing my body past the frame and landing painfully in blackness. The shotgun clattered against some obstacle on the floor. I have said that the cottage is halfway to being reabsorbed by the forest, and this is true, but the freshness of the woods has not yet entered the dwelling: inside it was unpleasant, close, with a faint odour like bladderwrack after a hot day on the shore. Creepers covered the windows, but a thin light came in through the big crack made by the landslip at the front, and via a hole in the roof. I had brought a candle and the tinderbox, but preferred to let my eyes adjust naturally; candles intensify the dark, summoning distracting phantoms out of shadow.

The dwelling comprised one room with a short corridor and a half-wall dividing what must have been the kitchen from a store. In the centre stood a broad ladder to the upper level; I climbed this first, and found myself inside the bedchamber I had glimpsed six years ago. The place was quite empty, however; swept clean. Back below I paced around, ruffling through a pile of sacks in one corner, bruising my leg on a dresser. My attention was caught by a large woodbox; I lifted the lid, gingerly, inch by inch, to find a pile of bark and a huge spider. It was only when I raised my eyes from the floor that I noticed something unnatural about the room. There was no hearth, no chimney breast. It should have been on the north wall, where the chimney emerged from the roof. The dim light made it difficult to determine whether the masonry was recent, so I crawled back out through the window, round to the rear of the cottage, and almost slid into a deep pit in the ground. Arthur, I recalled, had been talking about a recent landslip, and here the movement in the earth had continued up the north wall, splitting it in two places. I propped the shotgun against a tree and pushed my face into the larger and lower of these holes.

The dark within being impenetrable, finally I lit the candle. A narrow enclosed space, quite dry, soot growing off the interior walls like black fur. On the floor was a quantity of ruckled fabric. As I reached my arm inside to lift the material (coarse, brownish) I think I knew what I would find as the hood fell back: the piebald ruins of a face, some dark hair around it, young sapling bones creating undulations in the cloak below. Again I caught the seaweed reek I had noticed inside the house.

I was careful not to hurry, walking back; to look straight ahead. It has been there all the time, I told myself, I have walked past it a thousand times. Nothing has changed, other than a disturbance deep in the earth. I set my mind on home, the image of Geneva House pulling me forward as if I were Theseus following his string out of the labyrinth. About halfway along the path there is a section where the bushes condense to form a thick hedge on one side; the air was still, but I was aware of a subtle disturbance in the dry leaves. I had the impression that something was moving along the top of this hedge, on my right, keeping pace; something that bobbed up and down unevenly, like a coal-scuttle hat.

November 11

I shall not report it. Who would I tell? They would say I am crawling my way back to favour by accusing others, or that I must have known about it for years. They would very likely arrest me, not Matthew Hocking. He has grand friends, I have only Arthur, and Arthur is away – God knows how long for. They would certainly ask how I knew where to look for Eliza's body. And how would it help Eliza, now? I can think of more practical ways to justice; I have the weapon and the opportunity.

In any case I am less troubled by my melancholy discovery than I imagined I might be; no one should have to see what I saw that night, but the sight of death is familiar to me as it is to any man in my profession. And here by the Fall I see numberless deaths. Almost every day there is a dismembered rabbit, a mouse seething with maggots, a pile of feathers, a skeletal butterfly. Last week a small dolphin lay outstretched on the shore, still plumply burnished and perfect (how did he die?). They eat each other, or are struck down by God. Occasionally I prey on them myself. I am the only Christian witness to these quiet exits, and sometimes it seems strange to me that we expect the world to shudder and stop when a man dies. We pray, find money for the coffin, a black coat and a wake, even if they meant little to us in life. And if we loved them we are outraged by the persistence of normal things in their absence. Yet we ignore the speechless presences on the margins of our daily life, and I am like a man on a great ship who imagined himself alone and awoke one day to find it crowded with fellow passengers.

Part 4: Whistling Jack

Look, he passes by me, and I do not see him;
He moves on, but I do not perceive him.
He snatches away; who can stop him?
Who will say to him, 'What are you doing?'
Job 9:11
The New Oxford Annotated Bible

14

On the first-floor landing at the Bonaparte there was a framed photograph. Raymond Nankervis had found it in a junk shop somewhere and hung it up by the linen cupboard: 'a bit of local history, makes a change from Napoleon'. Penny never liked it, she said the faces 'looked like drowned people', so then I had to take a closer look. A group of men and women of various ages were sitting on cane chairs in the shade of a spreading cedar; there was a table with a cloth, blurred tea things on it, a blurred dog underneath, and two children, boys, standing. The house behind the cedar was one of the grander villas in Trebeere, and the people's clothes – high collars, wide straw hats and chin-tied veils – suggested this tea took place in the first decade of the twentieth century. If I put my hand over the clothes, though, the faces could have been people I saw in the street every day, and I wondered why on earth this should be surprising.

At seventeen I was sad for those men and women because they were certainly dead, and even more sorry for the pale serious boy and his frowning little brother, pushed to the front. Now, the memory of this photo provokes a harsher impulse. I stride across the grass to the tea party like a sadistic postman, interrupting these people who believed themselves to be at the centre of their own lives, of their children's lives, at the apex of history, and I slam my fist on the table and shout, brutally, 'This is all over, gone, past. It's all finished.' And today I have no wish to revisit what remains of Geneva; I have a fear, almost a conviction, that I would see the four of us still there in the white room beyond the veranda, laughing about seals and death in the greenish light, ruthlessly indifferent to the lumpen ghost from the future skulking around outside.

I assumed it was Raymond who offered Tracy a place to stay at the Bonaparte, but later I discovered it was Penny. It made sense, all those empty rooms, and Penny always had a conscience. Or perhaps Kerenza said something to her mother. No doubt Mrs Carpenter, Mrs Barfield and the shadowy chorus of social and psychiatric services were grateful for the chance to offload an unresponsive adolescent, to deliver her into the hands of a respectable family from the girl's home village. They may have been under the impression that Tracy would be staying with Penny, rather than in an empty hotel with a recently separated older man, a man who had been living with Carole Carr, a girl in her early twenties, and had been interviewed by the police over the murder of a schoolgirl of Tracy's age. Perhaps they did not think at all, after Tracy left care. Tracy had been at St Levan House for seven weeks. I never found out what happened to Mrs Tabb's painted furniture, or Tracy's iridescent shells.

When I try to recall the time that Tracy and Victor lived with Raymond Nankervis at the hotel, it is as if I am remembering a period of months, an epoch. It must have been less than four weeks. During those weeks, the revived investigation into Clara Selman's death was active, though we were only aware of it peripherally through the looks and whispers I have already mentioned. It was reflected in Raymond's sudden switches of mood, and in our shared paranoia about walking the streets of St Anthony and Trebeere, the fear of being seen. But it would be easy to exaggerate, to say we felt besieged there, or that the Bonaparte, with its decaying grandeur, felt like a sinking ship. It didn't, really. It was more of a reprieve. With every day that passed without the police calling us back, our indolent youthful optimism grew stronger

Tracy was not going to school. On leaving St Levan House she had slipped into some sort of bureaucratic vacuum. At first nobody noticed. Victor and Tracy were absorbed by their reunion and spent most of the time upstairs, either in the cupola (which Victor had named the Observatory) or the Neptune Room. Kerenza was amiable in her offhand way, and Raymond Nankervis a little less gloomy than he had seemed in recent weeks. He may have been relieved by Carole Carr's abrupt departure, or cheered to find himself suddenly among a group of noisy young people, penniless guests in his corridors of vacant eighteenth-century rooms. But it would never have occurred to us to speculate on his state of mind, he was far too old for that. When Raymond made some vague enquiry of Victor concerning homework, he discovered that Victor was refusing to go to school because someone had said that Tracy would not be coming back. Raymond, with uncharacteristic initiative, telephoned the school and was informed by Mrs Marsh that Tracy Pender's place had been closed, on the understanding that she had moved to Plymouth, and he would have to contact the local education authority. So he rang St Luke's Hall, but was told the local authority was based at Truro, and anyway he would want another local authority altogether if Tracy had been in Plymouth, which was in Devon. This finally defeated Raymond, so Tracy stayed at the hotel during the day, while Victor agreed to go back to Joseph Carne, which he did, intermittently. I often went over to the Bonaparte in the evening, sometimes staying overnight.

Victor's brother Paul rang me out of the blue and asked me out. He was still asking every girl he met out, reasoning quite sensibly that every now and again one of them would say yes. I said yes. He was tall and broad, eyes trained inward as he talked, and had become ponderously courteous. He drove us out to St Ives for a meal. I learned quite a bit about amalgams, malocclusions, anaesthetics, and CB radio. Then he asked me the question all readers dread.

'So, Sally, your hobby is reading, what type of books do you read?'

Hobby – the word sidled out on its stubby wooden legs and squatted on the tablecloth. I thought of my shelves at home and could think of no good reason to mention one book rather than another, and of course I couldn't talk about my A-level books in case he thought I was the sort of person who only ever read set texts.

'Thrillers.'

When I glanced up again, he was looking at me.

'I knew her a bit, you know.'

'Who?' Distracted by 'hobby', I had been mentally listing other words that provoked irrational disgust ('quaint', 'gorgeous', 'dainty', 'nestled', 'tongue'), trying to separate colour, meaning and texture.

'Clara Selman. We used to see her sometimes in Cinnabar's. She looked older than she was, so she used to get us in, swear we were all eighteen. An adventurous young lady.'

'Oh'.

He was expecting something, a revelation, details, a confession. When I remained obstinately quiet, he told me how upset his parents were about the police and Victor, which I already knew; he seemed about to say more, but checked himself, and after the pizzas were finished we ran out of conversation. He took a different route home, across the high moors. I hadn't realised he had known Clara, and should perhaps have been uneasy, but I only remember the narrow borderless moonlit road, prehistoric stones, emptiness, moths in the headlights.

Visiting Tracy's grandmother involved a detour via the hidden path behind the old parsonage and up the hill to avoid people and their watchful windows. Mrs Tabb's new sitting room had what Raymond Nankervis would have called a commanding view across the bay. A few ornaments had come with Hazel from Number Five: a bottled ship, a clock, three flowered plates. Abstracted from the penumbra of her old sitting room, stranded in common daylight, they looked anaemic, while Hazel herself was flushed by her new central heating and, like the residents I remembered from my mother's time at Willow Court, sat facing firmly away from the window and its panorama. She talked about her new neighbours ('most of them are terribly old, poor things') and her late husband. 'He's gone out without his coat again.' But when she asked after my mother she remembered accurately that she now worked at the museum, and praised a sculpture of a running woman I had shown her years ago. Just as we were leaving, though, she called Tracy 'Irene'.

We had the Bonaparte almost entirely to ourselves. By this time the staff, never numerous or permanent, had gone; the tables in the bar were now covered in books and last night's supper dishes. There were no guests after the Manchester couple left. Mavis still called in sometimes, just in case, and I believe

Raymond paid her. Now that Tracy was not attending school, Raymond had decided to educate her himself. The curriculum consisted of history, mainly Cornish but with detours into nineteenth-century England, and music, Mendelssohn and Schubert. History took place in the deserted restaurant, but for the music lessons he took advantage of the powerful acoustics in the Assembly Room on the first floor. He sat Tracy at a table in the centre of the graceful rectangular space, light falling through high arched windows on the mint-green panels below the gallery. He put the record player on the stage at the end of the room and turned the volume right up. I can't listen to Schubert's *Nocturne in E Flat Major* without seeing that room.

Kerenza was at the hotel often, to escape Penny and Mark. Mark was barely speaking to her ('a massive relief'), but she warned us to stay out of his way. 'He keeps saying that if it was up to him, I'd be forbidden to see any of you, you're all a bad influence. I'd love to tell him it was Mum who got Tracy back here, just to watch him blow up.' Kerenza made no comment about the squalid state of the bar, or the music floating down from the upper floors, and she spoke to Victor and Tracy with the cool, slightly exasperated tolerance I had always heard in her conversations with her father. I, on the other hand, found myself in favour. She asked me to read an essay of hers, brought coffee up to the Observatory, satirised the teachers and pupils at St Agnes for my amusement. She lent me political magazines, and books: Simone de Beauvoir, a book on evolution, a history of trade unionism, *Silent Spring*.

'You can't just bury yourself in the nineteenth century, Sally, you need to know what people are saying now, or at least since the last war.' I had a tendency, she said, simply to accept what I read, 'But you have to deconstruct it, look below the surface.' Perhaps she would help me form some convictions.

There ought to be a word in English to describe the disproportionate gratitude evoked by attention from those whose good opinion we are unsure of, a word that would encapsulate the whiff of servility and shame behind the desire to please. Kerenza was always waiting for me now, when I arrived; she came to fetch me if I spent too long in the Neptune Room talking to Tracy or Victor, she rang me at home, often keeping my mother on the line, making her laugh, and I was flattered.

This time I had some intimation of the reason for the change. She was glad I had won the history prize, because 'It shows you aren't falling into the trap. I was beginning to think you'd got lost in the woods.' She didn't elaborate, but I understood that she wished somehow to detach me from Tracy and Victor, or from whatever it was they represented to her. And so, gradually at first, then more consciously, I began to comply, to prefer her company to theirs, to ask myself, as my mother had suggested, if I really had so much in common with Tracy and Victor, who were doing everything too fast and risking... not a spectacular fall, but something more prosaic: a future submerged in surface noise, in a living room like Mrs Jordan's, orange curtains drawn in the daytime.

One evening Kerenza took one of the few remaining bottles of wine from the cellar and we shared it up in the Observatory, the light off, watching the lighthouses waking up along the coast. I asked why she had gone to the police, why she had shown them the photograph. 'It was because they wouldn't believe me at first, they wanted something definite. And I went to the police because, like I told you before, I thought they should know what we saw.' She paused. 'When I was younger, thirteen or fourteen, I used to get that photo of Tracy out and stare at it. I kept it in a drawer, underneath my lepidoptera files. After a while I noticed that I had two separate memories, both clear, as if I were two people. One of them is of Tracy kneeling in the water, with her hands round a woman's neck. I can see her big hands, and there are bits of seaweed in her hair, Victor is standing up, near her. In this memory, we – you and me – are watching from the trees on the edge of the beach. In the other one, I'm sitting down, my foot's hurting, and you and Tracy are just standing in the sea, near the woman. I can't see Victor. That's it, just pictures, scraps. I never knew whether the photo had made me remember something real, or if my mind had created the memory around the photo. It was maddening. I'm still not sure.'

I watched her light a cigarette and I remembered her once, two or three years earlier, looking at Tracy and saying, irrelevantly, 'What big hands you have, Tracy.'

'Also,' she continued, not looking at me, 'I was just curious. I think I wanted to see what would happen, if I went to the police.'

* * *

Victor had discovered a cache of old records on the Bonaparte's third floor, in a cupboard by the derelict bathroom with the Nazi radio. They dated from the 1950s and 60s, and were probably relics of Raymond's youth. If Victor liked a piece of music, he would hover over the record player and move the needle back, over and over again, to hear the same track until he had sickened himself on it (he hated tapes, which enforced patience). I had a puritanical objection to this approach; you should, I thought, be forced to listen to the whole record, savouring the favourite track in context. It never occurred to any of us that Raymond might not want to hear the music of his past playing on endless repeat.

That Saturday Victor had been playing 'Just Walk on By, Wait on the Corner' in the Assembly Room for an hour until Tracy, who was broadening her musical taste under Raymond's tuition, lost patience and sent him upstairs. We were sitting on the edge of the stage in the sudden silence when an irregular tapping, like hailstones, came from the window. I had to lean right out to see Denise Jordan looking up from the street, chucking peanuts at the glass. She was heavily pregnant, though none of her born children were with her.

'About time. Is Vic in there? Tell him to get home.'

'He's upstairs. Do you want to come up? The main door's open.'

'No. Just tell him to get home. And just Vic, not her.'

Victor came down scowling, but he went off with his sister without protest. I went down to the kitchen to make coffee.

I never saw Carole Carr come in. By the time I recognised her, which was not immediately, she was already seated at the bar. The others were quicker. Tracy fled somewhere upstairs, and Raymond had vanished, either into his office or down to the cellar. I had been waiting for Kerenza to turn up. She always used the back door; perhaps she had come in, seen Carole, and gone straight out again.

'Where is everyone?' Carole said, discounting me.

'The bar isn't really open at the moment.'

'Never mind, Sally. This time I've brought something. Can you at least find us some glasses?'

There was a half-bottle of gin on the counter, its top off.

She nodded at Raymond's office. 'Is he in?'

'No.'

'Just as well. Pass a couple of those tonics up.'

I put the glasses and tonic on the bar. I disliked gin, but didn't want to seem childish. There was an urgency in her manner, a feverish quality, so I sat. Carole looked crumpled and sallow. There were stains on her skimpy t-shirt, which stretched tight across thin shoulders and rode up above her jeans. She still smelt of patchouli, now layered with sweat.

'Look at you, Sally. Your face, your round cheeks. Maybe when you're a bit older you'll see that relationships are complicated. You'll find out how a person can invest everything, and then be completely let down, because people pretend to be one thing when they're really something different. They act principled, above it all, and forget about the others, the ones who have to face the consequences, deal with the muck they got dragged into.'

'Love isn't complicated,' I said, impressed by my own confidence. 'You love someone, and either they love you back or they don't.'

I understood she was upset about the break with Raymond and I was terrified she would start crying, a possibility that was the more awkward because of her usual insistence on her own maturity. Even if I had been able to think of something suitable to say, apart from 'sorry', the idea that Raymond himself might be listening from the office, or standing on the cellar steps with the trapdoor propped open, was inhibiting. Carole began to repeat herself.

'I don't know why I'm telling you, you're too young to know what I'm talking about. Where is he, anyway? Hiding in his crazy book? And where's Kerry vanished to? Could you just pop into the cellar, Sally, and get us some wine?'

To my surprise, the gin was nearly finished.

Raymond was not in the cellar. I found a dusty bottle of Liebfraumilch and brought it up. I uncorked it and told her I had to go, but she talked across me.

'Ray couldn't even give me a straight answer when I asked, wouldn't even talk about it. Ignore the papers, he says. And now look what's happened. Wait, Sally, you haven't seen what I brought.'

She held the bar with one hand and bent unsteadily over to retrieve a plastic bag from the floor, from which she retrieved a tabloid newspaper. 'Look,' she said, riffling through it to an inside page, 'can you imagine what I felt when I saw that?'

It was a photo of Raymond, with Tracy, by the front porch of the Bonaparte. Tracy was smiling, holding a milk bottle; he was holding the door open for her. There was just a short paragraph underneath it, about the ongoing investigation, and a caption, 'Hotelier Raymond Nankervis, with a friend'. It was an unremarkable photo in my opinion.

'They talked to Raymond I think, the police,' I said, 'that's probably why the paper took a picture.'

At that moment, Victor returned, obviously out of breath. I pushed the newspaper back at Carole. He strode across the stale bar, bringing the outside with him on his blue jersey – woodsmoke and seawater. His face looked altered, rigid and closed, the usual flush confined to the cheekbones.

'Where's Tracy?' he demanded.

'I don't know,' I said. 'No idea. Upstairs? Why do people always expect me to know where everyone is?'

'Well could you at least help me look?'

'No.'

Carole was talking again, but I heard only Victor, thudding across the Assembly Room over our heads, running up to the higher floors, down through the back kitchens, slamming doors, shouting for Tracy.

'When you see Tracy,' he said when he came back into the bar, 'tell her to come out and meet me.' He named a location. Then he walked straight out into the sunshine on John Wesley Street.

Carole was drinking the German wine as if it were fruit juice. I left her in the bar and banged through the double doors into the kitchen, where I nearly bumped into Kerenza. She was just inside, by the fridge. She touched my arm, rippling with laughter. 'You were quite good out there, Sally, very patient. I wouldn't have lasted two minutes.'

I swore, but was actually delighted to see her. 'Have you just been in here listening? I didn't know what to say to her. He's your father, not mine. Is she drunk?'

'Of course, who cares though. Did you see Victor? He's lost Tracy.'

My conversation with Carole, seen through Kerenza's eyes, suddenly looked quite different – there I had been, just a moment ago, substantial as a character in a play; the blameless and quietly dignified young woman dealing with a troublesome intruder.

The next hour or so, not more than two, I spent with Kerenza across the street in the house behind the hotel, in her mother and Mark's kitchen. We might have talked about books, or films, but the only thing I remember is making cheese-and-onion toasties on Penny's shiny new sandwich machine. We drank whisky with them; Kerenza had some idea that whisky was rugged and unfeminine.

When we returned to the Bonaparte in the afternoon, I glanced into the bar to make sure that Carole had left. She hadn't. She was slumped in one of the armchairs, her feet crossed on a table, still drinking, but if anything she looked more alert than before, certainly more than I felt. I watched Kerenza stride in ahead, pick up Carole's cigarettes and light one.

'Go home, Ca-*role*.'

'Charming. You should be celebrating, Kerry. Your old dad's going to get off. Escape unscathed. Too late for some. The cops are still there, by the way, up the hill.'

I was standing in the doorway. 'Has something happened?'

Carole twisted round to look at me, exasperated. She enunciated slowly, as if I were nine.

'I'm talking about the cops, like I told you before. They've arrested Keith Jordan. And this time they've found something definite apparently, evidence. I wonder what it could be, after all this time? Maybe a bag or a shoe belonging to the girl, underwear. Everyone knows. I just swung by to congratulate Ray.'

I looked at Kerenza, but she was looking past me, towards the staircase. 'Tracy. Where have you been? Victor's looking for you.'

'Here. Upstairs. I went to see Nan earlier, but that was ages ago. What are you all talking about? Where's Victor?'

I thought Victor knows. He's known for hours.

'He came back,' I said. 'He said to tell you to go and meet him, then he just went back out.'

Carole turned to look at Tracy. 'The police are turning over his house. His dad's nicked, so Victor will have legged it if he's got any sense. You better get your skates on, Tracy.'

Tracy said, 'Where? Where did he say?' Then she began to chant, where, where, where. And I could not remember. A grey space, a gap in the shelf. In my mind I saw Victor coming down the stairs, walking up to me and Carole, 'Tell Tracy to meet me', and then nothing, only an impression that the words, the name of the place, had left a bluish stain on the air: blue, with a splash of red, a touch of brownish black.

'It was outside,' I said lamely. 'It could have been the Fall.' Even as I spoke I sensed this wasn't right, although 'F' is indeed blue. If it had been Geneva, or somewhere else on the Fall, the memory should have clicked back into place. Kerenza smiled at me, encouraging, 'Yes, Geneva, that must be what he said.'

'Are you sure?' Tracy said.

'Have you got a better idea? Echolocation?' said Kerenza.

We started running, through Reception, out of the Bonaparte's door. We passed Raymond loping up John Wesley Street with a carrier bag, his jumper hanging off his shoulders like a flag. He opened his mouth, as if to say, 'What's happened?'

We went in single file, Tracy in front; along the sunken path behind the old parsonage, through Miss Rescorla's hens, up Torbett's Hill, across the plateau, down into the forest and the Fall. Kerenza and I had to stop several times, but Tracy never seemed to tire, she was relentless as a wolf. Once, on the Silent Road, she turned, frowning, and called back, 'Are you sure?' There was nobody at Geneva, of course. We searched the house, the shed, the trees, the shore. We split up; I went west, deep into the coombe and past the Shadow Pools, Kerenza climbed into the wooded hillside to the east, Tracy went along the shoreline, over the rocks, into the next inlet. Once, when I looked down through the trees, I saw her in the sea up to her waist. We shouted Victor's name into the calm of the May air until the trees rang with it.

Back at Geneva I found Kerenza spreadeagled on the grass in front of the veranda. We would wait for Tracy, and decide what to do next. It was a gauzy evening, the Fall luminous with a hundred separate greens, but there was something wrong with the sea horizon. A pall of grey was out there, some way off but coming nearer, contracting the view. I had the sense of a door closing in an empty room. I went into Geneva to get us some water. When I came out, Kerenza was sitting up, clutching her knees.

'Sally, I'm not sure if Tracy heard everything, when Carole was talking about Mr Jordan.'

'Yes she did, she must have. Why else have we been running up here?'

'She heard something about the police at Victor's house, about meeting Victor...' She stopped. 'What the hell's that?'

The panorama of the bay was gone, the sea itself reduced to the width of a river, a river whose opposite bank was a wall of fog, pushing forward, consuming the light. We were on an island of sunshine, and as we watched, curtains of white came pulsing into the trees, the sun glittering in the moisture for a second before greying out. Kerenza stood up, her face tight.

'Sally, where's Tracy? We have to go.'

It's just a sea fog, I said, recalling that day long ago, when Kerenza had shown the same uneasy reaction.

I called, 'Tracy!', my voice damp and small.

'Wait, shut up,' Kerenza clutched at my sleeve, speaking too fast, 'I think I might have made a mistake. I think Victor may have said Penglaze Point.'

Two blue capital letters, dominating the words, staining most of the other letters, but leaving a touch of red, a splash of brownish black. The memory snapped into place: of course, Victor had said Penglaze Point. I didn't pause to wonder how Kerenza knew what he had said, but I realised it was the first time I had seen her nakedly frightened. At last Tracy appeared out of the mist a few feet away, clothes soaked, her fringe in wet bronze strips across her face, and Kerenza shouted, 'We think it's Penglaze Point he said.' Her voice disturbed a nearby tree, which shrugged a patter of raindrops off its leaves.

'The hawthorn,' said Tracy, 'he means the hawthorn, just before you get to the Point. It's where we go when something's wrong.'

'Well, something's definitely wrong, Tracy,' said Kerenza. 'They think Victor's father killed Clara Selman.'

Tracy stayed ahead of us on the path back; I had a persistent stitch in my side and Kerenza had pulled a muscle in her leg. The fog however made little difference, we knew the way so well. On the Silent Road we started hearing the foghorn from Trebeere harbour lighthouse, a harsh boom every thirty seconds. In order to reach the rocks at Penglaze Point you have to return almost all the way to St Anthony and then double back westward along the edge of the beach where we had found the dolphin years before. Brown wigs of seaweed were strewn across the wide sands. Victor was not under the hawthorn tree. I stopped under it, bent double, breathing the sweet childish scent of its white flowers. We were not alone on the shore: a group of people, four or five, were standing below the jagged pyramid of boulders. Tracy stood outside this little circle. Victor lay on his front, his face twisted to one side. There was blood on his forehead, but that was not what drew the eyes of the watchers. His t-shirt had rumpled right up his back, and all of the exposed skin was crossed with scarlet welts: thick whiplashes from shoulder to hip, then a cluster of twisting red lines like roots up and down his sides. The violet bladder of the Portuguese Man o' War sat in a bank of seaweed a few feet away: a remarkably large specimen, long tentacles of blue hair spread out on the sand. Tracy began to walk back towards St Anthony. She looked at me as she passed by, her face empty. 'He's lost his jersey.' I started to follow but Kerenza caught my arm – 'Let her go.' The fog was lifting off the ground and now resembled a low ceiling, the harbour wall visible in the distance. Tracy's shape receded, shrank, lost individuality, until, quite soon, she could have been anyone.

Someone had already gone to phone the authorities, and Kerenza said she would wait with the others until they arrived. My legs were covered in stings and scratches, stiff as wood; by the time I hobbled into John Wesley Street the sirens were singing all along the promenade from Trebeere. I don't know if I really expected to find Tracy back at the Bonaparte. Voices came from the kitchen, Penny's and Raymond's. In the Neptune Room the ship's figurehead loomed with fatuous courage over the dry wreck of Tracy and Victor's bed. I climbed up to the Observatory: empty. I leaned over the banister under the skylight and shouted, Tracy, down the deep stairwell.

15

It was never established whether Victor had fallen on the rocks before or after being stung by the jellyfish, or, more accurately, the siphonophore, or which of these events had caused his death. The coroner was inclined to blame the rock and the disorienting fog, given that stings from *Physalia Physalis* are unpredictable in their effects and vary between people: usually, you suffer extreme pain for a few hours and then recover, but sometimes you die. Perhaps he was also reluctant to publicise the existence of potentially lethal creatures floating around St Anthony at the start of the holiday season. The verdict was accidental death. I used to try obsessively to identify the exact moment when Victor died. It would have been while we were searching for him at Geneva, sometime after the fog swept in. I don't believe he jumped deliberately from the rocks, or fought the Man o' War. When he thought Tracy was not coming, that he had lost her, he lost himself, and fell; it could have been either one, or both.

The arrest of Victor's father had been possible because of an incident quite unrelated to the inquiry, and if it had not occurred at a time of such intense interest, when the name Clara Selman lived again in people's thoughts, it would likely have remained a trivial matter. Two days before Victor died, a trio of young men stole a car in Trebeere. They were intoxicated, so their wavy progress attracted the attention of the police, who pursued the vehicle along the promenade. The boys then abandoned the car near the new harbour at St Anthony. They disappeared into the bushy waste ground between the new harbour and the old, as far as the disused quay, where they then stole a dinghy. This took them only just beyond the harbour wall, at which point the dinghy's outboard motor died and the ancient boat began to take in water. Both the car and the dinghy were damaged, and it was while inspecting the dinghy that the police found a book among a pile of pornographic magazines in a locker under the rudimentary cabin. Someone had re-covered the book in sticky patterned plastic. This had begun to unpeel and blister, but had nevertheless contributed to the preservation of the pages within. It was an illustrated history of German cinema, with Clara Selman's signature on the flyleaf. The dinghy was registered to Keith Jordan.

This was not, of course, proof in itself. It was Jordan's terror of authority that simplified matters, disabling any attempt he might have made to defend himself. The interrogating officers would only have needed to nudge and prod, to give the impression they already knew most of the story and merely wished him to offer his version of it, and this particular suspect would have jumped to attention, volunteering a memory of a hitchhiker on the road from St Dominic in the summer of 1976, then a description of attempted intercourse, to which Clara had, naturally, eagerly consented. From there, a smooth path was laid out before the compliant murderer: the cup of tea, the cigarette, the expression of rueful, manly sympathy, and he would have stepped on to it like a calf, confessing to panic when the capricious girl had changed her mind. The police concluded that Clara was killed, most likely by strangulation, probably in Jordan's van, the small red van I used to notice sometimes speeding along the lanes. Jordan had then driven six miles to St Anthony, on to the disused quay, where, screened by the thickets of elder, it would have been easy to transfer her body to the dinghy and head out along the tortuous shore of the Fall, where nobody ever went.

This was the official version, the one that secured Jordan's conviction, but he began to change his story, repeatedly, over the months before the trial, pleading not guilty, insisting that Clara had stepped eagerly into the dinghy and had been alive and happy when she stood up and jumped into the sea, so that by the time he came to court he seemed a man floundering in a dream, contradicting himself, lost in elaborate knots of occult conspiracy, wrong-footing his defence counsel, befogging prosecution, judge and jury. The journalists struggled to report the case with any coherence.

There was one matter on which he was consistent, however. He vehemently denied possessing or using a knife. Indeed the question of the knife seemed to obsess him disproportionately, even after it was pointed out to him that the wound was unlikely to have been the cause of Clara's death.

My impression is that I hardly left Pellow Street, except to go to school or the library, from the day Victor died in May 1982 until I left Cornwall for university in 1983. Within days of Victor's death, Kerenza Nankervis was sent away, first to her uncle Maurice and aunt Pamela, where she was to continue her A-levels at a Bristol college, then to a cousin in Wales for the summer. I had a surprisingly kind letter from Maurice, leading me to wonder if his boorishness at that awkward supper had merely been a cover for nervousness – the first in a long line of reassessments I've been compelled to make over the decades. The following summer, after I, like her, had won a place at university, Kerenza sent me a postcard – a day-glo beach panorama of Weston-super-Mare:

'Sally, you'd hate it here – the tide goes out so far you can't even see the sea. Dangerous mudflats. Well done, K.' The card came in an envelope, which also contained a photo of a huge owl with an irregular fan of erect feathers around its face. On the back she had written: 'It's not an owl, it's a Harpy Eagle (*Harpia harpyja*). One of the biggest of all eagles, lives in central and south America. It whistles. But why would a harpy eagle... I hear you start to ask. Answer: exotic pets. Plenty of idiots keeping them in Cornwall, especially in 1976.' The harpy eagle looked mortally offended, its face an umbrage of grey hat-feathers and censorious eyes, like a senile Edwardian countess. It might be frightening from a distance, but I felt the Owlman's spirit retreat, along with mine.

I didn't reply to Kerenza, because after that amount of time there seemed no way to ask if she had overheard Victor in the Bonaparte's bar, naming Penglaze Point as his meeting place, and had then forgotten it, as I had, or misheard it (she had been eavesdropping, I remembered, from the kitchen), or if she knew exactly what Victor had said, but had simply assented when I suggested Victor could be waiting at Geneva. Assented because she was curious, because she wanted to see what would happen. I wonder if she avoids the same thoughts I avoid, because she knows what I know – that if, with my famous memory, I had remembered the words 'Penglaze Point', or if she had, Victor might still be alive. Victor, waiting under the hawthorn as the hours ticked by, would have assumed Tracy had heard about the arrest of his father. He would have waited and waited while

Kerenza and I were making sandwiches and drinking whisky, while we were all running through St Anthony, up to Geneva, searching the Fall. By the time the sea fog came in, over five hours had passed since Victor gave me the message for Tracy. He was never patient. The suspicion would have grown, a shadow at first, then a terrible conviction, that Tracy was not coming to meet him, would never come to meet him again, because of what his father had done. Kerenza must also be aware, as I am, that Tracy knows that is what Victor thought.

On the other hand, Clara Selman's parents, Colin and Pauline, would not have cared less about Kerenza's motives. Without Kerenza, the cold case would have stayed frozen; it was Kerenza who resurrected it, ending the long misery of uncertainty about their daughter's death, Kerenza who focused, like the ants we studied when we were eleven, on putting things right.

During that final year at Joseph Carne I was adopted by a small group of conscientious, self-effacing pupils, all of whom were predicted to do well. They saved me a place in our corner of the library, shared their biscuits with me, their plastic folders, class notes and revision plans. Whether from kindly tact or incuriosity, they talked only about schoolwork, and even then quite specifically about the task in hand; there was never any danger that we would wander beyond the borders of each subject, that history, literature, biology, politics, French or physics might cross-fertilise, point to anything beyond examinations, or reach out and pull us in. I went to bed early, the sleep empty as anaesthetic, apart from once, just before the exams, when I dreamed of Victor and Tracy's wedding reception.

They are side by side on the raised platform in the Assembly Room, the painting of Napoleon at Arcola on the wall behind. Seaweed spreads itself all over the floor, bladderwrack, oarweed, kelp and emerald gutweed, the guests are slipping in it. Penny

Nankervis sends me upstairs to find a mop and I am confused by the corridors, which multiply, opening out on theatrical halls and grand spiralling stairwells whose existence I never suspected. People are unpacking suitcases in the bedrooms; none of them look up as I go by. On the third floor is the disused bathroom, the plastic curtain printed with gold stars. The big radio in the bath whistles with static, as if someone were turning the dial; any moment now, a voice will come out of it, jabbering unbearably fast or drawling slow, and I must run back down the stairs to avoid hearing the words. In the Assembly Room everyone has gathered around the windows, Tracy and Victor lost in the crowd. The wedding guests are watching the sea, which is surging right up the steep street, washing against the panes, each wave bigger than the last.

* * *

From a distance of thirty-five years, the search for Tracy Pender looks extraordinarily lackadaisical, though at the time I assumed this was normal. Perhaps it was normal and the desultoriness was natural in the circumstances: in May 1982, the police had just caught and charged a suspect in a murder dating from 1976, a case that had attracted unwelcome national attention as well as unnerving a whole community. On the heels of this success came the sudden death of the perpetrator's son, which had to be investigated in turn. The absence of this boy's girlfriend, now seventeen, a girl almost entirely without family, who had been in and out of the care system, who had a history of wandering off, whose actions or omissions had sown confusion and bad feeling during a murder investigation, was probably not a priority.

Nevertheless, when nobody had seen Tracy for three days, and Raymond had looked in vain for her bag and coat at the

Bonaparte, a search of sorts was organised. I had of course been up to Geneva myself, twice, and found no sign of her (*'I'd just go into the woods. They'd never find me'*). A couple of officers searched the Bonaparte, then trekked up to the Fall, checked Geneva, made a recommendation that the derelict property be closed off more securely, and tramped in and out of the trees along the forest path. I believe they also sent a launch along the shoreline of the Fall. I called once on Hazel Tabb, who suggested that Tracy had gone to Venezuela to see her father.

After two weeks, I went nervously to the police station with some idea that I would declare her a missing person, but was told that this had already been done, though they did ask me if Tracy had 'other boyfriends'. I wrote to Mrs Carpenter at St Levan House, assuming that she would know Tracy was missing. She didn't. Her reply was uncharacteristically concise: she would let Amanda Barfield know, though another social worker would soon be taking over Amanda's caseload, and I should feel free to come and talk to her at any time, which I never did. After that, nothing.

After I had left Cornwall, my mother moved from St Anthony to Trebeere, to an almost identical tiny terraced house. On visits home I was always alert for things to overhear. There wasn't much, but once, the librarian at Trebeere Library recognised me and started speaking under her breath as she stamped my books. 'I knew her mother, you know. Irene Pender. We were at school together. She was stunning, too, like Tracy was, full of life.' Full of life, a description only ever applied to the dead. I picked up my books. 'I'm looking,' I said, 'I'm still looking.'

I am certain that Tracy is still alive. I am as sure of it as I am sure Victor is not, as confident now as I was in 1982. At university I started making 'missing' posters: Tracy Pender, also known as Tracy Tabb, illustrated either with the photograph from the newspaper, with Raymond cut out of the picture, or the only other one I have, from a night out at the Ruby Tiger. I pinned them on student noticeboards. Later, when my job took me around Britain, I stuck them on lamp posts (where they joined lost cats), left them in bars and station cafes, on trains and ferries, in glittering city dance halls and at wintry bus stops in those bleak fenland villages strung out along flat car-ways, a line of minatory trees on a horizon straight as a ruler. If you're old enough to remember that decade, you probably saw one. After seven years, a missing person can be declared legally dead. In 1990, I checked, but no one had done this. Nobody else is looking for her.

There were some responses to the notices, from people who thought they might have seen her in a supermarket, at a motorway service station, on a beach in Italy, and these were of little use. One man, a persistent caller, was convinced that Tracy was his runaway wife, and even after we had established that this wife was born in 1954, not 1965, he kept phoning, 'Why don't you come for a drink anyway?' I was contacted by a clairvoyant from Sheffield, who assured me that Tracy was married and living in rural Denmark. Then a woman in Brighton wrote, swearing there was a girl matching Tracy's photo and description, of the right age this time, working in a café in the town. I took the train down from London, and the woman sat me in the dining room of her bed and breakfast and told me the story of her life and husbands. She lit cigarettes with ice-pink nails until smoke hung in layers over the reek of fat bacon, and she was sorry, but she couldn't remember exactly where the café was. 'It's definitely your friend, though. I saw the poster and I thought to myself, I was meant to see that. Everything happens for a reason.'

When I moved with my family overseas, I taped Tracy's untraceable image up in railway stations across Europe, and once, while changing trains at Munich, I found myself face to face with a notice I had put up three years before.

I have questioned this certainty, of course. My mother told me that everybody local had soon decided Tracy had killed herself, probably the same day Victor died, somewhere in the densest part of the Fall where nobody would dare to look. But no walker, no botanist or geologist, has come across anything on the Fall in three decades. And it is not so easy to walk into the sea like Whistling Jack; the will to live propels you like a cork back to the surface; the sea prefers to make its own choices.

It seemed to me that huge numbers of people went missing in the decade after 1982, but of course I was unnaturally attuned to the phenomenon. Bodies were discovered, murderers uncovered, people who had disappeared long ago turned up dead below fields and floorboards, in psychopathic cellars and under sterile paved back gardens. Every time this happened I prepared a room in my mind and waited outside it, patient and quiet, for news, but it was an academic, cerebral anxiety – I never really felt the victim would be Tracy or Tracy could be a victim, it didn't fit with how she outran and outswam us, the military order in the bedroom at St Levan House, the nights alone at Geneva, the way she skirted foxlike along the edges of things, transient and camouflaged.

After a while I stopped. Years were filled with people and events quite unconnected with this story. My 'search' has become less earnest, a refrain or motif running below the main business of life, and there is even, if I'm honest, a pleasurable dimension to it. It's a quest, a project, a promise; a refusal to admit that an actual return might be a revelation only of some terrible ordinariness and mutual incomprehension. On Google Street View I drop the little yellow figure on a random stretch of foreign road, the more remote and obscure the better. People appear suddenly by the sides of country lanes, or on urban waste grounds, pinned like moths by their geographical coordinates. You see them from behind, move ahead with the arrow, look back for another view; sometimes they are there again, sometimes they have vanished, sliced out by the cut of the photography. Artless and anonymous in a world of curated self-portraiture, they have a peculiar innocence, and though the faces are intentionally blurred, you would know them by their shapes. Most often I am drawn to America, the whole continent, where space is cheap and lost houses like Geneva are too commonplace to notice. On an empty highway outside Galveston, a woman who is not Tracy runs alone, racing the telegraph poles across miles of Gulf Coast marsh. I search in Venezuela, too, although much of it, especially in the Andes, is still hazy, unmapped.

Raymond Nankervis never really recovered from the backwash of suspicion that swept over him in 1982. I don't like to think about his tactful courtesy, his ectomorphic gestures and constant air of mild surprise, the terror he must have concealed during those last weeks at the hotel. He had a breakdown that winter, then moved to Fowey, and the Bonaparte was sold soon after. As far as I know the book about the Great Families was never published, though, surprisingly, he outlived Penny, who died of cancer in 1995, at the age of fifty-four. Hocking Nankervis (Mr Simpson moved to London) became one of the most successful estate agencies in Cornwall, and by the time Penny's tenancy on earth was cancelled she left a substantial amount of property above the ground. I assume Kerenza inherited it, though she would not have cared overmuch, she was never interested in money – I always liked that about her.

Miss Rescorla also died in 1995. She must be relieved to know that the battery-hen farm near Thomas Hardy's cottage is now a business park, though billions of other hens, and pigs, are born each year to live and die in hell, incubating pandemics. The Owlman has his own Wikipedia page.

The remaining members of Victor's family were transferred by the council to another town in Cornwall, except for Denise, who refused to be 'driven out by interfering bastards'. I believe she is still in St Anthony. Victor's other sister, Andrea, said that her father had sometimes been violent at home, though only to the children, not his wife. Nobody would dare assault Bridget Jordan. I remembered that evening when Victor had come banging and swearing out of the alley in St Anthony; he had not been fighting anyone – the injuries had been inflicted earlier by his father. Victor's brother Paul now has a dental practice in Norwich, where his wife runs a cattery.

16

In May 2016 I spent a month in Trebeere at my mother's house, much longer than my usual visits. By then she was eighty-two and had two years to live. At the top of her street, St Senara Road, there is an art studio named (I had to read it twice to check) 'Memento Mori', while the biggest trawler in the harbour at the bottom bears the name 'Resurgam'. My mother still smoked rollups, and fat packets of duty-free tobacco flapped through the letterbox on Mondays; 'I think the fishing boats bring it in from France.'

Trebeere is extraordinarily quiet after midnight, if you're not used to it. On a still night, you can sit in the courtyard under stars and washing lines and hear snails feeling their way across the wall (a subtle, irregular clicking), but the wind only has to ruffle up a bit and the sea is loud, close, even in the centre of town, as if it creeps inland in the dark. Masts whistle and chime like bells from the harbour, water laps at the end of the alley, almost at the back gate.

On my second morning, my mother announced at breakfast that a neighbour wanted to meet me.

'Sandra Menhennett. She says there are things she would like you to know.'

'Sandra Menhennett?'

'She used to be Sandra Jenkin. That poor girl's friend, all those years ago. I told her you'd call round at half eleven.'

I knocked, an ancient anxiety awake in my stomach, and Sandra opened the door. She is five years older than I am but looks younger; she has lived in the same Trebeere street all her life, works as a receptionist (at the vet, not the Bonaparte), is married to Terry, a fireman, has four children, the eldest of whom has left home to be a Media Project Manager (neither of us really understood what that was), and detests travelling. We have absolutely nothing in common, and I liked her immediately.

'It was so awful, that time in 1982, watching what was going on, and not being able to talk to any of you, but I couldn't. The police came here too, talked to me again, and interviewed my brother again – after six years, imagine. I remember a horrible atmosphere, people swapping stories about Tracy Pender, Mr Nankervis, as if Tracy was a sort of witch, and Victor Jordan a criminal like his dad, as if everyone wanted the worst things to be true, and I kept saying, they were only eleven when Clara died. I felt sorry for all of you.'

'What was Clara like?'

'She was clever at school, I often think about what she would have done later. And kind. But we were completely different. You can't talk about the difficult parts when someone dies, can you? We used to argue. She was very impatient, she used to snap at me sometimes, she expected you to remember everything she said.'

She had snapped, Sandra remembered, on that Saturday evening in 1976, the day before her death.

'Clara was keen on my brother Michael, though she wouldn't admit it, but he didn't fancy her. When Michael left Cinnabar's that night, she lost interest in the whole evening and wanted to go home. I didn't, and we had a stupid argument. On the Sunday she rang and said she was coming round, I said suit yourself, and when she didn't turn up I assumed she'd had second thoughts. It was so hot that day, I was relieved. I'm always replaying that afternoon, and I tell her, *Stay at home, I'll come up to your house*. That's what I live with.'

'Were you surprised she got into a van with a stranger?'

'No. We used to hitch around. And Clara did it alone, for the experience. If life offers you an experience, she said, you should always accept, and she was reckless when she was angry. I could even imagine her getting into Jordan's boat. If she was still alive at that point.'

I told Sandra about Geneva, what we had seen in 1976. When I finished, she told me about the couple who were living there until 1975, when a minor landslip made the house uninhabitable — 'they were German, I think, writers or students'. Then she started talking about her husband.

'Terry's dad has a mate who used to be a police officer. He was there when they brought Clara into the mortuary. She was in a body bag, and when they unzipped it, or whatever they do, there was still a lot of water in there and a fish came flapping out. The fish was still alive, but Clara wasn't. I never forgot that.'

I saw a good deal of Sandra that month. I told her about my search for Tracy, from the photocopied posters to the missing-persons websites. She was less optimistic than I hoped she would be.

'Did she leave a note?'

'No, nothing. But she took her bag, her make-up, and her coat. You don't take a bag and coat if you're going to kill yourself, do you?'

'Don't you think she would have got in touch by now, Sally? Or you would have heard something, even if she has a new identity? It's been more than thirty years.'

'Tracy has no idea of time.'

'But where do you reckon she is? What would she be doing?'

'She moves around. Along the margins. Off the grid, they call it.'

Did I realise, Sandra asked, how Tracy and Victor's story had changed since the 1980s, that their names are quite well known. 'It's become a sort of myth, something people tell visitors when they ask about the Fall.'

'Like Eliza Tabb?'

'Exactly. Or the Wandering Boy. The young people, they don't remember what we remember. They know there was a murder up there, but nobody talks about Clara Selman any more, as a person. Or about you and Kerenza Nankervis, for that matter. They want to hear about Victor and Tracy, the lovers, how they lived out in the woods, how Victor was killed by the jellyfish at the Point, and Tracy couldn't reach him in time and killed herself on the Fall.'

She paused. 'I'm sorry, I know you don't think that's what happened. I hope she's alive. But here, everyone thinks they know the story. Young couples go out there to take photos, they look for the tree with Tracy and Victor's names on it. Schoolkids scare themselves with ghost stories. We've had people, tourists, asking the way to the old cottage – we have to put them off, it's dangerous, and impossible to find. My mother used to go up on the Fall when she was young, she always called the house Geneva as well. But I've never wanted to see it.'

I didn't tell Sandra I thought the murder of Clara Selman must nevertheless be contributing to the interest in Victor and Tracy.

I took a bus from Trebeere to St Anthony. I wanted to go up to the Fall because I didn't remember any tree with names on it, I needed to check. On Cornish buses there is always somebody talking to a companion who is silent, indifferent, and on this occasion a woman on the seat behind me was describing a holiday in Canada, a train ride where she had looked out and seen a deer on an ice floe sailing down a river, 'a huge wide river full of broken ice and the deer was rushing along in the current on this one piece of ice, standing quite still and calm'. The woman was lit up with the memory; her companion barely managed a murmur in response. St Anthony was tidier than I remembered, and busy: bulbous, wide-hipped cars mocking the narrow streets. I squeezed past someone who looked like Andrea Jordan. It wasn't her, and I saw others who were not Maggie Hart, not Miss Rescorla, not Geoff the Pylon, and I wanted to say, like Carole Carr, 'Where is everyone?'

Number Five, Glebe Lane, has changed hands several times since Hazel Tabb and Tracy were evicted, and is now immaculately restored and renamed The Sail Loft. There is nobody living there. You can always tell when a house is a holiday let because there will be a wooden bird in the front window – a generic seagull standing on one leg – and the room beyond will be furnished in Puritan style and painted grey. I went up the (moss-free) slate steps and peered through the window. The wall separating Mrs Tabb's living room from the lean-to kitchen had gone, leaving one big space, clean as a seashell, with a view to the garden – which was no longer a garden, being covered in gravel like a patch of cat litter. 'Tidal Boutique Holidays' and a web address were carved on a slate plaque by the door. Three houses in Glebe Lane had Hocking Nankervis sale signs on them that day. In winter, they say, entire streets in St Anthony stay dark for months.

Places revisited after a long absence are supposed to look smaller, but if anything the sheer scale of the landslip shocked me afresh. Along the Silent Road and into the Fall, where the idea of cars becomes as abstract as dinosaurs, my shoulders unclenched and I came back to myself. I found the tree: a big smooth-barked beech near the first of what we used to call the Shadow Pools: 'Victor & Tracy 1981'. The letters were crudely carved, the ampersand more like a figure 8, and Victor's name being first, I imagined he must have done it. I thought of James Prideaux, haunted by the people who pass by leaving no trace. He wrote a lifelong journal and is quite forgotten; Clara Selman is nearly forgotten. Tracy and Victor, who used to insist that 'nobody will ever know we were there' when we went trespassing, are remembered. The world loves a dead lover.

I colour-in Clara's progress as the years pass. She is always ahead of me, always six years older, living in Berlin, making the films that Victor would never have made, though he might have written the screenplays. I miss Kerenza too; I argue with her in the wood, and about the wood, putting words in her mouth. If all this complexity, I say, is only epiphenomenal foam on the current of evolution, filtered through the senses of one species, why does it need to be so extravagantly various, so eccentrically beautiful, and why should we be compelled to notice it at all, when a woman and her man need only verify the presence of essential services – water, shelter, food – for the babies to come, survive and reproduce? But it's not always beautiful, Kerenza replies, remember the hagfish ('a swimming vagina with teeth'), the clever parasites, the fungating tumours and haemorrhagic viruses. Even the pretty things are often dangerous and always indifferent, a sea of fairground jellies, iridescent pulsing Medusae.

In the end, though, we agree on one matter: it is a terrible thing to be sitting indoors on a warm summer night, with your window open, your light on, and not one moth comes in. Better to tell yourself a fairy tale, say that the moths have finally wised up to our electric moons, than believe there is nothing out there in the dark.

The letters on the tree are too sharp to be thirty-five years old. Either someone has re-carved them, or they are an invention, a response to the myth that has grown up around the real Tracy and Victor. I saw no young couples taking selfies, though a sinewy man came by, belted onto a backpack, using two sticks to stamp doggedly along as if he were attempting to ski through the wood. He was followed half an hour later by two runners in black neoprene suits, like forest seals. None of them saw me because I was sitting in a yew tree, high above the path. Nobody expects to see a middle-aged woman in a tree like a woodpigeon, and few people ever look up anyway. Once they had gone, time drained away into roots and moss, birds crept out, and the Fall came back, smoothing every muscle, ticking along every nerve and vein.

That knife still prickles my conscience. Victor thought he remembered an actual mother-of-pearl knife. Then there was Keith Jordan's fierce denial that he had stabbed Clara, when it was clear this would not affect his defence. At eleven we were already one year past the age of criminal responsibility, old enough to be tried like adults in a formal court. Kerenza had owned a knife, but it was an ordinary penknife and I only saw her use it in the wood, in her experiments, not on the beach. My own memory of the mother-of-pearl knife is safely embedded in Tracy's story of Whistling Jack, but the image of Tracy and Victor bending over Clara persists, and I cannot know what they were doing while I was looking for whistling jacks to throw on Clara's dress. Did Kerenza really suspect Clara had still been alive when we found her, or that one of us, or two or three of us, had played with a knife and wounded or killed her? If we had, would it have seemed any more important, at eleven, than the selkies, the moths, the Owlman, the Mint Woman, the Knife-Sharpening Man? There is something I know for sure: even if Tracy or Victor, or both of them, had hurt or killed Clara that day, I would not love them any the less. Eleven was another place, where people rose out of cracks in the earth to spin in the evening air with the gnats, and Clara took off her sealskin before walking home to supper.

Geneva, Sandra said, is sinking into the Fall; I had no wish to see it, so I walked right past the concealed entrance path like a tourist. But there was one change I could not ignore: a new house had appeared on Torbett's Green on the borderline between the open plateau and the Silent Road, about halfway between Geneva and the outskirts of the village. It was large, low-built in traditional style, painted yellow, not unattractive. It was also abandoned – barbed wire wrapped around the gate. In the garden the grass was high and the whistling jacks were everywhere, crimson flags against the green.

What Sandra Menhennett told me about that house sent a hairline crack across the foundations of my modern orthodoxy – or so I tell myself. More truthfully, the feral flare of something unexplained was welcome, like an old friend. The land belongs to Mark Hocking, Sandra said, the title having descended through his family for generations. Land that does nothing is useless, so in 2011 Mark hired an architect to build a luxurious house with the best sea views in St Anthony, views which, it was hoped, would compensate for its remoteness. Technically, the site was outside the Fall, beyond the geological area of risk, and it was sold by Hocking Nankervis for nearly a million pounds. About a year later, rumours began to circulate about the middle-aged couple who had moved in, a retired neurologist and his wife, a popular author. On several occasions this woman had reported her husband missing.

'One time,' said Sandra, 'she came all the way down to the village at eleven at night and banged on the door of the Crabber, which had just closed. She said her husband had walked off into the woods that afternoon in search of a rare lichen, and had not returned. Very early the next morning she found him drinking tea in the kitchen, as if nothing had happened, with no memory of going out.'

They did tests (his wife suspected a stroke), but there was nothing wrong with his mind or his memory. He developed a new obsession with seals, risking his life tracking along the shore of the Fall, telling people he had seen hundreds of seals hauled out on the rocks and more in the sea, surrounded by green lights – stories that were hardly credible, surprising from a scientist. His wife became convinced he was having an affair, meeting someone down on the beach. In spring 2013, after a wet winter, she was on her own in the house in the afternoon when she felt a powerful tremor under her feet. Cups smashed, books fell off shelves. She ran out to find that the garden on the western side had sunk. The wall of the house there was buckled, convex, and a deep crack split the brand-new access lane, circling the property, annexing it to the Fall.

'This,' said Sandra, 'is where the story gets odd. The wife, I'll call her Mrs Smith, rang the emergency services. My Terry was one of them who went up there. When they arrived they declared the house unsafe and closed it all off, and Mrs Smith asked them to help find her husband, who was absent as usual. It was starting to get dark when they found him, on an isolated bit of shore, or rather they saw him through the trees from above, a long way down. Terry said Mr Smith was standing up to his thighs in the sea, fully dressed, surrounded by dozens of seals. They, the seals, were making a moaning, whistling sound, almost like a song, but not quite, and the sea was glowing with green light. Maybe it was phosphorescence. And there was a woman there with him. They don't know who she was, she never reappeared, but Mr Smith came back up the cliff by himself, quite unharmed. He remembered nothing.'

'What did she look like?'

'Mrs Smith?'

'The woman in the sea.'

'I know what you're thinking. No, she did not have fair hair. From what Terry could see from that distance, she was very dark.'

* * *

I no longer dream about executions, but of rising seas, tidal waves; sometimes I wonder if everyone in the world is having this same dream. I hear the sirens along the coast as the water in Lantern Bay drains out, far beyond the lowest of low tides; fish and fishing boats lie beached, a petrified forest is exposed, crabs are thrown from their beds, a wire sculpture of a running woman appears on the mudflats, dressed in seaweed. Then the sea pulses back, pouring over the harbour, smashing the tourist shops, evicting estate agents, carrying yachts and freighters over woods and fields. Beyond Penglaze Point, a wall of water pushes into the narrow inlets, gathers up Kerenza's jellyfish and dumps them on the rough moor high above St Anthony, where they catch on the prickly heather and shrivel in the wind.

I must return Prideaux's book – taken without permission and now around thirty-five years overdue – to the Branwell Library. I suppose I should also report the evidence about Eliza Tabb, one unreported body is enough for a lifetime, and though there will be nothing left of her, physically, Eliza deserves some formal acknowledgement.

There are two short entries in the journal after November 11, 1827, the first of these is dated November 22:

> I have stopped using the upstairs room. I moved the mattress downstairs a few weeks ago, and now I prefer to sleep under the glass of the veranda, where I can see the light change. I leave the doors open. I wish to remain close to the woods, to feel the trees breathing in the dark. It is astonishing how little space a man needs, and I cannot understand why I ever thought Geneva House small. Every night before I retire I set a small glass out on the grass, with a little of Arthur's spirit in it. The glass is always empty by first light.
>
> The strange confidence I experienced after I shot the rabbit is not simply connected with hunting. Until recently I had avoided the landslip scrupulously, as everybody does, especially those of us who saw the Great Fall just after it occurred, we who have a vision of destruction and collapse inscribed on our dreams. The Fall begins about a quarter of a mile to the west of the house, a short walk. I never went near it when I stayed out here with Geneva, and, unusually for her, she expressed no curiosity, no desire to go there alone.
>
> The first time, I tricked myself. It was late in September. I went down to my miniature cove at around five o'clock to see if the seals had returned, which they had not, though I hear them at night. What a pity, I told myself, that I cannot walk a little further west, to see if they have another, more private retreat up there. Perhaps I should walk in that direction, but keep to the thickest part of the wood, taking care to fix my gaze southward to the sea; that way, I might glimpse the next

cove or inlet without having to look upon the Fall itself. Right up to the last moment, I believed I would not look at the Fall.

I looked. It had transformed itself. What lay before me in the evening light was a scene from the beginning of the world, or the garden at the end of Time. Every hard edge, every cliff and spur and jagged ridge ripped up by the upheaving, is now under a counterpane of green. No paths, no walls or borders interrupt the steeply undulating expanse of ferns, mares' tails, bracken, moss, young trees and late flowers. Saplings grow out of the towering pyramids of rock at sharp angles, creepers hang in veils from the summits. It is loud with bees, larks and blackbirds.

I go there often now, not every day, but when I need to. I sit with Ossian in a place where the sea, the Fall and the path back to the house are all in view, though I myself am hidden. I have this journal beside me, and the shotgun. I think about Maryann, fall asleep and dream of her. I am a guest at a large party; she is there with a formal husband, unknown to me. We find ourselves alone together just for a minute, on a seat in the porch, hidden from view by the throngs of party guests coming and going. The scent of cow parsley comes in from the dark, and there is a sudden bright joy, welding body, heart and intellect with an intensity I have never known in life. She turns to me and says, 'The strange thing about being dead is that you go on making exactly the same mistakes as you did when you were living.' She goes on talking but her words are drowned by the noise of the party, and she departs with the husband, both their faces stony, walking past me without a glance.

How easy it would be to track Matthew Hocking in the dense shade of the eastern woods. I would take my time aiming the shotgun through the leaves at the back of his head, one sharp bang sending the sleeping owls up out of the trees; I imagine Arthur's wordless regard, the next day. This is my temptation.

I see Jack everywhere. He has no fear. He leaps all over the Fall like a deer, flings up his arms and shouts as he jumps over ravines and dances along vertiginous escarpments. In the mornings he is high up in the ash tree by the house, reading. He floats out with the seals in the bay, sometimes he turns and waves, but more often he forgets. From a distance it is hard to tell him and the seals apart. I have not lost my senses, I know I have to wait. I will search and I will wait, and I know that Arthur, or some other benevolent spirit, will bring Jack to me. This is my faith.

The final entry is undated. I assume that his use of 'we all' refers to Ossian and, perhaps, the fox: 'The weather continues grey and cold, but I find I feel the chill less and less. Yesterday we spent most of the day on the Fall, and it was only when we returned after nightfall that I realised I had gone out without my coat. We all sat under the apple tree this morning and watched a big schooner sailing westward.'

James Prideaux died in February 1828. His grave is not at St Anthony but St Dominic, where he was born, right at the back of the churchyard, in shade between two lines of beech. Unlike Arthur Wigge's tombstone with its distinctive tree motif, Prideaux's has not worn well, but the dates are legible under the lichen, 1769 to 1828, and a Latin inscription, 'Lux Umbra Dei'. I have not been able to find any record of a son, nor any likely person named Jack Prideaux or Jack Tabb or Jack Pender – at least not in these three parishes, with dates that fit. The farmer Matthew Hocking also died early in 1828; a paragraph in the *Gazette* for January 10th says this occurred in 'a shooting accident just beyond his own lands, near the Great Fall', but there is no further detail on how it happened. I can confirm that Arthur Wigge was living in Paris in 1848 when he died, twenty years after his friend. Perhaps he went to lay his bones in a city convulsed for a second time by revolution, and his tomb here in St Anthony is empty, a mere memorial, like Napoleon's vacated grave on St Helena. Shortly after Prideaux's death, his widow Geneva Florey (she reverted to her first married name) left for Jamaica with her son Henry, taking Dinah Pengelly with them. She, Geneva, lived until 1865. I have no idea what happened to Ossian.

I saw Kerenza once, a few years ago in Barcelona, at a memorial service for a South American president. Not such a great coincidence: she was in the city for a conference at the university (on marine algal blooms), while I was living there at the time, and, for reasons I have explained, I take an interest in Venezuela. The church, Saint Mary of the Pine Tree, was appropriately resinous and dark, so I only saw Kerenza as we were all filing out, but I knew her straight away.

'What are you doing here?' I said.

'Nothing. I was just curious.'

Acknowledgements

First I must thank my editor Linda Cleary at Hypatia Publications for the huge contribution she has made to the publication of this book. Linda has a gift for holding the broad shape of a book in mind while attending to the detail. Her comments on drafts were insightful and precise; she was reassuring at all the right moments, her work during the production process always responsive, intelligent and professional. She has been a source of strength and her role has been essential.

I also want to thank my agent Philippa Brewster for her belief in *Whistling Jack*. I was amazed and flattered to attract interest from someone with such a distinguished record in publishing; she has been consistently perceptive and supportive. In our conversations she astonished me with her memory for every detail of the novel, and – most importantly – she seemed to understand exactly what I was trying to do in writing it.

I am grateful to all at Hypatia Publications for publishing this book, and to Miki Ashton in particular for the cover design. Thanks also to Ben Corrigan, of The Whole Proof, who prepared the 2023 e-book as well as the 2025 paperback edition, and to Phillip Bentley, who reworked the cover for the 2025 edition.

Jackie Malton provided invaluable advice on police attitudes and procedures in the late 1970s and early 1980s. She read an early version and has been encouraging and thoughtful from start to finish. Many thanks also to Christopher Good for his kind words and advice on an early draft, this was greatly appreciated at a difficult time.

Linda Williamson kindly gave permission to use the quote from Duncan Williamson's *Tales of the Seal People*, without charge.

I also owe huge thanks to the following people for their friendship, generosity and encouragement: Sarah Bentley, Phillip Bentley, Catriona Brodribb, Victoria and Bertie Richardson-Burton, Augusta Dorr, Vanessa Gardiner, Diane Hofkins, Alexander Lowery, Stephanie Northen, Delly Sayer.

It was my husband, David, who persuaded me not to give up. Thank you for that... and for everything else.

Printed in Dunstable, United Kingdom